AN OPERATIONAL NECESSITY

GWYN GRIFFIN was born in Egypt in 1922 and educated in England. During World War II he worked as an administrative officer in the depots of various colonial forces in Africa. Later he became a police officer on the Red Sea coast. He then spent a number of years in Australia, where he began his career as a novelist. Griffin and his wife eventually settled in Italy, in a small town in the Abruzzi, where he lived until he died in 1967 at the early age of 45. Despite a much too brief career, Griffin has, nevertheless, won recognition as a writer and story-teller of exceptional power. He wrote eight novels and a collection of short stories.

Gwyn Griffin

AN OPERATIONAL NECESSITY

THE HARVILL PRESS

LONDON

First published by Collins, 1968

This edition published in 1999 by
The Harvill Press
2 Aztec Row, Berners Road, London N1 0PW

www.harvill-press.com

1 3 5 7 9 8 6 4 2

A CIP catalogue record for this book
is available from the British Library

ISBN 1 86046 546 X

Printed and bound in Great Britain by Butler & Tanner Ltd
at Selwood Printing, Burgess Hill

(Written on the Eve of his Execution)

My prime of youth is but a frost of cares;
  My feast of joy is but a dish of pain;
My crop of corn is but a field of tares;
  And all my good is but vain hope of gain:
The day is past, and yet I saw no sun;
And now I live, and now my life is done.

My tale was heard, and yet it was not told;
  My fruit is fall'n, and yet my leaves are green;
My youth is spent, and yet I am not old;
  I saw the world, and yet I was not seen:
My thread is cut, and yet it is not spun;
And now I live, and yet my life is done.

I sought my death, and found it in the womb;
  I looked on life, and saw it was a shade;
I trod the earth, and knew it was my tomb;
  And now I die, and now I was but made:
My glass is full, and now my glass is run;
And now I live, and now my life is done.

CHIDIOCK TICHBORNE (1558–1586)

Contents

SOUTH ATLANTIC

One

Rayner and the child came up on to the fore well-deck just after seven. From the window of the radio-room Gaston watched them as they climbed over the canvas-covered baulks of wood composing the deck cargo and then settled wearily on No. 2 hatch. Rayner wore only the dungaree trousers of the stokehold, so thickly grimed with oil and coal dust that they had acquired a patina as dark and polished as his own black skin and, like it, glinted with red and copper highlights under the last rays of the setting sun. When he spoke he moved only his head, his hands lay relaxed and motionless in his lap, machinery at rest. By contrast the boy's small hands were never still, lifting and falling, opening and shutting, he seemed to gesticulate even while he listened—agreeing, negating, doubting. Gaston, whistling softly under his breath as he sharpened a pencil, wondered idly how they communicated—by facial expression, tone of voice, gesture perhaps, for neither spoke more than a few words of the other's language.

It had been the same a week ago in Conakry in front of Monsieur Lagny; despite the language problem translation had hardly been necessary. 'Mister, look. *Regard* s'il vous plaît. This one come for galley-boy, *n'est ce pas?*'

'*Non, non. Trop jeune.* 'Ow many year 'e' ave?'

'He say *quatorze ans.*'

'*Si, si! Catorze! Catorze!*'

'*Merde!*' The First Officer had turned his long, melancholy, weather-beaten face to Gaston. 'Gaston, you will translate if you please. Tell him that he is too young. I do not at all believe that he is fourteen.'

'I do not speak Portuguese, monsieur, I regret.'

'No, no. It is not to be supposed that you do. But you speak English. Tell this stoker that this boy will not do. He is still a child.'

'Mister says that this young boy is too young. He does not agree that he is fourteen.'

'*Si, si! Catorze! Catorze!*' And the small hands flew out in splayed demand for belief, the shoulders lifted almost to the ears, the eyes widened with the passionate desire that this lie should be accepted as the truth.

Gaston had sighed. Monsieur Lagny had sighed; and Rayner, thinking, perhaps, to ingratiate himself whatever happened, had sighed more deeply than either. The child's hands had dropped slowly, hopelessly, and his big dark eyes had filled with tears. '*Catorze*,' he had muttered. '*Catorze*.' Then, singing very loudly in his fine baritone voice, Captain Crawshaw had swung out of the fiddley—Heaven alone knew what he had been doing there, but after all it was his ship; he was entitled to be in even the most improbable places at any hour he wished—and requested to know what was going on. Gaston, of course, had had to translate. '...and so Mister says he is too young.'

Rayner had said suddenly, 'Got 'isself left behind, sir. Stranded, you might say—offen a Spaniard. 'E bin askin' all over for any ship going back to Bahia. Comes from Bahia, see? So when—'

The Captain had nodded and Gaston had seen at once that he would let the child come with them to Bahia. 'Well, come on now. How old *are* you, eh? Tell the truth and shame the Devil. *Nove? Dez? Onze?*'

'*Catorze*.'

'Don't believe it. Never mind; let him stay. Gaston, tell Mister that he can stay as galley-boy to Bahia.' The Captain had grinned. 'Know what age I was when I went to sea first, Gaston? Just on nine! Yes, that surprises you a bit, doesn't it?'

Gaston smiled back. He was the Captain's favourite and well aware of it.

'That was very young, monsieur. But—excuse—it was not in time of war.'

'No. No, it wasn't. That's true enough. But we're only taking young "Catorze" to Bahia—no farther. Is the Chief still ashore, you know?'

'He is returned ten minutes since.'

'Good, good.' And the Captain had nodded genially to Monsieur Lagny and strode off. They heard him burst into song as soon as he was round the deckhouse:

'Rattle his *bones*
Over the *stones*
He's only a pauper
Whom nobody *owns*!'

'The Captain—' said Monsieur Lagny sadly—'has a most kind heart. He is above all things a man of sentiment. *Alors*, Gaston, tell this boy he may stay as far as Bahia.'

The child appeared to be too overcome to do more than murmur, '*Obrigado. Muito obrigado*,' and wring his hands.

'*Quel nom?*'

'What name?'

In the end he had to write it down in large shaky capitals—FELISBERTO PANDIA. The First Officer had shaken his head. 'Philippe,' he had said. 'He will have to be Philippe—at least until Bahia.'

Two

Bahia was to be their main, although by no means their only, loading port. At Conakry they had taken on several tons of palm kernels and a quantity of evil-smelling hides now stowed in the tween-decks aft. Then, to the consternation of Monsieur Lagny, the Captain had announced that he was taking on a small amount of wood as deck cargo; west African hardwoods, expensive and valuable and with names that sounded like the roll-call of a Zulu army—Opepe, Iroko, Makoré, Agba. This was strewn about the forward well-deck wherever it would go, mostly between hatches Nos. 1 and 2 where there was a space of nearly twelve feet, and very slipshod and unshipshape it looked. But this was wartime and Monsieur Lagny had put up with so much since the war started, more than five years ago, that he could put up with almost anything now—or so he always said.

At Bahia they would take on many tons of rough rubber; great grey-white bales composed of tightly folded and compressed sheets of the stuff; a somewhat lesser amount of monozite sand and possibly some coffee and coco-fibre. Monsieur Lagny planned to place the monozite sand in the bottoms of holds 1 and 2 and the rubber aft in 3 and 4 above the palm kernels. The coffee and the coco-fibre—if taken aboard—would share the after tween-decks with the African hides.

Then at Georgetown there would be sugar—to go on top of the sand; and at Trinidad there would be rum—mostly for the British Navy but a small amount for Captain Crawshaw. Monsieur Lagny was not sure yet where he would place the Navy's rum—perhaps in the tween-decks if they were not already full, or he might make a deck cargo of it aft. Where Captain Crawshaw would stow *his* rum was not a matter for the First Officer's attention—in the fiddley, quite possibly, for the Captain, who had gone to sea in the days of sail and still thought in terms of long clean decks with the great polished trunks of masts rising from them, seemed to believe that the housing at the base of the tunnel was a place for the disposal of any of his personal dunnage that would not fit into his cabin. The First Officer was wondering about the stowage of the rum—the Navy's, not the Captain's—when he crossed the forward well-deck shortly after seven-fifteen on his way aft to find his assistant, Mr Slater the Second Officer, who should be on the poop superintending the painting of the stern rails.

But in fact the painting had been finished some ten minutes before and Mr Slater was in his cabin amidships, his ordinary spectacles changed for his reading ones, continuing the serial letter to his parents which would be posted when the ship reached Bahia.

. . . 'Seven days and probably another seven to go. Nothing is ever certain on this ship and the most uncertain things about her are her engines which are said to have been made well before the turn of the century and originally to have belonged to an even older ship before being installed in this one. I must say that I should not have thought such a thing possible myself and perhaps it is not true, but the Captain says anything is possible with a French ship and continually insists that we would go much faster if we had sails. We crossed the Line today and this makes the eleventh time I have crossed it (or recrossed it). The Captain says that if he had a pound for every time he had crossed the Line he could buy all the brothels in China . . .' Slater paused, wondering whether he should have put that in, but decided to let it stand. Coming from several generations of nonconformist forbears he strongly disapproved of lewd speech and writings, but he had been, until three years ago, a promising history student at Oxford and he possessed the true historian's implacable passion for accuracy. Captain Crawshaw had said brothels—not tea or rice—and he must be quoted accurately or not at all. Brian Slater shook his pen on to the blotting-paper, glanced at his watch, noting that the time was nearly twenty past seven, and wrote—'This will be my second visit to Bahia. It is ironical that I should so often visit these southern cities when all my true interests lie so much farther north . . .'

Three

Right in the stern, in the half-light of the after chain locker where the great rusty red links of the anchor cable were stored, Ignacio Roldan the lamp trimmer and Lin Hsiang, one of the Chinese stokers, were making love—that is to say they were performing the actions of sexual intercourse as far as their young male bodies would permit. It was not very satisfactory and each would have been happier, and a great deal more comfortable, if his partner had been a woman. But of course there were no women on board and so it was a case of half a loaf being better than no bread—for sailors on tramp steamers, like English public school boys, know that they must satisfy their sexual instincts among themselves or not at all. The difference is that the authorities of the former take the situation for granted while those of the latter do not. If Mr Slater, who had been to a public school before going on to Oxford and who was only a temporary sailor, had chanced to enter the chain locker this evening he would have been shocked and disgusted—particularly as he approved of both the Spaniard and the Chinese who struck him as being intelligent, polite and industrious boys, the type, he often felt, who might have profited by the sort of education which he himself had had.

Yet except for their ages (neither had yet attained his nineteenth birthday) Roldan and Lin had nothing in common with the sort of youth turned out by the institutions which had produced Brian Slater. The fathers of both young sailors had been practising anarchists and had been shot for it, after the customary preliminaries of torture, at the hands of the Spanish Nationalists and the Kuomintang. Their families had been duly proscribed and had broken up as each member sought what safety he could in flight and exile. Despite their extreme youth, despite the fact that neither had ever been guilty of anything save the petty larceny forced upon hungry and penniless refugees, both these two would have been executed if they had fallen into the hands of their respective governments. Coming from peoples who possessed a particularly strong sense of fatalistic resignation, Roldan and Lin accepted their position without rancour, almost with in-difference, seeing in it no more than the usual calamity of being born a human being into a world dominated by their own species. They would have been as surprised if told that this was not—or, at least, should not be—the case as they would have been derisive if informed that what they were doing in the after chain locker was generally considered shameful and even sinful.

But this evening their hearts were not really in it. Roldan, staring over the curve of Lin's shoulder at the churning tumult of frothy wake that boiled below the trembling hawse-pipe, was thinking that this time he had enough money saved to desert ship at Bahia. He did not know Bahia, but he knew Pernambuco and had several friends there.

One of them wanted to open an auto service station and there was the possibility of a partnership . . .

Lin, whose nature was at once more nervous and more intricate, felt the Spaniard's heart thudding against his own sticky flesh and with a gasping giggle twisted his legs sinuously between Roldan's thighs. Yet he was more than half distracted by the thought of red—brilliant firecracker red, less orange than vermilion, more glowing than scarlet. A shroud of such a colour was what he wanted most of all. He must have a shroud; all the Chinese seamen had their own—and that colour, that brilliant vivid red which he had only once seen (in a shop in Colombo when, infuriatingly, he had had no money in his pockets) was what he had set his heart upon. Perhaps when the ship reached Bahia . . . His almond eyes caught the glint of the Spaniard's wristwatch. He would like one himself. It was twenty-three minutes past seven. Perhaps in Bahia . . .

Four

Captain Christopher Crawshaw poured rum into a handsome glass tumbler and, after adding some sugar and the juice of one of the fresh limes which Mr Trupert, the Chief Steward, had taken on at Conakry, he raised it, as was his custom, to the coloured portrait clamped to the forward bulkhead of his cabin. '*Bonne chance, mon ami,*' he said. '*À la victoire!*' From his gilt frame Nicolas Charles Oudinot, Duke of Reggio and Marshal of the French Empire, stared doubtfully back with, as Captain Crawshaw often thought, the expression of a polite haberdasher listening to a customer's criticism of his goods. There was nothing soldierly about that square, bald-browed face above the immensely high gilded collar of the Napoleonic uniform; it was difficult to see in its possessor the famous leader of the Grenadiers of the Guard, the general who was regularly wounded in every one of his battles, the short dour soldier from Bar who, on occasion, would contradict the Emperor himself. Beside the portrait was a glazed frame of the same size containing, in very small print, a summary of the Marshal's career. Captain Crawshaw had made Gaston translate it for him and it had caused him to find still more oddities in the French character than he had already discovered amongst his officers and crew. Oudinot's conduct—at least according to the summary— seemed both bizarre and macabre. On one occasion, learned the

Captain, when the Frenchman's horse had refused to move forward
during an Imperial review held at the camp at Boulogne its furious
owner had stabbed it in the neck with his sword, killing it under him.
'Is that the way you always treat your horses?' Napoleon had asked
that evening at dinner. 'That is my way when I am not obeyed,' the
Marshal Duke had replied grimly. Captain Crawshaw had not credited
this story at first. Gaston had had to repeat it a second time.

The SS. *Maréchal Oudinot*, a freighter of some 7,500 tons, had been
built by Boucicault, Michelot, Bonpland et Cie. in 1904 at Brest, and
the origin of her coal-burning, triple-expansion engines, which was a
mystery to her present crew, must have been known to at least one
of those three long dead partners. Monsieur Yves Pionnier, the Chief
Engineer, had told Gaston, who had told the Captain, that he believed
that they had been made in Constantinople and originally intended
to drive three special locomotives ordered by the Khedive Ismail
but, after that thriftless prince's bankruptcy, sold and adapted for use
in a Dutch dredger. Monsieur Pionnier was, of course, joking but
Captain Crawshaw, who had never had the slightest interest in engines
and knew nothing about them, had, to Gaston's delight, accepted this
explanation as the truth.

The ship herself was typical of her period; too long for her comparatively narrow beam, with a high bow, a curious spoon-shaped
stern and deckhouses which looked like a collection of miscellaneous
iron crates piled one upon another. Her single narrow funnel was of a
dim mauve, splotched with rust and flaked with soot and surrounded
by a cluster of immensely tall buff-coloured ventilator shafts. She had
been owned by the Niort Steam Navigation Company of Rouen and,
being docked with engine trouble in Bombay at the time of the French
capitulation, had subsequently been taken over by the British Ministry
of War Transport, her crew being given the option of further employment or free repatriation to their various countries of origin. Her
captain and two junior officers had chosen to go back to France but
most of the remainder had accepted British employment, and though
throughout the ensuing four years many changes had been made, her
crew had always included a high proportion of Frenchmen. This
evening, a few miles south of the Equator and passing through the
neck of the South Atlantic between Freetown and Natal, there were
still thirteen of the original crewmen on board and these included the
First Officer, the Chief Engineer and all the cooks.

Captain Crawshaw got along very well with his crew even though,
as a Welshman, he had never before had much to do with the French

and spoke hardly a word of their language. He liked and trusted Monsieur Lagny, a quiet, rather gloomy man who collected carved ivories; he liked the Chief Engineer and assumed correctly that he understood his peculiar charges. He was tolerant of French foibles and he greatly pleased the galley staff by eating their food with genuine enjoyment and praising it with admiration (the previous captain, a Scotsman, had grumbled continually and once made them cook a haggis he had brought back from shore leave).

But the Captain's especial approbation was reserved for the young radio operator, Gaston Guéroult, a short, bull-necked, twenty-year-old Dieppois who, at the age of sixteen, had crossed the Channel to take up his technical training in embattled England and then to go to war under the Red Ensign. Gaston, though of course he could not know this, bore a strong resemblance to Captain Crawshaw as the latter had been fifty years ago. The Captain was some four inches taller, his nose not quite so snub, his mouth not quite so wide; but there was the same high colour, the same shock of tar-black hair, the same broad chest and short powerful thighs. There was, too, much the same flamboyance. Gaston's cap was always cocked at a slant on the side of his head; he wore—at least in the tropics—his white shirt open to the waist disclosing a fine portrait of Admiral Abraham Duquesne tattooed on his chest, and he habitually stood with his feet wide apart and his hands jammed on his hips. '*Je suis dur—moi*,' he would say, grinning, flexing his thick arms.

Being French, albeit a Norman, he had smoother manners, a more elegant turn of speech, than his captain and he boasted unself-consciously and with no inhibiting modesty about his bravery during the two occasions on which his previous ships had been sunk by torpedoes. On the first of these Gaston had remained at his post, rattling out the regulation SSS—SSS—SSS of a submarine sinking and giving his position, until the bridge and radio-room were a shambles of wreckage under the surfaced U-boat's angry gunfire. He had leapt overboard, the last to do so, just in time to save himself from the suction of the death plunge and then, being hauled on board the enemy submarine, had been savagely shaken and slapped by the furious commander before being kicked into the sea again to swim to the nearest of the ship's lifeboats.

Recounting this treatment, Gaston's face would seem to swell and become a dark red with indignation; he spluttered and trembled. This always amused Captain Crawshaw, who added to his radio operator's rage by saying, 'But what did you expect the fellow to do?

Give you a drink and some dry clothes? He might have shot you, after all.' The Captain did not realize that Gaston, in his own imagination at least, had been playing a role that day and one not far from the brink of hysteria. The U-boat commander's behaviour had, by sobering him up, both destroyed this role and frightened him far more than the shelling; it had wantonly damaged his *amour propre* and was consequently unforgivable.

Gaston, surprisingly, reciprocated the Captain's liking, finding at least one undoubted affinity with the old man, a shared pragmatism, a self-sufficient, self-regarding realism—a Gallic rather than an Anglo-Saxon attitude to life.

In common with most of his fellow countrymen Gaston's feelings for the British consisted largely of a mixture of derision, impatience and incomprehension. They were complicated, blank-faced, sly and had no proper feelings. By the stupendous folly of the Polish guarantee they had dragged a reluctant France into war to save a country which was already lost and then effectively destroyed their ally by refusing to commit their powerful air force in French skies in defence of French armies. Like the leader of the Free French, Gaston looked upon collaboration with the difficult British as the only alternative to collaboration with the impossible Germans—one did not much care for it but one had to accept it. And also, like the General, he made no effort to conceal this view.

But typifying and underlining all Gaston's anglophobic sentiments were the person and the personality of the Second Officer. Mr Slater was tall and thin and blond and reserved well beyond the point of taciturnity. He was, it appeared, a University student of great promise and Gaston, who had a correct respect for learning (though he himself had never attended any higher seat of it than the *École Communale des Garçons* in the Place Louis Vitet at Dieppe), would have liked to hear about his studies. But the Second Officer would never discuss these. Mr Slater was deeply religious—though since he was not a Catholic this only meant that he plunged himself ever deeper into a mire of heresy—and he held some views which seemed to Gaston so close to insanity that he often wondered how Captain Crawshaw could ever allow his Second Officer to have the watch.

For Brian Slater was a savagely militant pacifist and though not quite a conscientious objector he was as close to being one as made no matter. His main reason for being on the *Maréchal Oudinot* was that, owing to various causes connected with the ship's age and construction, it had been deemed impracticable to give her any defensive armament. Gaston, who longed above all things for a cannon to play with on the bow or the stern, had been speechless with surprise when the Captain had told him this and the Captain had taken advantage of the unusual silence to describe and animadvert upon the English non-conformist conscience in general and that of Mr Slater in particular. Gaston had grasped it all very well for a Frenchman—he was, as Captain Crawshaw always thought, an intelligent boy. 'It is not a mental disease but a—a *condition psychologique*. All the same, it is a madness. They should shut him away.'

'They can't very well. You see, there are a great many of them. Besides, it's religious. They do it to please God.'

'So? They think it displeasing to God that they should kill others, but pleasing that others should kill them. They must indeed have a sad opinion of themselves.'

Gaston had asked this question bluntly on the next occasion he had had to go to the Second Officer's cabin to retrieve Françoise, the radio-room cat, whose affections Mr Slater was attempting to alienate from their proper owner. Slater had stared at him with the surprised indignation of someone asked a most impertinent and indecent question.

'What business it is of *yours* I cannot imagine. But since you ask . . . I take it that the Bible has been translated into French?'

'Oh yes.'

'And—just possibly—you have a knowledge of it? At least you may have heard of the Sixth Commandment?'

'*Et alors—?*'

'Either you obey it, or you don't. Either you accept that life is sacred, or you don't.'

'*Mais* . . . *Écoute, mon ami*— If another should attempt one's life. . . ?'

'That is his affair.'

'Assuredly it is not!'

Mr Slater had shrugged, contemptuously silent, and continued to rub a forefinger under Françoise's left ear. Grinning angrily, Gaston had leaned forward and whisked the cat into his own arms. '*Alors— merde à vous!* This is my cat. You would do well, Monsieur Slater, to think also, sometimes, upon the *Tenth* Commandment!' Delighted with his own cleverness, he retired to the radio-room with Françoise.

The Captain had laughed a great deal over Gaston's description of this scene but, as if to show that he was not going to take sides in the matter, he had bought a bright orange-coloured cat in a Liverpool pet shop and presented it to Mr Slater with his compliments at the commencement of the present voyage. Gaston was more pleased by this gesture than the Second Officer. It was a practical and sensible one and confirmed his already high opinion of the *Maréchal Oudinot's* Welsh master. The Captain had 'proper sentiments'; he was not devious or reserved and he took the French view that a little personal enterprise was not unbecoming to his position. Both the forward deck cargo of African hardwoods among which Rayner and the Brazilian child were resting this evening and the extra rum—when it was loaded at Trinidad—were personal enterprises on the part of Captain Crawshaw.

Gaston wondered idly whether he himself might not take on something in that way. Bahia would offer a large assortment of American luxury goods, things almost unobtainable in present-day Britain. And there was plenty of room in the *Maréchal Oudinot's* capacious radio office. . . Putting down his newly sharpened pencil, he rose, stretched and glanced from the starboard window across the twilight sea, vast and empty and merging imperceptibly into the darkening eastern horizon. He began to sing softly under his breath. '*Comment épouser un soldat, moi qu'aime tout le régiment?*'—and then stopped, frozen in sudden shock.

Some forty metres off the starboard bow two long white streaks trailing bubbling wakes rushed towards the ship, plainer every second below the glint and gleam of the slow swell. He heard a frightened shout from the bridge and, knowing that it was far too late, that nothing, now, could be done, leapt around the table, tore open the door of the radio-room and was half-way out of it as the torpedoes, striking simultaneously one amidships and one on the starboard bow, tore the old freighter apart beneath his feet.

Five

The *Maréchal Oudinot*, whose long life was thus abruptly terminated at 7.28 p.m. on the 5th of January 1945, carried a crew of thirty-seven. Of these more than half died immediately. The midships torpedo, tearing through the old ship's rusty side two metres below the water-line, exploded in the engine-room which, at that moment, contained nearly its full complement of engineers and greasers since Monsieur Pionnier was holding one of his frequent inquests into the failure of some auxiliary machinery, and they all died, hardly knowing it, with their minds still engaged in puzzled speculations of a mechanical nature. The men in the stokehold were slightly less fortunate, but the bursting boilers, forcing super-heated steam into their clanging world of coal dust and roaring furnaces, allowed them only just time to scream briefly at the quick glimpse of Death's face before they were flayed and boiled to rags. And the three cooks died in the galley, roaring and struggling in a welter of food and burning coals as their kitchen disintegrated around them in fire and buckling iron.

The other torpedo, striking forward and exploding in No. 1 hold, tore the ship's bow completely off. It upended and sank, taking with it all the seamen at present off watch and in the fo'c'sle. Several, perhaps most, would probably have escaped if the starboard door opening on to the forward well-deck had not been jammed into its frame, or if the port one had not been blocked by the twisted bulk of a derrick boom ripped from its pinion-joint by the explosion. As it was, the occupants of the fo'c'sle were trapped in terrifying blackness and thrown in a sprawling jumble first to the port, and then, as the ruined bow sagged back on its sundered side, to the starboard bulkhead. After the first screams of surprised shock they quietened down, moaning and holding to each other, pressing closely together in an instinctive recoil from the loneliness of death and of the death-struggle which must precede it. Even so it was all over for them in a matter of minutes.

Monsieur Lagny, who had been half-way up the starboard bridge ladder with his back to the arrowing torpedoes when the look-out gave his belated shout of warning, was thrown overboard into the sea. He guessed accurately what had happened while he was still struggling to the surface, but no sooner had he reached it and taken a great gasping breath of air than the end of the derrick whose fore part was blocking the fo'c'sle door fell upon him, crushing his skull.

The after part of the ship suffered least and it was from the canting stern that most of the survivors of the attack escaped. These included Roldan and Lin, who rushed out of the chain locker naked as babies and, climbing to the poop, seized fire axes and began to hack at the ropes which held the aft lifeboat to its teak skids and chocks on the deckhouse roof. It was a heavy whaler-type craft which they had no chance of launching—but that did not matter. Hooked on to the gunwales of the boat at each end were gripes fitted with short pieces of chain; screwed into the skids were ringbolts. The ropes they were cutting connected the chains with the bolts on the skids and once they were severed the chocks would hold the boat until the ship sank when it would, with luck, float free since it was too big and buoyant to be pulled under by the death-drag. With the disappearance of its twin on the prow, it was the only properly provisioned and seaworthy boat now available and the prompt action of the young Spaniard and Chinese demonstrated not merely the intelligence which Mr Slater believed them to possess but the instinctive capacity for self-preservation which their bleak histories had inculcated so early.

Around them three or four off-duty greasers who had been in their quarters in the stern and had thus missed the massacre in the engine-room cut the lighter cords of Carley floats and emergency rafts and heaved them over the side. In this they were led by Reemann, Rayner's mate and, like him, a Jamaican Negro from Kingston.

There was not much time, only two or three minutes, before they must all leap into the sea, but if they could free a sufficiency of the buoyant rafts they would avoid being pulled down with the sinking ship, and if the lifeboat floated off they could then transfer into that and their chances of survival would be comparatively high. They were all of them, even the youngsters, experienced seamen—they knew this perfectly well.

Gaston was already in the water. The explosion of the torpedo amidships had flung him from the door of the radio-room down the ladder to the iron deck fifteen feet below, battering the breath out of his body and partially stunning him. He had staggered to his feet, barely more than half conscious, seized a lifebelt from its broad iron hooks and toppled with it over the side. Then he had paddled and kicked his way as fast as possible from the hissing, clanging, groaning wreck while debris and deck fittings crashed frighteningly into the water around him. Looking up, he saw two of the enormous old-fashioned ventilators that ringed the funnel swaying slowly towards him, right above him against the darkening sky, and for a moment he believed that it was all over. But the nearest missed him by some four feet, throwing sheets of spray high in the air and engulfing him beneath a frothy wave. As the backwash subsided he finally got his arms properly hooked over the lifebelt and, spitting and blinking salt water, still kicking away with his feet, turned to look his last at the *Maréchal Oudinot*.

The bow was in the act of disappearing. Upended, the stem a dark line against the sky, it hung for a moment seemingly suspended by the air within. Gaston heard the thin, unreal wailing of the men trapped in the fo'c'sle and then, deliberately and steadily the bow went down, passing below the surface with the smooth precision of a hotel elevator descending a floor. As it did so one great bubble of air broke the surface like an immense sigh of sorrow.

Now wreathed in a misty fog of steam, the stern gloomed unnaturally upward through the falling dark. Gaston could see figures frantically hacking at ropes and lashings, then slipping, sliding, leaping into the sea. And all the time this turmoil rang and echoed with the gonglike sound of falling metal, the banshee-screech of tearing iron, the roar and hiss of escaping steam and the huge burps of trapped air suddenly escaping below the water.

Fascinated, he stared at the spoon-shaped stern lifting rapidly ever higher out of the sea. Here came the great single screw with its huge blades still turning slowly, rising from the deep like some monstrous ocean flower. In seconds, now, everything would be over—already emergency rafts and swimming heads spotted the water.

Someone shouted from just behind him and Gaston felt a large hand grip his shoulder. He turned his head to see the Negro stoker Rayner—Rayner and, incredibly, the Brazilian child whom they called Philippe. Both of them were sitting on the loose, canvas-covered planks of the hatch cover—on the very hatch cover upon which they had been sitting three minutes ago when the torpedoes struck.

'You okay, mister? You all right? Here—pull up on this. That's it!'

With Rayner's help Gaston heaved himself on to the hatch cover and pulled his lifebelt up after him. Polite, unsmiling, the Brazilian boy made way for him.

'Christ, they done for us this time! Done for us proper!' Rayner's voice was shaky yet somehow jubilant as he stared back at the stern now empty of life and rising at a high slant for the plunge. 'Wonder if they got the boat free—if it'll float. This is your third time, isn't it, mister? An' my second—an' young Phil's first. Jesus, we're lucky sods! Jesus, we are that!'

'*Du calme, du calme!*' said Gaston impatiently. 'Demonstrate some calm. We must help these others.'

Small red marker-lights gleamed here and there on the rafts. Shouts and whistles sounded through the dusk. It was impossible to be sure how many survivors were swimming in the sea—perhaps a dozen. Gaston doubted if there could be many more.

'Look—she's going!' The black bulk of the stern was lifting fast now. Up, up, up it rose against the softer darkness of the sky and Gaston, breath held, stared entranced at that great looming hull so soon to vanish for ever from human sight. For years and years—long years before he was born—the *Maréchal Oudinot* had steamed slowly over the world's seaways on her amiable unimportant errands. Her paint had blistered in the tropics, ice had coated her ungainly rigging in the northern seas; she had lain indifferently at rainy French docksides, at the cheapest berths in great American ports and at the best, perhaps the only, ones in small African harbours. She had rusted gently at her moorings at the mud-banks of the Seine estuary during the long depression between the wars and come to wheezing rattling life again six years ago. And her crew ... If old houses held ghosts and memories of ghosts how much more so must be the case with old ships. Hundreds—thousands, perhaps—of men of every nationality had spent weeks and months of their lives waking to work on those iron decks, sleeping to the grunt and tremor of those engines, the thud and churn of that screw. And now ...

But Gaston never saw the death plunge of the *Maréchal Oudinot*. Even as the stern hung poised for it he felt a light grasp on his arm and Philippe's voice, urgent with surprise and delight, came from behind him. '*Monsieur! Monsieur, regardez!*'

He turned quickly—and there it was. Long and low and silent, it moved slowly towards them under the power of its soundless electric motors. Men stood on the fore casing and from the bridge, under the tall periscope standards, a voice called brief calm orders. It was only the second time in his life that Gaston had heard German spoken; he shivered with distress as though at the return of an ugly dream. Then the submarine was beside them and the hatch cover was bobbing and scraping along the bulging curve of its saddle tanks. A voice called in English, 'Is there an officer?' And its owner must have seen Gaston's black epaulettes against his white shirt, for almost at once it came again, 'Yes—you! Come here!'

It was not easy to climb the slippery sloping metal up to the hollow iron grid of the casing, but Rayner steadied the hatch as best he could and a blue-overalled sailor leaned down perilously far and grasped Gaston's outstretched hand. Then, for the second time in eighteen months, Gaston was standing on the deck of a U-boat facing a German officer.

It was an encounter very different from that first occasion, and every detail was to be firmly fixed in Gaston's mind until the end of his life —to remain exact and clear when the memory of that earlier experience at the hands of the furious commander whose anger he had aroused with his radio messages was difficult to recall in any but its broadest outlines.

The man who now confronted him had nothing in common with

that big, burly, red-faced, shouting captain who had shaken him and slapped him before throwing him back into the sea like an inedible fish. This man was small and young; smaller, and perhaps younger, than Gaston himself. Only his big high-fronted gold-badged cap showed his rank as an officer, for otherwise he was dressed in the same dark-blue overalls as the sailors around him. But his overalls were new and clean and fitted his small frame so well that they gave the wearer an appearance of neatness and smartness for which they had never been designed. He smiled at Gaston from a face as smooth and round as a coin—a cocky little dandy smelling strongly of scent.

'What is the name of your ship?' The English was stilted, a sentence learned from a book of instructions, and badly accented—though not, it seemed, with a German accent.

'*Le Maréchal Oudinot.*'

The German's eyebrows lifted in quick surprise. '*Française?*'

'*Oui—française.*'

'*Et—vous?*'

'*Moi aussi.*'

And now the German spoke in French—French as fluent and clear as Gaston's own. 'I see. Then tell me, if you please, to where you were bound, from whence and with what cargo. And your name and rank, too, of course.' He smiled broadly as if all this was a joke between the two of them, not to be taken seriously.

These were routine questions and Gaston gave routine answers; there was nothing in the least secret or important which need be concealed. While he spoke he wondered with a mixture of resentment and curiosity whether the officer before him was partly or wholly French. This was not by any means impossible and was shortly to be confirmed. A voice from the dark height of the bridge called 'Emil!' and Gaston's interrogator lifted a hand in acknowledgment. 'One minute. I shall be back.' He turned and went aft along the casing, his small dark figure fading quickly into the falling night.

The sailors spoke softly to themselves in German and shifted their feet—they all seemed extremely young and smiled at Gaston with shy yet inquisitive embarrassment. He grinned back without warmth. Then the officer returned, walking carefully, carrying something in one hand. 'Here is something for you that I think you will like— French cognac.'

Gaston accepted the enamel mug and swallowed its contents in three gulps. It did him a great deal of good.

'You feel better, eh?'

'Yes.' Gaston wiped his mouth with the back of his hand. 'But this is my third time, you comprehend. I am used to it, therefore.'

'*Mon Dieu!* Three times!' The German's round face held a look of slightly shocked admiration. 'You are certainly most unfortunate, are you not?' Then, as if wishing to confide something in his turn, 'This is my first patrol—and your ship the first one I have seen sunk. It is a pity it was a French one.'

'You speak very good French,' said Gaston carefully.

'Because I am French—or three-quarters French. My home is in France.'

Gaston, the brandy hot in his stomach, felt a sudden exasperation rising within him. Despite his fury at the German captain who had slapped him and kicked him into the sea, he had been impressed by the man's size and power and force—and his sailors had seemed to be men, too, from what he could remember of them. But here, tonight, he was surrounded by a group of awkward adolescents; giggling teen-age boys playing at pirates. It was somehow humiliating to think that the *Maréchal Oudinot* had been sunk by a gang of children. And now, apparently one of the gang leaders was claiming kinship and wanting to make friends.

'Well,' he said coldly, 'if that is the case what are you doing in that uniform?'

But instead of being taken aback the German only smiled. 'And what are you doing sailing under that flag? No, no—it is not so easy to answer such questions, is it? So I will ask you some easier ones. What ships were in Conakry last week? Were there any warships? Also, is it true that convoys are now escorted by carriers?'

Since these questions were not routine ones Gaston, who had a fertile imagination, gave a series of highly mendacious answers. He doubted if he deceived his interrogator, who merely smiled and nodded but took no notes; he did not seem to be paying much attention.

As Gaston finished one of the juvenile sailors said something and pointed down at the hatch cover which still bobbed and scraped gently against the submarine's swollen metal flank. The officer nodded and turned to Gaston. 'There is a lifebelt down there with your ship's name on it. You will not need it and we do. We are expected to bring back some proof of a sinking if possible.'

Gaston called down to the glimmering canvas-covered hatch and in a moment Philippe clambered up the saddle tanks with spidery agility, lugging the old cork lifebelt after him. The Germans looked at the small thin figure in the wet shirt and shorts with surprised distress and the officer said, almost reprovingly as if the fault were Gaston's, 'We did not know that you were carrying *children*.'

'This is the only one. We were taking him to Bahia, where he lives. He is Brazilian.'

'And now . . . of course . . .' The German shook his head, frowning. Then he said, 'One minute . . . I will see . . .' He disappeared for the second time towards the bridge. One of the sailors took a slightly battered piece of chocolate from his pocket and offered it hesitantly to Philippe. Philippe shook his head. Then the officer was back. 'Listen. It is probable that you will be picked up tomorrow— or the next day at the latest. There is a good deal of shipping in this area; also airplanes. But of course it might be longer. We are strictly forbidden to take survivors on board unless they are valuable prisoners. This boy is obviously not a valuable prisoner. None the less, the Captain has ruled that he may come with us if he wishes—or if you think that is best. We are also in danger, of course. And if *we* get sunk there are very seldom any survivors at all . . . Well?'

It was no use asking the child. Even if the alternatives could have been coherently explained in Portuguese he was too young to weigh up the chances of survival in either case. Gaston must do it himself. And now that he had to make the choice for someone else, to take the responsibility for another's life in his hands, he realized for the first time how grimly perilous was the life of these foreign youths on the submarine's casing; how weighted and fraught with danger their work. He did not know—and certainly would not be told—whether this boat was outward bound or returning to its base, but from what the German officer had said about this being his first sinking Gaston thought the former more probable. Philippe, if left aboard the U-boat, would be treated with great kindness, but he would have to endure many weeks of constant, and at times very great, danger. A day or two adrift on a life-raft—four or five days, even—could not compare to that. And it was very probable that the *Maréchal Oudinot*'s stern lifeboat, fully watered and provisioned and with sails, awnings and compass, was floating near by, soon to be reached and boarded.

Gaston shook his head decidedly. '*Non, mon lieutenant.* I think he is safer with us.'

The German smiled. 'I, too. And—all will be over soon.'

'But it was kind of you—and your captain—to offer it.' And now

Gaston looked at the small figure before him, whose white-topped cap glimmered in the darkness, without any of his former rancour, with something which, approaching understanding, went further and became for a moment a sad affection tinged somehow with a benign amusement. 'Yes. Well, should we meet after the war I hope to tell you that he reached home safely.'

'I hope so, too. Then that is all and you can go.'

Gaston, preceded by Philippe, climbed down the sloping hull of the submarine and back on to the hatch. Shoving off with his feet, he heard the German's voice once more from the darkness above. '*Bonne chance—et au'voir, Monsieur Guéroult!*'

Gaston laughed suddenly. He only knew the German's first name. '*Au'voir, Emil!*'

And now, as the low loom of the submarine faded into the night, came the work of collecting the rest of the survivors and trying to locate the lifeboat. Gaston had assisted in this before, though both his earlier experiences had taken place in daylight and there had been officers senior to himself from whom to take orders. But for the present at any rate he must assume that he was the senior survivor. Yet since there was no way of propelling the loose planks of the hatch cover it was the others who came to Gaston and with the first float, which held Mr Slater, one of the bridge look-outs and a couple of Chinese greasers, the main responsibility for giving orders devolved upon the Second Officer. 'You'd better come off that,' he said, his voice even now retaining the note of impersonal disapproval which was its normal tone. 'It might break up at any moment.'

'It has not done so yet.' Gaston was annoyed in his turn. After all, this was the *third* time for him while it was only Slater's first. 'And that raft cannot accommodate more than one more person. I know, because—'

'It can take six. And Philippe is too small to count.'

'I know that it is written so. Nevertheless—'

'Please do as I say, Guéroult! Rayner—help me hold on while—'

'Mister Slater, I tell you—'

There was a shout, a bump and another raft, a far heavier one, looming out of the darkness struck the hatch planks and knocked three of them away. Gaston and Rayner slid into the water while Philippe was lifted by one of the stokers on to Slater's raft.

Angrily, followed by the big Negro, Gaston climbed aboard the new arrival. The Second Officer had not said, 'I told you so,' but he was certainly thinking it. And fleetingly through Gaston's mind passed the wish that Slater and the French-German officer could be changed about. 'Emil' had undoubtedly been *sympathique*; no one could say that about Mr Slater.

The raft into which Gaston had climbed was one of those cut loose from the stern and it contained four men among whom he recognized the young Spanish lamp trimmer Roldan and the second Negro stoker Reemann. The Spanish boy was violently excited. He grasped Gaston's hand in both his own. 'M'sieur Guéroult! Ah, how glad I am to see you safe! We—I and Lin—we cut free the lifeboat. Did you know? If it still floats . . . Tell me, you sent a message?'

'No, no. There was no time at all. Now we must help. It is not the time for talk. There are others swimming . . .' And even as Gaston spoke the raft gave a sight lurch as a hand reached up from the water and grasped the lifelines. Then, together with the Spaniard and Reemann, Gaston hauled the groaning, life-jacketed figure of Mr Trupert, the Chief Steward, over the side. A small grey-haired Londoner, it was his first voyage on the *Maréchal Oudinot* and no one knew much of him save that he had been on permanently bad terms with the cooks since the ship left Liverpool. He was suffering from severe shock and appeared to be in great pain. Gaston bent over him. 'What is it, mister? Where are you hurt?'

'My hand—hand.' Feeling carefully in the darkness, Gaston found that his left wrist was broken. Well, there were bound to be some casualties; it was surprising that of the survivors so far located none other had been hurt. But there was nothing to be done for Trupert until the full medical equipment on the big lifeboat was available. Meanwhile there were still men in the water, for two more small red lights blinked through the dark and a distant voice was shouting. A voice—Gaston's heart leapt. Yes, surely that was the Captain's voice! But where . . . ?

'Mister Slater! The Captain—I hear him!'

'What's that?'

'The Captain! Listen—!'

But the voice was silent and in its place Gaston's straining ears caught a new sound—the sound of engines approaching. Quickly through his mind flashed the possibility of immediate rescue. A ship was at hand. In a few minutes they would be safely aboard with decks once more beneath their feet, with help for those still in the water—above all, with light to see by.

And even at the thought of light, light appeared; a shaft of gleaming white which sprang suddenly from the darkness three hundred metres away and swung in a swift arc thrusting back the moonless night. That long narrow fan of light moving quickly across the still water held everyone silent. Gaston, watching it with fascination, knew that they ought to shout in unison. It was almost certain that they would be found but, as he was well aware, no chance was too impossible to be disregarded. Ships in the past had run down life-rafts and still failed to see them.

Then out of the empty blackness the moving light illuminated Captain Crawshaw. There he was, a bulky white-clad figure, sitting on several heavy planks—part of his own deck cargo—and lit up like the central figure on a theatre stage. Gaston gave a gasping sigh of relief. He had not realized, until that moment, how much the Captain meant to him, how deeply he would have felt his loss. His heart went out to that plump old man squatting on his baulks of expensive —and now lost—hardwoods, as it had done for a strange second to the enemy officer on the casing of the departed U-boat. The Captain would be taken aboard first. He would be there to greet them when, a few minutes later, they too had climbed the rope ladders.

The engine noises were louder now and Gaston thought that he could make out the ship's bow wave, a faint white glimmer below and far in front of the searchlight. Then two things happened with shocking abruptness. A voice—a voice which despite its amplification through a megaphone Gaston recognized all too clearly—shouted 'Get off! Get off!' And at once the still night was ripped by a long burst of machine-gune fire which tore into the sea a dozen metres away from the crouching figure on the makeshift raft.

'Get off! Go in the water! *Sauve-toi, imbécile!*' And another burst of fire—closer this time so that the spray from the torn sea, splashing up in a glittering haze, obscured the white figure of the Captain. And when it fell the dark logs were empty. No one sat there. The Captain had gone.

Gaston watching, mouth open in horrified wonder, saw the white bow wave rushing at the logs, saw the low stem of the U-boat smash into them, knocking them apart as if they were slats of a fruit crate— scattering them to bob and heave and bump along the wide metal flanks. But what—? And why—?

And now the searchlight swung viciously across the water and Gaston was himself illuminated, his seared eyes shutting against the blinding white beam. 'Into the water! Quick—*into the water!*' But this time it was Mr Slater's voice, high and strident with urgency. Even as he spoke the machine-guns roared out close at hand and bullets tore over the heads of those in the two life-rafts. No one needed further warning; they leapt and tumbled over the side and began to swim frantically away. Only the Chief Steward, in too much pain or too handicapped by his broken wrist to move quickly, was still on the raft when the next burst, long and sustained, ripped into the wood and canvas and flung him dying on to the slatted floor.

Then the U-boat struck both rafts together, overturning them and ploughing on through a jumble of minor wreckage, its light probing and searching back and forth and at last steadying upon a large single object which floated, buoyant and motionless upon the calm water, less than a hundred and fifty metres beyond the capsized, broken rafts. The stern lifeboat. Spitting water, clinging with one arm to a floating crate, Gaston watched with frightened, despairing fury as the machine-gun bullets—burst after long burst and each at an ever decreasing range—destroyed the lifeboat. The boat which the enterprise and quickness of young Roldan and a Chinese stoker had freed in time and in so doing had saved—*should* have saved—all the survivors. The boat which had been waiting for them close at hand with water, provisions, medical supplies—which undoubtedly they would have found by the light of one of the flashlights with which all the rafts were equipped. Now the submarine was upon it . . . Now it was under that crushing iron stem—gone—destroyed—sunk.

Holding to his crate, Gaston watched the long searchlight beam swing and turn restlessly across the wreckage-strewn water; saw it illuminate what appeared to be a large empty raft and saw the submarine turn to ram it. But even as the bow struck it the raft parted in the middle and Gaston heard the clang of great baulks of hardwood against the iron sides. The U-boat turned again as the questing light picked a small float from the blackness to the left of the scattered timbers. Two figures, quite still, were clearly visible upon it and this time no one shouted from the oncoming submarine. Instead, a long burst of bullets tore the sea to foam some ten metres from the float's side. At that the two occupants came to sudden frantic life and paddled with all their might. Surely they must know that they had no chance—that there was no escape that way. But they would not leave their float—perhaps they could not swim properly—and a second burst of fire flung them dead and still across the punctured buoyancy tanks and spun the float itself around in a sudden mad gyration as if it had been caught in some unnatural vortex of the waters.

Then, once more, the light was in Gaston's eyes, once again the throb of the diesels was loud in his ears and growing rapidly in volume as the U-boat bore down for the second time upon the upturned and bullet-shattered rafts, to the sagging lifelines of which a few men still clung.

Gaston, who had dragged himself half out of the water so that most of his body was lying across the crate, slid quickly back into it again. As he did so fire from the U-boat's bridge ripped close overhead while the prolonged roar of the guns momentarily drowned the thunder of the diesel engines. Then the U-boat, moving at its full surface speed of nineteen knots, thrust past him, burying him beneath its bow wave, whirling and tossing him and dragging him under in the eddying turbulence of its churning screws.

Gaston had swum and dived as soon as he could walk, and despite several of the alarmingly close escapes usual in an amphibious coastal boyhood he had no fear of the sea. But now, struggling blindly against the tug and spin and swirl of the U-boat's passing, he had a quick horrifying vision of those racing screws slicing the water beside him, of the long blades of the after hydroplanes cutting smoothly through it. At any second his kicking, jerking legs and arms might be severed by the whistling propellers, his skull shattered by those great horizontal rudders.

Then he was tossing, choking and gasping and retching in the white wake and the heavy fumes of the engine exaust gases. The submarine was past and he had survived the second attack. But it seemed that no one else had done so. There were no little red lights spotting the water now—no shouts or whistles or cries. The sea, save for himself and the submarine, seemed empty. Gaston turned slowly on to his back and rested motionless, except for his heavy breathing, upon the subsiding darkness of the water. From far away came the sound of two sharp detonations and then a thin screaming followed by a further burst of machine-gun fire. Then silence again save for the distant throb of diesels.

Had the sinking and subsequent attacks by the submarine taken place in northern latitudes Gaston would have been dead long since, his short body now sinking slowly into the profounder depths. But here upon the Equator the sea was not the implacable enemy which it became in the icy north. Still more important, Gaston was wearing light cotton clothes which hardly hampered his natural buoyancy at all; and instinctively he had kicked off his shoes within seconds of leaping from the *Maréchal Oudinot*'s canting deck.

Yet the shock of the two attacks, the terror of his own complete helplessness and vulnerability under the U-boat's glaring, cyclopean searchlight, had partly numbed his ability to think. All he knew was that he must stay as he was, with nothing but his face above the water, until the Germans gave up hunting for him and left the area of the sinking. For, alone and with death closing in upon him, Gaston was filled with the instinctive belief that it was he only, the radio operator, who was the submarine's quarry and intended victim. For more than another hour, for nearly two, though he did not know this, he lay supine, his body just below the surface and kept in position by the continuous finlike motions of his spread hands, his face staring upward at the star-filled sky. Six more times the searchlight passed over him; six more times he waited, his body cramped and pulsing with fear as the engine noises grew greater and then diminished. And all the time there was firing—irregular, intermittent bursts, all apparently from the same guns—never ceasing for more than a few minutes at a time. In the end Gaston's nerves were in such a state that it was only with great difficulty that he stopped himself screaming every time the light passed near him.

But at last it was over. The U-boat's engines faded until they were no longer discernible and the darkness was once more absolute except for a growing radiance upon the horizon where the moon was about to rise. And with the moonrise came the possibility of finding some wreckage upon which to climb. Gaston, aided by the continual circling menace of the searchlight, had kept his mind resolutely away from the thought of sharks, but that these were around and would increase rapidly in numbers he had no doubt. He must get out of the water, get on to something as soon as there was light enough to see by. And as the moon lifted, white and glowing from the dark rim of the sea, he trod water and rose as high as he could from the surface. A sinking always left a wide area of wreckage, though the submarine had almost certainly destroyed all the larger pieces . . . And now, under the growing moonlight, Gaston made out, with quick relief, a variety of irregular floating shapes marking the tranquil surface of the suddenly silvered sea. He swam to the nearest of these and discovered an upturned float, one side shot away but still buoyant enough to support a single body. And as he grasped the ragged canvas of its broken side he saw that it was already supporting one—or most of one, for the slumped figure sprawled face down across the shattered cork lacked its left shoulder and arm and where the back of its head should have been was a cavity filled with sea water. Gaston thrust it off, eyes partly averted; he was determined not to see its face and know its identity. It slid smoothly into the water and disappeared below the surface, leaving Gaston bobbing precariously on the wood-and-canvas stretcher which formed the float's bottom, but out of the water and free at present from the peril of sharks or slow drowning.

So convinced had Gaston become that he was now the sole survivor of the *Maréchal Oudinot*'s crew that when he saw something moving on a tangle of minor wreckage a dozen metres away he at first believed it must be some sea creature—a giant squid come to the surface to search with mindless curiosity among the flotsam for food. He shuddered and, had he had the means, would have propelled his broken float farther away. Then through the fear and exhaustion which filmed his mind, he realized slowly that this was nonsense. None of the sea animals inhabiting the depths which the *Maréchal Oudinot* had now plumbed for ever approached the surface in a living condition; parts of their decomposing bodies alone would sometimes rise sluggishly to the surface to make a meal for sharks. Whatever lay on that obscurely floating mass must be human. Gaston called softly—even now his instinctive terror of the U-boat's return made him keep his voice needlessly low—'Who is there? Is someone there?'

An odd grunting snort was his only answer, but from the jagged outlines of splintered woodwork the unmistakable head and shoulders of a human figure lifted slightly and turned towards him. Quickly Gaston pulled a broken piece of planking from its canvas rungs on the floor and, using this as a paddle, thrust his float clumsily across the water. And, lying as if crucified upon a waterlogged collection of broken crates which were held together only by his wide-spread arms and legs, Gaston found the stoker Rayner. The Negro turned his head, his eyes glinting in the moonlight; he grunted and gobbled and for a moment Gaston thought that the long hours of terror in the water under the charging death-blows of the submarine must have driven him out of his mind. For Captain Crawshaw had once told him that, while it took much more physical damage to kill a Negro than a white man, it took much less mental strain to drive him mad. But as the float touched the stoker's wretched raft he saw that Rayner's mouth was a mangled mess of torn flesh, his lips pulped, his teeth shattered stumps.

Gaston stared down at him for a long time and Rayner, speechless, stared back from agonized eyes. 'See what they have done to me!' those eyes, moving slowly in the black face, seemed to say, and, 'There is nothing you can do.'

But at least Rayner could be taken, somehow, on to the float. Gaston grasped one wrist and pulled and slowly, reluctantly, the Negro turned, and as his boxes slid and bobbed beneath his shifting weight he clambered up beside the radio operator. The float sank perilously low in the water but it supported them both. In fact the added weight of the Negro helped to raise the broken prow out of the water and there, clipped to a wood stay, was the rubber-covered flashlight with which all the rafts were supposed to be, and a few actually were, equipped.

A radio operator's work in wartime was long and arduous; also for the past two days Gaston had been having trouble with his emergency sender and had spent most of his off-duty hours taking it apart—and thus missing out on sleeping time. He had very recently been thrown down fifteen feet of ladder on to an iron deck, fallen half stunned into the sea and swum for hours under constant attack and without any support save his own moving arms and legs. Now, crouched in eight inches of water beside the slumped black body of Rayner, he was so exhausted that he could only think very slowly. Though he did not realize this, he had been nearly five minutes staring down at Rayner's prostrate body before the idea of taking him into the float had sifted into his fatigue-clogged mind. It took him quite as long to realize that if he had that flashlight and if, which was not very likely, it worked, he could signal. On that calm night sea the flash and gleam of a light would carry a long way. Somewhere, at present far out of sight or hearing, a ship might be moving steadily through the darkness, look-outs alert on the bridge. A prick of light on the horizon, the dots and dashes as his thumb pressed the button, could bring that ship's helm hard over, could bring her ploughing rapidly towards him . . .

But to reach the flashlight was another matter. Gaston tried to tell Rayner what he wanted; which was that the stoker should pull himself up on to the raft's side and lean back—counterbalancing Gaston's weight as he edged down towards the shattered end—but it seemed impossible to get any sign of comprehension out of the Negro. As Gaston was to realize later, the blow—caused by a baulk of wood hurled sideways by the charging U-boat's bow—which had shattered Rayner's mouth had also partially concussed him. Yet Rayner must do what was required. Otherwise any forward movement by his companion would force the broken end of the float under water and capsize it, throwing them both into the sea and making it impossible ever to reach the flashlight. In the end, with tears of frustration trickling down his cheeks, Gaston half pushed, half lifted Rayner dangerously on to the float's edge and placing his hands on the lifelines forced his fingers around them and clenched them shut. Then at last he was free to wriggle down the floor into the water and, as the crushed bow sank deeper and deeper beneath his weight, to feel for the big flashlight and work it carefully from its clips. Then slowly he inched his way back.

'All right, Rayner. Now you may return. Descend, now, into the raft!'

But the Negro took no notice; perched on the rounded canvas-covered edge with his bullet-round head fallen forward on his chest, he seemed asleep.

Gaston turned to the flashlight and with his teeth pulled the tough rubber protector from its face. The glass front was intact at any rate. Breath held, he pressed the button and jerked in quick shock as the flash leapt out full in his face. So now . . . Easing himself back into the curve of the stern, drawing up his knees to support the heavy light, Gaston started to work carefully, slowly round in a circle of 180° sending his SOS flashing out into the night again and again and again.

The flashlight should, of course, be used sparingly. A quick circle of signals every ten minutes—or even fifteen or twenty. After all, there were no fresh batteries for use tomorrow night or the next when the present ones became exhausted. But Gaston knew well enough that unless help came very soon there would be no tomorrow night for himself or Rayner. But on the second circle there came, from far to the west, a faint shout. Gaston paused a moment and then, breath held, pressed down the button and shot out one long steady beam. Again that shout—someone was over there, perhaps half a mile away, across the water. Another survivor. But whoever it was would have to come to him if he could for Gaston could do no more than indicate his own position by continual guiding flashes. He settled to this and for a little while he believed that he heard faint sounds of splashing and once again that shout. But the flashlight was heavy on his knees and his head was still heavier. The flashes became fewer and more and more erratic and a few minutes later they died out alto-gether. The batteries were by no means exhausted but Gaston was. Crouched huddled in the curved stern of the float with the motionless form of Rayner bowed brooding above him, he slept.

Six

'. . . *the son of a respectable brewer, and his uncle on his mother's side was M. Adam, Mayor of Bar-le-Duc, his native town. Here, in a dwelling of somewhat gloomy appearance, he was born on the twenty-fifth of April, 1767 . . .*' But from the frame the Marshal, his whiskered face no longer expressing a bland, slightly deprecatory surprise but an odd, inward, sinister glee, was beginning to smile and Gaston hurried on more and more rapidly yet knowing that he would never succeed in reaching the end in time . . . '*a colonel at twenty-six, he even risked leaving the city under the most venturesome conditions to go himself in search of news of General Suchet . . .*' No, it was going to be no good. Already the cabin was tilting sharply downward as the stern rose high . . . '*The army advanced east across Lombardy driving the enemy before them . . .*' The ship was below water level now and in the green and silent gloom a giant squid passed slowly, tentacles waving, beyond the cabin window. Everyone else had gone long since. Gaston alone remained, translating rapidly from French to English. But the Marshal's gold-braided uniform was darkening and changing, and as the glass of the picture cracked under the enormous pressure of the main deep he stepped out of the splinters—small, round-faced, smooth-chinned, in blue overalls with a high-peaked cap . . .

Gaston opened his eyes, groaned with pain and heard the Captain saying, 'Try to get that rope, Slater, and—no, wait! He's all right. It's the other one . . .'

Gaston shook his head. 'Emil—' he said and felt a hand on his shoulder in the darkness. 'Gaston! It's me, the Captain. Are you hurt? Are you—'

'Monsieur! But—how? I thought—I saw them kill you.'

'No, no. The bastards tried all right, but they didn't. I'm fine. Lost all my bloody wood, though. What about you?'

'Nothing. Nothing at all. But—' Shaking his head, Gaston tried to stare around him but could see only a looming shapeless mass. The moon was down so several hours must have passed since he had clambered on to the broken float. 'How—What happened?'

'In a minute I'll tell you. It's taken us a hell of a long time to reach you. We lost you when you stopped flashing. But I've got one of the big rafts here and it's more or less intact. Thing is—what about yours? Is it worth keeping, you think?'

'One end is quite destroyed.'

'There may be things worth salvaging. We'll keep it till dawn. Now come in with us. You got that flashlight?'

'Yes.'

'Good. The one in this raft doesn't work—otherwise I'd have returned your signals. Give it here.'

Gaston and the Captain fumbled in the blank dark—it was not for the former, now, to make light without the latter's permission—and as soon as the Captain felt the heavy rubber-covered cylinder in his hand he switched it on and Gaston saw that his own broken float was being held against the side of a larger craft by a long, pale, bloody arm. The Captain must have felt this called for some explanation, for as Gaston climbed over the canvas dodger he said, 'Slater's been hit—but not badly. They threw grenades. You heard that?'

'Yes. I thought it must be—'

'If you're unhurt, Gaston, then you and I are the only ones that are.' The Captain flashed the torch briefly around the interior of the raft and for the first time Gaston saw the other occupants.

'Roldan—leg broken above the knee. Chinese stoker—arm broken and some ribs *and* a bullet through his f—ing shoulder.' Gaston saw the small, agonized face of Lin Hsiang, the eyes narrow slits screwed against the light. Then the beam swung away to show Rayner crouched bloody-faced in the stern, staring up like some great bemused night-bird, and then touched a small figure lying on its side, the left leg of its shorts red and wet.

'Not—They did not shoot him, *too!*'

'A bit of grenade in his bottom. Nothing too bad. It was the one that got you, too, wasn't it, Slater?'

'Yes.' The cold voice of the Second Officer held its usual calm. 'But luckily their aim was bad. They were close enough to have blown us both to fragments. But they were really trying to destroy the rafts, I think.'

The Captain flashed his beam along the bullet-tattered canvas dodger and then down to the deck boards. 'We've done all we can at present, Gaston. I don't think there's any more left alive. But we can't waste light searching now. It'll be dawn soon anyway. What you've got to do—' he handed back the flashlight—'is to go into the bow and get off a signal every ten minutes fore and aft, port and star-

board. And quick as you can so's not to waste it. If you hear anything
—well, I don't need to tell you that. O.K. ?'

'Yes, monsieur.'

'Good.' The Captain sat down beside Gaston and there was silence
save for the moaning hiss of Lin's breathing. The others, despite their
pain, were very quiet, for on this still night the noise of a ship's engines
could carry a long way and since all Allied ships steamed without
lights it was by engine noise alone that they could be detected.

Gaston threw out his first series of quick, exact SOS's and as the
rapid clicking of the flashlight button ceased the Captain said, 'We've
been lucky—this raft. Slater had it first, but when he jumped out and
they rammed it, it just overturned. Couldn't have hit it properly.
Then they must have missed seeing it upside down. Slater and young
Phil got under and inside. I found them there. We dodged around it
every time they came near. When they went off we all got on one
side and turned it over again. It's hardly damaged at all. Yes, we're
lucky—so far.'

'But Roldan and—'

'They swam to another—after the first attack. There were three
more with them. Two were killed in the next attack and these two
lads wounded. Only one was unhurt—the other nigger.'

'Reemann?'

'Yes, that's the name. Well, that raft was smashed-up and sinking,
so Reemann finds some planks—probably my stuff—and lashes them
up with the raft's lifelines. He gets these two boys on to them and
then he finds a bit more wood and he's trying to add that when that
f—ing boat comes back. The gun cuts him in half but though they
hit the planks they didn't break up . . . Later I and Slater saw them
floating near us. Roldan's not so bad. But the other . . .' Gaston,
pressed close to the Captain, felt his heavy shoulders shrug. Shifting
the heavy lamp on his knees he said suddenly, 'I—I talked to them,
monsieur. To one of them. He gave me a drink and offered to take
Philippe on board and said *Bonne chance* . . . And then— Why?
Why did they do it? Why?'

Seven

'. . . this decision with a very heavy heart. In the circumstances there was no choice. I can only add that those men who died tonight as a result of my order were—whatever their country's propaganda alleges to the contrary—as much our combatant enemies as any Tommy or Ivan on the land fronts. They knowingly risked their lives in war just as we are doing, and they lost them—just as we may lose ours. We attacked them in the course of our duty and—and regrettably were forced to destroy them in self-defence. The enemy air forces which are even now destroying our cities, and killing thousands of women and children in the process, cannot claim as much.'

Those words had been spoken nearly six hours ago but they still sounded in Emil's ears as he stood on the dark bridge peering out into the blackness across the now moonless sea. The crew had listened and had accepted what they were told without comment—at least those in the control-room. Emil had watched their faces as the Kommandant's voice had come amplified from the loudspeaker system. No one had shown much expression—they seemed to be reserving judgment—except Huberein who, as so often, looked in mortal anguish, his eyes screwed up, his mouth twisted as if someone was ramming a bayonet into him. Sehlte, pale, heavy and sad, had stared down at the iron deck plates, nodding resignedly. Kalewski alone had lifted his gleaming head and stared across the crowded room, his eyes meeting Emil's in a glance at once sulky and defiant. Emil guessed that some of the other under-officers had been criticizing him —obliquely, at any rate. Whether or not the Kommandant's speech would convince his own—and Kalewski's—critics, it would probably silence them. After all, to argue against such plain good sense would be irrational. Now, in the humid, salt-smelling darkness, Emil went over the whole thing again, once more justifying all that had happened but somehow feeling no better when he had done so.

They had sighted the ship, far to port and steaming on a course almost at right angles to their own, at 6.58, and the Kommandant's first decision had been to let it alone. They themselves were submerged and would remain so until dark and by that time the ship would be miles away. Also she did not appear a particularly valuable prize and the great, red-painted section of her hull above the waterline showed

41

clearly that she held little, if any, cargo. Far more important victims awaited their torpedoes in the Indian Ocean, upon the crowded sea lanes which converged on Aden. But instead of disappearing quickly over the horizon she seemed to be almost motionless. Emil, taking a quick look through the periscope, had seen no bow wave, merely the water-ripple at her stern. And as the submarine, running quietly on her batteries, slid at four knots below the slight swell it soon became obvious that even running at their submerged speed they could overtake that old freighter with ease. There she was, sitting duck-like on the still water, practically demanding to be sunk. In the end the temptation became too great. No one said anything, but the atmosphere in the control-room grew more and more tense, more and more expectant—and would, if thwarted, become frustrated, sulky and disappointed. Later those feelings would penetrate throughout the length of the boat.

Emil had seen the Kommandant struggling with this problem; had watched his eyebrows rising higher and higher above his pale horn-rimmed spectacles while the wide, well-shaped mouth which was his most attractive feature thinned to that look of dubiety and primness which meant that he was balancing still more than the usual juggler-like quantity of considerations in his slow but devious mind. Few people, and surely no naval officers, could take so long to come to a decision as Kapitänleutnant Eugen Kielbasa—nor change that decision so often.

'Very well—' Kielbasa might have been agreeing unwillingly to a spoken request—'very well, we'll sink her, then—since she's not an oil-burner.' And immediately the sullen tenseness in the control-room relaxed and was replaced by an air of excited expectancy, of joyful anticipation. Emil himself had been by no means immune from this sensation, as he realized uneasily afterward. It was true that a very old empty freighter—not even a large one, either—whose speed seemed to be that of a hired rowboat on a public pond was not a spectacular victim, but she was lawful prey by standards which even the enemy now grudgingly accepted. If she was empty today, there was no reason why she should not be carrying aircraft engines or their spares across the North Atlantic to England in two or three weeks' time. Unsunk she might, despite her appearance, be ferrying thousands of rounds of ammunition from Britain to triumphantly advancing Russia within a month. Yet as Emil knew, the Kommandant had taken the decision largely as a matter of morale. The patrol had been disastrous so far, and they had not even reached their proper area of operations yet. To wipe out the disappointment of ships seen, stalked, and for one reason or another left unsunk; to wipe out still more the fear and panic of the air attack which had cost the lives of two seamen and the First Lieutenant and destroyed the snorkel, the young crew needed above all a taste of victory.

Emil also knew that the Kommandant's reluctance to attack this ship had been due to its—and their own—present position, almost equidistant from Freetown and the British air base on Ascension Island, from which two points British air patrols covered wide miles of sea. It was a most unhealthy area and one in which four other U-boats had recently disappeared without trace.

Yet in less than half an hour it would be dusk, in little more completely dark. It would be simple to creep up on that ugly vessel dawdling across the evening sea and then, attacking with perhaps only one torpedo, sink her and run far and fast through the night. Standing beside and slightly behind the short slender figure of the Kommandant, watching the daylight from far above glinting through the eyepieces of the periscope to flash from the heavy lenses of his spectacles, Emil had felt, as so often before, that the decision which had just been taken was now being regretted, and this distressed and saddened him, for although he had only worked for Kielbasa for the past six weeks he was already his ardent admirer.

'We will use the attack table, Emil. It is not necessary, of course; but for practice. And two torpedoes. I want—it is important to destroy her entirely. To blow her to bits.'

From then on it had been a matter of mechanical routine. Emil, at the attack table, had worked deftly setting range bearings and distances according to the Kommandant's quickly spoken directions. Huberein, his small rubbery face contorted with concentration, had watched irritatingly over his shoulder and had himself drawn down the switch handles which angled the two torpedoes. Because of the smoothness of the sea it was only possible to use the small periscope, and then for a mere second or two at a time. 'Up periscope!' was succeeded immediately by 'Down periscope!' and Emil wondered how, in those quick glimpses above the water, the Kommandant was able to give accurate range bearings at all. Yet they must be very accurate and the submarine must be brought unnoticed so close to its intended victim that the torpedoes would be fired at what amounted to point-blank range—yet not so close that the great shock wave would damage the boat itself. For one thing above all was vital; that old ship up there must be so violently struck, so torn apart and disintegrated, that her radio operator, if he survived the attack, could have no chance at all to reach his key and stammer out even one dying message to the enemy air bases waiting vengefully so close at hand. Emil, standing back from the attack table, was seeing more clearly with every passing minute the number of calculations which Kielbasa had been computing and balancing before his attack decision. But not, as yet, all of them.

'Stand by!' And everyone was suddenly rigid, breath held. For the great majority of young men in the control-room this was the first time they had participated in a sinking.

'Fire One! Fire Two! Down periscope!' The light on the little panel of the torpedo firing indicator had glowed and two quick shudders had passed through the boat. 'Torpedoes running.'

'Up periscope . . . Down periscope . . . Up periscope.'

Emil found himself counting quickly under his breath. The range had been minimal, slightly less than three hundred metres. Those torpedoes rushing at thirty-five knots below the calm surface could not miss. They did not miss. A sudden booming explosion shook the boat like the distant eruption of an underwater volcano.

'Both torpedoes have hit. One on the bow; one amidships.' To Emil it seemed that the Kommandant's voice held a note of relief rather than exultation and he turned quickly to Huberein, the acting First Lieutenant, 'Christ—take a look. Then let Emil have one.'

Huberein, his tongue right out of his mouth, glared through the twin eyepieces. 'My God! Have we hit her! *Have* we hit her! She's come right apart. She— Quick, Emil, or she'll be gone!'

And then he was at the periscope—the large one now, for there was no further reason for caution—and there she was, so close seen through the high-powered lens that one felt one could reach out and touch her —what remained of her. Emil, seeing that ruined canting deck through the haze of smoke and vaporizing steam, watching that tall funnel topple and crash, felt a quick shudder of panic. It suddenly and for the first time struck him that people were dying—dying at this very moment in mortal agony and fear—because of what he and his colleagues had just done. The thought made him momentarily sick with fear as if he had committed unthinkingly, but nevertheless wantonly, a terrible crime for which he would inescapably be made to pay in full. He turned away smiling a little weakly and Kielbasa was back at the periscope anxiously searching the evening sky. 'All right, we'll go up. Stand by to surface. Gun crew at the ready.'

The thunder of compressed air bursting into the ballast tanks, the long needles of the depth indicators moving swiftly back across the numbered dials; the Kommandant, signalman and look-outs climbing into the tower and then the sudden rush of fresh air as the hatch was opened. Emil, called to the bridge, had watched with awed fascination as the stern of the broken ship had lifted slowly, then seemed to steady itself and hang poised for the death plunge. There had been figures on it, too, but even as he watched the angle of the decks grew impossible and they leapt or fell into the sea.

It was then that the Kommandant, peering worriedly over the wreckage-strewn water, had told him to go forward and find a survivor—an officer if possible—and interrogate him.

So then there had been that odd encounter with the radio operator. A Frenchman, too . . . Guéroult. A northerner; probably a Norman by his accent. And that little Brazilian child . . . Bahia. But they could have taken him aboard. They had offered to do so. He himself had asked the Kommandant, who had agreed readily—almost eagerly. Emil moved restlessly in the dark between the two look-outs and started to bite the nails of his left hand, then quickly stopped. He had been a compulsive nail-biter from childhood but his last employer, Konter-admiral Waldenkolk, had nagged him relentlessly until he had broken the habit. So—even then, even when he was telling the Kommandant about the child, Kielbasa had already known, or at least guessed, what he might have to do. Through the Captain's brain had been passing the various permutations of probable future events which had pro-duced a most unpleasant fact. There was far too much floating wreck-age; far more than he had anticipated. And it should—it *must*—be destroyed. It was nearly dark and the surfaced submarine could now run on her diesels throughout the long night before dawn forced her once more below the waves. But with dawn would commence those air patrols between Freetown and Ascension and the mass of flotsam left by the *Maréchal Oudinot* could not be missed. Under her full power the submarine, running on the surface, could travel no more than some one hundred and fifty sea miles during the night. And that was no good at all. To an aircraft one hundred and fifty sea miles was negligible. As soon as the morning came and the wreckage was sighted the hunt would be on and enemy planes, armed with quick-sinking depth charges, would be searching the ocean with every newly perfected detection device in a great doomed circle. Then the sub-marine would have little more chance of survival than a tadpole in a puddle surrounded by boys with sticks and stones. And—and there were the survivors, too. Guéroult in particular. If there was any sort of flashlight in the rafts floating among that debris Guéroult would be able to speak to the circling aircraft as clearly as if he was conversing in a quiet room. Even a bit of mirror or a tin plate—broken glass, even—and the exact time and position of the sinking would be in enemy hands. And then—Emil remembered the panic fear of the first air attack sixteen days ago. This time it would be still worse.

But if the wreckage was destroyed; if the larger pieces were torn apart, sunk and scattered, and if there were no survivors . . . If that was done the position would be very different. For after more than five years of war minor wreckage of every sort was strewn over the seven seas. A floating wooden grating, a few broken spars or a couple of rusty drums lashed together—these, even if they were seen, gave no information. Perhaps they came from a sunken ship, but the ship might have been sunk months ago and a thousand miles away. No concentrated air search of a particular area would be undertaken on the evidence of such insignificant remains. And all this had been going on in the Kommandant's head and probably he had already known what he was going to do when they sheered off into the night and Emil himself had called, '*Bonne chance—et au'voir, Monsieur Guéroult!*'

For when, after that, he had gone back to the bridge and reported—tried to do so, rather—to the Kommandant, Kielbasa had not been listening. He had stood staring aft, his arms widespread, his hands clamped to the steel rim of the bridge, not listening to a word. Emil had fallen silent, and there had been no noise from below where, awaiting further orders, the engineers stood ready and expectant to change from the electric motors to the diesels. Still on her batteries, soundlessly and slowly, the U-boat had crept away into the darkness of newly fallen night with her captain, rigid and motionless, staring aft.

They must have progressed thus for almost a thousand metres before the Kommandant had turned and called down the voice pipe for Huberein. And as soon as the ginger-haired, red-faced Austrian had appeared on the bridge, leaving Sehlte in charge below, he had told them calmly what had to be done. He had not said 'What I intend to do' but 'What must be done,' as if he was speaking of some action to be taken in conformity with an immutable physical law.

In the half-dark of the dim blue bridge light Huberein had stared up puzzled, then aghast. 'You—you mean we must kill them all? But we *can't* do that! They are not even military personnel. And even if they were . . . And if we destroy their rafts they will drown. Even the ones who have life-jackets will drown because those kapok things are good only for eight hours. No, no—we can't! There must be some other way—something else—*anything* else!'

Emil had glanced from Huberein's anguished face to the Kommandant's patient spectacled one and had felt an annoyed contempt for the First Lieutenant which was new to him. For everyone liked Huberein, good-natured, tolerant, endlessly kind; the crew doted on him. But could he not see? Could he not understand? Surely he must realize that the Kommandant had worked out the matter for himself and had taken, with obvious reluctance, the decision which, as captain, it was his duty to take. Surely Huberein must know that all he was saying now could make no difference to the facts which they had just heard so plainly stated. In fact Emil had intended to protest himself. After all, he had talked personally to one of the survivors and in an inexplicable way he looked on Guéroult as a newly made friend. But now he decided that he would say nothing. He believed he understood the Kommandant; at least he felt for him nothing save approval, admiration and trust. It was something, at this stage of the war, to be in the hands of such a man rather than some grimly suicidal maniac determined to carry his boat and his crew with him into the fake glories of a noisy Nordic Valhalla. Eugen Kielbasa had a proper sense of self-preservation which met with Emil's wholehearted endorsement.

And when at last Huberein was silent the Kommandant had said, 'It is our lives or theirs, Christl. And if you would prefer it to be ours I can only say that I think very differently—luckily for everyone else on board.'

'But—but they are human beings, too!'

'Yes, indeed. I wish they were fish. Then the problem would solve itself.'

'What do you want me to do?' Huberein had asked wretchedly.

'Oh, go below and take over from Walter. Tell him and the underofficers what we are going to do. Just say "destroy the *Überrest*— the remains." And try, my dear Christl, not to sound as if you were on your way to the gallows; it is disheartening for everyone.'

And then, as Huberein muttering miserably to himself had descended the ladder inside the tower, the Kommandant had turned to Emil. 'You are the Gunnery Officer, Emil. Order up the two M.G. 15s and ammunition. Have grenades and Schmeissers ready, too.'

'We are to—?'

'You are to destroy the *Überrest* by gunfire. Yes, I know what you

are thinking. Very well. Shout at them first to jump in the sea—
then destroy the rafts and all the larger pieces of wreckage.'

'I suppose—' Emil's voice had been uncertain and the Kommandant
had interrupted him at once. 'That was an order I gave you.' And he
had felt the Kommandant's hand suddenly hooked into the open collar
of his overalls and his voice, when he spoke, was slow and firm.
'Did you like that air attack—the time Chirol was killed? Do you
remember what he and the look-outs looked like after the cannon
fire had struck them? And the depth charge—you remember that?
The one that you thought was so close? It was not really very close
but you and the others who had not heard one before thought so. Do
you remember waiting for the others which—most fortunately for us
—never came?' At each question the hand hooked in his collar had
pulled him gently forward, then pushed him back.

'Yes—yes.'

'What you are going to do now is going to prevent that—and, oh,
very much worse than that—happening to us tomorrow. Now hurry.
Kalewski and Wutsdorf are to man the guns.'

And as Emil in his turn had descended the tower the Kommandant
had turned to the bridge telephone and was already giving the necessary orders to Walter Sehlte in the engine-room.

And after that . . . But Emil's mind could only recall—*would* only
recall—confused pictures. An old man in white squatting on an
arrangement of planks which resembled a farm gate floating on the
water. 'Get off! Get off!' Emil had shouted urgently into the electric
megaphone and then given the sign for Kalewski at the starboard gun
to fire a long burst into the water near by. 'Get off! Go in the water!
Sauve-toi, imbécile!' And the large figure in white had tumbled swiftly
off the planks and when, seconds later, the stem of the U-boat had
struck them they had crashed emptily apart. Emil had sighed with
relief.

Then the rafts . . . But in most cases the survivors on them had
jumped into the sea after the first warning shots. Without their rafts
they would certainly drown, but that was knowledge which one
might push aside—at least for the moment. The important thing was,
as Emil quickly discovered, to destroy the rafts and larger wreckage
while leaving the destruction of the living men upon them to the sea
and the sharks. But in the event neither proved possible. Emil realized
to his rising horror that the old freighter must have been carrying a
cargo of wood—probably a deck cargo—unseen below her high, old-
fashioned gunwales. The sea was a mass of floating logs and planks.

And some of the survivors refused to leave their floats and life-rafts in which case Kalewski or Hansi Wutsdorf shot them as ordered.

Up and down, round and round, went the submarine. That big, empty lifeboat was soon sighted, riddled and rammed. It was their only real success in the attempt to destroy the wreckage for the cork- and kapok-filled floats, though ripped and broken until they were useless as lifesavers, would not sink. The guns fired until they overheated and one—Wutsdorf's—jammed. Sweating, trembling, Emil had helped the young under-officer clear the blockage.

The Kommandant then sent for the grenades and himself trained the big signalling lamp, which acted instead of the searchlight the U-boat did not carry, over the wreckage-scattered sea, but with the exception of the lifeboat, which had disappeared, there seemed no visible diminution of all that floating wood and broken yet buoyant flotsam; it was impervious to bullets or bombs. But the *Überrest* meant more than only wreckage, it meant survivors, too. And in that respect the U-996 had succeeded fully. There were no more cries and shouts, no more small red lights bobbing on the water. Once the signalling lamp lit up a sprawled figure lying headless on a timber baulk and once a body, supported by a ripped and sodden life-jacket, bobbed and jolted down the curved hull, but otherwise the sea was lifeless. And in the end they had to give up. There was nothing else to do unless they intended to thresh about all night parting wreckage with their bows which only tossed and closed again indifferently in their wake. Yet for some time Emil wondered if the Kommandant, under the influence of the bitter frustration which must be filling him, did not intend to do this, so that dawn and the enemy would find them ploughing the sea in useless furrows among wallowing planks and joggling shark-torn corpses. But at last, when it was obvious that neither machine-guns nor grenades or—the suggestion had come from Emil—the 3.7 cannon—could sink the floatsam, there was nothing for it but to go.

After one last run through that indestructible mass the Kommandant gave the orders that brought them back upon their true course, gave the orders to take the machine-guns below and unship the signalling lamp—then handed over briefly to Huberein, whose watch it was, and left the bridge.

Half an hour later, as Emil lay sleepless on his curtained bunk in the wardroom, the loudspeaker system had given its preliminary warning crackle and then—'*Achtung! Achtung! Der Kommandant spricht . . .*'

And now, except for the muffled thunder of the diesels below his feet, there was silence. Silence and emptiness and somewhere far back behind the glimmering wake those dead bodies, ripped by bullets, torn by sharks, would be sinking down into the depths to join that broken old ship. Down, down, down—descending unimaginable fathoms of blackness lit only by the phosphorescence of passing angler fish, the glowing vertebrae of the deep sea eel. The bodies of Guéroult, the radio operator with whom Emil had so recently talked, of the little Brazilian boy whom he had tried to save, of the fat old man on the raft of planks . . . And it had all been in vain; so much horror and despair and panic and blood—for nothing at all. The U-boat's chances were still less now than they would have been had she left the scene of the sinking at once. Emil shivered. In not much less than two hours the first glimmer of light would edge the eastern sealine and then some airman on Ascension Island or at Freetown would be sighing and stretching, tumbling sleepily out of bed . . .

Beside him Emil heard the starboard look-out humming beneath his breath and caught the tune of an old song, 'On a sailor's tomb no roses bloom.' Angrily he snarled the man to silence.

Eight

Dawn, advancing at the rate of fifteen degrees of longitude every hour, brought slowly to an end the longest night which any of those crouched in the bloodstained, bullet-scarred life-raft had ever known. It came coolly out of the east clothed in low grey cloud and bringing with it a dank, gusty, fitful breeze which made Captain Crawshaw frown up at the lightening sky. 'It'll rain before noon, Gaston. We'll have to be ready to catch as much of it as we can.'

'But—then it will clear?'

'Perhaps. But it's more likely to keep on for a couple of days. At least it's better for us than rotting here under the sun.'

'But the aircraft—the patrols! In this weather—so low is the cloud —they will not see us!' Gaston's hoarse voice was urgent with distress but the Captain only shrugged; to him all aircraft were venomous and unreliable things about which he had neither interest nor understanding. While the word 'rescue' really meant 'aircraft' to Gaston, it meant 'ships' to Captain Crawshaw.

The Captain was an old man who had been born and reared in what were now considered the immensely peaceful, civilized and ordered times of the late Victorian and Edwardian ages; a period of history which Gaston's equally old grandmother invariably referred to as *La Belle Epoque*. He ought therefore, felt both Gaston and Brian Slater, to have been shocked into a daze of disbelief and horror at the past night's terror. Were not all old people on both sides of the Channel continually throwing up their hands and deploring that they had lived to see such dreadful times and to witness the degradations and enormities of modern man? But the Captain, far from being lashed into unbelieving fury or stunned into numb despair by the cold-blooded savagery of the German submarine, seemed to take the whole thing for granted. He deplored the loss of his deck-cargo but otherwise seemed much less outraged than the young men themselves. For Captain Crawshaw had sailed seas—the Arabian, the Java, the Yellow—when slavers and pirates still plied with grim trade in all the gruesome bestiality of an otherwise bygone age. While still a young boy he had seen the results of coastal raids in the Sunda Straits; had seen men dying after red-hot ramrods had been thrust up their rectums, women still alive though skinned from the hips down, various victims of 'the slicing process'—and once a whole village doomed to inevitable starvation since the thumbs of the entire population, regardless of age or sex, had been chopped away. One did not experience such sights while still in one's teens and retain many Victorian ideas about the nobility of man or the ordered progress of the universe under the eye of a beneficent God. And, quite apart from these horrors, some of the details of existence in the fo'c'sle or the roundhouse of a late-nineteenth century windjammer would have come as a considerable shock to Gaston or Mr Slater.

Nor was this by any means the first time that the Captain had experienced shipwreck and the fact of being adrift on the open sea held no immediate terrors for him; he had survived it before. In fact, as soon as the U-boat had left the scene of the sinking and subsequent slaughter, as soon as he and Slater had managed to right the life-raft, he had believed that the worst was over. At the moment his greatest worry was the big black stoker Rayner who sat crouched at one end of the raft unmoving, his battered face downturned towards the slatted floor, his great arms rested on his drawn-up knees. Rayner was still, the Captain guessed, in a state of shock from the impact of a shattering blow; one which would have killed a white man and which had probably injured the Negro's brain. Rayner was, in the Captain's eyes, the greatest danger he now had to face; a potential and ever-present menace who could destroy them all. For, as the Captain knew well, survival in a shipwreck depended more upon the behaviour of the victims than on that of the elements. Their attitude rather than their equipment was the vital factor. The Captain as a boy had known an old sailor who had been a member of the crew of the brig *Argus*; who had, in fact, claimed to be the look-out who had first sighted the great raft of the abandoned frigate *Medusa*. This raft, originally holding one hundred and forty-nine souls, had only been adrift for twelve days—a very short ordeal by any shipwreck standards of the times—yet the rescuing ship had found only fifteen crazed and dying survivors upon the bloodstained planking, together with pieces of drying human flesh intended for food. And the Captain knew of plenty of other examples on a smaller scale but teaching the same lesson. With the exception of Rayner the rest of the survivors would certainly do as they were told and remain under the Captain's proper control. Gaston and Slater because they were educated officers, Roldan and the Chinese because they were immobilized by their injuries, and Philippe because he was too young to think of doing anything else. No—if there was trouble it would only come from Rayner. The Captain wished that Gaston had not found him and brought his looming twilight presence into the raft.

Meanwhile there was much to do, and assisted by his radio officer he proceeded to do it. The wounded men must be properly examined and, where possible, treated. Lin Hsiang's injuries were by far the worst. At least four ribs were badly broken and the flesh above them pulped into a purplish mess—this too had been the result of a hard-wood log hurled violently aside by the thrusting stem of the German submarine. And with his right arm fractured near the elbow and the ragged hole torn by a heavy machine-gun bullet through his left shoulder below the clavicle it was unlikely that he could live many more hours. Only immediate treatment in a properly equipped hospital might have saved him. Meanwhile he lay naked, sodden and crumpled in four inches of sea-water, and breathing in quick shallow moaning gasps, his small face already thin and hollow with death. The Captain realized that there was nothing that could be done for him save to leave him alone. Any attempt to move him or to straighten his legs and shift him to a more comfortable position—suggestions which Gaston made at once—would only bring forth screams of pain as he was dragged back to a brutal awareness of the broken body he was now trying to leave. The Chinese, in the Captain's opinion, had little tenacity to life; once badly hurt, they resigned themselves to death and died quite quickly.

And in fact Lin's mind was, as it were, half out of his body already. He was moving through the streets of all the ports he had ever visited and they were all one street and full of shops, each one packed with the most desirable objects. For, unlike Gaston or the Captain, the sea had meant little to Lin, who had never noticed its beauty or understood its danger. It was not a way of life to him, he did not particularly like it and never thought of it as more than his place of work. It had always been the ports which fascinated him; he arrived at each one with eager expectation and left it reluctantly and with regret. And the bigger the port, the noisier and brighter it was, the better he liked it. Twice he had deserted ship, and on both occasions because the vessel was leaving before he was ready to do so himself. The first time there had been a festival with a procession on the evening of the day of departure; on the second a travelling circus, due to arrive the next morning, had plastered the walls with inviting posters. Lin could not have borne to have missed either event.

So now in his last hours he thought lingeringly of circuses and fairgrounds and stalls selling coloured drinks and sweets, cotton candy and popcorn, of shooting booths and cockshies and betting wheels in striped tents under bright lights. Dully he was aware of sickness and pain, but as long as he did not move and breathed only very lightly it was bearable, it did not shriek through his whole body in sheets of all-obscuring agony as it had done when they lifted him from the planks where he had lain, supported by the lower half of Reemann's dead body, and into the raft. Perhaps he was dying, but if he was then the worst part, the physical pain, was already over. He had never been frightened of death in the abstract since he had never conceived of it. But the process of dying—and he thought of it always as a violent one —was preceded by bodily agony and he knew enough about that to be properly terrified of it. If he was really not going to suffer much more . . . He drifted vaguely off through an arcade of bright shops searching for his red shroud.

Ignacio Roldan, though less badly injured, was in a much more pitiable condition. His left leg was fractured above the knee, the femur completely shattered for some six inches of its length, and the powerful thigh muscles had pulled the splintered bones sideways and by contraction had forced the jagged edges deep into the tissue. Though neither he nor the Captain now examining him knew this, he was just as certainly doomed to death as Lin if he did not receive proper treatment in a short time. Since the rest of his strong young body was undamaged he would live longer, but that only made it worse. A good

eighteenth-century surgeon on a line-of-battle ship would have unhesitatingly amputated that leg and cauterized the butt with boiling
pitch. The shock would have been appalling but, with the advantages
of health and youth and a nervous system partially paralysed by a heavy
dose of Navy rum, Roldan would have had a good chance of surviving it. As it was, his only hope lay in rescue within the near
future.

Captain Crawshaw's attempt to splint the leg with a pair of the
miniature oars of which the raft possessed one and a half—the fourth
oar had been smashed by bullets—was entirely unsuccessful. Roldan's
screams ripped the nerves of everyone and the leg, refusing to
straighten, remained as bent and bulged and rope-taut as before. 'No
good.' The Captain sank back on his knees, red-faced, angrily perplexed, a little flustered it seemed by his mistake. And it suddenly
struck Gaston, kneeling faithfully beside him, that this was the first
time he had known the Captain to fail in anything he set his hand to.
What the young Spaniard needed above all else was morphia, but the
small box of medicines which should have contained, among other
things, a dozen syrettes, had been lost when the U-boat smashed into
the raft and overturned it. There were no medicines or medical
equipment of any sort on board.

Leaving Roldan, his face livid and gasping in the aftermath of his
agony, the Captain turned to Philippe, a damp draggled little monkey
whose dark eyes seemed huge in his narrow olive face. Philippe,
luckily for himself, could swim like a dolphin; otherwise the Second
Officer would certainly have drowned him. For when the submarine
had charged toward the raft, firing over the heads of those sitting in it,
Philippe had been the first to jump off. He had slipped quickly over
the side, submerged and swum away under water as fast as he could.
It was a sensible thing to do but Slater had believed he was drowning
and had leapt after him. And as soon as Philippe had come up for air
he had grabbed the boy and started to apply the lifesaving techniques
he had learned as a Sea Scout. But he had taken his lifesaving lessons in
a swimming pool and these, applied in the blackness and terror of
shipwreck in mid-Atlantic, had very nearly destroyed both himself
and his victim. The Second Officer, though a man of great courage,
was neither a strong nor a confident swimmer and his gaspings and
threshings and unintelligible cries of 'Stay still! Turn over and lie on
your back! Don't struggle!' had naturally made Philippe believe that
he was drowning in mad panic and intended to take with him anyone
near enough to grasp. Wailing '*Ay, Jesus!*' Philippe had fought back

ferociously and, intertwined together, they had sunk and risen and sunk again until their strength was gone and Slater, sobbing with exhaustion, had pulled himself and the boy on to a floating mass of planks upon which they had lain sprawled and unconscious of the returning submarine until a grenade had exploded near by, throwing them both once more into the water and—providentially—within three metres of the capsized raft from which they had jumped. Though they had been partially shielded from the explosion by a hardwood log, Slater's legs and feet had been badly gashed by fragments and one piece had hit Philippe.

It was to this that the Captain now turned. 'Let's see what's happened to you, Phil,' he said with as much geniality as he could manage; but Philippe shrank away. He had all the primly purposeless Victorian prudery of his Portuguese ancestry and had no desire to have any part of his body examined by anyone, even the Captain—particularly the Captain, of whom he stood deeply in awe. '*Non, non*—' he stammered in the French of which he had picked up a surprising amount during his few days in the galley. '*C'est M'sieu Slater qui souffre.*' And he edged away, pointing to the Second Officer.

'But we'll deal with you first,' said the Captain decisively, and when, with extreme reluctance, Philippe had pulled down his shorts and was staring fixedly at the floorboards the Captain and Gaston found a three-inch gash high up on his left thigh. It was deep and blue-edged but seemed clean enough and the piece of fragmented grenade had not lodged in the flesh. The Captain tore a handkerchief in two and made a rough bandage. 'Well, *he's* not too bad. That's something. What about you, Slater?'

'Much the same, only more so,' said Slater. He was cutting off his sodden trouser-legs above the knee but the Captain stopped him. 'Don't do that unless it's really necessary. Otherwise you'll be sorry when the sun comes out. Just slit the seams.' But when the wounds in Slater's legs and feet were examined the Captain looked more dubious. 'I'd say there's some bits of metal in some of these. Well, we can't get them out. Perhaps they'll work out themselves. But— Here, what's this?'

'Oh Christ!' Slater's face whitened as the Captain unlaced his left shoe and eased it slowly from a swollen foot. 'But—but I never *felt* anything!' For of all the toes on that foot only the large one was left intact; the rest were either missing or mashed into blood- and water-sodden pulp. 'I never felt a thing!' Slater said again in tremulous wonderment

The Captain said nothing but took the piece of cloth which Gaston had ripped from the tail of his shirt and quickly covered that gory and deformed foot. 'They'll all have to come off as soon as we're picked up. It won't stop you from walking or anything—still, it's back to your history books for you, Slater . . . That's it, Gaston. Not too tightly, though.'

And then the Captain, clambering back into the bow of the float, began to take stock of their position. Seven survivors, one of whom was clearly dying and only two of whom were completely uninjured. Well, the chances for Roldan, and perhaps even for Slater, depended on being rescued within a very limited period. The boy's wound was nothing, so long as it did not become infected. He glanced across at the great Negro. Rayner alone had received no examination of his wounds and though the Captain would not admit it to himself, this had been because he was too frightened to attempt it. Rayner had not moved since he was pulled into the raft. He sat there, a great black brooding image, staring downward while thick drops of dark blood fell from his crushed mouth to the water-covered floor slats. If only, thought Captain Crawshaw—if only Rayner had been Lin.

For the rest of the morning the Captain and Gaston worked to set the raft to rights, to check what equipment it possessed and to salvage anything of value from the wreckage which bobbed around them over a continually increasing distance, by now almost two miles in circumference. To Gaston's distress, though not to the Captain's, the cloud-filled sky loomed lower and lower and the horizon all around them was lost in a grey misty haze. The air was dank and humid, the sea a dull pewter with occasional gleams of dead green as ugly and disconcerting as the phosphorescence of a waterlogged corpse.

The life-raft itself, inadequate and infinitely inferior to the boat which Roldan and Lin had managed to launch from the *Maréchal Oudinot*'s sinking stern, was less harmed than they had at first suspected. The damage done by the submarine had been largely superficial—bullet holes through the canvas dodgers and a badly buckled but unbroken starboard bow where the submarine, striking it, had overturned the raft but failed to break the hollow metal floats which lined the interior. It was three and a half metres long and two metres wide with an extremely blunt round bow and a square stern and, as Gaston remembered, it was one of four carried by the *Maréchal Oudinot*—two lashed to the rails of the poop and two at the side doors of the fo'c'sle. There was a mast which, detached from its lashing on the floorboards, slid into a hole in the short foredeck and was secured in a metal foot below. To this could be rigged a wide-bellied red jibsail which had been gnawed here and there into ragged holes by some of the *Maréchal Oudinot*'s rats. The Captain shook his head over this. It would not last long with those rents in it; a good strong breeze would blow it to tatters. He did not look reproachfully at Mr Slater, but none the less the Second Officer's pale face coloured slightly. The never-ceasing task of harrying the rats had been his duty. And surely he could have kept them out of the life-rafts. Fortunately the food and water supplies were all in metal cans—the rats could not get at those. But several seemed to be missing; probably they had become detached from their fastenings when the raft had been struck and overturned. What was left was part of the disconcerting mixture which the conscientious Monsieur Lagny had acquired from various sources over the past years. A square can with a complicated patent opener which took nearly half an hour and much of Gaston's temper to understand—this held six pounds of wheaten ship's biscuits: American, perfectly preserved and, unlike most other ship's biscuits, actually enjoyable to eat. A much smaller can contained four boxes of concentrated meat extract cubes, and a rat-gnawed canvas packet which had originally held a dozen cans of French sardines now held only seven. One metal box held hard chocolate and another twelve boxes of matches. There was also a single two-gallon can of water; the sole remainder of a rack of four.

These supplies, with a small hatchet, a cork-handled knife, a fishing line and two hooks, an eyeleted canvas awning, badly rat-gnawn at one end, a tin bailer and a box of dangerous-looking French fireworks labelled in Monsieur Lagny's handwriting 'Flaires of Safety', were all the raft contained. It was not a very imposing equipment but, except for its total lack of drugs or medical equipment, it was a good deal more than might have been hoped for in the circumstances.

And additions might perhaps be made to it from the flotsam scattered across the grey uneasy swell. At any rate Captain Crawshaw felt this to be worth trying and for nearly five exasperating hours he and Gaston attempted to manoeuvre the clumsy raft alongside any floating object which looked as though it might contain something useful. Since they only had one and a half pairs of oars they each took one and set Slater in the stern with the third to act as rudder. In this manner, and very slowly, they made their way to the upended wreck of a raft which before the attack had been the twin of their own and of which only the bow and short foredeck now lifted from the dull grey sea.

But it was chiefly in the stern that the supplies were stored and there was no way of getting at them. Gaston might have tried diving for them, but the fins of at least three sharks had already been sighted and the slender chances of managing to find and release firmly fixed objects six or more feet below the surface made this risk a bad one. Instead they had to content themselves with one more two-gallon can of water, and a further box of French flares.

Nor were their further efforts much more profitable—an empty five-gallon oil drum, a kapok life-jacket and another oar. Once they found a partially sunk crate containing the bodies of six drowned chickens—fowls taken on at Conakry by Mr Trupert—but no one was yet hungry enough to think of eating raw, sea-sodden poultry. Just before noon they made two other finds. The first was a very small and primitive life-float of a sort designed to be thrown quickly from the deck if a man fell overboard. It was in the form of a hollow metal square with the interior floored by a piece of stout rope netting. One of the sides had been punctured by a machine-gun bullet so that it floated partly submerged, but the Captain dragged it to the raft's side and, emptying the flooded portion, plugged the hole with a piece of canvas. He still had hopes of finding useful articles and if he did this float might be used to carry them, leaving the raft free for the survivors. He attached the float by a short line to a ringbolt in the raft's stern and it floated lightly behind them over the swell.

The second find was much more rewarding—eight oranges bobbing gently like abandoned Christmas decorations upon the metallic water. The Captain decided that those who wished should have one each immediately, and though Slater proposed that they should be kept for the two badly wounded boys the Captain turned this idea down. And he was proved correct since though both were offered pieces of orange neither would eat. In any case Lin had already been given the only thing he wanted—water. And given more of it than the Captain entirely approved and in fact only sanctioned because of his certainty of coming rain.

The rain came half an hour after they had collected the oranges. It blew up quickly from the north-west, a darkening sky, a grey mist advancing rapidly across water which turned white with dancing spray, sweeping in a great semi-circle from horizon to horizon. 'Here it comes!' shouted the Captain. 'Get out that canvas sheet! Gaston—Slater—you each hold a corner. Phil, you and I will hold the others. And we'll have the oil drum between us—under the worst holes.'

Then, with a soft hissing roar the advancing wall of spray was upon them; the raft spun, rocked and steadied, lurching a little as the rain cataracted into it.

That squall lasted half an hour, enabling the five-gallon drum to be filled to within eight inches of its top. It also killed Lin Hsiang. For the canvas sheet which was being used to collect the rain was supposed to be the stern awning of the raft, the cover under which the wounded or the sick or those seeking some shelter from the elements might take refuge. Without this roof over him the dying stoker was unable to continue the difficult and exhausting work of breathing in the short shallow respirations which did not expand his chest and grate together the broken edges of his fractured ribs. Under that torrential squall rainwater entered his open mouth and his nose. He choked and the movement, flooding him with fiery pain, caused him to scream. But it was only a feeble scream for most of his strength was gone now, and only Rayner, crouched above him in the stern, heard it. He looked down at the Chinese and in that moment Lin's eyes met his in what the Negro rightly believed to be an appeal for help. Lin's gasping choke as the rainwater entered his nose and throat had brought him sickeningly back from his world of innocently avaricious and acquisitive dreams to the world of the raft. He had been in a great emporium in some South American city trying on and buying the most beautiful clothes before a tall pier-glass in whose reflected depths he preened himself in vivid silk shirts and slick-hipped American slacks. Now the cold rain restored him to a short-lived but clear awareness of his present nudity and it filled him with a shame and distress which for a moment almost blotted out his pain. Here he lay, before his captain and two officers, with nothing on at all—naked as a fish. He had been happy enough to kick off his dirty stoker's trousers in the privacy and gloom of the after chain locker when he and Roldan had commenced their makeshift and violently interrupted sexual games yesterday evening, and since that moment he had never given them a thought. Now, with the rain hissing down and beating a cold tattoo on his bare stomach and thighs, he longed for them or some substitute covering even more than a release from pain. He could not speak loudly enough for Rayner to hear him above the drumming of the rain, but weakly he put up a hand and tried to grasp the big Negro's. If he could make Rayner kneel down he might, perhaps, be able to whisper . . . Rayner did not understand. He himself was suffering badly now from his smashed mouth and, though he did not know this, a broken jaw; but he saw only that Lin was suffering still more—and obviously on account of the rain. He needed cover, needed that canvas sheet above him. Water or no water, he ought to have it.

Rayner leaned forward and touched the Second Officer on the arm and, when Slater turned his head, pointed to Lin and then to the canvas sheet which sagged above the slowly filling drum between the three officers and Philippe. Since Slater did not appear to understand Rayner reached out and plucked at the canvas. He had intended it only as a gentle tweak, an indication of the object which his ruined mouth could not articulate. Unluckily his movements, coinciding with the lift and sink of the raft over a swell, unbalanced him and the light tweak inadvertently became a savage tug. The canvas awning was ripped from the hands of Slater and Philippe and its contents cascaded uselessly into the sea-water slopping across the floorboards.

The Captain, for the first time in anyone's experience, let out a bellow of rage and followed it by a stream of the sort of curses which his Second Officer, despite nearly three years at sea, had never believed existed. Rayner quickly regained his place in the stern. He lifted hands and eyebrows in urgent but mute apology, and as if to explain his action pointed to Lin on the floorboards and the canvas sheet in the Captain's hands. But the Captain suddenly dropped the awning and, seizing a heavy piece of wood—a tiller-bar which an hour before Gaston had wondered to see him bring carefully aboard—he thrust his way in two strides down the swaying raft. 'Any more trouble from you, you black bitch-born bastard, and I'll smash what's left of your ugly nigger head in with this!' He swung the tiller-bar twice in a fast low curve over Rayner's cowering form and then held a clenched and quivering fist an inch from Rayner's bloody mouth. 'Right! Now stay *still*—see! Quite still, so I can keep an eye on you!'

Gaston and Slater glanced quickly at each other and then away. No one had ever seen the Captain in such a furious rage before, and though of course the clumsy spilling of precious rainwater was a serious matter, they could not account for it now. They said nothing as, red-faced and muttering to himself, the Captain returned to his place in the bow, but Philippe shrank slightly away from him as he sat down once more and grasped his corner of the canvas sheet.

It was some five minutes later that Slater suddenly realized what Rayner had been after. 'Captain, sir! I think he wanted something to put over Lin—the Chinese. I—I think that's what he was after.' Slater had to shout through the hiss and drum of the rain even though this was noticeably decreasing. For a moment the Captain's hot brown eyes met his in an angry stare. 'We've got to have this water. The man must wait.' Then he thought of something else. 'All right, he can have the sail. We don't need that yet.' Holding his edge of the canvas sheet with one hand, he rummaged behind him under the little foredeck with the other and, bringing out a loose red bundle, tossed it to the Second Officer.

It was almost too late. The rain in his mouth and the consequent coughing had nearly finished Lin. He was existing now only in hazy sensations—pain, coolness, breath-struggle. But as Slater unfurled the vivid sail and as it settled over him in all-embracing folds he seemed to smile very slightly. So he had his red shroud, after all; he must have had it all the time without knowing it. When the rain ceased entirely ten minutes later and Slater lifted the soaking sail, Lin was dead.

In the damp silence which succeeded the passage of the rain-squall they looked down at the broken body of the Chinese boy—the small head rolling gently to the rocking of the raft, the black hair swaying in the bilge water, the gory hole in the shoulder and the swollen green and purple flesh over the fractured ribs. None of them except Rayner —and Roldan, sick and exhausted on the other side of the raft—had really known Lin at all. Until this morning the Captain had not even known his name. Now, more than the sunken ship, more than the men who had gone down with her, he seemed a symbol—a symbol both of their own plight and of what had been done to them.

In the anger and bitterness of his heart Gaston, staring down at that battered body, said, 'They made him die like that. They did that to him.' He lifted his eyes to the Second Officer. 'If I find them one more time I shall kill them for it. Particularly one of them—most especially a certain one of them! But you—you do not think it correct to do that? Or perhaps *this* changes your ideas a little—yes?'

But Slater, glancing bleakly from the short, broad-shouldered, angry Frenchman to the naked body at their feet, said only, 'Why should it? Surely to a rational man it could only emphasize them?'

And now behind the squall came the wind; no longer in sullen, gusty puffs but in a strong, full breeze which veering erratically from quarter to quarter, piled the sea in sharp, short swells and drove the lacy caps of waves in spinning spray to rattle on the raft's canvas dodgers and to whistle over them. The wind did what the U-boat had been unable to accomplish—it dispersed the wreckage, driving and scattering it across leagues and leagues of tossing water under the scurrying leaden clouds. The last they saw of it from the raft was a wooden grating upon which Slater's ginger cat stood wet and draggled and mewing pitifully—but it was soon swept away with the rest and disappeared into the haze of mist and spray.

Until the wind settled in a steady direction there was no point in trying to use the sail. The Captain and Gaston lifted the dead stoker by his arms and legs and rolled him over the side, then they rigged the canvas awning and carefully eased the wounded Spaniard under it. Slater pillowed the boy's head on the life-jacket and wrapped him in the red sail. Then he, too, took shelter under the awning and Philippe crawled in shivering and huddled against him for warmth.

The Captain, still squatting in the bow, had pulled a sodden envelope and a stubby pencil from his pocket and was working out a sum. When he had completed it he said, 'The rations are going to be as follows: three biscuits, half a sardine and half a meat cube and a piece of chocolate for everyone each day. Water will be three ounces each, twice a day. The rest of the oranges will be kept for Roldan if he wants them and he will also have double the water ration. If there is more rain the water rations will be increased according to how much we catch. If we catch any fish they will be shared between everyone.' The Captain shook his head. 'We made a bad mistake when we let those dead fowls go, Gaston. Bait! Why didn't we think of it?'

'God—yes!'

'Too late now. Well, there it is.'

For the rest of the day and all the night the wind and rain blew in veering squalls over the tossing sea. The swells became long whalebacked rollers, corrugated and ridged upon their weather slopes, with sheets of stinging spindrift torn from their tops. The motion of the raft was sickening. It laboured up the swells, teetered in the wind's teeth upon their crests and then, swinging wildly from side to side, slid down their lee slopes like a bob-sled on an ice embankment into the gloomy, windless caverns of their troughs. Ascent under the howl and whine of the wind, drunken imbalance, then stomach-lifting, breath-snatching fall. Hour after hour and all night long. . . .

The second dawn, breaking wanly through an eastern rift in the tumbling grey clouds, showed an empty, heaving sea without a sign of the wreckage which had surrounded the raft twenty-four hours ago. Everyone was sick and exhausted and numb with cold and fatigue, for what clothes they had had been soaked through and through since noon of the day before. They had all, even Gaston and the Captain who were otherwise unwounded, suffered bruises and lacerations

during the sinking and the subsequent attacks and these were now inflamed and swollen by the salt water and the continuous rubbing and
knocking against the interior of the raft. Everyone was in pain and,
notwithstanding the fact that they had had no rest for more than
thirty-six hours of fear and danger, only Philippe had slept, crouched
in a sodden ball and held in place between Gaston and the Captain.

As soon as it was light enough the Captain gave out the first of the
day's rations—a biscuit and half a sardine split lengthways and a
couple of spoonfuls of water. Despite their exhaustion, all of them were
hungry and this meagre meal increased rather than allayed that hunger.
Partly to forget it, partly because they were also bored, frightened and
nervously exhausted, Gaston and Slater began bickering over the
latter's pacifism; Gaston alleging vehemently that if most people held
the same views as the Second Officer the world would be populated by
servile slaves under the savage rule of gangs of bandits, and Slater
wearily pointing out that if *everyone* held his views war of any sort
would be impossible.

'But that will never happen, I think. So there will always be wars.
So—'

'Wars, my good Guéroult, are *not* caused by persons wishing to kill
each other. They are caused by ridiculous rivalries promoted by unscrupulous and ambitious politicians. Killing is merely the means by
which they are carried on and, in due course, completed. You confuse
cause and effect.'

Gaston's sore unshaven face broke into an angry grin. 'I am aware
that I have not the great education of yourself! My time at school was
not long. But to me it appears that I have seen—oh, much, much more,
of the world—of men—of many things than you. . . .'

'Then you have profited less than you should from your experience.
You are a Frenchman, and you should think logically. But it has been
my own experience that Frenchmen can think logically about almost
everything except France. When it is a question of France, or French
interests, or French prestige or something equally idiotic, they lose
their heads completely. And that is something which you undoubtedly
share with the men who are responsible for our present position. There
is no—'

'You say we are like Germans!' Gaston exploded with rage. 'My
God! You say that we and the Germans—'

'Shut up—both of you!' growled the Captain angrily from his
sodden place in the prow. His bloodshot eyes glared from under his
heavy brows. 'Shut up and keep quiet!'

Slater shrugged and Gaston relapsed into sulky silence. Yet after a few minutes he said, 'The officer I talked to was French—or mostly French,' and the bitterness in his voice was so great that Slater felt suddenly embarrassed and stared down silently at his knees. Slater and Gaston hardly spoke again that day but crouched opposite each other trying to prevent the erratic motion of the raft from throwing the injured Roldan from side to side. It was a hard and exacting task, almost impossible to perform successfully. Sometimes they could hold him still for almost as much as ten minutes at a time, but at last a sudden lurch of the raft in an unexpected direction combined with a momentary slackening of their tired muscles caught them unawares and the Spaniard was thrown sideways across the wet slats. Every time this happened he gave a gasping yelp of pain which, by constant repetition, rasped the nerves of the others. It was clear that under the present treatment he was undergoing he could not live long. He was being tortured to death by the sea. Unless the weather moderated he would die quite soon; and, as Gaston darkly guessed, it might be better for him if he did so.

But by evening the wind had dropped; in the west the clouds had parted and through them a clear, serene sunset glittered and gleamed across the troubled but subsiding sea. It glowed for what seemed a long time upon the little raft and her battered crew and by its golden light Captain Crawshaw issued the second meal of the day—two biscuits, a piece of chocolate and half a cube of concentrated meat extract—cutting up the latter with a small pearl-handled penknife borrowed from Slater. The meat cubes were salt and the water which was doled out with them was completely inadequate to allay the thirst which they produced, yet now, with the rain storms over—as the Captain had predicted—within forty-eight hours, they did not dare drink more. When the sun at last sank behind the wide backs of the slackening swells they tried to find such positions as they might in which sleep would be possible. All, that is, except the Captain. For when Gaston had asked if he could not keep the first watch the Captain had refused. 'No, no. I don't feel sleepy, boy. No, you rest if you can. I'll wake you at midnight to take a spell.' But though Gaston woke himself at midnight the Captain would not be relieved. Humped up in the prow, gazing aft through the blackness, he growled, 'I'm all right. Get back to sleep if you can.' And, puzzled, Gaston did as he was told, wondering when, if at all, the Captain intended to take some rest.

Captain Crawshaw had asked himself that question a long time

before. Asked it and silently answered it. Never at night. Not in the
dark while the great black body of Rayner loomed motionless, invisible, but tinglingly present across the length of the raft, crouched in
the stern.

Nine

In his cabin, a tiny cupboard containing a bunk, some lockers, a tip-up
washbasin and a miniature desk and separated from the control-room
by only the regulation green curtains, Kapitänleutnant Eugen Kielbasa had been trying to sleep, but without success. He had not slept
properly since the death of his First Lieutenant weeks ago, for the rest
of his crew were so inexperienced that only someone possessed of a
fatalism of Oriental completeness could have rested tranquilly while
the boat was in their hands. Oberleutnant Chirol, who like himself
had survived four war patrols, had felt the same. 'At least you and I
will be able to sleep alternately,' he had said the night they had left
Kiel. But now Chirol was dead—through the fault of a seventeen-
year-old look-out who had failed to notice an attacking aircraft in the
cold light of an early Arctic dawn—and though Christl Huberein and
Emil Kümmerol did their best and were learning quickly, they were
still novices for all practical purposes.

And because one could listen to everything that went on in the
control-room through the separating green curtains, one could hear
their deliberations, their questions and doubts. Sometimes these were
of such a speculative nature and had such frightening implications that
the Kommandant had difficulty in restraining himself from leaping
through his green curtains and taking up the direct command he had
laid down some twenty minutes before. He could not do this, save in
a serious emergency, since neither of the two junior officers would ever
learn if prevented from working things out for themselves—but he
could not sleep either. Now, as so often before, he gave up the
attempt and lay, his hands clasped behind his head on the pillow,
staring up at the sweaty, white-painted deckhead above him, resigned
to a weary wakefulness.

It is natural, according to Plato, that man should seek to escape from
evil and tragic circumstances and so survive them, and Eugen Kielbasa
had spent many sleepless hours on his bunk pondering his own chances

of surviving the war which now, in mid-January of 1945, was so very evidently lost to Germany. He himself, though a career officer, had taken a singularly inactive part in hostilities until twenty months previously, when he had been transferred from the Copenhagen office where he had assisted in administering the supplies and equipment of Baltic minesweepers and sent to the U-boat service. It had been one of many such transfers as both submarine losses and submarine production steadily increased, and each newly commissioned boat was commanded, officered and manned by sailors ever younger and less experienced than those who had gone before.

Eugen Keilbasa came from a family of prosperous Hamburg lawyers and had joined the Navy in an unusually prolonged fit of adolescent rebellion against the prospect of a life spent in offices and law courts. He had regretted his action soon afterwards since he was, as he shortly discovered, much more suited for the quiet and intricate life of a lawyer than the active and decisive one of a naval officer. But by then the European scene was darkening with ominous clouds of conflicting fears and pressures and it would have been unwise, perhaps even impossible, to have resigned his commission at such time. Since he was, even by the high standards of his nation, a competent and painstaking bureaucrat, he had applied for a shore posting and worked inconspicuously behind his desk, shunning both notice and promotion until his youth and his health—at twenty-four and in full possession of all his limbs he was bound to stand out among nothing but grey-haired cripples—brought him to the undesired attention of one of the numerous manpower committees engaged in finding combat replacements.

And now, after four war patrols and eleven attacks by the enemy, he had his first operational command, a *Seekuh*—one of the largest types of submarine designed for long cruises and commerce raiding in the farthest seas. Under different conditions he might have been pleased and proud and happy, for he was still young enough to feel excited and flattered by the very fact of being a submarine captain. But in the present circumstances he felt none of these things. For what was the use of this cruise upon which he must daily risk his life and the lives of his young crew? Even if each one of his twenty-four remaining torpedoes destroyed a fully laden Allied merchantman— which was a wildly grotesque fantasy—this would make no difference to the now irretrievable ruin of Germany. The only possibility of averting or modifying that was a negotiated peace—although every opportunity for one seemed already to have gone.

From somewhere on the other side of the curtains he heard a crew-man's voice raised a moment in sudden pleading query and Emil's surly '*Quatsch! Lass mich fertig sein mit meine Arbeit.*' He sighed briefly. That was no way to treat these boys. They could only learn if people answered their questions, however stupid. He would have to speak to Emil again. But what was the good? By the time the crew learned to be even moderately competent, if they ever did, the war would be over.

And what then? Who could say? It was being seriously alleged at home that the triumphant Allies intended to dismember Germany, to destroy every industry and let the people starve. It was said that the nation was to be entirely eliminated, and though this was more difficult to believe, it was lent a grim touch of veracity by the appalling casualties inflicted night after night by the Allied bombers. It was also said that when Germany was completely conquered the officers of all her armed forces were to be handed over to the Russians for mass execution or slave labour beyond the Arctic Circle. And it could happen— the Russians had destroyed the Polish officer corps in that way. . . .

Eugen moved restlessly on his bed, rubbing one hand across his tired forehead into the thick shock of pale hair above, and like the sudden reawakening of an old pain came once more the thought of Brazil. Far away to the west, yet separated by nothing but unobstructed leagues of sea, lay that huge, half-known land of which he had heard so much. He groped upwards to the shelf of one of the lockers, reached down a wooden box, then opened it on his chest and, sorting through four or five envelopes each bearing Brazilian stamps, selected one and slid out a photograph. A spectacled woman, a dark man, a little boy in tropical white stood in a garden below two palm trees and behind them rose the corner of a white house . . . his sister Viktoria, his Brazilian brother-in-law and his unknown nephew. The last letter was dated more than two years back, but only the child would have changed—ten years old now, rather than eight. As so often before, he let his mind linger in a dream of São Paulo—wide streets, palm trees, tropical flowers, a dark-skinned people moving always in hot sunlight and dark-blue shadow. His brother-in-law had once offered him a position providing only that he took his law degrees first. How he wished that he had accepted that offer. Even now the remembrance of his refusal made him shiver with remorseful distress.

Supposing he rose, parted the curtains, went into the control-room and told Emil to lay off a course for Rio? It would be done, of course, for he was the Kommandant whose orders must at all times be rigidly and unquestioningly obeyed.   And it was well-known that Kommandanten often sailed with sealed and secret orders to be opened only at a given latitude.   These orders, marked *Geheime Kommandosache* were handed over just before a boat left its moorings and invariably contained positions and dates for meetings with other boats, with submarine tankers for refuelling or with German agents abroad.   The crew knew such orders existed; they would work the boat unquestioningly to Rio and not until Brazilian naval authorities were on board and the German ensign was hauled down would they realize they were prisoners.

Of course it could not be done . . . at least, not yet.   To hand over to the enemy an undamaged, fully armed and crewed submarine in a most desperate period of the war would be for the Kommandant to cover himself with eternal infamy.   Not, thought Eugen, that he would particularly mind that; but back at home every Keilbasa upon whom the State could lay its hands—his parents, two other sisters, uncles and aunts—all would have to pay with their lives for his treachery.   Probably, too, the relations of Huberein and Schlte and perhaps of the two junior officers would also be killed—one could not tell.   And even then there still remained the threat of extradition to Russia as soon as the war was over.

But to fight on uselessly in a hopeless cause, a foredoomed effort to avoid defeat—this was almost equally intolerable.   And today the U-boats were as much quarry as hunters.   One had to accept the fact that any attack by a U-boat against any Allied ship could only be made at an ever-growing risk to itself.   And U-996 was particularly vulnerable since the cannon fire from the enemy aircraft which had torn both arms and shoulders off Oberleutnant Chirol had also destroyed the snorkel, so that the boat could no longer run submerged on its main engines and must surface to charge its batteries.   The snorkel was an unwieldy and awkward device but its destruction greatly enhanced the submarine's peril.

And once they reached their operational zone in the eastern part of the Indian Ocean on the approach routes to the Aden Straits, the risks were too great to contemplate without a turning of the stomach.   With this large, slow-diving and vulnerable boat, and with a crew such as he had today . . . Eugen felt the sweat break out on his chest and forearms. Used to thinking in figures, he calculated that he had no more than a twenty per cent chance of ever reaching home again—probably less. And once more the weary cycle commenced as he strove to think of some way out of his lethal impasse, shut off here and alone in his tiny cubicle behind the green curtains.

They sighted the tanker soon after noon and in Huberein's watch. They had risen to periscope depth, for though still several thousand miles from their target area and running fully submerged during daylight, it was the Kommandant's order that the periscope should be raised briefly at intervals during each watch on the chance of sighting a worthwhile target. Now, deep in the southern latitudes preparatory to rounding Cape Good Hope at a safe distance, the chances of such a target were not great, since enemy shipping still preferred to hug the African coastline under the protective umbrella of shore-based aircraft and submarine chasers. Huberein himself was not in the control-room at the time. As acting First Lieutenant since the death of Oberleutnant Chirol, the position of medical officer had also devolved upon him and it was one which he liked. His kindly and compassionate nature found great satisfaction in administering first aid—though, as Emil had said, he appeared to suffer vicariously all the pain of the minor injuries he treated—and at the time the tanker was sighted he was in the ward-room sweating and groaning with distress over a crushed finger suffered by Letzer, the assistant engineer officer.

Thus it was Kalewski, the under-officer of the watch, who raised the periscope and saw the unmistakable long, low silhouette on the horizon. 'Down periscope! Kommandant in the control-room!' said Kalewski briefly and then waited, taking no notice of Huberein as he rushed from the wardroom still holding scissors and lint and stammering questions, until Eugen was beside him before announcing, 'Target right ahead, sir. A small tanker, probably about three thousand tons, range three thousand metres.'

Eugen gave the order to raise the periscope and, not waiting until the eyepieces had risen to his own height, stooped down and snapped open the handles as soon as they were out of the well. Rising, with the cold daylight from far above glinting on his glasses, he was uncomfortably aware of Kalewski standing respectfully two paces behind him, regarding him unflickeringly from those pale blue eyes.

Of all the crew, Eugen knew well that while Emil Kümmerol was his greatest admirer Geniek Kalewski was his chief critic. It was an odd reflection that neither of them was even half German by blood, Emil being three-quarters French and Kalewski an Estonian Danziger, one of whose grandparents had come from Tashkent. Both expected a great deal of him and, in Kalewski's case, this expectation unfortunately centred on a properly ruthless ability to sink enemy shipping.

Kalewski enjoyed destruction and killing, innocently and for their own sake, in the same way that a dog enjoyed killing rats. He bore no personal or political animus towards the enemy, for he was not, by any ethnic standards, a civilized Western European but an Easterner, a man descended from a basilisk mixture of Tartar and savage Norseman. His ancestry was plainly to be seen in his high-cheekboned, broad-nosed face, his tilted arctic-blue eyes and astonishing corn-gold hair. The crew had nicknamed him 'Vanya'—and it was true that he would have appeared a much more probable figure in a Russian soldier's blouse, fur cap and felt boots than he ever did in the shore-going blue of an under-officer of the *Kriegsmarine*.

Eugen, still mentally flinching from the grim memories of the destruction of the *Maréchal Oudinot*, would have liked to have allowed this new potential victim to proceed on her way unharmed, thus making, as it were, a posthumous reparation to the men he had killed ten days ago. But with Kalewski waiting confidently behind him he knew this to be impossible. At least there would be no necessity to destroy the *Überrest* this time, since they were far from the danger of shore-based aircraft and in any case sunken tankers left carpets of oil, often miles in width, across the sea's surface for days afterwards.

Now he swung the periscope in a quick search through 180° of cloudless, empty sky and then brought his gaze back to his steadily approaching victim. 'Action stations!' And as the klaxon blared through the boat. 'Helm—port ten . . . Steady.'

'Steady, sir. Course two-four-zero.'

'Right. Steady on two-four-zero.'

The attack developed quickly and, to begin with, in accordance with the correct principles inculcated at the U-boat school at Kiel. Eugen's helm orders brought the U-996 to a position in which the tanker would present her entire starboard side to his torpedoes, of which—thrifty by nature and never forgetting that they cost more than twenty thousand Reichsmarks apiece—he would expend three. The target's bearing, speed and range were read calmly off the periscope and fed by Emil into the attack table, the complex electrical machinery which computed from these data the angle of deflection for the torpedoes. The tense silence of the control-room was broken only by Eugen's quick 'Periscope up! Periscope down!'—the sea was far too calm and flat for him to allow himself more than the briefest glimpse of the rapidly approaching tanker before retracting that long cyclopean eye beneath the glassy pale green surface.

Emil, clicking the dials of the attack table, found his mind an odd jumble of fear and exultation—and hate. He hated the unseen target and he hated her crew, identifying them, obscurely, with the massacred survivors of the *Maréchal Oudinot* towards whom, with the exception of Guéroult, whom he tried not to think about, he now bore a deep if irrational resentment. For, like the Kommandant had he known it, he had felt an immense moral relief when, on the morning after that frightening massacre, his actions had been proved correct by the total lack of hostile air search. *Kriegsräson geht vor Kriegsmanier*—a load of guilt had fallen from his shoulders and had been replaced by a peculiar martyred indignation. For had he not been forced to take part in a horrible act in order to save his own life and the lives of fifty-three shipmates? Who had forced him to this? The Kommandant in the first place, but also his own position as gunnery officer and his own immediate understanding of the terrible alternative. He and Kielbasa and the two under-officers had done the job, since it had to be done. They had saved the others and subsequently been covertly criticized by them. Since he could not blame the Kommandant and would not blame himself, he could only blame the survivors for their presence which had made their killing necessary. If they had all gone down with their ship, as they were meant to have done, it would not have happened. He was reminded of a time some four years before he had joined the Navy when an owl had entered the dining-room at lunch-time and, despite open windows and everyone's shouts, had failed to fly out again. It would not go out into the bright glare of the summer noon but flew round and round, knocked over some valuable china, and frightened his aunts so much that in the end he had been forced to kill it with a tennis racquet. It had lain on the floor, dying, staring up at him with huge shocked eyes—and for days afterwards those eyes had haunted him. He had soon begun to hate that owl bitterly—in self-defence.

Now he hoped that these torpedoes, whose angling and aiming were largely his responsibility, would send the new victim up in one great sheet of flame and leave no single survivor, even though in this case survivors would be more or less immaterial to the U-boat. 'Deflection three-zero degrees, Herr Kommandant,' he said, his voice cold and hard. This attack was going to be a set-piece and within minutes that tanker would cease to exist.

But it did not turn out like that. Eugen's voice snapped, 'Stand by, tubes one, two and three!' and everyone froze, knowing the moment at hand. Though only the Kommandant was at the periscope, all the officers and most of the crew had a perfectly accurate mental vision of what he was seeing. The large bow would be entering the left-hand side of his circle of vision and within a few seconds it would touch the vertical hairline of the periscope's aiming sight. When that happened . . . 'Fire One! . . . Fire Two! . . .' The tanker's midships were now cut by that hairline '. . . Fire Three!' A quick pause, then, 'Down periscope! No—wait! God—she's seen us! She's turning!' For Eugen had kept the periscope up too long and some vigilant look-out on the tanker's bridge had caught sight of the small white smear on the glassy smoothness of the sea. Now the torpedo wakes would be seen instantly and the ship would turn in time to avoid them. As if to confirm this, the sliding door of the radio compartment aft of the control-room opened and an operator called, 'Enemy radio sending fast, Herr Kommandant! Submarine attack and position.'

'*Also?* Stand by to surface. Gun crew at the ready. Blow main ballast.' The hum of the motors grew louder, drumming in the ears, and then came the whistling rattling roar of high-pressure air forcing the sea-water from the great saddle tanks. The bow of the submarine canted steeply and Eugen was already up the ladder, his hands gripping the wheel that operated the conning-tower hatch, with the gun crew at his heels. Then they were on the surface and out in the fresh air under the bright sun.

The tanker had turned right away from them and had avoided all three torpedoes. Watching her through his big binoculars, Eugen was angrily aware that he should have retracted the periscope after his first fire order and timed the other two missiles by stop-watch. That mistake had cost sixty thousand Reichsmarks. But he was shortly to have more than the loss of his three torpedoes to think about, for the tanker had a gun on her stern and it was manned and ready for the U-boat as it surfaced. Even as the throb of the electric motors gave place to the clattering roar of the diesels that gun flashed and jerked and a shell whined overhead to tear into the sea fifty metres to port. Again—but short this time. Through his binoculars Eugen saw the gun crew moving like frantic ants on the tanker's stern above the white-painted name *Empire Advance—London.*

Then 'On target!' from Wutsdorf, the gun captain.

'Good! Permission to fire.'

And immediately from below: 'Range eight hundred metres. Fire!'

There came the splitting crack as the gun opened and its recoil jarred the plates beneath the feet of the bridge personnel. Both ships were now coming on to parallel courses, for the tanker's captain, who must be a man of resolute disposition, had seemingly realized that his only chance of survival was to sink the U-boat by gunfire before she could once again point her bow or stern at him and loose her torpedoes. And now—what was that? What was happening as the tanker's bow swung into line? A *second* gun—camouflaged, this time among the deck machinery on the prow. Eugen felt the sweat break out on his face. He would have to break off the action—he could not fight two guns with one—but would he be able to submerge without being hit? And that devil over there was sending fast all the time and—God in Heaven, he was beginning to turn! Was he going to try to *ram*! Anything seemed possible with this ship. For a lost and impotent moment Eugen stared hopelessly at his intended victim now turned assailant, wishing passionately, and for the second time on this patrol, that he had let a merchant ship alone. But suddenly a flash of bright red winked from the tanker's superstructure aft and was followed by a thick cloud of black smoke. Eugen sighed with shaky relief. Wutsdorf was a good gunner. He shouted, 'Well done, Hansi!' and from below Wutsdorf grinned up at him triumphantly. But it was ill-timed triumph for immediately afterwards the tanker struck back vengefully. The air was suddenly sucked out of Eugen's lungs and he was flung to the deck of the bridge as something exploded with an appalling detonation against the armoured conning-tower and shrieked away in metal fragments into the clear bright sky. He was on his knees gasping and coughing up the stink of high explosive, his head a hollow ringing void. Emil was beside him, heaving him to his knees.

'Are you hit? Are you hurt? It didn't—'

'No—no. Emil, the gun—!' For if the shell had struck the side of the conning-tower sufficiently forward, its explosion would have been deflected across the bow, scything down the unprotected gun crew. It had. Staring over the coaming of the bridge, the two officers saw only Wutsdorf, bleeding and blackened, his overalls ripped to rags by the blast, swaying drunkenly over the breech, fumbling with a shell between his bloody hands. Wutsdorf, and some dreadful pieces of his crew.

Two more shells screamed overhead so close that both Eugen and Emil fell back below the coaming with the other bridge personnel, half hearing Wutsdorf's angry, wailing shout, 'Come and *help* me, someone! Come and help—instead of hiding in the tower!'

It was suicide out there on the unprotected fore casing; but Emil was the gunnery officer and knew quite well that it was his duty to get down and man the gun with Wutsdorf until a reserve gun crew could be summoned from below. And Eugen, as Kommandant, had the same plainly obvious duty to order him to go. Their eyes met in one brief understanding glance and in that moment any lingering doubts they might have had of each other were destroyed for ever. Each knew the other was intent on personal survival above all things, and each respected and approved that intention. Now Eugen would no more order his young gunnery officer out on to the casing than he would go there himself. And in that case . . . 'Break off the action! Clear the bridge—quick!' And as the look-outs tumbled rapidly down the open hatch: 'Wutsdorf! Wutsdorf, stop that! Get below!'

But Wutsdorf would not stop. The shock of that explosion had jarred and partially numbed his brain; it had also temporarily deafened him so that he could not, in any case, hear the Kommandant's voice. He was working the gun automatically and without any conscious thought or effort while he swore repetitiously and obscenely at the top of his voice; seizing shells as they were passed to him up the ammunition hatch, slamming them into the breech and aiming and firing all in one movement.

Shell after shell tore into the sea around the boat but the tanker's gunners were unpractised and she was only hit once again—at the very moment when Eugen, his voice cracking with near-hysteria, was threatening to leave his recalcitrant gun captain where he stood and submerge the boat beneath his feet. The tanker's shell struck right astern below the water-line. It jarred the boat as if she had been punched by an armoured fist and jerked her around—even in the instant of the explosion Eugen guessed that it must be on or near the rudder—and it threw the cursing Wutsdorf off aim so that he loosed his own shell prematurely and fell to the deck. And that shell, an explosive incendiary, tore across nine hundred metres of water which now separated the two ships, plunged into the tanker's side, entered her largest fuel tank and exploded.

Only Wutsdorf, dazed and blinking and lying among the horrible human remains below his gun; Wutsdorf, an ugly, lanky nineteen-year-old from Karlsruhe, saw the tanker go up in one roaring sheet of flame. For Emil was already down in the control-room and Eugen, furious and white-faced, was halfway through the hatch.

Ten

Hot, silent, very quiet and glinting back the burning sunlight, the sea stretched endlessly, emptily around a tiny dark spot—the *Maréchal Oudinot*'s single remaining life-raft. And the interior of the raft was as still as the motionless air surrounding it, the motionless water upon which it lay.

Four figures slumped on the sun-warped, salt-caked boards and canvas. Crouched in beaten, twisted postures, their ragged clothes stiff and shiny with dried brine, their skins patched with sea-water sores and their eyes bloodshot between thickened lids, they hung for hour upon hour in a drowsy haze of dreams and long vague reveries in which the past was recalled, relived, altered and amended, and Time was no longer a stable dimension but dwindled or expanded erratically, endlessly. It was the twenty-first day.

Philippe alone of the raft's crew sat cross-legged on the short foredeck, crooning to himself and trailing a string, with a small piece of rag attached to it by way of a lure in the water. A gaunt brown little scarecrow in nothing but his ragged shorts and with his black hair falling over his eyes, he alone of the survivors retained a full semblance of humanity—after all, he was not getting much less to eat now than he had been accustomed to receive during most of his childhood in a Bahia slum. But he was bitterly bored.

In the raft Mr Slater, who was dying rapidly and certainly, was having one of the lucid periods which interspersed, more frequently now that the remainder of his strength was gone, the long spells of semi-conscious delirium in which the last days had been spent. His left leg was dead and rotten almost up to the hugely swollen, discoloured knee-joint, while the darkening red patches, unmistakable indications of the onset of gangrene, expanded ever farther up his right calf. Even should rescue come now, at this very moment, it would make no difference at all to him. His life was over and, because he had realized and accepted this, his nerves were calmer than those of the others who still had hope. 'Nothing—' he quoted wryly to himself—'concentrates a man's mind so well as to be told he will be hanged in a fortnight.' Though of course he did not have anything like fourteen days' further expectation of life—four at the very most, he thought.

What a waste his long years of education and scholarly study had turned out to be! If war had not intervened he would, by now, have been commencing a career as a historian which would have brought him fame and honours before his middle years—and a name, stamped upon the spines of many large books, which would have gone, respected and admired, echoing quietly but persistently down the centuries after his death. Slater's *Early Slavic Emigrations*, Slater's *Indo-European Traditions Exemplified in the Grave-fields of Southern Scandinavia*, *The Search for Vinland—Slater on the Seaways of the Early Norse*. None would now be written; the world would be poorer for their loss and he himself would die as anonymously, as pointlessly, as the sacrificial victims strangled and flung into bogs to appease the pagan northern gods of whom he knew so much.

Slater was not a modest man, since scholars seldom are, and it was the thought of those unwritten books which grieved his heart most deeply in these last hours. He should, he realized now, have overcome his vanity and submitted himself to a Conscientious Objectors' Tribunal. But since he would certainly have been asked a great many very stupid questions by persons immeasurably his intellectual inferiors, and since it was his habit to reply to stupid questions with coldly sarcastic rudeness, his plea would probably not have succeeded in any case. Hitler, he would have been told, persecuted intellectuals. Hitler would make him accept—if, indeed, he did not actually make him write—entirely fictitious history glorifying the origins of the German race. It was as useless to argue such questions as it had been, under First World War Tribunals, to argue about the hypothetical German rape of one's hypothetical sisters—for the interrogators, like those in the enemy's unpleasant organizations, were also the judges.

And yet . . . Two hundred years ago no one would have dreamed of making a someone such as he, a scholarly student of Oxford, take up arms to fight Louis XIV. And—unless he had been stupid enough to get drunk in a Portsmouth tavern and fall a victim to the press gangs— he would have been equally safe and respected during the Napoleonic wars. The world today was turning rapidly back to those long-distant dark ages of barbarism which it had been his intention to scrutinize and examine. Perhaps he was best out of it all. It would not be much longer now and he was so tired and sick that it was too much effort even to feel frightened for more than a minute or two at a time. And yet he would have liked to have seen the end of this nightmare. Particularly with regard to the Captain . . .

The Captain . . . Gaston dragged himself back from the summer evening streets of Dieppe, the crowded sidewalks, the inevitable surge of day-trippers from across the Channel, the fishermen lounging over their glasses of Calvados outside the tavern Au Grand Duquesne . . . For the hundredth time he struggled with the problem and for the hundredth time he came to no conclusion. For what, alone, could he do ? If Slater had been uninjured— But Slater was dying. Slater knew; he was sure of that . . . Together they might have . . . Hardly moving his head, he glanced from puffed red eyes to Slater's skull-thin face hanging by its stalk of a neck upon his skeletal chest—brooding, it seemed, over those dreadful legs. Together they might have . . .

For there was no longer any doubt that Captain Crawshaw was taking far more than his just share of the dwindling supplies of food and water. He had probably commenced this practice when the young Spaniard, Roldan, had died a week ago. Not before that, surely . . . but could one be sure ? Gaston hated to think of Roldan's death, which had been terrible, but until then the Captain had seemed to be be-having as normally as any of them. Or had he ? It was a struggle to think back against the great tide of weakness and torpor which flooded him, but Gaston could remember clearly that in those first days on the raft the Captain had seemed more controlled, more calm and competent, than any of the other survivors. It was he who had fashioned a harpoon out of the cork-handled knife and an oar, and who had actually speared a fish with it. And though he had scrupulously divided this up between everybody, he had not eaten his own share but had used it as bait for the fishing line—and then, catching three further fish, he had portioned these out justly, too.

For the first two weeks things had seemed completely under the control of a man who was completely in control of himself. Except for that sudden outburst against Rayner on the first day—and that had been due only to anger at the spilled water—the Captain had done all that the most exacting standards of maritime behaviour could have demanded of him. He had—and perhaps this was his only error, un-selfish as it seemed—taken far more watches than the rest. 'I'm an old man—' he had said gruffly—'I don't need sleep like you youngsters.' And, indeed, he had hardly slept at all . . . or only in the briefest snatches. His big, bulky, wakeful presence had watched over them from the raft's bent and stubby bow, a salt-caked, narrow-eyed, sel-dom-moving presence by day; a black and looming shadow by night. Of sleep—the one condition in which the pain and misery of their present plight might most easily be borne—he had forgone almost all.

Then . . . why? And . . . when?

It was on the eighth day that the harpoon had gone. Gaston remembered the school of dolphins and the Captain's determination to spear one. He had cut a hole in the oar-haft of his harpoon and riven a rope through it, fixing the other end to a metal cleat in the raft's bow. He had hung over the side for nearly an hour, making ineffectual stabs at the swift, flickering shapes in the water below. Then, suddenly, he had succeeded; the harpoon was torn from his hand, the raft jerked wildly and Roldan screamed weakly. Then the cleat was ripped from the bow and both rope and harpoon disappeared into the deep. And next day the fishing line had been lost, too.

Since the Captain had been the sole fisher, his occupations were completely gone, as was the chance of obtaining anything to eat save what the raft still contained. But it was not until the night of Roldan's death that Gaston had wakened in the stillness to hear the faint but unmistakable crunch of someone eating ship's biscuit. Was it dawn already? Was the first meal of the day being handed out from the bow? No—nothing but black night and the slumped, still figures of Slater, Rayner, Philippe. And no noise save that quiet, almost inaudible munching from the bows. Gaston had remained mute and motionless, head sunk on chest, and later there had come the stealthy clink of someone moving the water container—a soft gurgle. . . .

Next morning when the first rations were handed out Gaston had tried to take a mental inventory of what remained, only to find that the Captain's movements were such as to largely shield from view the stocks of food and water still unconsumed. Of course it might easily have been unintentional . . . And last night *might* have been a dream. One dreamed so much and, because of the constant nagging thirst and hunger, so invariably of food and water.

And two nights later it had occurred again. And the next day the Captain had announced that the concentrated meat cubes were finished. Gaston had tried all day to work this out. It was a highly complicated business since Roldan had ceased to eat at all for the last three days of his life and during the times when they had had fresh fish the Captain had correctly decided that the meat cubes should be preserved. In the end Gaston worked out that of the original number of cubes at least five and a half should be left—say four, anyway; there could not be less than four.

At noon he had conceived the idea of asking for the empty tin box. 'I could make it into a heliograph, m'sieur. To signal a plane.'

The Captain had given him a long, suspicious stare and Gaston's heart had sunk. He was sure, now, that the box was not empty. 'We may need it—for other things. I'll see.' Captain Crawshaw had turned his heavy face away and stared stonily down the raft's length to the crouched form of Rayner.

But next morning the box—quite empty—had been given to Gaston. He had worried about the rations ever since, and in the weak, light-headed state to which they were all reduced, his suspicions had become ever more entangled with grotesque fantasy. The sardines had gone, of course . . . but had *they* been shared out fairly? Gaston had visions of the Captain eating them all very quickly, gobbling up a can at a time while warding off the others with his tiller-bar. He had shaken his head and remembered perfectly clearly how the Captain, as each of the cans became empty, had given it to Philippe, telling him to lick up the half-spoonful or so of oil which remained within. And yet now—for there was no real doubt in his mind any longer—the Captain was himself stealing the food, and, more important still, the water, which should have gone to Philippe and the others.

And there was nothing that could be done about it. Nothing—unless he himself could think of something. But his weary mind, beaten down by the exhausting, burning glare of the sun, could not think even moderately clearly for more than a short stretch of time. He drifted once more back to Dieppe; the deep notes of the bells of St Jacques chiming behind the Palais de Justice; the old women offering their *oeufs du jour* from baskets under the bright green horse-chestnuts, glinting in the May showers . . .

There were four and a half meat cubes left, about twenty biscuits and some three litres of water. Philippe knew the locations of all these things. He knew, for example, that the meat cubes were all carefully hidden between two iron brackets below the starboard side of the tiny foredeck. Four of the biscuits were in one box of safety flares and another two, wrapped in a scrap of canvas, were wedged between the floorboards. About one litre of water was stowed in an allegedly empty container now jammed right under the Captain's seat. The rest of the biscuits and water were where they should be and were brought out at the right hours for distribution.

Philippe had seen, at various times, the movements of the Captain's hands and the jealous glances of the Captain's eyes towards these various caches. He had the quick, watchful alertness of a mouse and nothing escaped him. He was also fairly sure that Monsieur Guéroult and Monsieur Slater guessed that something of the sort was going on. He was equally sure that they did not know for certain.

Philippe was envious of the Captain but not condemning. It had been his experience for most of his twelve years—for he was only two years younger than he pretended—that power alone entitled its pos-sessor to anything he could get, and by power alone could he retain it. If, instead of being a child—and a rather small one, at that—he had been the biggest man in the boat *he* would have had the biggest share of food and water—naturally. As it was, he remained sincerely grate-ful to the others for giving him anything at all; had they decided not to do so he could have done nothing whatever about it.

If he had a grudge against anyone it was against Monsieur Guéroult. For had it not been for the radio operator he might now have been in that submarine. He had understood enough of what had been said on the casing to know that the small German officer who smelled so beautiful had suggested it—a suggestion for which he could never be sufficiently grateful—and that Monsieur Guéroult had refused it—probably as a punishment for something he had done. For most of the time on the raft Philippe had gone over and over his period as galley boy on the *Maréchal Oudinot*, scrupulously examining his conduct to find out in what way he had offended, in what way he had so failed in his duties or his behaviour as to merit the bitter deprivation of the chance of a lifetime—a trip in a submarine. But he could find nothing.

To someone born into the crowded stink of Bahia's grim *favelas*, into a country where five per cent of the population was responsible for one-third of all personal expenditure—and those the parasites of a savage and corrupt dictatorship—'justice' was a word which had no meaning. And since Philippe's education, such as it was, had been gained in one of those Latin-American Catholic schools which never preach doctrine since they know how productive of heresy this can be, he had not even a superficial understanding of good and evil. But since children, unlike adults, think and react in much the same manner all over the world, he had acquired the natural idea that he was punished, in the main, for offences of commission or omission against grown-ups. But try as he would, he could think of nothing he had done which could have annoyed the young radio officer who had been, next to Rayner, the adult he had most liked and admired on board the *Maréchal Oudinot*. It was inexplicable.

Unlike the rest of the survivors, Philippe's physical sufferings were not a constant torment. The wound in his left thigh had healed quickly and cleanly and his dark skin accepted the sunlight and neither sloughed off nor erupted into suppurating sores. He was perpetually hungry, but he was so used to that that he hardly noticed it, and his mouth was sticky and foul with thirst, but his greatest distress was the immense boredom of days which dragged past in great gulfs of yawning emptiness. He had examined every piece of the raft and its equipment a thousand times. He had found a short piece of string and had spent days knotting it and unknotting it until the Captain had growled at him to desist, and since then he had sat on the foredeck waiting for some fish as bored as himself to snap the small piece of handkerchief he trailed over the side. Silence and stillness and the sea perpetually glaring back the shining empty blue of the sky. It was the twenty-first day.

Eleven

Captain Crawshaw lived much of the time in a world containing nothing at all—except Rayner. Rayner was no longer an individual, not even a mortal man—he was Satan and much worse than Satan, for he existed all too materially and was a deadly threat to the Captain's corporeal being rather than his soul.

Captain Crawshaw had never liked or trusted Negroes; they made poor sailors. To a lesser degree he disliked and distrusted Chinamen and the various Goanese and East Indians who went under the general name of Lascars. Yet a Chinaman could often be intelligent, quick and able—and he was invariably very clean. Lascars, though dirty, were hardworking and obedient. Both races might, by a fairly strong effort of the imagination, be accepted as human beings; different and distinctly inferior to oneself yet members of the same species.

But Negroes—no. Indolent, piggish, clumsily cunning, they were something different altogether. They were a horrible half-step between the great apes whom they so closely resembled and human beings, and this showed particularly in the powerful physique of their great black bodies. When they got out of control they were a supreme danger.

Throughout his long years at sea Captain Crawshaw had been present at several minor mutinies. These had always been abortive, but none the less extremely unpleasant, occurrences. Yet he had seen an officer, a young Dutch mate armed with a single oar, put a whole pack of screaming Chinese to flight and had watched admiringly while a tough little Welsh captain, a pistol in each hand, had cowed an entire crew of Lascars, forced them into the hold, battened them down and, with only three officers to work his ship, get her across a thousand miles of ocean and into port. But he had also seen a single Negro go berserk, charge up the bridge ladder and, despite five heavy bullets from an old-fashioned service revolver, kill two officers with an axe and throw a six-foot steersman overboard—and even in his death agony he had fixed his teeth so firmly in a seaman's leg that his jaw had had to be cut away to free it.

Fortunately Negroes were not a sea-going race like Chinese and Lascars and there were seldom more than two or three among a ship's crew. But in times of difficulty or danger they had to be classed as a perpetual menace of the first order and kept under continual surveillance. That was why he had placed Rayner in the stern. That was why he sat in the prow with the teak tiller-bar always within a few inches of his right hand. That was why he at first would not, and later could not, sleep in more than stretches of ten or fifteen uneasy minutes —to wake with a startled jerk and a hand leaping automatically towards his club.

The Captain found a cause for additional fear in Rayner's smashed mouth and probably damaged head. He would have much preferred it if the stoker had suffered a broken leg or arm. In that case the danger from his presence would have been immensely diminished, and thus it would have been possible to give him proper and considerate treatment. As it was, his wounds, which were in no way incapacitating, made him appear more fearsome than pitiable, a great silent brooding presence with a hugely swollen jaw and bloodshot eyes closed to the narrowest slits. As the days wore on and the Captain's nerves stretched continually tighter under the strain of sleeplessness and thirst and hunger, his fear of Rayner, growing ever greater as the supplies of food and water diminished and his own and Gaston's strength dwindled with them, became the first and most terrible of all their perils. For by the fourteenth day the Captain knew exactly what was in the big Negro's slow but cunning mind. Rayner was waiting. Rayner's wounds were, in reality, far less severe than they looked. He was keeping his face puffed out with air to give the impression of a smashed jaw. That way he need not talk and perhaps unwittingly give away his plan. For of course he had a plan—and the Captain knew what it was. Rayner was waiting until the rest were weak enough from thirst and hunger and exposure to be disposed of by his greater strength. It was true that Rayner had no more to eat than the others— considerably less, in fact, since he could not eat the biscuits. But Negroes possessed immense physical endurance and he would still be strong and powerful when the strength and power of the others was all but gone. And then—then he would rise slowly from the stern and come up the raft. He would throw Slater, Gaston and the child into the sea and stand grinning over the Captain, savouring for a long moment the terrible power that was now his own. If he had a concealed knife he would use it; otherwise he would crush the Captain's skull with the tiller-bar or strangle him with those gorilla hands. And when, supplied with all the food and water remaining, he was eventually picked up by a passing ship he would say plausibly enough that he had always been alone on the raft—the sole survivor from the sunken *Maréchal Oudinot*.

The only man who could prevent this was obviously the Captain himself. He must hold out, unsleeping, ever-watching, until it was possible for him to reverse Rayner's plan. Until it was possible for him to rise from his place in the prow and go down the raft, tiller-bar in hand, to dispose of Rayner. To do that he must keep up his strength and that meant he must have more food and water than the rest— taken secretly and carefully at night so that the Negro down in the stern should never guess that instead of weakening daily he was storing vital energy for the ultimate encounter. In taking the extra food and water the Captain knew that, far from cheating the others out of their fair chances of survival, he was doing the one thing which might save them from certain death.

Twelve

Two days later at sunset Brian Slater died. He died unnoticed by the other survivors, for he had hardly moved nor been properly conscious for nearly twenty-four hours. He died in the midst of an acrimonious debate concerning the early Icelandic settlements in Greenland which was being carried on before a Conscientious Objectors' Tribunal whose members, exasperatingly, quoted continually from large books which they denied the defendant and which they refused to identify. But Slater died knowing that he was right and the opposition wrong— which was exactly how he would have died even if there had been no war and he had lived to become a famous scholar eighty years of age instead of a promising university student of twenty-four.

It was not until nearly midnight that his death was discovered. A movement of the Captain's knocked the tiller-bar across the floor-boards and his quick jump—almost a pounce—to retrieve it caused the raft to sway suddenly to starboard. Slater's body fell sideways, tumbling to the bottom.

For almost a fortnight he had seldom moved at all, and though the others had become used to the dreadful smell of his putrefying legs the ghastly charnel stench which they gave off when disturbed by the fall of his body choked them all with stomach-twisting nausea. Gaston recovered first and, lifting the skeletal head, realized that for another of them the long torment was over. He had deeply disliked Slater in life but now he felt only sorrow and pity and admiration for the stoical courage with which the Second Officer had observed, almost scientifically, the onset of his certain death. Slater had been a bigoted, wrong-headed and conceited man—he had actually dared to compare the French to the Germans—but he had deserved a better fate.

'We'll have to put him over the side.' The Captain's voice from the dark bow was hoarse but firm. 'Take his left arm, Gaston—that's it! I'll take the other. Don't touch his legs. Out of the way, Phil—get on to the other side. All right—let him go!'

A soft splash, a sudden sparkle of foaming phosphorescence, and the remains of Slater were gone for ever. But it was not for some time that the others were able to get the stink out of their nostrils and throats.

For forty-eight more hours the raft lay still under the silent glare of the windless sky, but on the third day after Slater's death dawn broke to a sparkle on the water, a light but steady breeze from the east. And for the first time since the sinking of the *Maréchal Oudinot* the air was full of the cries of gulls and the gleam and glitter of their swooping flight.

The breeze did an odd thing to Captain Crawshaw—it made him want to sleep. For more than three weeks he had hardly slept at all and he had thought that he could never sleep again. But now, taking in great mouthfuls of the suddenly fresher and cooler air, he knew that he *must* sleep. He would raise the ragged little red sail and with his prow pointing towards the nearest land, which was, as far as he could judge, the coast of Brazil—not too far off, either, if the sea-gulls were anything to go by—and the sheet firmly in Gaston's hand he would lie flat on the salt-stained boards and sleep for hours. Yes, but Gaston's place must be in the stern, and for himself—he could not sleep quite yet. Something must be done first, and now was the time. He rose, gripped the tiller-bar and took the three steps down the raft to Rayner.

Gaston was often to blame himself for what happened then. Despite the weakness and exhaustion of more than twenty days' semi-starvation and exposure, he still had enough strength to have intervened in time. But though he had been uneasily aware for days past that something was wrong with the Captain, he had not realized what that something was. Except for his single outburst long ago at the time of the rain squall Captain Crawshaw had given no open indications of his increasingly aberrated obsession with Rayner. Or if he had given them they were not of a sort which Gaston and the others were in a fit condition to notice. But now—was it truly happening or was it a hallucination born of what had gone before?—the Captain was standing over Rayner, his tiller-bar uplifted, and ordering him into the tiny square float which still bobbed at the end of its length of fraying rope behind the raft. 'Come on—get out of here! Pull that float up and get into it!' His voice was hoarse and the words themselves, struck from a thick tongue between dry teeth, were guttural and jagged, but their meaning was plain enough and he stood, his ragged clothes fluttering and blowing in the increasing breeze, towering above the bewildered Negro, who raised an arm above his head and blinked his swollen eyes but remained seated.

Though the Captain believed Rayner to possess the strength of a gorilla, anyone in his right mind would have seen at once that the stoker was now the weakest of the remaining four on the raft. His great shoulders and chest had sunk to sagging folds of cracked and lifeless black skin draped over his barrel-like rib cage. He had eaten hardly half the scanty rations doled out to the others and weeks of continual pain added to this starvation had brought him to the very brink of death. Far from being able to stride down the raft, throw the others into the sea and then stand grinning over the Captain before cutting his throat, Rayner was too weak even to be able to rise from the stern thwart at the Captain's order. He stared up dumbly and shook his head.

But the Captain was not seeing Rayner; he was seeing the incarnation of absolute evil—as frightful an ogre as any to be met with in the wickedly labyrinthine corridors of the worst nightmares. By being so close to Rayner he was stretching his very considerable courage almost to snapping point. He took a deep breath and, grasping the worn line which sagged from the raft into the water, he pulled the float up sharply against the square stern. 'In!' And with one vicious blow across the chest he tumbled the dying Negro over the raft's edge and into the bobbing life-buoy.

Gaston struggled to his feet, realizing too late that the Captain was out of his mind and must be stopped. The freshening breeze caught the raft, now dangerously unbalanced by the two standing figures, and tilted it suddenly and sharply on to its port-side, throwing Philippe across the floorboards against Gaston's legs. Gaston and the Captain both fell; Gaston back into the raft—Captain Crawshaw into the sea. The breeze was strengthening fast and even in the short time it took the Captain to come to the surface the raft was drifting quickly away. Spluttering, he trod water and shouted, 'Get out the oars, Gaston! Quick! You and Phil—you'll have to—' But his words ended in a gasping choke as the rising slop dashed a small wave in his face; he was very weak, despite the extra rations he had eaten, and he was far older than the others. He knew, suddenly, that it was probable that he would drown. And this knowledge, coupled with the shock of the fall into the water, temporarily drove away the black, torturing hallucinations of the past weeks. He was in the sea, the raft was drifting rapidly away, and in his hand he held—he was not quite certain how or why—a rope. On the other end of the rope the little square float with Rayner huddled on its netting bottom rose and swayed over the increasing swell. For a moment the Captain looked at Rayner with clear eyes and saw that the vast Negro, the all-powerful black devil of his disordered fancy, was a crumpled wreck of a man who could be of no possible danger to anyone. Then why—? He did not know. A mistake of some sort . . . But he did know that his fear of Rayner had gone. He would cling to the float and stay there until Gaston and the boy had somehow manœuvred the clumsy raft back across that twenty-yard gap of choppy sea and picked them both up. He pulled himself to the side of the float and said, 'Here, Rayner—give me a hand!'

But if the Captain's fear of Rayner had evaporated, Rayner's fear of the Captain was now intense. He was very weak and knew that he could not survive much longer. He also knew that the Captain had wanted to set him adrift to certain death less than two minutes ago and believed that he now wanted to throw him out of the float, which in any case could only hold one person within its narrow interior. He lifted one thin leg over the edge and drove his heel into the Captain's face.

Captain Crawshaw went under for the second time. But he still retained the line in his hand. When he surfaced he was on the other side of the float and Rayner had to shift his whole body to bring his feet once again into operation to repel the old man struggling in the sea. He succeeded in this, but as once more he drove his heel into the Captain's face the latter's grasping, despairing hand was holding on to the bung of cloth with which he himself had plugged the bullet hole in the float's side at the time of its salvage. The cloth tore out; the water flooded in, and at the recoil of Rayner's frantic kick the rope netting, rotted by long immersion, broke. The float swung up and capsized as the Captain, now at the end of his strength, once more came to the surface beside it. Gasping, livid-faced, he had just time for a last glimpse of the bright sky, a sky full of the quick swoop and glitter of gulls, before the float with Rayner entangled like a great black spider in its torn netting, turned over and fell upon him, driving him below the surface finally and for ever.

Gaston and Philippe had tried, with what strength they possessed, to row back to the two struggling drowning men and the float, but they were too weak to do anything more than partially delay the raft's progress as it drifted away. They were more than thirty-five yards off when it capsized. Panting, gasping and exhausted, they ceased to row and looked back. The float lay upside down on the rising swells, its bottom gleaming with streamers of green weed and clusters of goose-barnacles which had attached themselves to it during the last weeks. From the torn netting of its centre one of Rayner's legs lifted grotesquely, the big splay foot waving like a flag at the end of a stumpy mast. Yet within seconds that foot was still and the float with its gruesome underwater burden was fast diminishing to windward.

Thirteen

That day began for Gaston a short period to which he would later look back as a curious interlude of happiness set in the middle of a nightmare. At the time he was too tired and weak to wonder why this was so, but afterwards it became obvious. Since the sinking of the *Maréchal Oudinot* the raft had continually carried Death as one of its passengers. It had been certain, even on the first day, that Lin Hsiang must die. It had been increasingly obvious in the days that followed that first Roldan and afterwards Slater were equally doomed unless speedy help came. For days Gaston had watched their slow but inevitable end, and for the last week he had also had to contend with the knowledge that his admired captain was stealing rations and losing his reason.

Now all that was over. The horribly maimed, the dying and the crazy had disappeared as if blown away by the wind which now drove steadily from the east. He and Philippe, thin and weak with hunger and exposure, but unhurt and sane, remained in the raft—and with greatly increased chances of survival. He felt nothing, now, but an immense relief. Before that float was entirely lost—a small, ugly speck on the eastern rim of the sea—Gaston had rigged the tattered red sail, and as he turned from the mast Philippe emerged from below the foredeck grasping three meat cubes, four biscuits and the can which all had thought empty but which, grinning painfully with cracked lips, the boy shook till it gurgled and splashed.

They said nothing, but in unspoken agreement they ate a meat cube and two biscuits apiece and drank half a litre of water. It was an expenditure of their supplies which could not have been considered before, but it had an immediately reviving effect physically—and, still more, mentally.

The raft was clumsy, squat and unwieldy; but now, lightened of most of its original load, it moved at an increasing speed under its red sail, driving, Gaston reckoned, due west and towards the Brazilian coast. If only this wind remained steady and did not increase to a dangerous degree two or three more days should see them approaching the shipping lanes of the coastal waters.

And that afternoon they had a further piece of luck. Out of a rolling swell to starboard suddenly tore a shining silver spray—flying-fish leaping in maddened panic from pursuing dolphins. They shot across the raft like gleaming bullets and five of them struck the sail and fell stunned to the floorboards. Both Gaston, releasing the sheet, and Philippe flung their worn bodies upon them. The raft swung around dangerously and toppled on a wave but until the fish were killed and safely in their possession neither of the last two survivors of the *Maréchal Oudinot* gave anything else a thought. Laughing delightedly until their lips cracked and dribbled blood, they thrust their catch under the foredeck and brought the raft back once more into the wind. Those fish meant almost certain salvation. With what remained of the rations and water they would provide enough food for another week.

That night the wind eased to a light but steady breeze still blowing from due east and for three more days the raft moved slowly towards Brazil. On the third afternoon Philippe discovered that the raft was surrounded by a shoal of bluish fish, most of them about half a metre long, swimming at the same speed as the raft and only just below the surface. There were no fish hooks or line left, but remembering how the Captain had made a clumsy harpoon from a knife and an oar, Philippe tried to make another. The belt which held his ragged shorts was made from a dozen thin strips of plaited leather and by taking these apart he was able to tie his own small clasp-knife to an oar's haft. Gaston watched him with a mixture of indulgence and pity. It was extremely unlikely that even if the harpoon held together he would succeed in spearing a fish, but it gave him something to do and allayed the deadly monotony which must have been his worst suffering during the burning endless days which had gone before.

So Philippe lay across the raft's lee side peering down into the water and Gaston sat in the stern wondering how it was that this small Brazilian child should have suffered so little physically or mentally compared with himself and the others. Philippe was extremely thin, though in Gaston's recollection he had always been so, but it was a proportional thinness, a fining down of all the flesh rather than, as in his own case, the skeletal caving-in of the body over its bone cage. And Philippe's skin had remained a sun-browned dark olive while Gaston's was broken and cracked and scarred with eruptions. And even now Philippe retained enough strength and interest in external things to make that useless harpoon and to try to stab fish. Comparing his own exhausted state with the child's, Gaston felt an odd superstitious awe. Philippe had been sitting on the hatch cover of No. 1 hold when the torpedo had exploded within. He had survived that—God alone knew how for the matter had never been discussed—and been found in the sea still on top of that hatch cover and entirely unhurt. He had been machine-gunned and bombed at point-blank range, hurled into the water amidst great whirling logs of wood—and had suffered only a flesh wound in the thigh, which was now nothing but a small pink scar. He had subsequently watched men die in great pain and had been deprived for over three weeks of everything a growing child needed to sustain it. And yet he appeared to have emerged from the ordeal unharmed in body or mind. Even at that moment, as his arm plunged down with the harpoon, missed the fish and withdrew, he turned a smiling face to Gaston. And Gaston, smiling weakly back, waited until the child was once more staring down into the sunlit water, and then furtively, quickly, crossed himself.

That evening they saw their first ship. It was, of course, Philippe who saw it first and called to Gaston urgently where he drowsed in the stern, the strain of the sheet taken from his arm by a turn around a cleat. He rose shaking to his feet, rubbing his sore eyes, and saw the smudge of smoke on the horizon beyond the raft's port bow. Smoke—and below that would be a ship and in that ship would be fresh water, as much as one could drink, and food and—above all—safety and the future.

Gaston struggled under the foredeck and pulled out the boxes of flares. Both of them were rusty and salt-corroded and his heart sank as he broke them creakingly open and looked at their damp and discoloured contents. And, as he guessed, none of the flares would ignite; he tried one after another and then threw them all furiously into the sea. Perhaps the *Maréchal Oudinot* had possessed some better ones, but if so Monsieur Lagny had stowed them in the big lifeboats. There was no possibility of altering course to port since the raft was incapable of doing anything save sail before the wind. There was nothing to do but hope.

For nearly half an hour they drove on steadily under the breeze, their red sail bright and hot in the light of the westering sun, with Philippe standing on the foredeck, steadying himself against the mast and staring urgently at the horizon. 'It is increasing, Monsieur Guéroult! It approaches! Certainly they will see us soon!' And then 'Yes, yes—it comes nearer. Surely, now . . .'

And still later: 'It is going. M'sieur, it is becoming smaller. I think that—that they cannot have seen us, after all!'

For a long time Gaston watched the little Brazilian outlined against the fading sky and the red sail, his copper body glinting in the sunset as he peered under a raised hand at the place on the horizon where the ship had been. At last:'It is no good, m'sieur. It has gone. It has quite gone. *Ay, Jesus!*' But only when the light had failed and the first stars shone out in the darkening sky did Philippe descend disconsolately into the well of the raft.

'Do not distress yourself, Philippe. Tomorrow we shall see more.'

'*Vraiment?*'

'Yes, truly. We must be in the coastal shipping belt now. Tomorrow —or at the latest the next day—we shall be picked up. Now let us eat.'

But Gaston's words were braver than his feelings for it was possible, with ill luck, to pass unseen through even the most crowded coastal waters in a craft as low and small as this. Yet even so there was the coast ahead and they were bound to reach that—if the breeze kept up.

The excitement of the last hours, the hopes raised and then disappointed, had left Gaston more exhausted than he remembered being during the whole time in the raft. Exhausted, but also strangely elated. The end was not far off now. Tomorrow—or even tonight.

He smiled at the small boy sitting beside him and put an arm around his bare shoulders. 'We'll be all right now, Philippe—truly! It is nearly over now.' And for the first time he thought of the future without picturing, as he had done for so long, his personal vengeance on the crew of the U-boat. For by now they might all be dead. They might,

he hoped, have been found by an aircraft or a chaser and perished as
miserably, trapped in their iron coffin on the bottom of the sea, as Lin
or Roldan or Slater in the raft. Meanwhile there was tomorrow to look
forward to. And there was Philippe. Sitting in the dark with his arm
about the child Gaston thought that he could not let him go—at
least not back to the squalor of a Bahia slum. He deserved—perhaps
he had been preserved for—a future much better than that. Something,
surely, could be done. Vaguely Gaston thought of taking Philippe to
Europe and educating him properly. He pictured him clean, well-
dressed, well-fed, on his way to the *Ecole Communale des Garcons* in
the Place Louis Vitet at Dieppe . . .

He pulled himself up with a jerk. He had nearly fallen asleep. He
peered over the dark sea in search of lights but could see none.
'Philippe, I must sleep now. You can take this watch, eh? Don't
touch the sheet but wake me if the wind increases. And keep a good
lookout, understand? If you see a light anywhere wake me at once.
We have matches still and will burn a piece of canvas. But do nothing
by yourself.'

'No, m'sieur.'

'Very well, then. And wake me in two hours.'

'Qui, m'sieur. Dormez bien.'

Gaston grinned. 'We shall make a Frenchman of you yet, I think.'
Then, using the kapok life-jacket as a pillow, he lay down on the
floorboards and was asleep in an instant.

He dreamed vividly as he had done on every occasion that he had
slept, even in snatches, since the sinking of the *Maréchal Oudinot*. But
this time his dreams were of rescue. It seemed that he was still awake
and sitting in the stern of the raft under the light of a falling sun which
struck gleams of orange and gold from the calm opalescence of the sea.
Up on the foredeck Philippe stood, staring out at the horizon, his small
body still, statuesque, gilded by the warm light. Everything seemed
hushed in an evening calm and Gaston was aware of neither hunger
nor thirst nor tiredness, but only of a joyfully contented peace. It was
absolutely still yet the raft, as if propelled by invisible angels, moved
forward smoothly over the mirror-calm water. Unbroken silence,
silver-blue space where sea and sky dissolved and intermingled with
each other so that one might be sailing in the sky—into heaven.

Then Philippe turned, smiling, to descend into the raft, and his face
was no longer the thin, dark-eyed olive one which Gaston had come
to know and love so well, but the face of 'Emil,' and even as Gaston
jumped to his feet and caught up Captain Crawshaw's tiller-bar he

heard that unforgotten voice speaking in quick, unaccented, spiteful French, 'It is probable that you will be picked up tomorrow or the next day. There is a good deal of shipping in this area—as you can see.' And he pointed across the raft's bow to where, rushing across the water towards them, the U-boat threw up a seething wave from its sharp stem. Gaston shouted, raised the tiller-bar for one shattering, face-smashing stroke—and then fell heavily to the deck, and awoke. The sun was bright overhead and for a moment he could not think how evening had turned so suddenly into broad day. He blinked and rubbed his eyes, sitting up painfully and stiffly. With the automatic reflexes of years at sea he noted that the breeze was still blowing, though less strongly, from the east and the raft moved on before it over a diminishing swell while two sea-gulls dipped and mewed about the mast.

But—why had not Philippe wakened him hours ago? They might have missed half a dozen chances of rescue. He must have fallen asleep, too, and be asleep still. 'Philippe!' Groaning with the pain of his stiff body, still peering from eyes not yet accustomed to the bright sunlight, Gaston stared around the raft. 'Philippe!' He shook his head and as his vision cleared panic skewered him like a knife in the stomach. Behind, the stern was empty; in front on the warped floorboards lay Philippe's harpoon. The foredeck . . . nothing underneath . . . 'Phil—' But there was no one. The raft moved on gently across the bright morning sea guided by no hand—and it was empty of all life except his own.

Fourteen

In the small cluttered wardroom of U-996 Ingenieur Oberleutnant Walter Sehlte glanced up angrily from the book he was reading at the flushed face of Emil Kümmerol, who stood on the other side of the narrow table. 'And what do you expect *me* to do, eh? Put him under arrest, I suppose? Well, I'm not going to.'

'But he said—'

'I don't care what he said. You had no business to be in the motor-room in any case. It was not even your watch.'

'I went in to see Letzer; only he was not there, and so—'

Sehlte sighed with weary exasperation. 'I will not have you

quarrelling with the engine-room staff, Kümmerol. You—I do not know what is the matter with you these days! You seem quite incapable of being civil to anybody.'

'But he said—'

'Oh, *for God's sake!*' Sehlte banged his book hard on the table and Kümmerol sat down sullenly on the farther side and with lowered eyes and trembling hands began to leaf through a tattered cope of *Der Seeflieger*, pretending, presumably, to memorize aircraft silhouettes. Despite his words, Sehlte did not attach too much importance to the quarrels which were continually flaring up and dying away among the U-996's crew. The strain and tension generated by the exhausting and unnatural life of a submarine on an extended patrol were enough to set the Holy Family themselves tearing one another's eyes out. None the less the officers, above all, must control themselves, however difficult that might be. And it was true that Emil Kümmerol had changed a great deal since the commencement of this voyage. He had been very different in the early days, the long journey from Kiel up into the icy seas just below the Arctic Circle as the submarine struggled northward in the teeth of winter storms, to turn south-west at last between Iceland and the Faroes. In those bitter days of darkness and cold he had shown a competence and an easy ability to deal with the sea-sick and miserable crew which had earned him even Sehlte's qualified admiration. The engineer knew that he had been some sort of staff officer whose department had been closed down, if not exactly in disgrace at least with an ignominious abruptness. It was a fate which had overtaken many shore-based establishments during the last year as Germany strove to replenish its thinning combat ranks with men who had striven to pass the war in decent obscurity. It had given Sehlte, who knew that the Kommandant had been just such a one, a certain dour amusement to see how he and Kümmerol had immediately taken to each other. In those early days, as Sehlte had guessed, Kümmerol was uncertain of his new position and was feeling his way carefully, determined if possible to make neither mistakes nor enemies. But later, when the formidable presence of Oberleutnant Chirol had been removed, he had become more assured—and more demanding. He himself had struggled to learn his new job more or less successfully and he expected the rest of the equally inexperienced crew to do the same. But since none of them had Kümmerol's quick intelligence this was an expectation that was disappointed more often than not. Yet it was only after the sinking of the old French freighter that Kümmerol had begun to close in on himself in a sullen withdrawal, to snarl and snap at any crewman who failed in immediate comprehension and obedience to his orders and to slash at them with a peculiarly vicious—probably French, thought Sehlte—sarcasm.

But it was one thing to treat teen-age seamen in such a way; quite another to use the same language to older and more experienced engine-room artificers. No wonder Brandschied, a man at least five years older than Kümmerol, had answered back. Yet to use the episode of the sinking of the old French ship and its aftermath had been an unforgivable weapon to employ against Kümmerol. Particularly since the Kommandant had made it plain that the matter must not be discussed and had laid a ban of silence upon the whole incident. 'Neither now, nor at any future time and under any circumstances whatever, will that sinking or what occurred afterwards be spoken of—by *anybody*. It was something which had to be done, like a—a necessary but unpleasant surgical operation. It was done. Now it is best forgotten.'

Not that it could be forgotten, thought Sehlte. He would not forget it for one—any more than he would forget the great Hamburg air raid in which his two children had been killed and his wife so badly burned by phosphorus that she was now a horribly fire-scarred idiot in a mental asylum. One did not forget horrors, much as one might wish to do so. But one could refrain from mentioning them; particularly when ordered to do so. According to Kümmerol, Brandschied had turned away from him muttering 'Gunning people in the water is one thing—but where were you when Wutsdorf sank that tanker?'

Yet Kümmerol had only obeyed orders in the first place, and in the second—well, no one seemed certain exactly what had happened in the short two minutes between the death of the majority of the gun crew and Wutsdorf's fluke shot which had destroyed the tanker. It was hinted that not only Kümmerol but also the Kommandant himself had been crouching behind the armour-plated bridge . . . And it was certain only that whatever had occurred had done nothing to enhance the reputations of either of them. Sehlte realized with mounting irritation that Kümmerol would very probably now take his complaint to Kielbasa. That meant that he himself had better speak to Brandschied first. He would take him aside at the first opportunity and tell him sharply to control his tongue in future.

Yet as the oldest officer in the boat and as an engineer of long experience it was not the behaviour of the U-boat's crew which worried Sehlte this evening but the effect of that last encounter upon the boat's hull. The last shell fired by the tanker's bow gun ten days ago had damaged both the rudder and the port screw. The rudder would no longer answer to full port helm, and though this was not a crippling disadvantage it could, in certain circumstances, cause a dangerous predicament in manœuvring the submarine in combat. But the damage to the port screw was worse. The shaft had been wrenched out of true alignment and even at the slowest speeds the boat vibrated noisily to its rattling revolutions. This meant that should the U-996 find herself in the position of having to slide soundlessly away from a listening enemy she would be unable to use more than one motor. And it was now obvious that the screw gland had been damaged. Water was leaking in through it—and therefore, in all probability, oil was leaking out. And even the merest trickle of oil rising to the calm surface in a submarine's wake could arouse the suspicions of an alert observer in an aircraft, for, as Sehlte well knew, the tiniest quantity of oil rising to the surface would spread upon the seawater into a long glistening ribbon. . . .

Sometimes, when he was more than usually tired and depressed, he seemed to see a thin rainbow snail-track of oil spreading across the open book before his eyes. Tonight, unthinkingly, he tried to wipe it away with his hand, and catching himself doing this he glanced up quickly, furtively, to find young Kümmerol staring at him across the table with a sullen, alien hostility in his big dark eyes.

Fifteen

Emil Kümmerol was the precocious child of an unhappy and swiftly dissolved marriage. His mother, the youngest by many years of the three Mlles Coucy of Grévilly-le-Gros-Moulin, had married a German who was himself half French and at that time resident in Paris. When after two years the marriage broke up on the rocks of Dr Robert Kümmerol's continuous and flaunting infidelities, he returned to his paternal home in Hamelin and his wife, taking her baby with her, went to her sisters' at Grévilly, where she soon died of despair and unhappiness since she still loved her husband and her child merely bored her. She might have married again; she had only to say the word, for Paul Amoret-Labonde had been steadily in love with her since her childhood, undeterred, in the contemplation of her beauty, by either her vanity or her shallow stupidity. But the Colonel was nearly fifty then and with his limp, his medals, his iron-grey hair and stern moustaches he already possessed the full aura of an *ancien militaire*. She might just as well, as she told him cruelly, marry her own father. He was a devoted and lifelong family friend and godfather to her own baby—he must content himself with that.

After her premature death Emil was reared by his two spinster aunts with help and advice from the Colonel. Dr Kümmerol had married again and had moved to Berlin, where he was now treating his second wife in the same way as he had treated his first. It was out of the question that Emil should return to such a household, though as he grew older he was permitted to visit there once or twice a year. The Coucys, though they had all the appearance of well-to-do bourgeois, were living on a continually dwindling private fortune which dwindled still faster when the two sisters began accepting well-meant but injudicious advice concerning their investments from the Colonel. But for Emil, growing up in the green beauty of the Franche-Comté, there were no financial worries, everything he wanted was his at once; the aunts doted on him and would if necessary have sold the whole house and its contents to see that he lacked nothing.

It was not until he was fourteen that the question of his nationality caused any concern. The face that he was legally a German rather than a Frenchman had seemed to be as irrelevant as the fact that his surname was Kümmerol and not Coucy. He was a Frenchman by blood, birth and upbringing. And yet, as the Coucy sisters then remembered, not by birth for he had been born in Hamelin during one of the only two visits his mother had made to her parents-in-law. Now, with the political situation ominously worsening, it seemed that something should be done to clear up his anomalous position as soon as possible. Inquiries proved beyond a doubt that Emil was a German citizen. Had he been naturalized during his mother's lifetime and after her divorce, there would have been no difficulty. Now it was too late, for until he came of age Emil was theoretically, at least, in the custody of his father who, being a German, could not make his son a French national even had he wished to. There was nothing to be done but wait until the boy came of age.

But war came first. And with it came a most sensible suggestion from Colonel Amoret-Labonde. Emil should be sent to Switzerland to carry on his studies in peace and neutrality. But the Mlles Coucy, to their considerable embarrassment, had to admit that they no longer possessed sufficient means to do this. And, after all, it would not be necessary. Everybody in Grévilly knew that Emil was French—just as

French as they were themselves. And this time there was the Maginot Line and no chance of invasion. . . .

And then it was too late. France was defeated and partially occupied and Emil was in the peculiar position of being an enemy conqueror occupying his own home.

Eighteen months later, during the supremacy of Darlan and the closest period of Franco-German collaboration, Dr Kümmerol decided to do something about his son. As ever, his motives were largely actuated by self-interest since at the time it was both fashionable and politic to display friendship for France. He visited Grévilly where he was received coldly by the Coucy sisters but warmly by Emil who had always admired his suave, ambitious and opportunist father. The question of the boy's ambiguous position was gone into again and Dr Kümmerol pointed out the unpleasant fact that within little more than a year Emil could be—and would be—conscripted into the ranks of the German army, at this time massively invading Russia.

The thought of their Emil in field-grey, jackboots and coal-scuttle helmet was intolerable to both the Coucys and to Colonel Amoret-Labonde, and Dr Kümmerol, looking at his small, dark-skinned, handsome son, agreed. Emil was far too good for the oafish lot of a German infantryman. But this could be avoided. The doctor had friends in the higher echelons of the *Kriegsmarine* and if Emil was to volunteer for the Navy before his draft it was certain that a place in an officer training school could be made available to him. And after that —there were plenty of shore positions for officers with influential friends.

And so it had turned out. Emil did as he was told; Dr Kümmerol did all that he had promised. Within a few months of taking a tearful farewell of Grévilly and the aunts and the Colonel, Emil was back on leave, beaming and proud in a smart blue uniform with a single gold stripe below the star on his sleeve, and with a position on the staff of a certain Konteradmiral Waldenkolk working on some obscure intelligence project in Paris.

France was still officially collaborating with the Germans, and since naval uniform is very much the same the world over Emil's blue suit gave no offence to the wealthier residents of Grévilly, who had known of his ambiguous nationality all his life; while the local peasants, who had not, but who had never seen a sailor, presumed he was in the French service.

Emil's own feelings were fully collaborationist. He behaved sometimes as if his destiny was to amalgamate France and Germany into one nation in his own image. And for a little while—the last months of the enforced and uneasy honeymoon between the two countries— he was the praised and petted example of mutual integration both at Grévilly and, to a lesser degree, in Paris.

But France and Germany had as little in common as Emil's own parents and as the war began to turn ominously in favour of the Allies, French opinion hardened rapidly against occupation and exploitation by her earlier conqueror. Now when he came on his frequent week-end leaves to Grévilly, Emil met scowls where so recently he had been greeted with smiles. People whom he had thought his friends crossed the street in order not to meet him and shopkeepers who had served him benignly ever since he could peer over the tops of their counters affected not to notice his presence. For a long time he failed to under-stand what was happening, and when at last he fully realized it he was shocked and frightened. For it was becoming more and more certain not only that Germany was losing the war but that France—his own country in everything but name—was coming back into it against her. The Armistice, the Collaboration, the legal government at Vichy, meant nothing in the face of a French army across the Channel and the Resistance at home—both determined to avenge the defeat of 1940 and to liberate the land. And he, Emil, as French at heart as any of them, was an officer in the service of the enemy; an enemy becoming ever more ruthless in repression as the tide of sabotage and terrorism rose throughout a now fully occupied France.

The weekends in Grévilly became fewer and were spent entirely in the house of his aunts or of the Colonel. These three alone were left to him—for his father had died in one of the first of the great air raids —and even they paid for his inconspicuous visits by threats and dark looks from their neighbours.

Then, in the spring of 1944, Konteradmiral Waldenkolk's intelli-gence department—a peculiarly valueless organization which had spent its time in examining pre-war archives in the French Ministry of Marine—was abruptly closed down. The admiral was retired and his staff was sent back to Germany for training and combat duty. Emil, given the brutal choice between the U-boat service and a naval brigade fighting as infantry in Russia, quickly chose the former.

And so at last here was war—dangerous and very frightening. War for a country which was not his own and whose language he spoke im-perfectly and with a foreign accent. A country whose ideas and ways of thought were alien to him and, worst of all, a country which was heading ever more plainly for the abyss of complete and final ruin. Emil, who had participated safely and voluntarily, if rather tardily, in Germany's victory was now to participate, dangerously and involuntarily, in her defeat.

Sixteen

It was the oil from the damaged bearings of the port screw which betrayed them. A week earlier they had cautiously closed Cape Ste Marie, the most southerly point of Madagascar, and slid submerged into the Mozambique Channel. The other officers, knowing the Kommandant's caution, had expected him to swing in a wide arc to the east, keeping far out in the Indian Ocean beyond the normal range of air patrols from either Madagascar or Réunion. But Kielbasa had decided that such a course would be too wasteful both of time and fuel. There was always the chance of finding a valuable target in the Channel and with the possibility of the war ending within weeks, if not days, it was reassuring to have the long coastline of neutral Portuguese East Africa on his port beam.

It was the intention of keeping a neutral refuge at hand as long as possible as much as of conserving his precious fuel which induced him to take the passage up the thousand-mile channel at a leisurely speed. Sehlte should have mentioned the possibility of an oil-leak from the port screw's damaged gland, but he did not do so since it was merely an ugly hypothesis of his own and he did not wish to add a further, and perhaps baseless, worry to all the others with which his young captain had to contend at the present time. For soon they would be in their main target area and victims must be found for their remaining torpedoes. Days of acute danger lay ahead of them as soon as they had recrossed the Equator into the Northern Hemisphere.

But they never got there. At 7.30 p.m. on the night of the twelfth of February they surfaced some eighty miles south-west of the Grande Comore and proceeded on a northerly course closing the Mozambique coast. Soon after 2.0 a.m. the next morning, in Huberein's watch, they altered course to the east and when Emil came on to the bridge at four they were heading out into the Indian Ocean to swing wide of the hostile coastline of Tanganyika.

Emil turned his night-glasses in a perfunctory arc through the encircling blackness. Nothing. Only the phosphorescence of the tropical sea sliced by the submarine's stem and sent in two glimmering, sparkling lines of light coursing down the rounded bulk of the outer hull to meet in the turbulence of the wake. Breathing in the cool sea air, he listened to the rumble of the diesels and the vibrating rattle of the damaged port screw.

So now they were moving up once more towards the Equator. They had been at sea for three months and it seemed, in muddled retrospect, a lifetime of cramped discomfort, fear and ugly awakening. For this was warfare at its worst, useless and pointless—doomed men of a doomed nation killing and destroying because no one would allow them to stop. And he, Emil, who had always been a landsman from the depths of the French interior was now a sailor, standing in German naval uniform on the bridge of a German submarine. For a long unreal moment he stood outside his body gazing at himself in despairing perplexity. What was *he* doing here? Then the incongruity of his predicament filled him with a sullen rebellion. After all, he had only done as he was told—obeyed his elders and those with authority over him. The Mlles Coucy and Colonel Amoret-Labonde had been sincerely devoted to him, but at the same time they had always exacted careful obedience. His father too; careless, sardonic, kindly enough in an off-hand way where his own whims were not concerned, had expected the same. Emil had been brought up in the twin old-fashioned beliefs that one's elders always knew best and that docility was the most charming virtue of youth. Now he realized fully and for the first time how badly he had been misled. Everyone had given him the wrong advice and urged the wrong courses upon him. He had taken that advice and adopted those courses—and this was where they had brought him. In the darkness he sighed angrily, his small mouth hardened and he kicked with pent-up irritation at the steel side of the bridge.

And as if that kick had fired an electric contact there came a brittle crash overhead followed by the dull thud of a gunshot. At once the bridge, the submarine and the sea for hundreds of metres around were bathed in vivid violet-white light and as Emil and the look-outs jerked their heads upwards they were blinded by the aching glare of a star shell beginning its slow descent at the end of its miniature parachute. And another crackling burst like breaking glass high in the sky, and a new magnesium flare doubled the brightness of that terrible, shadowless, naked light. Then a shell came screaming over the bridge and plunged off into the distance, followed rapidly by a second—both from almost directly ahead.

Emil, shouting 'Dive! Dive! Dive!', fumbled for the button of the klaxon and sent its nerve-tearing note blaring through the boat beneath his feet. The look-outs were slithering down the ladder in the tower and somewhere close in front but unseen below the blinding luminescence of the star shells a ship—perhaps two ships—was closing the range rapidly. As Emil gave one last terrified glance over the side a shell, plunging into the water hardly more than twelve metres away, sent a shower of spray over the bridge, blinding him with stinging salt. Then he too was in the hot dark tower, pulling the heavy hatch down over that eye-searing incandescent glare, feeling, even as he did so, the boat canting steeply as the forward hydroplanes dug deep and she plunged her bows beneath the water.

In the control-room he found the Kommandant, white-faced and sweating, giving quick orders and countermanding some of those given by the under-officers, in an atmosphere of controlled but trembling panic. Despite their lack of experience, it was obvious, to the officers at least, that the boat had thrust her way into some sort of trap, though how and why they did not know. Alone among them Sehlte guessed accurately what had happened, guessed it even as he ran through from the wardroom buttoning his overalls. That tiny smear of oil from the port propeller gland had left its glistening line on the quiet sea and had been noticed by a low-flying airplane. The plane had probably sighted the oil streak just before dusk, and in any case that little ribbon glinting in the twilight down there on the calm evening water could only be taken as a suspicion at best . . . Even so, a radio report had been thought worth while and somewhere off the Grande Comore, probably, or perhaps from a Tanganyikan port, one or more fast submarine chasers had thrust out through the night to place themselves in the path of a hypothetical U-boat before dawn. They had waited in the blackness, their radar scanners turning and turning, until at last approaching dawn brought the first shining speck upon their screens, a speck growing steadily larger and more distinct until the range was close enough to fire their star shells. Only bad gunnery or bad luck or a combination of the two had prevented the U-996 from being struck and probably mortally hurt before she was able to dive. But to the frightened sailors in the control-room of the plunging submarine that would be little comfort, since they had only escaped the danger of shells for the still greater danger of depth charges.

'Take her down to ninety metres,' Eugen, standing on the tilting steel deck, had sniffed, raised his eyebrows and assumed that look of slightly insulted, sulky resignation with which he met dangerous emergencies. 'And shut off for depth charging,' he added, almost, it seemed, as an angry aside.

The heavy watertight doors were swung shut and clamped and silence fell in the control-room. Huberein, his red hair glinting in the bright light, his tongue half out of his mouth and caught between his teeth, was anxiously watching the depth gauges. Ten seconds . . . twenty seconds . . . thirty seconds; fourteen metres . . . twenty-five metres . . . forty metres. The angle of the boat steepened as she continued her dive into the darkness of the deep waters. Now all eyes were fixed upon the clicking needles of the depth gauges as taut nerves struggled with the suspense of wondering how deep the boat would be and how accurately placed the depth charges when the first of them exploded. Those ships—destroyers or chasers—must be right above them by now. Somewhere overhead heavy metal canisters packed with high explosive and fitted with automatic detonators actuated by the pressure of the water were sinking down swiftly towards them . . . Forty-five seconds . . . fifty . . . fifty-five . . . A thunderclap, a great crash as if a giant blacksmith's hammer had struck the outer hull, was followed quickly by two more and then a fourth. The boat rocked and staggered, reeling over on her starboard beam as the crew cursed and screamed and shouted their terror, the lights blinked out and the glass faces of the gauges, shivering to fragments, tinkled to the steel floor plates.

Emil was thrown to his knees and then in the darkness hurled against something angular and protuberant which drove into his back, causing him such pain that for a moment even the sickening fear of death was driven from his mind. Then the emergency lights flickered on and he was pulled groaning and whimpering to his feet by Kalewski, whose almost transparent eyes glinted eerily in the dim bluish light. The sounds of those terrible explosions were still booming beyond the hull, echoed back, now, from the sea bed far below. Then the next pattern exploded. But these were farther away; they shivered the boat throughout its length and shook out the few jagged pieces of glass from the broken dials of the gauges, but they gave a small, wan hope to the shocked and terrified crew. For everyone was still alive, the boat was steadying now and though most of the men in the control-room had suffered minor cuts from the splintered glass and were bruised and bleeding—blood which looked quite black in the weird lighting—no one had been badly hurt.

Eugen, swearing shakily under his breath, turned from the barefaced depth indicators. 'Check the hull and replace all broken lamps. Christl, find out if the—' The telephone buzzed and he seized it. 'Yes, yes. Well done, Walter. No—only our dials and lamps. We are at ninety? The gauges are all to hell. Yes, yes, very well.' He clamped back the telephone with a trembling hand and turned, his pale face marked by a smear of dark blood. 'Now stop all fans. Keep absolute silence. We will stay here at ninety metres without moving. If we are lucky they will go off searching for us elsewhere.' And as if to lend corroboration to his words a pattern of depth charges exploded harmlessly far away to port. A few grains of cork insulation fell from the ceiling but the lighting did not even flicker. Then the telephone buzzed again; reports were coming in from the other sections of the boat, compartments clamped away behind the heavy, hermetically sealed watertight doors. 'No damage' . . . 'Minor damage' . . . 'Lamps and dials' . . . 'A broken arm and a sprained shoulder' . . . 'Cuts and bruises.' There were still plenty of explosions as the ships above raced frantically through the breaking dawn searching for the quarry they believed was slipping through their fingers, but they were far away, unimportant and continually receding, adding a comforting reassurance to the crew's shaky hopefulness, their returning belief that they were, after all, to live—or at least not to die just yet.

Seventeen

In less than half an hour the last faint pattern of explosions had rolled its echoes to the silent submarine, still and motionless ninety metres below the surface of the Indian Ocean. Up there beyond all those suffocating tons of water it was already day. But what lay on the surface in the early sunshine? Was the sea calm and empty save, perhaps, for one or two rapidly disappearing ships somewhere on the horizon? Or was there a long low shape, as quiet and still as the U-996, riding silently on the surface like a basking shark, waiting and listening for the least noise in the depths below?

Quietly, almost in a whisper, the Kommandant gave the orders to unclamp the watertight doors and silently this was done. Then, together with Huberein and leaving Emil in charge in the control-room, he padded off on a personal inspection of the boat. The young crewmen were all in their places and from time to time he stopped to speak softly to them. Most of them had been slightly damaged, cut or grazed by the fittings and machinery against which the shocks of the depth charges had thrown them, but they had all been a great deal more frightened than hurt. Strangely enough, their small wounds moved Eugen far more than serious mutilations would have done, for they were of the sort which children so often inflicted upon themselves or one another by acts of folly or unmeaning violence, and it was difficult, watching a seventeen-year-old sailor dabbing at a bleeding elbow with a folded handkerchief, to realize that such trivial pain had been caused by an enemy intent on blasting fifty human beings to immediate death. He felt a touch of the same angry ridicule as the packed spectators at a bullfight when the matador has clumsily wounded the bull but failed to kill it.

Once more back in the control-room, Eugen glanced at his watch and decided that another half-hour would have to be sufficient. If there was a ship waiting for them up there it had only to wait long enough and listen carefully enough to find them eventually. For it could remain for a week or more if necessary, whereas they themselves had air for twenty-four hours at the most. If they could not surface within that time they need not worry about surfacing again. It was best to make the attempt to creep away as soon as possible.

Accordingly, after a further half-hour during which Huberein and Emil managed, with much acrimonious whispering as to how it should be done, to set and splint the broken arm of one of the engine-room ratings, the Kommandant sent for Sehlte and gave him his instructions. These were to start up the starboard motor and, using only the undamaged screw at its slowest and quietest speed, to move gently ahead. There was no point in altering course, they had run blindly into the trap and blindly they must make their way out of it.

Once more, very softly this time, the watertight doors were closed and clamped; once more the long pressure hull was hermetically sealed into half a dozen compartments, each divided from the other by a bulkhead as strong as the three-centimetre-thick hull itself and in communication only by telephone.

Everyone stood silently in his place, waiting, sweating with nervous apprehension, the Kommandant at the telephone in direct communication with his Chief Engineer; Huberein, with his eyes on the readjusted depth gauges ready to check the trim, behind the hydroplane operators whose hands gripped their brass wheels.

Then, far off in the motor-room, the great switches of the starboard motor were thrown and with a purr so soft as to be hardly audible within the submarine itself the U-996 began to creep slowly away. Quietness of the profound depths, motionless and dark and silent save for that faint purr as the long steel shape slid slowly through a gloom peopled only by the greater fish of the middle deep—porbeagle shark, manta ray and giant squid.

Two minutes . . . Emil glanced at his gold wristwatch—a present from his godfather upon his twentieth birthday—and saw the sweat glinting upon the back of his hand. Lifting his eyes, he met those of Hansi Wutsdorf beside the panel of wheel valves and levers which controlled the vents of the ballast tanks and the batteries of compressed air bottles below the deck. Wutsdorf was staring at him with a probing, almost surgical interest and when his gaze was returned he did not drop his eyes or shift his glance. He was taller by some six inches than Emil, thin, muscular, with over-lax features and tow-coloured hair; big-handed, loose-limbed. Emil had always disliked him; now he hated and feared him. Yet Wutsdorf was, as Emil knew well, generally liked, and since the sinking of the *Empire Advance* he had become a hero to the even younger sailors who made up the majority of the crew. He would receive an Iron Cross First Class for his escapade with the tanker and that set him apart from the others. Though what good such a decoration could possibly do him in the circumstances—even if he survived to receive it—was not clear. And now he was waiting, watching the gunnery officer to see how he would behave in their present mutual danger. He knew that Emil had been on the bridge when the gun crew had been killed by that lucky shot from the tanker; he knew that Emil should have climbed down to the exposed gun, but had not . . . his eyes said as much now.

Emil felt a nervous frightened exasperation filling him. Let Wutsdorf have his Cross if it meant so much to him, certainly. He himself coveted nothing at all save a safe return to Grévilly, to the comforting presence of both his aunts, to those long summer evenings which ended at last in a green afterglow watched from the window of his bedroom above the lilac bushes. His back still hurt badly and for a moment he forgot his present danger in an acute wave of self-pity which brought hot tears pricking to his eyes and forced him to look down at the deck.

Four minutes . . . five. They were going to get away after all . . . Six minutes . . . And then the quick metallic echo of something seeming to touch the hull for a second with a wire brush. Ten seconds. . . . Then again that odd, unreal, yet undoubted *zip*—and immediately afterwards from Federsen at the hydrophones: 'Propellers closing quickly from dead ahead! One-zero-six revolutions.' The enemy had been waiting and had found them.

And then even with their naked ears they could hear the whistling churn of the propellers overhead—right above them. There was nothing to be done now but pray—for death was upon them. Emil had been reared a Catholic and now he pushed a trembling hand into the front of his overalls to clasp the small gold cross which lay on his hot damp chest. '*In manus tuas, Domine . . .*' Dry-mouthed, he tried momentarily to commit his soul to God—and then stopped, suddenly struck by the vast unfairness of it all. What had *he* done that he should ask forgiveness for *his* sins? Caught up in a ridiculous, lethal dilemma which was in no way his fault, bruised, bloody, filled with fear and despair, without hope and knowing not which way to turn for help and at last, and inevitably, face to face with a horrible choking black death. It was for God to ask *his* pardon—not the other way about. He withdrew his hand from the front of his overalls and his mouth hardened sullenly. If he was going to die he would die repenting only that he had been so badly treated. Across four metres of deck space Wutsdorf slowly grinned at him and with a small, angry, hopeless shrug of his shoulders he smiled weakly back.

Then the depth charges began to explode. They came rapidly in towards the boat, detonating in pairs. The submarine vibrated, shuddered, then was flung sideways and forward, tossed by the pressure waves in sickening lurches from side to side. Those lights which had been repaired went out immediately and the control-room echoed to the terror-filled screams of men thrown about like dolls kicked across a room by an angry child. The last twin explosion was one which they all felt rather than heard, so deafened had their ringing heads become. It came as one appalling crash forward and for a single second the boat shot up and seemed to be trying to stand on its stern while everyone in the control-room was thrown aft in a heap of tangled bodies. Then the bow fell; for a moment it regained its proper level and then dipped steeply down at an ever-increasing angle. The compass bell, the alarm, was ringing wildly. The steering and hydroplane controls, unmanned but now certainly useless, spun loosely. All the gauges were out and in the black bell-filled chaos the battered, bleeding bodies of officers and men rolled once more over the glass-cluttered deck as the boat's angle, steepening every moment, took her plunging to the bottom completely out of control. Above the tumult one voice rose in a horrified wail of anguish: '*Ich kann ja nicht sehen!*

Ich kann ja nicht sehen!' Then it was drowned as something broke in the maze of telemotor pipes and with a continuous ear-splitting scream the whole complex system went berserk, while deep below every other noise sounded the loud rumbling hiss as compressed air escaped into the stricken pressure hull from ruptured valve connections.

Down—down—down with the air pressure building up inside the hull and the immense pressure of the water outside increasing every second. Soon, very soon now, it would all be over, the hull would collapse and under the force of the black inrushing water they would all be crushed to immediate death among the ruins of their machinery. They knew this, but only vaguely, so hurt and shocked and deafened were they by what had gone before. The mass of overalled bodies twitched and writhed, cried and moaned, but made no attempt to disentangle themselves from the composite heap.

It was the Kommandant who moved first, and only after the significance of the dull, crunching thud which he had felt through the deck plates beneath his battered body had carried its slowly deciphered message to his shocked brain. They were on the bottom— and still alive. The bottom. But the bottom was far below the depth to which a submarine might dive. If that thud forward had been—as he instinctively felt it must have been—the bow striking the sea bed, then at the most they were at a depth of something like two hundred and thirty metres, the absolute maximum to which a submarine of U-996's construction might, perhaps, descend uncrushed. The only assumption was that some undersea hill of rocks and shale caused by an uncharted eruption had received their broken bow, and upon this they now lay.

That sudden jar had stilled the telemotor's eldritch shriek and brought on the emergency lights. Eugen struggled upwards from the pile of bodies and lurched over the steeply angled deck to the support of the forward periscope standard, where he hung shuddering and gasping. He was alive—for the present—and thus still captain of whatever remained of U-996 and whoever still lived within her. He supposed he would have to do something and through the dazing shock and pain of the last minutes he tried to think what it should be.

Damage—first find out the damage. He moved slowly to the telephone and slowly he eased it from its clamps. If it was working it would tell him very soon whether or not he still had a chance of life. Licking a trickle of blood from the side of his mouth, he tried to get through to where he believed the depth charges had done their worst

—the bow. Nothing from the tube space forward—that was hardly to be expected. Nothing, either, from the stowage compartment, the fore ends. Only the under-officer's mess space immediately forward of the control-room replied—a hysterical voice shouting furiously that no damage had been sustained and demanding the opening of the water-tight doors. Eugen recognized the voice as that of a dull-witted sailor named Prinz, the look-out whose slowness and ineptitude had been mainly responsible for the death of Chirol. Sharply he told the man to control himself.

Now he must try the compartments aft, commencing with the engine-room. If any of them were flooded . . . But in a moment he heard Sehlte's voice, high, shaky, immensely relieved. 'Engine-room! Engine-room here! Are you—'

'Walter! You are all right, then?'

'Thank God—yes. No hull damage. And except for a broken leg no one is badly hurt. And you?'

'I don't know yet. I think we're flooded forward—right up to the fore ends bulkhead probably. Have you a depth gauge working?'

'I do not know about *working*. It reads two hundred and fifty-three metres. That cannot be right.'

Dizzily Eugen shook his head. 'I think perhaps it is! My God, Walter—we are deeper than any boat of this type has ever gone before! I—I will get the doors open between us as soon as possible. A lot of air has escaped into the boat. We shall have to equalize pressure carefully.'

The tangle of bodies on the floor was sorting itself out, the unhurt men struggling back up the control-room deck which was listing heavily to port and sloping forward at an angle of about fifteen degrees. There was no longer any doubt in Eugen's mind what had happened. The last pair of depth charges had ripped open the bow and flooded both the forward tube space and the torpedo stowage compartment, bringing the boat plunging bow-heavy to the sea bed. In that case an immense amount of water must have entered the boat and . . . Once more the telephone buzzed and he seized it. 'Kalewski—in the forward stowage compartment.' The voice was slow and slurred and Eugen stared down at the instrument in his hand with the fascinated fear he might have shown if addressed by a ghost. 'But—but—are you all right?'

'I could not reach the telephone before this. My foot is caught under a torpedo. All right—me? I am the only one alive, Herr Kommandant. No—wait! Rann is still alive. There's an eel on top of him. But the rest were killed. The whole bow has gone for'ard, I think. Our forward bulkhead is leaking—but it is holding at present. It is jammed by the eel that is on top of Rann.'

Eugen shook his head. That bulkhead must be properly shored up at once. It would mean opening the watertight doors between the control-room, the under-officers' mess space and the fore ends—risking immediate death for them all—but it would have to be done nevertheless. Besides—he smiled weakly—he wanted to see Kalewski again.

The other officers and under-officers were on their feet now and with the rest of the control-room personnel they limped up the tilted deck and gathered around the Kommandant—bloody faces, torn clothes, most of them nursing hands or elbows or knees. Eugen sniffed, glanced around him and breathed deeply. 'Well—well, that is over. We are not so easy to kill as they think up there. Now those of you who are able must work, and work quickly if we are to save ourselves. Listen—' Still holding to the telephone bracket, he gave his orders, speaking slowly and carefully and in the simple words which his shocked and shaken sailors might understand and obey. By the time he had set them to locating and reporting the more important defects in the machinery of the control-room, damage reports from other sections of the boat were coming through and Eugen, piecing them together, was able to form a coherent picture of the present condition of the U-996.

As he had feared, the bows had been blasted to pieces, perhaps torn off. That none of the torpedoes in the four bow tubes had exploded was a minor miracle, for some at least must have been torn to pieces. According to Kalewski, the forward torpedo stowage compartment, the section of the boat immediately aft of the destroyed tube space, had been turned into a shambles. Two spare torpedoes had been wrenched from their burst cradles and thrown diagonally across the compartment crushing three sailors to death and gravely injuring a fourth, and it was one of the great gleaming greasy cylinders, jammed firmly against the forward bulkhead, which had prevented that buckled steel wall from collapsing under the growing pressure as the boat sank.

From the fore ends only Kalewski emerged when at last the watertight doors were opened and a torpedo levered off his right foot. With a crushed and broken ankle he had been enclosed in agony and complete blackness amid the crashing torpedoes and the screams of the dying—trapped in a compartment which could have flooded at any moment. Yet by wrenching his broken ankle almost out of its socket he had managed to reach the telephone at last and make contact with the control-room. He was carried back through the under-officers' mess, now a shambles of broken crockery and tumbled bedding, to the Captain's cabin and laid on the narrow bunk.

The damage to the rest of the boat was much less than Eugen had thought and appeared to be confined to the more delicate and complicated machinery. There were no leaks in the hull and the painful increase of pressure within the boat indicated that the escape of compressed air had been mainly internal.

Damage-control parties were set to work under Sehlte and shortly both the main lighting and the ventilation systems were once more working and the injured were given the only valuable treatment available—injections of morphia.

Yet one injured man still remained to be dealt with; Rann, a young seaman from Cuxhaven, one of the few crewmen with previous experience of the sea and one marked out by Kalewski for promotion at an early date. Eugen had been first at his scarlet-faced, screaming, weeping side when the watertight door of the stowage compartment had been opened—and had hurriedly left again after ordering a heavy dose of morphia. Now, with Emil and Huberein, he stood looking down at the overalled body which breathed in long rasping respirations, unconscious and out of pain. The torpedo which acted as a shore to the forward bulkhead lay across Rann's thighs and to extricate him that torpedo must be raised by block-and-tackle. But to shift it, even by a few centimetres, was to risk the collapse of the forward bulkhead with the consequent immediate death of those working the tackle and the slower but equally inevitable doom of the rest of the crew. For Eugen considered that there was still a good chance of raising U-996 to the surface once more—but only provided that the bulkhead between the stowage compartment and the destroyed and flooded tube space forward held firm. But if that bulkhead gave way and the fore ends flooded, the amount of water in the boat would be such that she would never again leave her present resting-place on the sea bed.

So for the second time on this patrol he was forced to take human life in order to save it. And this time it was no enemy, but one of his own men, who must die. For a long moment Eugen stared down at the seaman whose suffused and snoring head was pillowed on a bunch of cotton waste, while the torpedo lay like a felled tree-trunk across his thighs. There was no alternative—any more than there had been in the case of the survivors from the *Maréchal Oudinot*—to what he had to do now. Turning to Huberein he said tonelessly, 'Give him some more, Christl—enough to put him out completely.'

'I don't know how much that is.'

'Then fill him up with it. Give him four full doses—more if you like.' Eugen turned away abruptly, his face pale and sweating, while Huberein, tongue-tip between teeth, began to fill his syringe.

Returning quickly to the control-room, Eugen realized that whatever happened now he was not going on—on with the meaningless self-immolation which was all that the war in its last stages could mean to a German officer. If he could get U-996 to the surface again he would surrender to the first enemy vessel he could find. Whatever happened, he was not again going to be forced to make the sort of decision he had just been bleakly faced with.

But it was done now and, as always, he had the lives of the rest of his crew to think about, as well as his own. He glanced at his watch. Six-ten. Broad daylight somewhere above—very far above if the engine-room depth gauge was to be believed. Would the enemy still be there? Had the destruction of the U-996's bow sent up a big enough air bubble, a large enough patch of oil, to give the impression that the submarine had been entirely destroyed? Down here on the bottom they were safe from detection but once the boat started to ascend, if it ever did, they would once more be vulnerable to the enemy's Sonar—and the U-boat could not stand any further damage. For if their opponent was still there it was not, as he realized with a cold returning fear, a simple question of surfacing and surrendering. In their present condition and at their present depth the ascent might take a considerable time, and since the German U-boat service had always been regarded with a peculiarly bitter hatred by the British it was very probable that the enemy captain would prefer to destroy them in the middle depths rather than make them prisoners on the surface. So this time there must be no early attempt to move at all. They must wait here on this providential rise in the sea bed for as long as they dared—at least until night had fallen once more, and—Eugen suddenly swung around and took three quick paces to the navigator's table. The charts upon it had been thrown to the floor and were crumpled, cut by glass, smeared with oil and blood. Falling to his knees, he sorted quickly through them, found what he wanted and, rising, spread it on the table. Then with a stub of pencil and a pair of dividers he laid off a course to the nearest point on the mainland. They had been sunk some one hundred miles north-west of the Comoro Islands. Slightly under one hundred miles to the west Cape Delgado jutted its blunt spur into the Indian Ocean to mark the frontier between Mozambique and Tanganyika. He paused, dividers in hand, staring down at the creased and grimy chart . . . Portuguese East Africa—internment in a neutral country. Safety—and a future, after all. Later, when the war was over, he could go to Brazil. For a second the old coloured dream of São Paulo flickered across his mind but he dismissed it abruptly—first he had to get his boat to Cape Delgado.

He sniffed, raising his eyebrows, wrinkling his broad forehead above his glasses. On the surface and in proper working order U-996 could have made that landfall in eight hours—nine at the most. But with a crushed bow, and at a speed which would not seriously endanger that forward bulkhead . . . fifteen hours . . . fourteen at the very least, might see them in territorial waters.

But that would mean running on both diesels—an infernal noise. Then the batteries? These had been fully recharged during the past night but they could never drive the boat at even a quarter of the speed of its massive twin diesels. Yet if he could get the submarine off the bottom now, and proceed under water during the day . . . surface after dark . . . they could be beached on the neutral coast by dawn. But—but he *dare* not move for hours, and with nothing except that buckled bulkhead between himself and certain death he dare not progress submerged at anything below periscope depth—a depth at which the boat's dark oblong form was easily visible from the air.

He rubbed his cut mouth distractedly. The ideal course would be to surface after dark and then, with the boat ballasted down so that only the bridge showed above the dark water, to move as far as they could from the area of the sinking on their batteries and then to switch to the diesels until dawn. After that they would spend the daylight hours submerged at some forty metres, just too deep for an aircraft to make out their shadowy silhouette, and complete the journey on the following night. It might be done that way—if he was very lucky. Tapping the pencil against his teeth, he shrugged and became aware of Emil standing beside him, of the crewmen farther back but with their eyes fixed upon him. He licked his lips, breathed deeply and spoke. 'Listen, everybody. We are on the bottom at a depth to which I think no operational submarine has dived before. Only the magnificent work of the men who designed this boat and the men who built her has saved our lives—that and a great deal of luck. Our bow is probably entirely destroyed and thus our fighting value is finished—at least for the present.'

His eyes slid quickly to Emil's, read immediate understanding and moved away over the strained and blood-streaked young faces of the crew. Wutsdorf, he thought, was staring at him with suspicion already in his eyes. Wutsdorf wanted to get home, receive his medal and be a hero. But Wutsdorf was only nineteen and without Kalewski to back him he was no real danger. Even so there would be some twelve hours of inactivity before they might begin the nerve-racking test of blowing the tanks . . . It would be best not to say too much for the present . . . 'Until we surface again and can ascertain the full damage to our bows I cannot tell what we may have to do. We may—' he licked his lips again—'be able to make sufficient repairs to get us home. But I fear that is not likely. Or, alternatively, it may perhaps be possible to contact other boats and to receive some help from them. But for the present there is nothing to be done and we must conserve our air supply. Everyone not engaged on repair work or other duties will go and lie down on his bunk and keep still. Emil—you will see that that order is obeyed.'

And now for nearly twelve hours they must wait here silently on the sea bed, and for the captain and his chief engineer who—perhaps fortunately—were the only ones who fully comprehended the situation, this meant twelve hours of acute suspense. For it was by no means certain that U-996 would ever surface again despite the Kommandant's confident assertion. Weighed down by her water-filled bow and her heavy, undischargeable torpedoes, with her No. 1 main ballast tank smashed, her bow trimming tank and her forward hydroplanes probably destroyed, she would have to blow everything she could, and even then . . . And in any case no one living knew how a submarine would function at their present depth.

Yet with the exception of the men in the forward torpedo stowage compartment, now sealed off and silent except for a periodical visit to examine that bulkhead by one of the watch, none of the crew had been killed or even badly injured; and they were no longer being depth-charged. To those of them who were still capable, after the past terror, of any sort of speculative thought, the great depth at which they now lay served as a shield against the enemy above rather than an entombing peril.

As the damage control parties completed their work and returned to their pipe-cots the boat became quiet and still. There were always one or two blue-overalled figures padding up and down checking the hull anxiously for leaks, but soon most of the crew, exhausted by the experience of the last hours, slept, returning in dreams to the childhood which in most cases lay so recently behind them.

In order to save precious electricity only the emergency lighting was kept on and in the small wardroom the officers lay in their bunks aware of the figure of the Kommandant sitting at his usual place at the head of the table. For Eugen had declined to have Kalewski shifted back to his cot in the restored under-officers' mess space. Kalewski should stay in his own cabin where he was at present under heavy sedation. With a smashed ankle it should be possible to keep Kalewski out of everything until the boat was safely aground on the Mozambique coast—then he could say what he pleased.

Emil lay flat on his back staring up at the bottom of Letzer's bunk thirty centimetres above his head. He had readily accepted the Kommandant's assertion that they would surface at nightfall and was now wondering with an excited speculation whether he had understood Kielbasa's glance towards him over that chart. Was the Kommandant really going to take them to internment and safety in Portuguese East Africa? It seemed extremely probable. Emil remembered Kielbasa talking nostalgically about his sister and brother-in-law in Brazil. Brazil had once been part of the Portuguese Empire and then an Empire in its own right ruled by the royal house of Braganza. There were many close ties, including that of language, between the two countries, and even though Brazil was at war with Germany there was little doubt that Kielbasa's Brazilian relations would be able to lend him some assistance once he was on Portuguese territory. So in a few hours it might be all over—the increasing fear and strain and despair of the last months. All over and done with—war and death and the continual suspense of mortal danger under which he had somehow existed ever since leaving Paris. Let them fight it out to a finish since they were so eager to—Germans and Frenchmen, English and Americans and Japanese. He himself would wait with Eugen Kielbasa in Mozambique until the last shot had echoed into silence and then . . . Home, if possible, certainly, but if not—the world was wide and he was young. . . .

Glancing covertly at the hunched form of the Kommandant at the wardroom table, Emil wondered what was going on in that big, broad-browed head; what calculations of distance and speed, what balancing and choosing of possible courses? Or perhaps—merely dreams of a new life in Brazil with his sister? For if Emil had suffered severely himself over the past months he knew that this cruise had been one long nightmare for Kielbasa. Though he was a capable submarine executive officer he was the only one on board, and with none but half-trained officers to help him and with a crew most of whom were no more than recruits he had not been able to relax for an instant. His sole genuinely useful support, Oberleutnant Chirol, had died two weeks out of the Kattegat and since then Kielbasa had seldom had more than two hours' uninterrupted sleep at a time—often much less.

Then there had been the sinking of the old French merchantman and the grim decision to eliminate the survivors—Emil stirred uncomfortably in his narrow bunk—Kielbasa had never got over that, despite the fact that his action had proved justified. The attack on the tanker, bungled and only made successful by the insane behaviour of Wutsdorf and his fluke of a shot . . . And then this morning, and what they had found in the fore ends; Emil would never forget the look on the Kommandant's face as he ordered the death injections for that boy jammed under the torpedo. And glancing sideways at that still, patient figure, eyes hidden by the dull reflection from his spectacles, Emil found his earlier liking and admiration for his captain increasing to something greater, a compassionate understanding which seemed to swell his heart. For despite all that had happened, Kielbasa had never lost control of himself nor blamed his often culpable subordinates. The immense strain under which he had existed for months had turned him into neither a brute nor an idiot. And to whatever problem he had to solve, however horrible or grotesque it might be, he brought to bear upon it the calm, rational logic of an intelligent civilian. How or why he had joined the Navy as a career officer was a mystery which nevertheless did not change the fact of his basically unmilitary personality. Yet perhaps it was not such a contradiction after all, for Kielbasa had probably seen himself as a land-based bureaucrat rather than a sea-going officer. Yet his attitudes, once at sea, were neither those of a landsman nor a pacifist. It was merely, Emil saw, that he received no pleasure from the submariner's task of destruction and killing, that he possessed the civilized man's instinctive repugnance at taking life—an attitude totally out of keeping with the doctrines preached in Germany during the last twelve years. Lying back on his pillow, Emil wondered if he himself possessed it. Certainly he hated the childish vainglory of Wutsdorf and Kalewski, who seemed to look upon war as a competitive game with medals for prizes, and he had hated the incident of that old French ship. He wished suddenly that the survivors of the *Maréchal Oudinot* had been the men who had lain in wait in the darkness of today's early dawn—he would have felt no compunction at all in killing those. But instead it had had to be harmless civilian sailors and Guéroult—a Frenchman of his own age . . .

'*Au'voir, Emil.*' And afterwards . . . But he must not think of that; he thought about it far too often as it was.

But he was too tired, it was too much effort to think coherently, and he drifted off into vague daydreams and from them into deep sleep.

Eighteen

By mid-afternoon the air in the boat was deteriorating rapidly. The interior of the submarine always smelled of paint, of diesel oil and damp; it smelled strongly of sweat, too, except in the wardroom, whose officers disguised the smell of their own bodies by a liberal use of eau-de-Cologne. Now, with the forepart of the boat sealed off, there was less air circulating and a consequently quicker decrease in its oxygen content, which had a soporific effect on the crew. They sprawled, inert blue figures under the dim blue lights, and most of them slept heavily.

The watch in the control-room changed quietly and Emil, half waking, was vaguely aware of Huberein sliding from his bunk and clambering to the floor. Huberein's watch—that meant that there must be about another four hours to go before the preparations for surfacing could be commenced. Three minutes later, as he was sinking once more into sleep, a sharp bang echoed through the hull bringing everyone instantly to his feet in white panic. 'Something has given way!' was the immediate reaction of officers and men alike. 'Something has broken under the pressure.' Then the Kommandant was in the control-room, with Emil pressing behind him followed by Letzer and Sehlte. 'What—? Where is the officer of the watch? Christl—'

Huberein was suddenly in the doorway of the under-officers' mess. 'Prinz. He's in the fore ends. I sent him there as soon as I took over from Letzer—to check that bulkhead. He shut the door after him. I was wondering . . . I was just going to look . . .'

Eugen pushed through the startled group of under-officers who had risen from their bunks and stood staring at the heavy steel door leading into the fore ends. Carefully he opened the test cock. Nothing. Nothing in there had broken or given way. He swung the door open and there lay Prinz, a gaunt thin sailor of nineteen, sprawled across one of the fallen torpedoes with no back to his narrow head and very little left of his face. Blood, brains and bits of shattered bone were spattered everywhere and a Luger lay partly concealed below his crumpled body. At the Kommandant's elbow Emil said disgustedly, 'One might have expected that from Prinz!' Aware of the crowd pressing behind him, he turned. 'All right! Nothing has happened except that Prinz has shot himself. Get back to your bunks.' Then he pulled the heavy door shut and for a moment he was alone in the wrecked torpedo stowage compartment with Kielbasa. They stood together in that narrow, dimly lit space surrounded by dead men and displaced torpedoes in a stench of grease and fuel oil and fresh blood. Swiftly Emil said, 'When we surface—are we going to beach? This side of Delgado?'

Eugen smiled slightly. 'Is that what you want?'

'Yes, it is!'

'Good. It is what I want too. And now let us get out of here. Prinz is no loss, God knows, but this place is getting like a butcher's shop.'

But before they left both officers stepped carefully over the bodies and torpedoes to examine the forward bulkhead. Two small leaks which had appeared at midday had been patched and the metal was holding, firmly shored now with iron cross-beams fitted by Sehlte's artificers.

'We ought to manage, I think.'

'Prinz apparently thought otherwise.'

'Imbecile! If he could not have waited to find out he might at least have cut his throat quietly instead of risking all our lives. That bullet could have ricocheted and might have done anything. As it is, he has given everyone a bad shock—and just when I wanted them all calm.' Eugen's voice was bitter and he stared down coldly at the gory head of one of the least satisfactory of his crewmen. 'He was incompetent and stupid, but I did not think he would lose enough control of himself to do this!'

That suicide altered the whole mood in the boat. Before it occurred the crew had largely recovered, so resilient is youth, from the terrifying events of early dawn, and the calmness of the Captain and his Chief Engineer had greatly assisted in reassuring them. But now that someone, even if it was only the unhappy Prinz, had despaired so completely that he preferred to die by his own hand now rather than await the outcome of this evening's attempt to lift—this put their future prospects in a new and much bleaker light. They had worked beside Prinz, eaten with him, talked to him—and now he was a bloody corpse up in the fore ends. Had he—could it be that he knew of something still kept from them? Could Prinz have somehow stumbled upon some new danger so acute that the officers were keeping it a grim secret among themselves? As the afternoon drew on and the air became increasingly foul they edged together in pairs or small groups, each seeking out his closest friends for mutual reassurance or low, whispered discussions of the plight which so few of them comprehended.

The officers were more fortunate since they could spend the time openly discussing the ways of raising their boat and listening to the Chief Engineer's comments upon them. No longer attempting to sleep, they sat around the wardroom table while Sehlte, with Letzer's capable assistance, drew sketch plans of the hull and of the supposed damage and worked out an elaborate system of coupling up little-used cross-connections in the pumping and draining systems which, by ejecting every litre in the trimming tanks and most of the drinking water and fuel oil as well, would bring the boat to maximum buoyancy. Though some of the air flasks had been damaged, they still retained enough pressure to blow the remaining ballast tanks and should be able to lift despite the heavy weight of water in the bows. 'Only, of course,' as Sehlte said in a voice so carefully matter-of-fact as to send a sharp stab of panic through Emil, 'if we have not buried our bow too deep in the sea bed. We shall have been about thirteen hours on the bottom and we struck hard. A certain amount of silting-up may have occurred. For instance—' he paused dubiously, glanced at the Kommandant sitting opposite him, and continued—'one of the reasons those small leaks in the fore ends bulkhead have ceased may be because that bulkhead has now sunk below the level of the sea bed.'

For a startled moment everyone sat silent; then Eugen said, 'That would mean that approximately nine metres of the bow has sunk in mud. I suppose that *is* possible?'

'It is possible. And if the bow has been blown open, as we must assume it has been, then the mud will be inside it, too—acting as an anchor to hold us down.' Sehlte's voice was apologetic, as if the matter was somehow his fault. He pushed back his overall cuff and looked at his watch. 'It is four o'clock—just past. It is not my duty—' he spoke gently now—'to make decisions in anything but engine-room affairs, but I think I ought to say that if our hypothesis with regard to a soft bottom and the consequent sinking and silting is the right one—then every hour we remain here substantially lessens our chances of rising.'

'None the less we must wait.' Eugen glanced around the table and tapped its edge gently with a pencil. 'Every hour we wait makes it more likely that our friend up above will give up and go home. He may have gone now—or he may not. But he is much more likely to leave at sunset. It is human instinct to retire at night. He has probably already decided to sit out the day and, if there is no further sign of us by dark, to assume that he has destroyed us. In all probability we will have to use the motors to drag our bows clear; and, as you know, the port screw makes enough noise for ten. Unless he has gone he will be listening; and if he is listening he will hear us as soon as we start the attempt. And then, of course . . . No, we must wait.' Emil felt the sweat sticky on the palms of his hands and below the wardroom table he rubbed them furtively on his overall trousers. He wished Sehlte had kept that idea about silting up forward to himself.

They were all breathing with an almost conscious effort now. They were used, during most of the recent voyage, to spending as much as thirteen or fourteen hours submerged and today they had, so far, spent only eleven; the air, if foul, should not as yet have been any cause for serious physical discomfort. But two things had altered this position for the worse. The interior space of the boat had been decreased by the destruction of the bow and the leak in the compressed air system had heightened the pressure within the hull—a process which, for technical reasons, alarmingly increased the toxic effects of the carbon dioxide released with every exhalation of every member of the crew. And this was something which would build up at an ever-increasing rate. Emil knew just enough of the physiological conditions involved to realize that within another two hours they would all be finding the act of breathing both difficult and painful.

The Kommandant at one end of the table; Huberein, Letzer, Sehlte and himself—and the empty place which no one had occupied since Chirol's death so long ago. Empty, that was, unless Death sat there, silent and invisible. Sehlte, with his family destroyed, did not, perhaps, care much about dying himself. Huberein would accept it with the simple, almost animal innocence of someone who had never considered his own right to individual importance, and Letzer would probably retain his indifferent, enigmatic calm. He himself? How often in childhood he had thought, 'Whenever I shut my eyes it is night. If I died the world would no longer exist.' It had been a game then—to shut one's eyes and try to feign death. But it was not a game now . . . And the Kommandant? How would he take it if—and for the first time Emil allowed the words to form consciously in his mind —*If we are quite unable to surface . . . Entombed finally on the sea bed?* Would he sniff and turn from the useless controls, his eyebrows high above his glasses, his mouth thin and prim with displeasure, and go to his bunk—or, rather, to Chirol's—and lie down silently, composing himself for ever, hands crossed on breast? Emil gave a short gasping sigh and, aware that Keilbasa was looking at him, smiled nervously. He must not think like that, must not fall into premature despair in the manner of Prinz. For after all, in some four hours' time they might be on the dark surface heading west for the Mozambique coast. He must think of that, and only that, and meanwhile wait and watch the minutes crawl by on the smart flat dial of his gold watch.

And for nearly three more hours the five officers sat at that table under the dim emergency lighting. They spoke seldom, and never of what was foremost in their minds. Once every twenty minutes one of them made a tour of the boat, checking the streaming hull, upon which condensation had gathered in drops that turned into thin runnels so that the whole deck was at last damp underfoot, speaking briefly to the under-officers in charge of each compartment, seeing to the injured men and, worst of all, steeling himself to open the heavy door into the fore ends and struggle over the bloodstained torpedoes to examine that buckled bulkhead which might be burying itself ever deeper in the heavy mud of the sea bed.

Yet when at last Kielbasa rose and said, 'Very well, Walter. We'll try it now. Christl—give the order for surface stations,' Emil felt a sickness in his stomach which almost doubled him over the ward-room table. All afternoon he had waited longingly for this moment; now that it had come at last he wished desperately that it could be put off, even for another half-hour. He was not ready . . . Let them wait a little longer—give him time to gather himself together. But he said nothing, following the Kommandant and Huberein into the control-room.

As Emil had guessed three hours before, the air was now very bad. The young crewmen in their dark overalls were breathing with difficulty and their pallid damp faces, the mouths open, the nostrils wide, betrayed the fact that the vitiated air which they tugged into their straining lungs no longer contained even the minimal amount of oxygen which their bodies needed to function properly. Unless they could rise to the surface very soon a high proportion of them would be unfit to undertake the various tasks necessary to reach it.

'Stand by to surface.' The Kommandant glanced at his watch, noted the time was two minutes after seven and then said quietly, 'Surface.' 'Surface,' repeated Huberein mechanically and immediately afterwards commenced giving the prearranged blowing instructions for the main tanks. The under-officers at the control panels opened the valves as Huberein's voice, higher and more unsteady than usual, called the numbers and there came the reassuring hissing, whistling roar of high-pressure air bursting into the great ballast tanks. The men at the after hydroplanes' controls swung their wheels and lifted their eyes to the glassless dials overhead. No needle moved, no needle even quivered. The boat remained as motionless as a bedded rock.

Kielbasa wasted no time. 'Group up. Half astern together!'

The boat shuddered as the motor switches were thrown and the screws began to revolve. There was the usual clattering vibration from the port one and the thought crossed Emil's mind that if the enemy was still above them the man at her hydrophones would be shouting for his captain. But it was a passing thought and one which hardly worried him at all. His whole being was violently engaged in willing the U-996 to rise.

'Full astern!'

The propeller noises redoubled, echoing through the quivering hull. The boat shuddered and it seemed that the deck angle increased for a moment, but no needle moved on the pallid faces of the depth gauges. It was as Sehlte had guessed—the shattered bow was sunk and silted up in metres of clinging mud.

'Cease blowing. Stop main motors!' Silence fell quickly as the motors whined down, the screws ceased to vibrate and the rushing air was stilled. For a long moment the Kommandant kept his eyes on the needles of the dials, and no one moved in the control-room. Then with a sulky shrug he said, 'We are still too heavy in the bow. But I think our friend of this morning must have departed. Otherwise we should have been made very aware of his presence. That is something, at any rate.' He glanced slowly around him at the young faces crowding the control-room, peering in from the after passageway. 'There is no reason for undue distress just because this first effort has failed. We are not finished yet by any means. But one thing I want to say. When I was passing through the engine-room half an hour ago I heard someone mention the escape apparatus. If any of you think that we can leave the boat by that means—and conceivably some of the less experienced of you may—I had better tell you that it is completely impossible. We are very much too deep to have the slightest chance of even opening the hatches. To do that against the pressure of water outside we would need a hydraulic ram; and if anyone got to the surface after *that* he would do so only in small pieces—each piece as flat as a sheet of paper. No—we are going up together in this boat. Walter—' he turned to Sehlte, patient and grey behind him—'pump all trim tanks according to plan and prepare to blow all after fuel tanks and the midships freshwater tanks. Report when you are ready and we will make another attempt.'

The pumping took some time and it was not for nearly half an hour that Sehlte returned with the information that the interior tanks were empty. During that half-hour they all remained in their places, patient, pale, breathing with ever-increasing difficulty, leaning against the dripping walls and dank machinery. The time crawled—and yet it went too quickly. The looks turned on Sehlte as the engineer officer climbed back down the angled passage and into the control-room were sick with apprehensive fear, for even the youngest and most inexperienced member of the crew now knew that, with some of their compressed air supply destroyed in the morning attack, the U-996 could blow her tanks fully but once more. At this new attempt they had to rise.

The Kommandant wasted no words. 'Listen. This time we are already much lighter, and we are going to blow most of the fuel and drinking water as well as ballast. Also—' he paused—'if we do not commence to rise immediately the motors are full astern I shall release the drop keel.'

To many of the crew this last remark was an unmeaning mystery. But the more experienced knew that U-996 carried a heavy weight, a solid but detachable iron keel weighing some twenty tons, along her bottom. In an emergency this could be released, but it was a measure which could only be taken as a desperate last resort—like abandoning ship, a course which it closely resembled. For since, without this great weight, a submarine could not dive, the jettisoning of the drop keel was tantamount to surrender anywhere other than in home waters. Emil wondered momentarily what Kalewski would have said had he been on his feet and in his usual place in the control-room. Would he have dared question the Captain's decision? In the circumstances he would have had the entire crew against him, so probably he would not.

'Very well . . .' Once more the Kommandant gave the brief orders to surface; once more Huberein repeated his blowing instructions. Once more the compressed air roared into the ballast tanks and the hull shook to the vibrating propellers . . . And once more the needles stayed motionless on the dials.

'Drop the keel! Keep on blowing! Walter, get every bit of power into those screws!' The Kommandant's face was a strained stiff white in the eerie light, his voice hoarse and cracked.

And then there was a sudden bump, a lurch and a sound of grating, tearing metal which made itself heard even through the roar of the blowing tanks—a roar beginning to subside as the supply of compressed air at last gave out.

'We're moving!' Someone's voice tried to shout and was cut off in a fit of coughing, The needles on the dials were flickering and the boat shuddered and shook throughout her entire length. The keel was off, the tanks empty, the motors tugging backwards at full pitch. Another shuddering lurch and an ominous cracking from somewhere forward —and then suddenly the needles began to move steadily upwards . . . 250 . . . 245 . . . 240 . . . 230 . . .

The crew was panting, trying to laugh and choking blue-lipped in the nearly oxygenless air, reeling dizzily and clinging to anything that would support them; but all grinning, all exulting in this escape from the cold slow death which had seemed so close a minute ago. And still the needles swung over the great blank faces of the dials. Up, and up, and up.

Nineteen

An hour later, at moonrise, they were on their way, the site of their sinking left far behind them in a huge misleading patch of oil. They were running silently on the electric motors and at the greatest speed which the Kommandant and Sehlte had calculated the exposed forward bulkhead of the torpedo stowage compartment would accept without too great a risk. In silence and in darkness they had slid away from the area in which one of their enemies might still, perhaps, be lurking, and until the moon lifted its rim from the sea it had been impossible to make out the damage to the bow. The behaviour of the boat upon the surface had indicated that the main destruction was to the portside, but neither the Kommandant nor his Chief Engineer was prepared for what they found after they had walked carefully along the forward casing while the sea swirled softly over the bulge of the saddle tanks below. The submarine's prow had disappeared entirely, and so had eight metres of hull plating on her port bow. To starboard the jagged edges of twisted metal, splayed out sideways, hindered by their resistance the boat's progress forward and necessitated the rudder being kept continually at an angle of ten degrees to port.

Back on the bridge after Sehlte had gone below Eugen accepted a cup of coffee from Hessel, the officers' steward, but would not eat. Hessel told him that a meal was being served to the other officers in the wardroom and he smiled slightly, wondering if Emil had any more appetite than he. For Emil's mind, too, must be engaged in the calculations which filled his own—how to get within Portuguese territorial waters without being caught in daylight on the surface by an enemy chaser or airplane. At present they could make no more than six sea miles an hour—sixty miles in ten hours. Dawn would have broken by then and they would still be some thirty-odd miles from Cape Delgado with another five hours to go before they could consider themselves safe. For without the drop keel there was no longer any possibility of submerging and passing the daylight hours forty metres below the surface. Now they must make the whole journey fully exposed upon the open sea. Yet considering what they had already survived there was no reason to think that their luck would desert them now, and if it did not they should be safely ashore by tomorrow's noon. In his imagination Eugen leapt forward some fifteen hours and saw them closing the gold-green African coast. He would have to check the charts for depth, and even then it might be wise to have a man up on what remained of the bow to take soundings. U-996—his first and last command—should be scuttled, preferably about half a mile off shore, after the crew had left in rubber dinghies. He felt no sense of regret at the approaching loss of his boat, and when he considered what the forward torpedo stowage compartment contained he wriggled his shoulders under his sticky overalls. All the watertight doors would be left open, the green sea would flood in and even if the depth was insufficient to explode the automatic demolition charges as the boat settled, the fish would soon come—the slow, pulsing squids, the clicking crabs—and within a week or so there would be only a litter of bones among those broken torpedoes . . . *On a sailor's tomb no roses bloom.*

In eight more hours it would be nearly dawn—bringing new danger. For a tired moment Eugen's mind groped with the idea of flooding the torpedo stowage compartment, thus partially making up the weight of the lost keel. It might work . . . Then he remembered that without forward hydroplanes to guide the boat such a measure would, in all probability, end in a second uncontrolled dive to the sea bed. Under the present circumstances it would be too risky even to ballast down. The moon was climbing up the sky now and silvering the empty sea for miles around. Empty and still, and far to the west, invisible

and approaching only with unbearable slowness, the loom of Africa—
a neutral shore.

Eugen realized that he was trembling with fatigue—and not only
with fatigue but with excitement. For there could no longer be any
objection, even from the *Seekriegsleitung* in far-away Berlin, to the
course he was taking—the sole alternative was surrender to the enemy.
He could even send a coded signal to explain his position and request
official confirmation for his proposed action. U-996, unable to dive,
unable to proceed at more than a fraction of her normal speed, with
practically all fuel pumped out and with her main armament entirely
destroyed, was no longer a weapon of war. Her commander had but
two duties to fulfil now: to prevent his broken boat falling into enemy
hands and to save the lives of his crew. Yet at this ultimate stage of the
war any such signal was bound to be regarded with the gravest
suspicion by the authorities. Irrespective of the danger of breaking
radio silence in such hostile waters, it would undoubtedly be best to
wait until the boat was within sight of land before informing Berlin;
and subsequently he must try to ensure that the Portuguese press gave
full publicity to the ruinous state of U-996 and the impossibility of the
boat remaining at sea. This meant that he must bring her into shallower
water than he had intended and leave the pistols of the demolition
charges firmly capped, thus making the boat available for inspection
by neutral and, if possible, German consular authorities . . . It came as
a sudden shock to Eugen to realize that it was, after all, by no means
yet certain that he would reach Mozambique territorial waters.

Yet he did reach them. Through all the hours of bright calm moonlight the U-996 drove forward, changing from electric to diesel power
well before midnight and raising the speed to a dangerous 7.2 knots as
soon as Sehlte's men had shored still further that exposed forward
bulkhead. Eugen refused to leave the bridge but at midnight he was
joined by Christl Huberein, the officer of the watch.

Huberein asked at once if they were not making for the coast with
the intention to beach.

'Of course. What else can we do?'

'Nothing—nothing at all. Only—' the Austrian had hesitated,
staring out over the starboard side of the bridge.

'Only . . .?' Eugen had prompted. 'Only . . . what?'

'I wondered whether you intended to send a signal. . . .'

'I do. But not yet. There is no knowing whether we shall succeed.
I do not wish to confuse headquarters. I shall signal when we are in
territorial waters. Of course my action will be confirmed.'

'Of course.'

Neither stated the obvious fact that long before such hypothetical confirmation could be received the U-996 would in any case be firmly aground on some coastal sandbank.

Later Huberein said, 'I am sorry that this cruise has—has not been successful. For you, I mean . . . You must feel . . . That is . . .' He had stammered into embarrassed silence.

Eugen dared not smile as he would have done if he had been invisible in full darkness. Instead he answered carefully, 'Everyone has done his best—except that idiot, Prinz; and he does not matter. The behaviour of the crew, yesterday in particular while we were on the bottom, was excellent. It was much more than I expected. When one considers their lack of experience and their average age . . . No— no one is to blame for what has happened.'

'You are right, of course. I only wish—' Huberein paused a second and Eugen completed the sentence for him. After all it did the look-outs no harm to overhear their officers uttering patriotic platitudes, however insincere—'that we were still undamaged and approaching our area of operations? Yes, indeed.'

'No. No, I did not mean that.' Huberein's voice was apologetic. 'I was thinking of—of something else. I meant I only wished we had not had to do that to those men of the French ship.'

Emil took over from the acting First Lieutenant after moonset. There was no real need for a watchkeeper on the bridge while the Captain was there but, as Eugen guessed, the younger man had been unable to sleep. 'And when I'm in the control-room I keep thinking of what's up forward.'

'Well,' said Eugen dryly, 'now you are here you can think about the approach of dawn and the chances of a sighting by enemy air-craft.'

It was a remark which would have offended Huberein but which, as the Kommandant knew, would not offend Emil.

'Sehlte says that we are quite safe. It is God's will that we shall not perish—otherwise we should still be on the bottom.'

'And if we had not got off the bottom—that would have been God's will, too, I suppose? God's will is much too unascertainable to give me comfort—or you, too, I think.'

'Yes—as I told him.' Emil grinned in the darkness. 'Poor Walter! Yet he needs something, of course—after what happened to his family. He had to choose between religion or revenge, I suppose. He was right to choose the former. You remember how distressed he was when—when we had to eliminate those sailors from the French ship?'

Angrily Eugen said, 'You are the second person to remind me of that tonight! Huberein spoke of it, too. Can we not forget it—after all that has happened since?'

'I—it was only thinking of Walter that made me say—'

'Then don't! We have plenty of other things to think about as it is.' Eugen pointed astern where in the east the sky was beginning to show faint streaks of grey. 'Look! Dawn is coming.'

And both officers, turning towards the stern, watched silently, apprehensively, as dawn broke slowly and a first shaft of rose-coloured light from Madagascar far away heralded the sun.

Twenty

Four hours later, but now over a bright clear sea etched with ripples under a light breeze, the U-996 thrust her mangled bow towards the invisible shore somewhere beyond the western horizon. Soon after eight Hessel brought more coffee to his grimy, red-eyed but exultant captain. The steward's happy grin showed that the crew now knew, and excitedly approved, the plan to beach their boat on a neutral coast. Eugen, seeing Hessel's face, would very much have liked to ask how Kalewski, Wutsdorf and some of their engine-room artificer friends were taking the news, but he refrained. Whatever the under-officers might feel, they were powerless to do more than sulk in the face of the wholehearted approbation of the rest of the crew. He gave the empty cup back to Hessel and as he did so lifted his eyes and saw, still far away, tiny and high in the north-west, an airplane circling. The port look-out saw it at the same time and cried out and within an instant alarm bells were jangling throughout the boat below—uselessly, for there was nothing that could be done save to man the guns.

And as the gun crews rushed to the 1 x 3.7mm and to the flak twins Eugen lifted his high-powered glasses and examined the approaching plane. British. That was certain. Shore based. A fighter-bomber . . . The worst that could befall. He swung around and faced the west and his lips parted in a quick gasp. There it was, a low smear on the horizon —the first faint loom of Cape Delgado visible at last. He dropped his heavy glasses on to his chest and seized the telephone. 'Engine-room!'

'Engine-room here, Sehlte.'

'Listen, Walter. We are probably going to be attacked—one aircraft. I am sure he has seen us. We will have to hope that we can drive him off with the guns—or better, bring him down. But he will be radioing our position. We *must* get within territorial waters before he can bring up chasers. We will increase speed to eight knots. Can you do that?'

'Yes. What about that bulkhead?'

'It will stand it.'

'I hope you are right.'

'Of course I am!' Eugen grinned briefly. 'It is God's will.'

Then the plane was upon them. Its pilot must have known all about yesterday's events for he neither circled nor made any attempt to ascertain the submarine's identity. It struck Eugen immediately that not only did the pilot know who they were but he had also accurately guessed their intended destination. Around him the flak opened up with a shattering roar and that roar was answered, was overwhelmed, in the fury of the diving plane. Eugen fell to the deck and lay pressed to the base of the forward periscope standard beside the trembling body of the port look-out as the plane's cannon and machine-guns swept the boat and as two bombs thundered into the water within twenty metres of the starboard bow. Then the plane was screaming upward into a shuddering, twisting climb and the bridge telephone was ringing shrilly. Eugen, clambering to his knees, wrenched it from its clips. 'Huberein here. Radio-room reports that plane is sending. Undoubtedly our position and calling up chasers.'

'Yes? Listen, Christl. Delgado is in view. We are not far off now. If we can beat off this plane we will get there. He killed the gun crews. We must have more. Volunteers. Get them up here quickly!' For the gunners at the flak twins lay dead, torn to pieces by the fire of the plane already returning for a second attack upon its immensely vulnerable opponent.

That second dive brought a bomb within seven metres of the submarine's stern. It exploded in a great cloud of spray and jerked the boat out of its true course, and once more the exposed hull, the still unmanned guns, were raked with armour piercing cannon fire. But by the time the aircraft plummeted down in its third dive the flaks were once more swung up and firing ferociously. This time Eugen, his face laid open from cheekbone to chin by a flying metal splinter, stood beside the juddering twin guns and watched, breath hissing through bloody teeth, as the plane thundered in upon them. This time the bombardier would make no mistake . . .

But no bombs fell and as the plane howled away into a frustrated climb Eugen guessed, with a quick rekindling of hope, that the bombardier was dead—killed by their own fire. He turned to congratulate the gunners, and saw that one of them was Emil. Emil. dirty, hatless, his black hair falling over his eyes, his mouth fixed tightly in a grim vindictive determination . . . Emil with, of all people, Hansi Wutsdorf as a companion. For a moment their eyes met and, as they smiled with a sudden half-amused embarrassment, it struck Eugen that the present scene would make an excellent illustration for the cover of one of the more stridently patriotic magazines at home—the bleeding captain on the open bridge, the bodies at his feet, the young officer personally manning the guns . . . But now the fourth dive of the attacking plane flung Emil sprawling to the deck and there was no more time for ironic speculations. Eugen dropped to his knees, shouting above the fading scream of the plane's engines, 'Wutsdorf! Take his shoulders—I'll take his feet. Wutsdorf—stop firing, damn you! Oh God—his leg!'

Emil, white-faced, flat on his back, moaned for a moment and then wailed, 'Hansi—get me out of here! Why do you *never* do what you're told in action?'

But Wutsdorf was shouting wildly, 'I've got him! I've got the bastard! He's on fire! Look! Look! He's coming down . . . Now! There he goes . . . into the sea . . . all pieces!'

Pale with rage Eugen rose and, grasping the tall sailor's shoulders, shook him savagely. 'Wutsdorf! If you don't obey me at once—'

But the young gunner, suddenly contrite, was on his knees beside Emil. 'Where is it, Leutnant? Your leg . . . Hold still. We must get a tourniquet on before we move you. It won't—'

But Emil suddenly sat up, blinked, and then, as the world of bright sky, grey steel plating, bullet-scarred, scarlet-spattered guns lurched and darkened before his eyes, frowned uncomprehendingly and fell back limply against Wutsdorf's chest.

Twenty-one

'We are making water almost too fast for the pumps,' said Sehlte half an hour later on the bridge. 'Some of those cannon holes could be plugged better from outside. We would have to heave-to, but—'

'No. Look!' Eugen raised an arm and pointed to the shape of Cape

Delgado rising from the sea some four miles away. 'We can make another mile or so as we are.'

'I do not say we are sinking. It is not that. It is the batteries.'

'I see.' Eugen's voice was coldly desperate. 'How much longer can we manage as we are—without stopping?'

'Roughly fifteen minutes, perhaps.'

Eugen lifted his eyes to the approaching land. Fifteen minutes . . . fifteen minutes. As soon as the sea-water entered the batteries the boat would fill with chlorine gas and become completely uninhabitable. Somewhere over the horizon behind them submarine chasers would be racing through the calm sea throwing up high white bow waves . . . Another air attack might be expected at any time . . . No, they must go on. He dare not order increased speed for fear of accelerating the flooding of the punctured pressure hull, but within fifteen minutes they might just be inside the three-mile limit. They could abandon the boat on a fixed course for the beach and take to the rubber dinghies. He dare not stop now. 'We must go on, Walter. Do everything possible to keep the water down. And get ready to evacuate the engine-room and motor-room immediately it becomes necessary.'

And as Sehlte descended the tower he called Huberein in the control-room, waiting patiently until his First Officer could be brought from attending the wounded. 'Listen, Christl. I want the rubber dinghies brought up and made ready on the after casing. And I want the badly wounded brought up, too. We will probably have to abandon ship in about fifteen minutes. Pass the word to stand by for that order.'

And now . . . now there were just these few more minutes, these last few miles. Bright sunlight and a calm, sparkling sea rippled by a fresh breeze over which a submarine, incredibly battered, her bridge a bloody shambles, her interior filling with water and at any minute ready to fill with poison gas, limped slowly towards the low green loom of the nearby coast.

Eugen was suddenly aware of a great thirst. He must have lost a lot of blood from his gashed face, the left shoulder of his overalls was soaked and sodden with it. He rang down for the steward to bring him some water and then leaned against the coaming, staring alternately at the approaching land and, behind him, apprehensively at the north-east.

When Hessel appeared he carried not only a mug of water but a canvas bag. 'These are the secret documents, codes and ciphers, Herr Kommandant. Obersteuermann Kalewski had them collected and sent up. The log is not included because—'

'Aircraft approaching fine on the port quarter!' shouted a look-out and, forgetful of the mug of water Hessel was holding out, Eugen grabbed the weighted sack and flung it into the sea. Then he whipped up his glasses and focused them in the direction of the look-out's pointing finger.

Two of them . . . approaching fast and low over the water. No hope now—no hope at all. Eugen swung desperately around and grasped the range-finder. Were they within three miles of the tip of the cape? No, not yet. Not quite . . . And for a second he wondered whether it would have mattered, even if they had been.

But to be so near—to be so close to success and to fail now . . . There must be a way . . . Run up a foreign flag? Baffle those planes for two or three more minutes? Useless. They would not be deceived for a single second. No—but a white flag. The planes would not fire upon a surrendered boat, at least not at once. And there was the possibility of misleading signals . . . 'Hessel! Something white—a sheet—the wardroom tablecloth. Be quick!'

And as the steward disappeared down the hatch Eugen turned to the remaining bridge personnel. 'Get down! Lie down! We may be gunned again.' The planes were climbing. Now they had sighted their victim and were sure of him they wished to gain height for their power-dive. Hessel, panting, was back with a bed sheet, but there was no time to fix it to the flag halyards. Eugen gripped one end and, telling Hessel to hold the other high over his head, clambered up the forward periscope standard.

Far above him the first of the planes tilted itself nose downward, gleaming brightly in the sun, and began to fall. The improvised white flag bellied out in the breeze between the two hands which clutched it. Eugen shut his eyes as the rising crescendo of the airplane's engine shrieked in his ears. At any second the cannon and machine-guns would open up and he would be torn to pieces as the gun crews had been torn to pieces less than an hour ago. Death and ending . . . Oblivion for ever. Eternal night. Eternal peace. Why had he struggled so hard against it? But even now he had no real belief in his own death. It would not happen because it *could* not. . . .

The first plane howled in one nerve-rasping roar overhead and its open throttle boomed through the thunder of the exhaust as its pilot put it once more into a climb. He had seen the flag, the wounded and the yellow rubber dinghies on the after casing, the unmanned guns. Then the second plane pulled laterally from its dive and followed suit and the submarine had won a breathing space however short.

Eugene knotted the white sheet to a halyard and tumbled back to the bridge. 'Fix your end, Hessel!' And . . . now, what?

Signals. The first plane was coming in low, a lamp blinking rapidly from its cabin. Eugene did not even try to translate the message since he knew well enough what it was—'Heave-to immediately.' Two steps took him to the range-finder. He bent, checked. They were within the three-mile limit; only just, but within it certainly. And now in theory he was safe. Legally, by all the tenets of International Law, he was within Portuguese waters and by firing upon him those British planes would be breaking that law and violating Portuguese neutrality. To Eugen Kielbasa, born of three generations of lawyers and intended from birth for the legal profession, the law was power. It was omnipotent; a weapon which in the right hands—a lawyer's—was far more deadly in attack than any military missile, far more sure in defence than armour plate. He did not stop to think that this might not be the view which the crews of those two British aircraft, now circling his boat, might take of the present situation. He himself would never have attacked an Allied ship in neutral waters—would, in fact, have been only too glad of the excuse to avoid doing so and might well have stretched the area outward by a prudent hundred metres or so to meet the circumstance of a doubtful case. For, as his family had never tired of quoting, a lawyer might manipulate the law but he must never break it.

So now his first reaction was to order up the signal lamp and explain to those two circling planes blinking their lights at him that he was within neutral waters and must be lawfully accorded the right to proceed unmolested to land. But though he seized the telephone to shout his order down to Huberein he never gave it, for at that moment the bridge was suddenly filled with men bursting, choking and coughing from the conning-tower while other reeling, blue-overalled figures scrambled from the after hatches. There was no reason for inquiry—the fierce stench that rose with them explained the position clearly.

Huberein was the last out of the control-room, and he had to be hauled half-conscious up the top rungs of the ladder. His face was blue, his eyes popping, and bloody saliva dripped from his gaping mouth. Eugen guessed that he had stayed below until the last of the crew had climbed the ladder, and in the engine-room Sehlte would have done the same.

And now he noticed that the deck beneath his feet had ceased to vibrate. Unable to man his engines, Sehlte, lacking the order which

Eugen had intended but had failed to give him, had closed them down rather than leave them running in a deserted engine-room. Inadvertently rather than purposely the U-996 had obeyed the order of the circling aircraft.

But the lights still blinked out and Eugen realized that the enemy had not done with him. Yet since without a signal lamp he was incapable of explaining his own position there was only one thing to do to ensure the crew's safety. 'Abandon ship! Get the wounded into the dinghies and then get into them yourselves. An officer or under-officer must go in each dinghy. He will be in command and is responsible for reaching the beach.'

Quickly the first dinghies were inflated—ballooning out under the hiss of their pressure bottles—and slid down the curved hull plates into the sea. The wounded were lifted in and laid on the bottoms and like great yellow flowers dinghy after dinghy pushed bobbing from the submarine's side. The calm sea made the launching comparatively easy and the losses among the crew meant that although the wounded took up more than their correct share of space there was ample room in the escape craft for everyone. Yet it was nervous work, under the uncertain menace of those circling planes whose signal lamps still blinked out overhead.

Stepping into the last dinghy, held ready for him by Wutsdorf, Eugen gave a quick glance back at the abandoned submarine rocking on the still sea. Empty—except for dead men lying in a now unbreathable atmosphere of poison gas. The long cruise was over and the U-996, which had accomplished only the destruction of one ancient freighter and a small tanker—nothing of the slightest consequence at this stage of the war—had been reduced to a sinking wreck in the process. All that terror and pain and death had gone for nothing at all.

The men at the paddles dug their blades into the water and the bobbing yellow boat slid over the calm sea heading for the land which, now that Eugen saw it from the water level rather than the eminence of the submarine's bridge, seemed farther away than it was. An hour or more of paddling, perhaps, and they must be careful how they approached the beach . . .

It was then that the first plane, apparently tired of signalling, roared in from a turn far out to sea and thundering low above their heads let loose a burst of fire which slashed the water less than fifty metres in front of the most advanced boat.

The paddles stilled, the crewmen and their captain stared up open-mouthed. What did it mean—that burst of fire? They had abandoned their submarine. They were shipwrecked sailors, unarmed and defenceless, within neutral waters and making their way in life-rafts to a neutral coast. Surely—legality apart—the enemy planes did not mean to massacre them on the open sea?

Then the second plane came in, this time across their bows and parallel with the shore. Its cannon fire tore up a stretch of water which subsided in mottled, lacy foam leaving a white demarcation line across the sea some thirty metres forward of the wallowing U-996 almost, it seemed, to the point of Cape Delgado. And that line spoke more clearly to Eugen than any words. That line they were forbidden to cross. They were not to approach the shore but to remain near the abandoned submarine. Why? The answer, too, was obvious; somewhere a chaser was approaching at speed to collect them. The British were not going to allow them to become internees of a neutral power. They had surrendered to a British aircraft and they were to be made British prisoners.

And at last Eugen's self-control, exerted so long and so successfully, snapped. It was too much. To be thwarted in this way—within hardly more than three thousand metres of safety—of neutral internment followed by a journey to Brazil . . . São Paulo . . . freedom. He rose in the rubber dinghy and shouted at Wutsdorf and the others to row forward. They were within their legal rights to do so! The law should not be broken—flagrantly flouted—in this way! Who did those English up there think they were to violate international rules of warfare? His torn face aflame with unusual rage he stood in the rocking dinghy as the planes tore in for the third time and waved his fists and screamed at them, his puny voice lost immediately in the thunder of their engines, the roar of their multiple guns. '*Du lieber almächtiger Gott!* What are you *doing!* What—' Then the whole left side of the dinghy was ripped to yellow tatters, the right side at once lifted vertically into the air and Eugen, with a sudden half-inverted glimpse of Wutsdorf, open-mouthed, clutching a bullet-torn shoulder, was thrown head-first into the sea.

Twenty-two

And far away—thousands of miles away to the west—another ship, the *Hipòlito Irigoyen*, a smart new Argentine freighter which had been attracted out of its course by a small patch of red bobbing above the waves far to starboard, was slowing to pick up a single skeletal survivor slumped inert on the slats of a salt-stained, weed-caked life-raft, one sun-blistered hand still clutching the rotten carcass of a flying fish.

BEYOND DELGADO

One

Mr Spencer was in Emerald's zoo, waiting for the pangolin to unroll itself and complaining in his soft, oddly accented voice about his sciatica and the unsatisfactory treatment he received for it from Emerald's father. 'Sometimes it is quite impossible to sit down—even in the *toilette*. It is like a very terrible toothache, and it goes on and on and on. Nothing seems to help—at least nothing your father has given me. Sometimes, dear Emerald, I become so depressionate that I think to myself that I will have my leg removed at the hip.'

'But if it is *in* your hip that wouldn't help, would it? You would have to have your hip removed. And I don't think one can do that.'

'Perhaps not. I told your father that if orthodox medical assistance could not cure me I must try other things. I said "I know you doctors distrust all who are not certified and label them 'quacks,' but the next time I am in Dar-es-Salaam I shall search out a reputable psychopath and see if massage helps."—That pangolin never liked me. It knows I am here and it will not unroll itself.'

'It will get over it. It wouldn't unroll itself for Tony to start with but it does now. It unrolls for Tony, for Mrs Shellybeare and—'

'It has a bad nature, I think.'

'No, a sensitive one is all. It unrolled when Patience Singlefield came to see it, but she took one look and said "Oh, God!" and it rolled itself up immediately and stayed like that for half an hour after she'd gone away.'

Mr Spencer nodded sombrely, his sad and handsome face bent a little over the chicken-wire front of the cage. Late afternoon sunlight filtering through the heavy leaves of the mango trees glowed on his new rose-coloured silk shirt and his bronzed and muscular arms below the short sleeves. Emerald envied him the shirt and wondered if she could induce him to buy her one like it next time he went up the coast. It was unlikely, though, since she was already in trouble over the pangolin. And it was the pangolin he mentioned next. 'Your father is still angry with you—about that?'

'Continually.'

'Five pounds is not a lot of money.'

'*He* thinks it is. He is so mean about money. He resents it that the dustmen aren't still looking pleased about last year's Christmas tip.'

139

'It came all the way from Malaya on a boat. The sailor wanted ten. He thinks I cheated you?'

'No, of course not.' Emerald gently kicked the bottom of the cage but the pangolin remained a tight, scaly ball. Dr Zared was certain that Mr Spencer had cheated her and she was fairly sure he had, too. But Mr Spencer always took a commission—he never said how much—when bringing things back from Dar-es-Salaam.

Around them in two long lines various monkeys, bush-babies and an assortment of brutal-looking parrots yawned, scratched and stretched or made bids for human attention. Some of the cages were new but most were old and dilapidated, the remains of an earlier zoo collected by a long-departed medical officer whom no one save Mr Gopal, the harbour-master and port pilot, could remember. Emerald had added the new cages and rapidly filled them. Zoology was an expensive undertaking and her mounting costs were a source of continual friction between herself and her father.

A car hooted angrily outside in the road and then they heard it turn in at the doctor's gates and the crunch of its wheels as it swept, unseen behind the high poinsettia hedge, up the drive.

'Tony?'

'I expect so. He wants me to play tennis.'

'Tennis, tennis, tennis!' said Mr Spencer angrily. 'Always it is tennis. Does he not know that there is a war on?'

'It's nearly over, surely.' Emerald eyed Mr Spencer's trim and slender figure. 'You would play tennis beautifully, if it wasn't for your sciatica.'

'I have never played, so you cannot tell. In my youth I played ice hockey—never anything else. There was—'said Mr Spencer moodily—'nothing else to play. Now I am far too old and far too busy for games.'

Then the oleanders behind the last row of cages were thrust suddenly apart and Tony Brickler, Mr Shellybeare's Assistant District Commissioner, pushed through them. He was in white tennis clothes but his shirt was unbuttoned, his face flushed. For a moment the falling sun, glinting through the mango trees, caught his glasses in a glare which dazzled him. Then he shook his head and made out the two figures beside the pangolin's cage. 'Oh, there you are, Spencer!' His voice was breathless and exultant. 'Look—we need your—your boat. Is that O.K.? The police launch is out of order again. Listen—they've caught a German submarine down the coast. I don't know the details, but it was somewhere off Delgado. They wanted to tow it back to Dar-es-Salaam but it's too badly damaged, so they're bringing it in here. We got a signal about it. Mr Singlefield's got to get all his police ready as a guard for the crew—and there are some wounded, too, so your father's standing by, Emerald. I'm to go out and meet the chaser that is towing it, the D.C. says. So we'll want to borrow your —your—'

'But of course! Of course, my dear Tony!' Mr Spencer's face was alight with joy. 'And I'll come, too—if you will arm me with a pistol or something.'

'That's not necessary.' Tony grinned and Mr Spencer flushed slightly. 'The fighting's been done. We can go just as we are. Emerald —you'd like to come, too?'

'Surely.'

'Fine. Well, let's get going. There's room in my car—I've only got the driver. Emerald, how would you like to add a German U-boat man to your zoo? You've got an empty cage.'

Two

Like most African territories under British colonial rule, Tanganyika had achieved order and tranquillity, but only at the cost of not achieving anything else; stagnant, rather than dormant, its people drifted drowsily through the long equatorial years lost in the dreary content-ment of mass failure. Consequently the arrival, off the little port of Masondi, of a battered and sinking German U-boat towed by a chaser full of surrendered German sailors was an event of unprecedented excitement and stimulation which affected everybody—except Dr Zared who was obsessed by the cost of the ant-eater to the exclusion of all else—from ageing, grey-haired Mr Geoffrey Shellybeare, the District Commissioner, to small, round-bellied Mr Serit Gopal, the harbour-master and port pilot. Mr Gopal was so overcome that he was quite incapable of taking in the facts about the long waterlogged grey hulk sagging behind the chaser which the latter's captain attempted to impart to him. The result was that the submarine grounded half a mile off shore on the reef and poor Mr Gopal was furiously attacked in a torrent of terrifying abuse by the chaser's skipper, aided by some cold remarks from the pallid, exhausted young man whom he understood to be the captain of the surrendered boat. For an hour he had tried to free the submarine but he was too upset to think clearly and in the end the English lieutenant commander had pushed him roughly aside, taken the wheel himself and casting off the tow had brought his own ship neatly and angrily to the side of the mole, upon which were ranged a double file of black policemen under a white officer.

Two hours later Mr Shellybeare was sitting on his veranda listening to an account of the U-boat's surrender from the chaser's captain. A bottle of whisky, half empty, stood on a table between the two men, and it, and the timely tact of the District Commissioner, had done much to assuage the anger of Lieutenant-Commander Barragold, who had originally come to lodge a bitter complaint against the harbour-master. Mr Shellybeare was a man of wide sympathies who, unlike most British residents in East Africa, liked Indians; and he particularly liked Serit Gopal. He knew, too, that a report and a subsequent demand for a naval inquiry into the professional conduct of the harbour-master in the matter of the grounding of the submarine outside the lagoon could wreck Gopal's future prospects in the service and might even be the cause of his dismissal. Gopal had seven children, thin, long-legged, timid creatures with great sad eyes, the eldest of whom was just sixteen, and that this family might suffer very real impoverishment if the chaser's captain put in a ferocious report about their father was intolerable. It was also unfair. Gopal was a competent enough man for the daily duties he had to perform but to deal suddenly with the extremely difficult job of manœuvring a towed and sinking submarine through the narrow entrance of the harbour lagoon was asking too much of him. It was something which needed luck as well as skill. It was true that Gopal probably had not the requisite skill, but with a little luck . . . However, there it was—and all that could be done now was to try to calm Barragold's anger.

Mr Shellybeare could sympathize with the naval officer even though he could not like him. Barragold was a burly red-faced man, a hot-tempered disciplinarian by the look of him, who had had a chaser captain's dream come true—only to be cheated out of the best part by what seemed to him the inexcusable incompetence of a civil service port pilot. For what Barragold had wanted, of course, was to take the U-boat back to Dar-es-Salaam for a triumphal entry behind his own ship. If the enemy vessel could have been brought safely into Masondi harbour it would have been simple enough to patch the holes in her hull and pump her out. Then the tow up the coast could have been accomplished without difficulty. But as it was . . .

Mr Shellybeare had made all the excuses he could think of for his poor Gopal and Barragold had seemed to accept them, albeit with reluctance and impatience. But the District Commissioner doubted

whether such an acceptance tonight would prevent him from de-
nouncing the Indian when he made his entry—with the German
officers, certainly, but without his precious trophy—into Dar-es-
Salaam harbour. He sighed, shaking his big grey head, and said,
'Another whisky, Commander, before we eat?'

'Thanks—I think so. But it must be the last because—Who's
this?'

Both men looked up as a car's headlights swung a double beam of
light through the darkness outside and a car's wheels rattled the gravel
drive before the porch. Then Mr Shellybeare heard his police officer's
voice raised from without. 'Are you at home, sir?'

'It's Singlefield,' he said, and called back, 'Yes, yes—come in!'

Mr Singlefield was tall and thin and in his late thirties. Though his
uniforms were smart and carefully tailored, they never looked right on
him—or, more correctly, he never looked right in them—and he
went about his duties with a peculiar air of wary yet malign suspicion which lent him, as Emerald Zared had once said, the expression
of a bird held in the hand to be photographed.

Now he saluted and said, 'Good evening, sir. 'Evening, Commander.
I hope I'm not disturbing you, but I wonder whether you would have
time to see the U-boat captain. He's been asking to see "the British
Governor" ever since the prisoners were landed and I took charge of
them. He won't say what it's about, but I suppose it might be important. He speaks a bit of English.'

Mr Shellybeare raised his eyebrows. 'Wants to see *me*—does he?
I can't see what good he imagines . . .' He broke off and, glancing at
Barragold, noted a look of angry embarrassment on the naval officer's
florid face. 'Well—all right. Bring him in, Singlefield.'

'Yes, sir.' The police officer withdrew and Mr Shellybeare, refilling
his guest's glass with whisky, asked casually, 'Any idea what this is
about?'

'Oh, some trumped-up nonsense, I expect.' Barragold's voice held a
resentful but slightly uncertain note of anger. 'Some complaint, I
imagine—just to save his face for surrendering. You don't have to
take any notice.'

Mr Shellybeare was about to remark that, as the embodiment of
H.M. Government in Masondi, it was not his practice to allow
others to tell him of what he should, or should not, take notice when
he remembered that since he was trying to win Barragold's favour
such a remark would be out of place. So he merely sighed again and
listened to the clink and rattle of rifles and the crunch of policemen's

boots as the prisoner and his escort were brought from Singlefield's car. He had caught a brief glimpse of the German before, kneeling on the dock beside one of his wounded men, and now he wondered why Zared had not kept him in the hospital, too. Never had he seen such exhaustion as that upon the swollen, bandaged face of the submarine commander in the blood-and-salt-stained blue overalls who stood as though only an immense effort of will kept him from buckling at the knees and falling over.

Quickly, before this might happen, he indicated a third chair and as soon as the man collapsed into it he poured whisky into a third glass and handed it to Singlefield. 'Give him this.'

But the German only shook his head. 'Thank you—no. I do not drink distilled spirit.' The English was accurate—pedantically so—and the voice low and slurred with a terrible fatigue.

'You'd much better, you know.' Mr Shellybeare thought that the refusal of the whisky was merely a typical example of German priggishness, though in fact it was due to Eugen's fear of vomiting it up immediately he had drunk it. 'Well then? What is it you want to see me about?'

With a slight gesture of one hand Eugen indicated Barragold. 'This officer made prisoners of me and my men inside of neutral sea frontiers. We were inside of the Mozambique coastal waters. Inside such confines it is not legal to be made prisoner. That International Law this captain has unobeyed. Therefore I request that you will make all correct by sending myself and my men to Mozambique for internment by the Portuguese government. That is our legal right because of International Law.'

Barragold gave a brief grunt of impatience and turned to the District Commissioner. 'He's been on about that ever since we pulled him out of the water. He even tried to get us to land his men on Delgado—said we could have the submarine if we towed it back a couple of hundred yards but claimed his right to be interned in Mozambique. All balls, of course.'

Mr Shellybeare glanced from the German's white face to the red one of the chaser captain. 'Were they in territorial waters?'

'On the edge, perhaps. Our planes had stopped them going any farther. But really it's of no importance. I can't think why he's so worked up about it.'

'Did you take a sighting or something? In order to be quite sure?'

Barragold gave an amused snort of laughter. 'Really, sir—I hadn't time! I'd been after this fellow for over twenty-four hours. His boat was abandoned—full of chlorine gas as it turned out—and he and quite a lot of his men were in the drink. It was more of a rescue operation than anything else. If we'd started taking bearings and arguing the toss they'd have been drowned or eaten by sharks.'

Mr Shellybeare turned to the German. 'You say you were within neutral waters. That means within the three-mile limit. Are you certain of this?'

'Yes.'

'How do you know?'

'I made measurement by my range-finder before—before we were in the sea. At that point we were inside of the neutral frontier by more than one hundred forty metres. In the rubber boats we progressed approximate fifty metres more—but then I had no range-finder to make certain of this.'

Mr Shellybeare gave a sigh, and though neither of the naval officers knew it, it was one of deep content. He had found the means of saving Gopal. 'I see, I see. Well, Barragold, the fact is that he took a reading or a sighting or whatever you call it whereas by your own admission you did not. Undoubtedly there was not much in it, as you say—he was on the edge of Portuguese territorial waters. But it seems that he is within his rights in claiming that he was technically inside. That puts us in a somewhat—hmmm—more complex position.'

'Oh, come, sir!' Barragold was inwardly extremely annoyed at what he saw as a piece of typical portentous bureaucratic cavilling on the part of a civilian. Old Shellybeare sat here in this out-of-the-way corner month after month with nothing to do, and now of course he was revelling in the opportunity to attract notice to himself over something which was really none of his business. It was to Barragold, who had sunk the U-boat in the first place, and to the dead airplane pilot who had found it slinking away and homed the chaser upon it, that all notice and recognition rightfully belonged. He wished bitterly that he had lied stoutly a minute ago, told the D.C. that he had taken a sighting on Delgado and that, far from being three hundred yards within territorial waters, the U-boat had been five hundred yards outside them. Shellybeare would have had to take the word of a British officer before that of an enemy. But it was too late now. He must go carefully . . . 'Of course we can't tell whether he's speaking the truth—as I say, I did not take a sight—but I don't think we should put too much weight on a U-boat commander's word. We know too much about their methods to take them for paragons of virtue. Besides, there is no corroboration.'

Mr Shellybeare gave a carefully dubious shrug of his shoulders. 'We can't say that with certainty. The Portuguese may have measured from the cape. Who knows? I can contact them about it, of course. I know their Resident over the border and he's a nice enough man, but a touchy one.' Once more he sighed gently. 'So many of them are, you know.' After a pause he said slowly, 'If the Portuguese corroborate what this officer says I'm afraid the Resident would raise a yell about it. We might have to hand them back in that case.'

'Oh, surely not!' Barragold grinned but his eyes glinted with anger. 'Not at this stage of the war, Mr Shellybeare. We're hardly frightened of Portugal, are we?'

'That point does not arise. We are not, I presume, frightened of Portugal; but we are, I hope, interested in the maintenance of International Law.' Mr Shellybeare's voice had taken on a sterner tone. 'If Senhor Azeredo corroborates this officer's statement I'm afraid that you'll have to explain to your own people why you took the action you did—and I may say the Navy will probably be less amused than you appear to be if it finds itself in a position of having to apologize for violating Portuguese neutrality. You may be commended for your zeal but I imagine they will want to know why you failed to take a sighting.'

'I tell you, I hadn't time! They were in the water! Good God— what was I expected to do! To radio Lourenço Marques, or—'

'Please don't shout, Barragold. There's no reason for it.' Suddenly Mr Shellybeare smiled. 'We have an extremely odd man living here in Masondi—an agent of Gillespie & Sankey, the shippers. His name is Spencer, though he's certainly not English. In his office hangs a little plaque which reads: *Do not enrage yourself—you will only shorten your life.* Let me offer that sage to advice you now.'

'But—'

'No, no. Just listen to me a moment. Your failure to take a sighting was obviously one of those minor errors of which all of us are capable but which sometimes cause troublesome results out of all proportion to their intrinsic importance. For instance, look what happened this evening to my poor port pilot, Gopal. A single mistaken helm order— something which in most cases would not matter at all—and that U-boat swung out of line and grounded on the reef. It's just the same with you—if you see what I mean.' Mr Shellybeare ended slowly and deliberately.

For a moment Barragold seemed about to continue his angry protests and Mr Shellybeare thought that his point had not been taken.

Then the Commander's mouth, which had opened to speak, shut again and he slumped back in his chair, picked up his glass and drank from it. When he spoke once more it was slowly, with an effort, and his eyes were averted from the District Commissioner's amused ones. 'Yes, I see. I suppose you're right. Mistakes occur . . . I—I've no intention of making anything out of your pilot's. I expect he did the best he could.'

'I'm sure of it.'

'And—and it was just bad luck. I've no intention of stating more than that in my official report.'

'I'm extremely glad you see it in that way. I'm sure you're right to do so. And I'm sure Gopal would be most grateful.'

Barragold muttered something which Mr Shellybeare did not catch, for now he must perform his own part of the unspoken bargain. He turned to the German. 'Now, Captain—What is your name?'

'Kielbasa—Eugen Kielbasa.'

'I see. Well, Captain Kielbasa, you were quite within your rights to make a formal protest since you believed yourself to be the victim of a technical illegality,' The District Commissioner saw the German struggling against his weariness to translate and for a moment pity moved him. This man had gone through a terrible ordeal—much more terrible, he suspected, than was at present known—certainly far worse than anything that had ever happened to Barragold. But it was to Barragold that he was bound under their tacit agreement. He continued more slowly: 'If you want to pursue the matter I imagine your proper course is to get in touch with the Red Cross authorities in Switzerland. But I doubt if it is worthwhile.'

'I ask, please, to be sent back with my men to Mozambique. It is our legal right.' The voice was low but it had about it an urgency which Mr Shellybeare found it difficult to understand. Internment by the Portuguese in Mozambique would be only mildly preferable to the perfectly civilized treatment this young man would receive in a British prisoner-of-war camp. Surely his main concern at such a time should be that he was alive and safe and freed from all further participation in a desperately hopeless cause. 'Why do you want to be interned by the Portuguese?'

'Why—why?' For a long moment Eugen stared amazedly at this elderly, plump English colonial official who seemed so civilized and—almost friendly, it had seemed—and yet could ask such a question. He himself had not followed much of the dialogue between the District Commissioner and the chaser captain. His brain was clogged with exhaustion and the effort to translate into an unaccustomed though carefully studied language was, this evening, too great an effort for his physical condition. Yet now he had to realize that much of his reason for the attempt to gain Portuguese waters had been a private one—his desire to gain quick contact with his Brazilian brother-in-law and the comparatively rapid freedom that he believed would result from it. He could not explain that now—it was too personal and too irrelevant. He paused, then said, 'It is less bad to become the prisoner of a neutral than of an enemy.'

Mr Shellybeare considered this a moment and put the wrong construction upon it. 'You cannot blame yourself, Captain. You have done all you could. Your boat was too badly damaged to fight again or to return to Germany. You had no choice except surrender. I should not have thought it mattered greatly to whom you surrendered, in the circumstances,'

Slowly Eugen said, 'Our government says that the British will send all German officers to the Russians—to be killed.'

'Good God!' said Mr Shellybeare taken aback. 'Do they?'

Commander Barragold nodded. 'I think so. To get them to go on fighting. Quite a clever idea. They would never believe that we would kill them in cold blood, but they can well believe it of the Russians.'

'Outrageous—but typical, of course.' The District Commissioner turned to Eugen. 'That is quite untrue,' he said firmly. 'What you are pleased to call your "government" may very well meet such a fate— and most deservedly. But German service personnel in our hands will be treated correctly under the International Conventions.'

'If that is so—' Eugen's voice was desperate now, for he did not believe the Englishman who had seemed to prevaricate and consult the naval officer before answering—'why will you not give me my right in International Law? If you break International Law today how would I believe you will not break it again one more time?'

But Mr Shellybeare was not prepared to be taken up in this manner. Like most Englishmen, he had a profound, if not entirely rational, disapproval of the type of war the German U-boats waged. It was difficult to see, in this worn-out, dirty young man before him, the typical U-boat commander of propaganda, but he belonged to a service well known for its ruthlessness and deemed by many to be piratical and a disgrace to the maritime traditions of civilized nations. Also, despite his present appearance, Kielbasa seemed to have behaved with all the tigerish resolution of his alleged type—fighting hopelessly back even when his half-destroyed boat was sinking under him and full of poison gas. A man of this sort might have been capable of anything. Pity should not be taken too far in such a case—it was all too likely undeserved. 'You must believe what you like. The fact is that you were *rescued* by Commander Barragold as well as taken prisoner. Now you will have to accept it and make the best of it. You are not likely to be a prisoner for very long, in any case.'

'You will not send us back to Mozambique?'

'No, I will not. I could not do so even if I wished. If that is all you wanted to say, you may go now.' The District Commissioner turned to his police officer who, throughout the interview, had been standing beside his chair. 'Take him back, Singlefield.'

'Yes, sir.'

For a moment he glanced at the sagging, blue-overalled shoulders of the German as he left the room between his guards and followed by the police officer. Then he turned back to Barragold. 'Well—that's that. You'll be taking him and the three unwounded officers with you tomorrow?'

'Yes, yes. Certainly.'

'Good. Let's go and eat.'

Three

Next morning Dr Zared was still preoccupied with the pangolin, as he had been for the last ten days. The crowded events of yesterday evening, the fact that his little hospital was now full of wounded Germans—even the exhaustion due to working in the operating theatre all night—none of these prevented him from bringing up the subject of the pangolin once more at breakfast. 'You don't seem to have the slightest sense of the value of money. It's one thing to buy a local bird from a native for fifty cents, or even a monkey for five shillings. But to buy an *imported* animal for *five pounds* . . .'

In an attempt to change the subject Emerald said, 'Last night I had a most peculiar dream. I dreamt that you lost control of your bladder and—'

But Dr Zared disregarded her. 'I suppose the next thing you'll want will be a Polar bear!'

Desperately Emerald said, 'Talking of Polar bears—do you know that I've really found out something at last about Spencer's origins? He let it slip by mistake. He started life as an Eskimo.'

'Nonsense!' said Dr Zared crossly. His small lined face lost none of its usual air of gloomy irritability but his eyes behind the steel-rimmed glasses held a gleam of interest as he asked, 'What on earth makes you think that?'

Emerald put down her coffee cup and started to peel a guava from the polished wooden bowl in the centre of the breakfast table. Her two little grey monkeys, Montgomery and Alexander, began jumping up and down on the back of her chair—they were not certain whether the guava was for them but they hoped it would be. 'Spencer let out that in his early youth he played ice hockey.' She paused. 'And he said that *there was no other game to play*. That must mean either the North Pole or the South Pole. At the North Pole they have Eskimos, but at the South only penguins. Even if he had been abandoned as a baby by whalers and reared by the penguins—like Mowgli by wolves—there wouldn't have been anybody to play ice hockey with. He certainly walks rather oddly, but that's due to his sciatica.'

'Quebec. He must be a French-Canadian—if he was speaking the truth.' Dr Zared pulled himself up. 'But that doesn't alter the fact that he asked for—*and you gave him*—five pounds for an imported scaly ant-eater. You can't do that, Emerald, you just can't! I haven't got the money. I have nothing but my salary. You know how much that is, don't you? Six seventy-five. We have to live on that. Can't you understand such a simple economic fact?'

'Yes, but—'

'I doubt if you do—if you *really* do. Otherwise you wouldn't go throwing money down the drain in this way. Listen: I am paid six hundred and seventy-five pounds a year. Those six hundred and seventy-five pounds have got to last three hundred and sixty-five days. Supposing that I spend, not six hundred and seventy-five pounds in three hundred and sixty-five days, but—say—*seven hundred pounds*—'

'Bloody smart,' said Emerald appreciatively.

'No—bankrupt! And you know what happens to government employees who go bankrupt in this country? They are fired—sacked—discharged!'

'Not necessarily. They can be undischarged bankrupts, can't they?'

Dr Zared made an angry noise in his throat and pushed back his chair. 'And who wants a pangolin, anyway? Tell me that.'

'I do,' said Emerald patiently. 'If I hadn't I wouldn't have bought it, would I?'

But her father, glancing at his watch, jumped to his feet and, striding rapidly to the radio, tuned in to the B.B.C. Overseas Service and at once the cool house was filled with the triumphant, strident music of 'Lillibulero'—heralding the early-morning news.

Dr Bernard Zared had lived most of his life in Tanganyika although by birth he was an Anglo-Indian and his maternal grandmother had been the wife of an English officer killed in the Mutiny. Like many of her kind, this unfortunate lady had lost not only her husband but all her worldly possessions in the course of that terrible event and had been left with three young children, all girls, to bring up as best she could on a tiny pension. She attempted, with only partial success, to run a dress-making shop in Bombay and as the years passed she and her family slipped slowly and uncertainly down the social scale like dinner plates sliding erratically downward into ever murkier dishwater. The two eldest girls married Anglo-Indians—nothing much better could be hoped for them in the circumstances—and the third married, rather late in life, a young Parsee who, like the rest of his tribe, had the ability to make money. Of this union Bernard Zared was born in 1890 and brought up both strictly and comfortably in Bombay. Given the choice of law or medicine, he chose the latter and, qualifying in London, entered government service and came to Africa as a colonial medical officer. He had taken this step upon realizing that his name, his accent and the slight tinge of golden brown about his skin would effectively prevent him from succeeding in a private English practice. Unfortunately he found that these liabilities weighed still more heavily against him in the Colonial Service. This caused him an early bitterness which, added to a naturally morose and suspicious disposition, went a long way to explain his continued failure to gain either friends or promotion. Yet since he was a competent doctor this latter would eventually have come his way had it not been for two interrelated acts of great folly on his own part. He impregnated an English hospital nurse for no better reason than that it had pleased his vanity to have a completely English mistress and that he had become careless in bed. And when, much to his dismay, he was forced to marry her, it was only to find that she was incapable of bearing children in the normal way. Emerald's appearance in the world was by means of Caesarean section —and it was then that Dr Zared committed his second and crowning act of folly. For rather than trust the local gynaecologist with whom, as with so many of his medical colleagues, he had quarrelled, he attempted to perform the difficult operation himself, panicked in the middle of it and then called in the gynaecologist—too late to avert a fatal result.

He had shown crass stupidity rather than culpable negligence and his superiors were sorrier for him than perhaps they should have been. His career was not ruined but his prospects were blighted. He was retained in government service but at fifty-four he was still only medical officer to the small southern harbour town of Masondi, some forty-odd miles from the border of Mozambique. And even that was a temporary posting from a somewhat larger station where he had remained second medical officer for nearly ten years.

Four

It was not until the morning of his third day in the Masondi hospital that Emil finally surfaced from the submerged twilight world of anaesthetics and heavy sedation. During that time, although he was not aware of this, he had undergone two operations at the hands of Dr Zared. The first saved his life and the second, and much longer one, would in due course probably save his left leg.

Meanwhile he lay, pale-faced and still and aware of a weakness so great that it was almost a negation of bodily life, in a room whose wide windows were covered by lowered venetian blinds which filled the interior with a soft gloom pierced here and there by thin, dusty rays of sunlight. Outside the windows there must be some sort of garden, for birds called and twittered continually and sometimes there came the sound of splashing water, as if from a hose, and the clink of a spade or rake upon gravel.

A bottle hanging above his bed was connected by a tube to his arm and for hours he lay unmoving, his mind as near a blank as possible, hearing only the bird noises, aware only of a dim warm greenness. Later the bottle was disconnected and taken away and soon afterwards a white-overalled dark-faced hospital orderly, a man whom Emil supposed to be an African but who was, in fact, an Indian, fed him very gently and delicately with soup. That afternoon he slept again and awoke in the early evening feeling considerably better but still so weak that even to turn his head on the pillow was an effort demanding concentrated willpower.

A doctor, a small man with steel-rimmed glasses, visited him accompanied by the same orderly and listened to his heart, pulled down his lower eyelids and then wrote something rapidly on a sheet of paper attached to a board by a large rusty paper-clip. Emil would have liked to ask several questions and he had phrased these in French before he realized that he would probably have to ask them in English if he was to be understood. Like most intelligent middle-class continental Europeans, Emil had taken his education seriously and understood— and in theory could speak—a good deal of English. But he had never been to England or spoken to English people so that his knowledge had remained theoretical. He was far too weak now to try out for the first time a difficult foreign tongue and so he kept silent, his questions unasked.

Later, there was more soup and he was carefully washed from head to hips and then he watched, with a detached interest as if it was being done to a waxwork, the Indian's slender-fingered, nimble hands insert a catheter into his penis and drain his bladder. Once more his pillows were skilfully adjusted to ensure the correct disposition of his weight and then the dark-eyed orderly smiled and left him to the deepening twilight and the twitter of birds arranging themselves to roost in the unseen trees outside.

For an hour Emil lay in a half doze of restful ease. For the first time since he had been wounded he was aware of sensation below the left knee, a mild, dull, but increasing ache. Then he drifted into sleep. Towards midnight he dreamed, falling at once into an incoherent and increasingly confused jumble of past events in which everything was hurry and distraction and foreboding, and in which he seemed to be struggling with immense complexities thrust upon him by nameless powers. Nothing remained constant except his own position as a suspect of some sort in the hands of accusers who were also judges. Sometimes these were his aunts, or even—ludicrously—his godfather and the Mayor of Grévilly, seemingly accusing him of having poisoned the Colonel's fabled and long-dead charger, Triomphe, and sold his silver hooves to the enemy. At other times his inquisitors were the in- structors at the U-boat training school, and once the main accuser seemed to be Kalewski. And he himself was always talking, fast and glibly and invariably untruthfully, to an ever larger, silent and un- believing audience. Within him hope, fear, a snarling defiance and pleading despair alternated with sickening rapidity—then, suddenly, he was alone on his back in the brightly lit forward torpedo stowage compartment of the submarine while a torpedo slid sideways from its cradle on to his left leg, crushing it, pinning him firmly to the steel deck in appalling pain. Blood was pouring from jagged bullet holes in the torpedo's side and he knew that it was in agonizing pain, too, for he could feel its pain as well as his own.

Emil screamed. And in a moment he was awake, gasping, sobbing with relief in the hospital bed. Hurried footsteps sounded in the corridor outside and the light blazed on, hurting his eyes, to disclose two dark-skinned orderlies twittering in soft worried voices, their compassionate faces bent above him. Emil tried to smile and then realized that his left leg was throbbing and aching and afire with pain. '*Ma jambe*—my—my leg!'

'Ah!' The dark faces nodded understanding and one of the orderlies left the room quickly while the other rearranged the bedclothes, hissing softly, soothingly, as he eased Emil into a more comfortable position and wiped the sweat from his face with a cool damp cloth. Then his fellow was back with cotton wool, spirit and a gleaming syringe. A prick in the arm and a slow ebbing of the pain, followed by a warm drowsiness seeping up and up until Emil fell into another, and this time black and dreamless, sleep.

Next morning at ten o'clock Emerald knocked lightly on the door, called, 'It's me, Patience!' and came in. But instead of Mrs Singlefield she found herself looking at Emil. 'Sorry—' she said. 'Wrong room.' Then she saw the framework which held the bedclothes off his left leg and realized at once that this was the German upon whom her father had operated and whose leg he believed he had saved. He had explained, with prideful satisfaction and a wealth of gruesome technical detail, how he had done this, interrupting his story from time to time to animadvert upon the hypothetical errors and confusions into which his various colleagues in the service would have fallen. 'Dr Mackintosh would never have thought of *that*, of course . . . Old Frewing would just have slashed it off at the knee and gone back to the whisky bottle. The man would undoubtedly have died in the hands of Thomas or Swayne—the first would have asphyxiated him with the anaesthetic—the second would have killed him through sepsis or gangrene . . . I, upon the other hand—' Emerald had encouraged him since anything which took his mind off pangolins was to be desired.

Now she said, 'How are you?' And then, doubtfully, 'Can you speak English?'

From his pillow Emil regarded her with astonishment. He saw a girl of sixteen or seventeen, dressed in a green shirt and white shorts, slightly built, narrow-hipped, long-legged, still almost flat-chested—the sort of figure described commonly, though erroneously, as 'boyish,' since it has about it none of a boy's muscled solidity. But it was not her figure but her face that held his startled attention. She could not be English—not with such Asiatically high cheekbones, such long narrow eyes and wide everted lips. And the eyes, black as his own, were outlined in green and silver, the thick lips painted a dead pale pink against the warm olive of the rest of her face. No girl in Grévilly, and certainly none in present-day Germany, would have dared to appear in public like that. Not even in Paris . . . Perhaps on the *Canebière* in Marseille . . . Her fingernails were painted a nacreous mother-of-pearl, and glancing down at her toes he saw that they matched them. The effect was not—as it might have been with someone of more European cast of countenance—either ludicrous or pathetic; it was one of distinct depravity which was heightened rather than diminished by the slender, sexless-seeming body. Emil, extremely aware of his own unusual and slightly ambiguous looks, was fascinated at once.

'Well—*do* you?'

'How—? Oh—I am able to understand. Also I speak a little. I have learned the language, you comprehend, but I have not had practice.'

'That's very good! You *do* speak it.' The girl nodded approvingly. 'The Captain spoke it, too—your captain. I heard him.'

'So?' Emil turned his eyes away. He did not want to think, much less to speak, about anything to do with his recent experiences. He had pushed it all into some subterranean cellar in his mind and closed the trapdoor above it. His world was now only his bed in the soft green gloom of this shaded room, outside which birds called and chattered, and the little silent doctor and the kind, soft-voiced orderlies—he wanted nothing else.

'They've all gone—three days ago. They went up the coast to Dar-es-Salaam.'

Emil said nothing, turning his face away to the other wall. The girl must have understood, for she approached the bed and standing over him said, 'You don't want to talk about it? You're going to have to, though. As soon as you're well enough they're going to send someone to question you.'

'Why?'

'Why?—Because you're a prisoner, of course. Prisoners are always questioned—particularly if they're officers. You're an officer, are you not?'

'Yes.'

'What rank?'

'*Leutnant.*'

'Lieutenant—yes.' The girl was at the foot of the bed now, reading something that was hanging there. 'Emil Kummerol.'

'Kümmerol.'

'Born June the tenth, nineteen twenty-four. That makes you twenty.' She paused consideringly. 'I shouldn't have thought you were as much as that. Have you been in the Navy long?'

Angrily Emil said, 'You are not right to come here! The doctor will be enraged that you intrude. You forget that I am most gravely hurt.'

'You'll live,' Emerald replied with the sardonic, public-school brutality she copied from Tony Brickler, and Emil stared at her in shocked unbelief. He had been treated with proper consideration ever since he had been wounded, and by the medical orderlies with a gentle kindness which his small size and childish good looks immediately called forth from their too-sensitive and responsive natures. Now he said, his voice shaking, tears of anger, self-pity and frustration gleaming in his eyes, 'Go! Go this moment—or I will summon the attendant!'

But the girl merely grinned, standing at the foot of the bed in the green gloom, thrusting her hands into the pockets of her shorts. 'Do not enrage yourself—you will only shorten your life. I will go when I want to. And the orderlies certainly won't make me. I'm the doctor's daughter.'

'The doctor's daughter—you!' Emil's voice was unbelieving.

'Yes. Who did you think I was?'

Emil was furious and very weak, but he was not a Frenchman for nothing. He gave the figure at the end of the bed a long look and then raised his eyebrows. 'I was thinking what most people would think upon your appearance. But also I think that it is useless. I am too ill— also I have no money to pay you.'

The girl grinned again. 'Good. That was the idea. I don't mean for you. I came here to see someone else who usually has this room— a woman.'

'*Saint Esprit!*' Emil was genuinely startled. He had heard often enough that the English were degenerate—but he had not expected to be given such early and flagrant proof. 'And—and this other daughter of joy. Why—'

'Patience isn't a daughter of *joy* at all. She's the most woeful individual.'

'Patience—?'

'That's her name. I can't think why they called her that—unless it's because she's always exhausted. She comes in here periodically to get a good rest—*she* says. But most people say her husband sends her in so that *he* can have the rest.' Emerald glanced at her watch, a gold one which Patience had gone to much trouble and expense to give her on her last birthday. 'Well, I'd better go and find her, I suppose.'

At lunch that day she said to her father, 'I saw your leg case this morning. He was in the room Patience generally has.'

'Umm. This meat is terrible, Emerald—really terrible. It could not be worse if we were eating your wretched pangolin.'

Hurriedly Emerald said, 'He speaks English. He spoke it quite well. He thought I was a daughter of joy.'

'A *what?*'

'He meant a whore. I had my special Patience make-up on— naturally, as I was going to see her.'

Dr Zared gave up attempting to eat his lunch and laid down his knife and fork. 'I wish you wouldn't do these things, Emerald, I really do! When Patience Singlefield is in the hospital you visit her specially to upset her, and now when I have a most interesting case—a case in which any other doctor would almost certainly have amputated at once— When I have almost certainly saved a limb, I say, you have to go and upset *him*. I was wondering why his temperature had gone up at midday—now I know.'

'I didn't mean to upset him. I was just—'

'You didn't *mean* to pay Spencer five pounds for that pangolin, but—'

'Oh God—not *again!*'

'Now see here, Emerald . . .'

Five

Mr Shellybeare was both intelligent and good-natured and had consequently risen almost as slowly in the administrative department as Dr Zared had in the medical one. The Colonial Service was reasonably tolerant of eccentricities and would undoubtedly have forgiven either defect singly, but joined together in one man they were impossible to overlook. Mr Shellybeare, at fifty-two, was still only a District Commissioner and had little remaining chance of promotion. Being intelligent, he was naturally a disappointed man, but being good-natured, he did not blame his partner in marriage and thus add a miserable wife to his other misfortunes. He received a considerable amount of amusement from his work and, unlike so many of his kind, the fact that he was undisputed ruler of several thousand square miles of African territory did not lead him to imagine that he was also God's right-hand man. For Mr Shellybeare had early learned—and, much more important, accepted—two truths of which, for his own good, it would have been better to have remained unconscious. The first was the fact that there was no mystique at all in the business of colonial administration. Any underpaid, half-educated, adolescent Portuguese infantry lieutenant over the border could, and very often did, administer a territory quite as large as his own and do it just as successfully. It was all a simple matter of power; power displayed at first by rifles, machine-guns and the ability to drop bombs from the air—and later by the universal symbols of such power, a white or whitish face above a khaki or olive-drab drill uniform. And secondly he had accepted the fact of undying native hatred and contempt, disguised always behind smiles and flattery but waiting with endless African patience for the never-doubted day when he and his kind might be returned—more, or less, forcibly depending on their willingness to leave—to wherever it was they had come from in the first place.

He had tried to impress these ideas upon his subordinate, but had only partially succeeded since Tony Brickler, though he agreed readily enough that it was wrong for the Germans to be in Poland or the Italians in Greece, did not think it wrong for the British to be in Tanganyika or the Portuguese in Mozambique. Yet he pleased his superior by demonstrating, in his turn, two things which were quite as unconventional by Colonial Service standards as Mr Shellybeare's twin heresies. While most young colonial officers had spent the war years wringing their hands in well-simulated woe at not being able to join the fighting services and in receiving condolences, congratulations, and sometimes promotion on the merits of this somewhat ineffectual patriotism, Tony had refused to do this. To speak the truth—that he was extremely grateful to be under no necessity of risking his life and considered himself most fortunate to be where he was—would have been impossible, of course. The outrage such a statement would have caused might well have incurred his dismissal and return to England—and thus been entirely self-defeating. But when older colleagues and their wives offered gratuitous commiseration upon his presumably frustrated desire for military glory he shrugged his shoulders and changed the subject with a terseness which led them to believe that it was too painful to dwell upon.

And secondly it seemed, at least to Mr Shellybeare, that he would shortly marry Emerald—assuming she agreed. To marry someone

who had an Indian grandfather would be flouting the strongest
traditions of the service and would perhaps demand more resolution
than Tony possessed—that remained to be seen. Meanwhile the
District Commissioner encouraged his assistant in various roundabout
ways and fell out mildly with his wife over the matter. For Mrs
Shellybeare did not see Emerald Zared in quite the same light as her
husband. A tall, thin woman with a beaky nose and a hairstyle which
looked as if it had been fixed for ever with glue, she had a judicious and
formidable mind which often severely hindered the D.C. in his work.
Emerald amused them both and, like Mr Spencer, was a useful,
because almost endless, conversational topic. But when it came to
encouraging Tony Brickler to marry her Mrs Shellybeare felt that her
husband was mistaken.

'Firstly she is much cleverer than he. He does not realize that yet,
but when he does he will not easily forgive her.'

'Oh, come! I forgave you, after all.'

'You are not Tony. You lacked male vanity. Tony has at least his
full share, if not more. He needs the sort of wife who will be his equal
most of the time but in the last resort look to him as the senior partner.
Emerald will never do that. I think—' Mrs Shellybeare had paused to
fit a cigarette carefully into her holder—'I think that even now she
despises him a little. Oh, she wants to marry him—I've no doubt about
that. She knows well enough how difficult it is for someone like her
to get a satisfactory husband. And of course old Zared would push her
into it even if she *didn't* want to. No, it's Tony I'm thinking of.'

Mr Shellybeare had laughed. 'And I of Emerald, you imply? That's
true up to a point. You see, my dear, an injustice was done—perhaps
it would be best to say a tragedy occurred—nearly ninety years ago
when Emerald's great-grandfather was killed in the Mutiny. Zared
showed me a picture of him once—a miniature. He was very young,
twenty-six, when he was killed and the picture showed him in John
Company uniform. He looked not unlike Tony except that he had
whiskers and no glasses and Tony has glasses but no whiskers. Had he
lived I suppose his daughters would have gone home and married
Englishmen of their own class. As it was—well, you know what
happened. But by marrying Tony Emerald could, as it were, put the
matter right at last.'

Mrs Shellybeare had coloured a little. 'I never heard such romantic
rubbish! What can it possibly matter to Emerald's great-grandfather
what she does! The fact is that Tony ought to wait at any rate until
the war's over and he can go home on leave and meet some

other girls. He'd easily find one who would suit him much better.'

'Why wouldn't Emerald suit him just as well?'

'I've told you. She despises him. Sometimes I think it is because he has not been in the war.'

'Good God!' Mr Shellybeare had stared across the coffee table at his wife with genuine shock. 'Surely you don't see Emerald as some frightful nineteen-fifteen "flapper"—handing out white feathers at London street corners? As far as I can see, most young people today —really young, that is—don't care a damn about the war. It bores them. It's only the over-twenty-fives—perhaps the over-thirties—who take it seriously. And that's largely because their age allows them to have more say in it—to get something out of it. Like that fellow Barra-gold. They are the ones who give the orders and it's the young who have to obey. But since the nineteen-twenties the young have got out of the habit of obeying—or, at any rate, of pretending to like it. What they are interested in is staying in one piece until the fighting's over and then leading their own lives in their own way. In fact it is just that attitude on their part which gives me some hope for a more civilized future.'

Mrs Shellybeare had listened patiently. Now she said, 'That is not what I meant. War—except from the very back rows—is the only male preserve left intact today. And since it is the only one it intrigues many women.'

'Horrible thought!'

'I mean that it is an experience they cannot share and therefore exaggerate and are curious about—as some men exaggerate and are curious about childbirth. Emerald has seen and done—or could see and do—everything that Tony has seen and done. For that reason he holds no real interest for her. She likes him up to a point but she is more interested in Mr Spencer.'

'We are all interested in Spencer. You feel that she should marry *him*?'

'I'm not joking, Geoffrey. No, of course she shouldn't—and won't. But she would probably make him less unhappy than she will make Tony. Emerald is excellent with animals, and since the English believe that to acquire the devotion of animals is a sign of sanctity she gets much praise for it. But she is somewhat different with human beings. Look at the way she treats Patience Singlefield.'

The District Commissioner sighed. 'Poor Patience!'

'You ought to get them posted somewhere else, Geoffrey—you really ought.'

'How can I? It would mean giving Singlefield a bad report—by inference at least. And he's a good officer.'

'You could write confidentially to the Chief Secretary.'

Mr Shellybeare gave an exasperated groan. 'There are some things a woman—even one of your intelligence, my dear—never seems to understand. If I wrote confidentially to the Chief Secretary it would be worse than giving Singlefield a bad report—and he'd probably think I was crazy into the bargain. And *don't*, please, suggest that I have a confidential chat with Singlefield himself, either.'

'You could.'

'I could *not*. He'd probably shoot me.'

'Then get rid of the Zareds.'

'Out of the question.'

'Not at all! Old Zared's always fighting with his D.C.s. He's been shifted for it several times before. You wouldn't be doing anything unusual.'

'What about Emerald? She's happy here. She's got her zoo and her friends—Tony and Spencer. She's been pushed around too much already.'

'Emerald—' Mrs Shellybeare had said, ejecting her cigarette and rising to go into the garden—'is a menace.'

Six

Emerald's attitude to her animals was largely the result of an upbringing which had been, as far as Dr Zared could manage it, along English lines, and it included all that patronage, that projection and rejection which in Britain make up the cosy cults of pony-worship, dog-devotion and pussy-love. Since Emerald lived in Africa the animals were of more exotic species but this made no difference to that formidable national idiosyncrasy of seeing all creatures as immature human beings and endowing them with rudimentary human feelings. The hopeless confusion and irrelevance of this idea was perhaps more excusable in Emerald than in her northern contemporaries since many of her pets were monkeys which, in their repulsive actions and impetuous instincts, often seemed to mirror aspects of modern humanity.

Like the majority of young animal lovers, Emerald had no taste for literature unless it concerned her hobby, and despite the fact that she was seventeen and a half her favourite reading remained the small, beautifully illustrated and precisely written works of Beatrix Potter. On the day after her first encounter with Emil at the hospital she sent him four of these books by the hand of her father.

Emil had recovered just enough strength to read, and the books gave him the greatest pleasure; their simple and elegant English made them easily understandable without effort and their stories took him far away from the terror of the last months—far back to his childhood in Grévilly when, indulged and petted by the aunts, he, too, had kept at various times mice, a hedgehog and a pair of rabbits. He lay flat on his back, his round face grave, his dark eyes moving slowly over the print and then sliding to the shiny watercolours on the adjacent pages . . . *Opposite him—as far away as he could sit—was an enormous rat. 'What do you mean by tumbling into my bed all covered in smuts?' said the rat, chattering its teeth* . . . Soft footsteps outside and the door opening. Absorbed in *The Tale of Samuel Whiskers*, Emil did not look up— the orderlies often came in to adjust the blinds or the overhead fan . . . *'Please, sir, the chimney wants sweeping,' said poor Tom Kitten. 'Anna Maria! Anna Maria!' squealed the rat. There was a pattering noise that—*

'Herr Leutnant!' Kalewski was in the room, leaning back against the door, supporting himself partly upon a rubber-shod walking stick. He wore the loose white hospital pyjamas and one of his ankles was heavily encased in plaster.

'Vanya!' Emil stared up with the old mixture of fear and distrust and, as of old, masked it with a tone of assumed cordiality. '*Was machen Sie hier?*'

'We must speak quietly. I am not supposed to be here.' Kalewski's voice was low but quick. 'There is no one about at present but at any moment one of the orderlies might come back. We are not supposed to see each other until we have been questioned. They had been waiting for you to recover sufficient strength. Tomorrow or the next day an officer comes from Dar-es-Salaam.'

'So? But there is nothing to tell him. They have the Kommandant and the Chief Engineer. They know what happened to us.'

'There is one thing you have to know.' Kalewski shifted his weight uncomfortably against the door. 'You remember that you were officially in charge of all secret documents?'

'Oh God! And so they were not jettisoned in time? Well—that is something which cannot now be—'

'They were jettisoned in time. I collected them and put them in the weighted bag and sent them up to the Kommandant by Hessel. The Kommandant threw them overboard himself.'

'Well, then—'?

'There was one thing—' Kalewski seemed to be speaking with difficulty—'that I refrained from doing. I am not an officer. I was not sure what the Kommandant was really attempting, you understand. I was not officially informed. Perhaps it was thought I would object . . .'

Kalewski stared for a moment at the small books, lying disregarded now on the sheet beside Emil's hands. Then he grinned widely, humourlessly. 'The war is over for us—and soon it will be over for everyone else. Because of that I will speak frankly with you, Monsieur Emil Kümmerol, and you will speak frankly with me. You and Kielbasa were going to surrender, were you not?'

Expressionlessly Emil said, 'The Kommandant had decided to enter neutral waters and scuttle the boat. He had every justification for doing so—you know that perfectly well.'

'No, no—I mean before we were damaged.'

'What makes you think that?'

'It was reasonably obvious—to some of us. It was obvious that you and he were interested only in saving your own lives. Had you not known the consequences for your families you would probably have surrendered at the first opportunity—and by putting an undamaged submarine into enemy hands you would have hoped for special treatment. Kielbasa had his Brazilian relations—Oh yes, I know about that —and you, now that Germany was dying, considered yourself French.'

'You assume a great deal.' Emil's voice was cold. 'It will not do you much good now though, will it?'

Kalewski shrugged. 'What I am saying is this. You knew I felt differently than you and so I was not informed about the attempt to scuttle in neutral waters. I thought that the Kommandant might have made a rendezvous with another of our boats. In which case he would have told none but the officers, of course.'

'Well—so?'

'I sent Hessel up with the codes and ciphers and the maps—but not the log book.'

'The log book *is* a confidential document. It should be—'

'It is irreplaceable. If we had been going to meet another boat—'

'You mean the British have got it?' Uncomfortably Emil felt a slowly dawning realization of what this half-whispered conversation might be leading up to.

'No, I don't think so. Not yet. I did not destroy it, but I hid it. I pushed it down behind the tip-up washbasin in Kielbasa's cabin. If they tow the boat to Dar-es-Salaam and take her apart they will find it. Of course they may not do that. But if they do—*if* they do . . . It might be unpleasant.'

Looking down at his hands, Emil said slowly, 'The first ship—the French one ?'

'Yes.'

'Sunk with all hands. I wrote that myself. I put also—"A short search for survivors was made. None was found." And you will remember Kielbasa informing the crew that the sinking was never to be mentioned in any eventuality. But they will only question the officers and under-officers. It is most unlikely that they will question the crew.'

'When we are questioned, tomorrow or the next day—'

'Vanya, you know the orders. Name, rank and service number. They cannot demand more.'

Kalewski grinned again. 'Perhaps—perhaps not. You are very like Kielbasa. You think that the rules of war are there to be obeyed—and are obeyed—except in cases of—of operational necessity. Listen. We sank one ship—that tanker. We blew her up. One ship—one ship *only*.'

'And later—if they find the log ?'

Kalewski shrugged. 'It would be necessary to admit to two, I suppose. Remember that we are quite entitled, once we have given our names, ranks and service numbers, to lie as much as we like. But probably they will not find the log. That is all that I came to tell you. Now I must go.'

'Yes. Well—we will meet again, Vanya.'

'Perhaps.' Kalewski gently opened the door, peered through, and then with a quick nod left the room. Emil heard the soft thud of his rubber-shod stick fading down the length of the corridor. Then he picked up the book he had been reading. '*There was a pattering noise and an old woman rat poked her head round a rafter. All in a minute she rushed at Tom Kitten and before he knew what was happening . . .*' But it was no good. That small, secret world of kittens in the chimney and rats behind the wainscot, of the innocence and simplicity of a childhood only ten years away, could not again be recalled. For the moment, at any rate, Kalewski had effectually destroyed it, his bleak presence a grim reminder that between past childhood and the present day lay the terror of a submarine shattered by depth charges and plunging to the sea bed, the stifling fear of those tombed hours on the bottom, the shattered hopes of freedom as the planes dived and roared above the loom of Cape Delgado . . .

Emil had had his brief hour of twilit tranquillity under the drugs and later the calm soporific of exhaustion. Now, or very soon, he must take up again the burden of his nationality and military rank. Wearily, angrily, he shifted his head on the pillow and pushed the books aside; and for the first time since he had lost consciousness in Wutsdorf's arms the scared questions formed in his mind: *What will they do to me? What is going to happen next?*

Seven

Two days later Emerald and Mr Spencer came to the hospital. Emerald carried a closed basket containing the rolled-up pangolin and four more copies of the works of Beatrix Potter. Mr Spencer, less exotically, carried a cloth containing a dozen mangoes and a bunch of zinnias. He looked mildly disapproving. 'The fact, dear Emerald—' he was saying—'that he told you to your face that he considered you a harlot does not seem to be a good reason for revisiting him.'

'You are quoting him out of context,' Emerald replied, using a favourite phrase of her father's: neither she nor Mr Spencer were quite sure what it meant. 'I annoyed him in error, you see.'

'How?'

'I told him that he would live.'

'But—does he want to die?'

'No, I don't suppose so.'

'Then I do *not* understand.'

'It's a remark of Tony's. It's difficult to explain. Anyway his temperature went up and my father was angry. I didn't mean to annoy him. So I want to show him that I bear no hard feelings, as it were. And in a way, it's rather complimentary to be called a harlot—at my age, I mean. Don't you think so?'

'No.'

'Oh, yes—in a way.'

Emerald led the way into Emil's room with a carefully assumed air of cheerful ease—as if she was visiting a friend she had known for some time rather than a foreigner whom she had offended once. But inwardly she was timid and uncertain, urged on by a curious, inquisitive fascination which demanded that she should discover more and still more about this peculiar and hitherto unknown species of mankind called 'the enemy.'

The war was something which had gone on for an immensely long time. It had begun æons ago, in her childhood, and was not finished yet; an unreal background to all her adolescence composed of B.B.C. news bulletins and reasons for not having certain things and not being able to do others. It was entirely remote, taking place in out-of-the-way spots on the globe of which otherwise she would never have heard and which could only very rarely be located in her school atlas. Dunkirk—for which she had searched in Scotland—Mindanao, Giarabub, Pantelleria, Orel, Kohima, Midway, Stalingrad—which was spelled 'Tsaritsyn'—all over the place, in fact, but always infinitely remote in space and, oddly, in time too, for she read about it with the same detached indifference as she read about the partition of Gaul or Waterloo. And suddenly, here in the old brick hospital at Masondi with its wide verandas and cool tiled corridors, was someone who actually took part in it—and on the wrong side, too. She could hardly have been more interested if a Roman centurion or an ensign of the Old Guard had been lying here. It was really her excited interest at actually seeing a *German* at first hand which had caused her to bungle her first visit. Now she wished to retrieve her failure.

In this she was entirely successful. Emil was both much stronger and in a much better frame of mind than he had been four days ago. His leg still hurt, a continuous dull ache, but he was becoming accustomed to it and Dr Zared assured him that it would decrease and did not consider that another operation would be necessary—at least for some time to come. And yesterday the British naval interrogator had come and gone. He had been a middle-aged commander of the reserve, a fat jovial man who spoke excellent German and who had used no hint of pressure but, on the contrary, had kept reminding Emil that he need not answer any questions he did not wish to. The conversation had been largely and gratifyingly about Emil—his home, his aunts, his schooldays in Grévilly. The Commander had appeared much more interested in all these things than in more recent events and he had listened sympathetically to Emil's disquisition on the difficulties of his nationality. 'But still, you'll be able to change all that soon—won't you?'

'Become naturalized? Well, I've always wanted to. But after being an officer in the *Kriegsmarine* . . .'

'Yes, yes. But you could not help that. And you haven't done the French any harm, after all. Tell me more about your friend Kielbasa; you say it was his first command cruise?'

Under the influence of the Englishman's sympathetic interest Emil had talked for nearly an hour and had, though he did not know this, built up an interesting and valuable picture of the personnel and morale of the U-boat service in the last months of the war while flattering himself that he had given away no technical secrets. They parted on terms of mutual content. The Commander had got exactly what he wanted and Emil felt very much happier about the future than at any time since he had become a prisoner of the British. He never had been taught, since the German authorities had never properly discovered, that the early psychological effects of falling into enemy hands are such as to make sympathy and kindness far more deadly weapons in the armoury of a skilled interrogator than either threats or physical pressure.

Thus he greeted the doctor's peculiar daughter and her friend with pleasure and a slightly shy amusement. This was the girl whom he had failed to insult by calling her a whore. But who on earth was the friend? This man with the kindly—'noble' was the only word for such Greek perfection of feature—face and the English which even to Emil's ears sounded odd—who could he be? Not her brother—far too old. Her lover, then? But if so why did she call him 'Mister' Spencer?

Emerald, for her part, was relieved and delighted that her reception was so cordial. She had not expected this and in order to disguise her pleasure she shook the pangolin out of its basket on to the bed, a tight scaly ball. 'I brought this to show you.'

'But—but what is it?' Emil eyed the reptilian little creature with doubt and a certain repulsion. He touched it; the scales were hard and curiously cool.

'It's a Malayan scaly ant-eater. The only one, probably, in Africa. It was brought from Malaya for my zoo,' said Emerald grandly.

'Oh—a sort of *hérisson*. I do not know the English word—this.' Emil pointed to the illustrated cover of *The Tale of Mrs Tiggy-winkle*.

'Hedgehog. Yes—in a way.'

'They also close up in this manner. I possessed a *hérisson* when I was ten years. It was called Sigismund and it would—would elongate only for me. For all others it would be like this. It consumed bread with milk—also insects.'

Emerald was delighted—as delighted as if her two martially named monkeys had suddenly developed the powers of speech and begun cursing each other in military language. Here was a member of that remote but vaguely threatening species 'the enemy'—someone who owed dark allegiance to a despot almost wholly evil and probably mad —who had kept a pet hedgehog called Sigismund and fed it on bread and milk. 'When you are better you must come and see the rest of my zoo. Mr Spencer is my chief collector. He finds things for it—don't you?'

Mr Spencer nodded gravely. 'Emerald's zoo is our main attraction here, I think. Certainly you must not miss seeing it. How is your leg?'

'It is better. I think the doctor is content. It does not cause me too much pain.'

'Excellent! Then you will probably be walking in a few weeks. When that happens you must come for a trip in my—'

'In his boat,' Emerald interrupted quickly. 'Mr Spencer has a very nice launch. We often go out in it. But perhaps you've had enough of the sea to last you for a long time?'

Emil glanced from one to the other. This man had a motor-boat— the submarine lay partly submerged on a reef at the harbour mouth; the log was jammed behind a tip-up basin—and he himself was completely immobilized in bed. He swallowed and tried to smile. 'I would like that,' he said carefully. 'There remain possessions of my own in the *sous-marin* which I desire to regain—clothes and some books.' He dropped his eyes to the still tightly rolled pangolin and waited with breath held to see if his hint was taken up. It was. Emerald said at once, 'Oh, that's easy. We'll go and get them for you. Tell us where—'

But Mr Spencer broke in. 'I am afraid not, Emerald. The U-boat is most strictly outside permitted limits. Tony told me two days ago. No one is to go near it. It is military property. Also—or so he says— it is dangerous. It is not secure on the reef and it could slide off into deep water and sink at any time.' He smiled at Emil. 'But never mind. We will supply you with books—and with clothes, too, when you are allowed up.'

Emil nodded and thanked them with an effort, telling himself that it was not really important and that there was still every possibility that the submarine might sink. Under the control-room, down on the bottom plating of the pressure hull, lay two demolition bombs actuated by depth charge detonators. In case of scuttling or abandoning ship it was only necessary to unscrew the protective caps of these and the boat would automatically be blown apart as soon as it reached a depth of twenty metres. This device was to prevent the enemy from salvaging a boat which was sunk or forced to scuttle in comparatively shallow water; but whether or not those caps had been removed before the sea-water entered the batteries and forced the immediate evacuation of the entire crew was something which Emil did not know.

Emerald said suddenly, 'I saw a most extraordinary man in the corridor just now. I think he had a broken ankle. He really was like—like nothing I have ever seen before.'

Emil smiled widely, 'No—I expect. That is one of our under-officers—Kalewski.'

'He is—is much more like a German—like I thought a German looked—than you.'

Mr Spencer coughed delicately. Emerald was often too outspoken for his taste; but then today so many young people were.

Emil said, 'Nevertheless he is not a German. And I, too, am not one.'

'But—'

'Kalewski is an Estonian and lived in Danzig. I am a Frenchman, *plus ou moins*, and live near Besançon.'

Emerald was incredulous. 'But why on earth are you both in the German Navy, then?'

'*Force majeure.* There is a Russian corps under a Russian general fighting with the German armies against Russia. I have heard also that there are many Indian soldiers fighting with the *Japonais* against the British. The *Finnois* commenced in the war allies of England, but then became instead allies of Germany. The *Italiens* commenced as allies of Germany—now they are allies of England.' He smiled sourly and shrugged his shoulders. 'That is the war.'

Mr Spencer sighed gently, 'Yes, yes. This war is a great mix-up. The radio news makes it sound so simple—but it is very far indeed from being simple. Here we have only the radio news. I often think—'

But the door opened and Dr Zared came briskly in. He glanced with irritation at his daughter and Mr Spencer. 'I have not given permission for this patient to receive visits. He is still far from strong enough. Emerald—who said you could visit him? I told you that—And, good God—what's that on his bed! No, Emerald—this is going too far! Your zoo is one thing and my hospital is another. I will not allow you to bring animals in here—especially that creature. And Spencer, really I must ask you not to encourage my daughter to behave as if—'

'All right, all right, all *right*!' Emerald picked up the hard ball of the pangolin and put it back in its basket. 'We'll go now. I only brought some more books because you said—'

But her father was hustling both her and Mr Spencer from the room.

'Now get along, Emerald, do! I've got to examine him and I'm extremely busy. And—oh, yes—Patience Singlefield has been asking when you are going to visit her.'

Emerald, glancing over her shoulder at Emil, saw that he was smiling at her amusedly and smiled back. Then the door shut firmly behind her.

Eight

For the rest of that morning Emerald dealt with the various chores incumbent upon even the most feckless zoologist. She cleaned the parrot cages, fed the monkeys, scrubbed the shells of the two giant tortoises which lived in the small birds' aviary and thus became quickly fouled, and then took her leopard Rose for a walk on its lead. Secretly she was very frightened of Rose, and though Mr Gopal said that people in India sometimes tamed leopards with considerable success when, as in the present case, they had been acquired as small cubs, she was always relieved when Rose was back in her strong cage with the door bolted. None the less, she liked to be seen out with Rose and to be, she hoped, admired for her enterprise and courage—for after all if Rose ever did turn bad, as Mr Spencer put it, it would be all up with whoever was holding the end of her lead.

Today as she walked past the hospital she wished she could take Rose in and display her to Emil. She already thought of him as 'Emil,' and had thought about him almost to the exclusion of all else since her first visit. Until today she had believed with some justification, that her interest in him centred around the fact that he was a German—an enemy national. There were still a few Germans in Tanganyika, but in the main they were elderly, kept themselves to themselves, were anti-Nazi, or said they were, and did not count as 'enemy.' The ones Emerald had occasionally met were dull and apt to be morose. But this little naval officer was quite different—and not surprisingly, perhaps, since he had turned out to be French. She saw continually that round dark face, that peculiar, rather ugly, smile, the quick movements of his hands when he spoke and the way in which he added nuances to his speech by changing the tone of his oddly inflected English. Emerald herself possessed much natural charm but she had been brought up among people whose instincts and training led them to suspect this attribute rather than to admire it, and to frown severely upon any conscious attempt to exploit it. In Emil she had encountered someone who had been reared in a completely opposed tradition. It was not surprising that she was fascinated.

In the end she took Rose to the Singlefields' house. Patience was sitting on the loggia under the purple shade of a heavy-foliaged bougainvillæa which exaggerated her high colour until she looked apoplectic. A heavily built woman in the early thirties, she had the jowls and sad, drooping eyes of a bloodhound, and suffered from a variety of complaints most of which had a nervous origin.

'Dear Emerald! I haven't seen you for days. And sweet, sweet Rosa! Come and shake a paw, Rosa! Come here and kiss me!'

But the leopard merely shook its head irritably and sniffed the ground near one of the white stucco pillars. 'What's wrong with her? Isn't she well?'

Emerald said, 'Her ears itch. I think it's canker. I've brought some Bob Martin's powder and I thought we might try it.'

Patience was the only person in Masondi who had no fear at all of Rose and it was this which formed, for Emerald, her main reason for visiting the police officer's wife. When it was necessary to give Rose a dose of medicine, to remove a tenacious bush-tick from her neck or to wash out an inflamed eye, Patience was an ever-ready assistant, holding the leopard, talking to her, soothing her or even, when Emerald's nerve failed, carrying out the operation herself. Now they both sat down beside Rose and cajoled her into letting them pour a little anti-canker powder into her right ear. It was not easy. Rose's ears were exceptionally delicate; they twitched angrily every time they were touched and before the second one was properly doctored the leopard was giving out low warning rumbles from deep within her throat, her tail flicking from side to side in growing exasperation. Pale-faced and sweating, Emerald said, 'Well—we'd better not do any more. She doesn't like it.' But Patience insisted.

'Rosa—you just stay still! Rosa, you bad girl—don't you dare growl at us! Go on, Emerald, pour it in—I've got her.'

With shaking hands Emerald obeyed and the leopard, giving a sudden roar, flexed its steel muscles and, bursting from Patience's grasp, rushed out on to the lawn shaking its head from side to side.

'Well,' said Patience equably, 'we did it, didn't we? Now tell me why I haven't seen you for such ages?'

'Busy. Work. And trouble at home.'

'Not the pangolin *still*?'

'Still.'

'Oh God! Really, it's too much. Look, if you gave him back his five pounds would he shut up about it, do you think?'

'No.' Emerald shook her head decidedly. 'It's the *principle of the thing* now. I told him I'd give him back his money if he wanted it. I said I'd earn it. If necessary I'd open a personal one-girl brothel beside the zoo.'

'Emerald!'

'Well, I'd recently been mistaken for a whore, you see. So naturally—'

'Who mistook you for one?' Patience flushed until under the shade of the purple leaves her face looked like a ripe plum. Her eyes were narrow points of anger. She was deeply, passionately in love with Emerald and would never tolerate the slightest criticism of her from anyone.

'No one you know,' said Emerald uneasily. 'Anyway, it was my fault.'

'Who? Who said it? Go on—tell me!'

'Don't take on about it, for God's sake. What happened was I went into your usual room in the hospital and found one of these Germans there. He was annoyed by something I said and threatened to call an orderly and have me turned out.'

'Have *you* turned *out*!'

'I said I was the doctor's daughter. He said, in so many words, that he had thought I was a local strumpet looking for custom.'

'My God! The filthy Hun! What incredible insolence. What did you do?'

'Just laughed.'

For a moment Patience looked taken aback. Then, angrily, she laughed too, and stroked Emerald's bare arm with fingers that shook slightly. 'How clever you are, Emerald! Of course that was the best possible retort, really. I'd never have thought of it myself. You've always been a clever little thing, though. I bet he—the German, I mean —felt a fool.'

Emerald said, 'I don't know. He's friendly enough now. I and Spencer visited him this morning and he was very friendly. I think it's because he's feeling better, probably.'

'Why on earth did you visit him a second time?'

'To show him the pangolin.'

Patience moved abruptly, glanced down at Emerald's face which held an amused smile of reminiscence and began to say 'I don't imagine that . . .' But Emerald, watching a recovered Rose rolling and stretching happily on the lawn, said, 'He turned out to be a Frenchman, not a German, even though he has a German name. I suppose he's a sort of mixture. Next time I see him I'll find out. I'll tell him about my Indian grandfather so that he shan't feel I'm being critical.'

'You ought to be careful. You don't want people to say you're fraternizing with the enemy. In fact, I'm not sure there isn't a rule against it. I'd better ask Clive when he comes in, perhaps.' There was an odd tone in the older woman's voice, a carefully modulated and controlled anger which made Emerald glance up quickly. 'Don't be silly. If I want to visit someone in my father's hospital I've got a perfect right to.'

'Not necessarily, my dear, I assure you. For instance, if Clive had a criminal from the prison in there you couldn't visit him.'

'I shouldn't want to—unless it was Spencer.'

'No one's talking about Spencer—don't be idiotic! If he's ever caught smuggling—and I'm sure he won't be, he's far too acute— Clive would only warn him to be more careful in future. No— But a prisoner of war is in the same position as a criminal. He's not a free person. You can't just go and see him whenever you like.'

'Hi!'—said Emerald angrily in her turn—'You Patience Singlefield! Just stop telling me what I can't do!'

'There's no reason to speak nigger-fashion, dear. Just because you're angry.' Patience's voice shook; she was near to tears and bitterly aware of it. Emerald was obviously going to make a friend of this creature in the hospital—just as she had made a friend of the impossible Spencer —and she would waste her time with him just as she did with Spencer—time when they could have been together as they were now.

Patience had been the first person in Masondi to take up Emerald on the Zareds' arrival twenty months ago. She wanted to keep Emerald for herself and had deeply resented it when Emerald, after some months, had begun to see as much, and later more, of other people. It was she who had helped Emerald establish her zoo, in the face of considerable opposition from Dr Zared. She had induced her husband to bring back animals for it from his tours of the interior and had herself bought several specimens, including two bush-babies, from natives as gifts for her young friend. For months they had got on splendidly and had drawn ever closer together, or so it had seemed. Then Spencer had started to take an interest in the zoo, or more

probably in its owner. Spencer—who had insulted the Bishop at the
D.C.'s garden party in 1942. Spencer—who had to be completely
ostracized for fear of mention being made of his wretched motor-
boat of which he was so proud. Spencer *sold* animals to Emerald whereas she, Patience, *gave* them. The only answer was illness and Patience
had entered Dr Zared's hospital with mild nervous prostration. But
Emerald had not come up to expectation even then. There was little
consternation, less sympathy, no loving visits. Though Patience did
not realize this, Emerald had no nerves herself and could not understand neurosis in others. By the time Patience had emerged Tony
Brickler was taking up Emerald—obviously for dishonourable
reasons. They played tennis continually. Then Emerald told Patience
that once she had suggested that they should play a set completely
naked under the full moon.

'But how on *earth* could you suggest such a thing, Emerald! How
could you!'

'I thought it would be fun. Tony refused, though—even though I
said that if he wouldn't I should not play with him again.'

But even Emerald's attitude to sex, which was both perverted and
prurient, could not destroy her vivid attraction for Patience but somehow seemed to heighten it. Looking at her peculiar, beautiful face, her
small breasts with the points of their nipples just discernible under her
heavy raw silk shirts, her long bare legs below the brief white shorts,
Patience would think yearningly and greedily, 'Oh, if only I were a
man! If I were a man I would . . .' And her nerves became worse than
ever.

Now she said casually, 'This—this German or French-German or
whatever he is—what's he like? To look at, I mean.'

'Well, I haven't seen all of him because he's in bed and one of his
legs is in plaster up to the hip. He's small and dark—as dark as me. I
always thought they were huge and blond. And—' Emerald's voice
suddenly changed—'my God, they've got something else there, too!
A petty officer. An Estonian or something. I've never seen such yellow
hair or such a face! He looks like a—sort of white Mongolian. I wish
I was a nurse—then I'd be able to have a real look at him. I bet he's
got a—a motor-launch like a—'

'Emerald!' Patience broke into shocked laughter. 'You know I
won't hear a word said against you, but—'

'Who's been saying words against me, anyhow?'

'No one. I mean I wouldn't let anybody.'

'I couldn't care less if they did.'

'But—' Patience persisted—'you do sometimes seem to have the—the mentality of a whore, if it's not being offensive to say so.'

Emerald, sitting back on her heels, glanced up, her heavy lips parted in a slight smile. 'Damn your impertinence,' she said gently. 'What the fucking hell do *you* know about motor launches, anyway?'

Nine

Four days later the plaster cast was removed from Kalewski's ankle and the same night he and Wutsdorf escaped from the unguarded hospital. 'Escape' was hardly the right word since they merely walked out—Wutsdorf half an hour after Kalewski—into the black dark of a moonless night. Kalewski had planned the escape for himself only and had talked it over with Wutsdorf as they lay in the small ward from which the other, more lightly wounded prisoners had now departed. But Wutsdorf, whose bullet-smashed shoulder was healing more slowly than he had hoped, insisted on coming, too. 'If I don't come with you, Vanya, I'll never get away. Once you've gone they'll put a proper guard on the place.'

Kalewski had shaken his head. 'You're not ready. Your shoulder is not even half healed.'

'Well, your ankle can't be—'

'I can walk on it. And as soon as they know that I'll be off to the cages—in a day or two at most. After all, they gave me these today.' Kalewski had pointed to the khaki drill shirt and shorts marked with big black cloth diamonds which hung on the end of his bed. 'You've only got pyjamas still.'

Wutsdorf had shaken his head. 'I'm coming, though,' he had repeated stubbornly. 'After all, if you find a truck—'

'That is a large "if." I'm not counting on it at all. I'd rather have a horse if I can find one, and keep in the bush away from roads and tracks. And you can't ride.'

'I can try.' Wutsdorf had levered himself into a sitting position. 'Vanya, don't leave me with *monsieur*. I don't want to go into the cages. And—and they might find out—about the French ship.'

Kalewski had stared at him for a long moment. Then he had sighed abruptly. 'Yes—yes I would take you if I could, if only because of that. But I'd have a better chance by myself.'

'I suppose so.' Wutsdorf's voice was miserable. 'But, even if you did—'

'And you haven't got any clothes. And you can't even drive a truck.' Kalewski had been speaking slowly as if trying to form a decision behind his words. Suddenly he said, 'Look—if I find a vehicle quickly you can come. Only like that—understand? If I find a truck or something before I've gone too far I'll come back and get you. Then we'll at least get close enough to the border to do the rest on foot. But you are not in a condition to do it any other way.'

'In two or three more days—'

'I'm not waiting two or three more days. I've got to go tonight— well?'

Wutsdorf had shrugged his uninjured shoulder. 'All right.'

'Good. And do not try to follow me. You would get lost. I've been outside, remember, and you haven't. If I'm not back in an hour—well, that means I haven't found anything close enough. And I can't spend too much time looking. I'll have to get as far as possible away from this place before dawn.'

And that night, as soon as the orderly had done his last rounds and turned off the lights in the small ward Kalewski had risen silently, and taken his shirt and shorts from the rail at the end of the bed. He had already carefully cut most of the stitches of the black cloth diamonds and with two or three quick rips he had the P.O.W. insignia off and thrust it under his mattress. He dressed and, lacing the rubber-soled army gym shoes, wished that they had given him proper boots or something which would lend more support to his bandaged and swollen ankle. But he was quite prepared to make do with what he had. To walk without the plaster cast and its iron stirrup was painful and he guessed that before long it would become very much more so— but then physical pain was something that he had never given much thought to. He had no money, no weapon and no food—nothing at all, in fact, save a bottle which he had filled with water that afternoon in the washroom, and even this lacked a cork and was stopped with a screw of paper. But the Mozambique border was barely forty-five miles away and Kalewski was possessed by an iron determination to get there even if he had to do the last part of the journey on his hands and knees.

Turning in the darkness, he limped to Wutsdorf's bed. 'Hansi, I'm going now. If anyone should come in, say I'm in the washroom. I'll be back within one hour for you—or not at all.' He felt for Wutsdorf's hand and heard his voice in the all-enveloping dark, strained and urgent. 'Try to get something, Vanya. Try to find a truck quickly! I'll be waiting . . .'

'Of course. Right—now I'm going.'

Wutsdorf heard the faint uneven shuffle as his friend crossed the tiled floor, the soft opening and closing of the door—then silence. In the hot blackness he lay motionless and sweating on his bed, his mind racked between hope and belief, doubt and despair. Vanya Kalewski had always been his friend, but he was not a German—and not even a proper European for he had told Wutsdorf that his maternal grand-father had come from Tashkent. He was only German by a sort of doubtful adoption and by his own hitherto unquestioning acceptance of his position and duties as a German national. Could one rely on such a man in the same way that one could rely on a fellow German? Wutsdorf doubted it, though without doubting Kalewski's good intentions. But instincts in the less civilized eastern nations, like the innate self-seeking hypocrisy of the decadent western ones, over-rode good intentions. Wutsdorf believed firmly and with the un-shakable complacency of the true German that only his own country-men could ever be trusted to keep their word. Kalewski might well find an unguarded vehicle; it should not be difficult in this sleepy tropical township far from the war. But would he then think of his friend and comrade lying waiting for him here in the dark? Or would he think only of his own escape and that by coming back to the hospital he might prejudice it? Wutsdorf turned his head wearily from side to side on the sweat-dampened pillow. He had no watch. How long was it since Kalewski had gone? Half an hour? Or ten minutes? He could not tell.

He should have insisted on going with him. He should have agreed to return alone to the hospital if a vehicle was not found—but he should not have trusted Vanya alone . . . And his presence beside his friend would have acted as a spur, an added inducement to find an unguarded truck. He had been a fool—he should have *insisted*. Had an hour gone yet? It seemed like two. Faintly he heard the sound of an automobile engine in the distance and his heart leapt, his breath caught and was held. The engine noise approached and then lowered and softened to the rhythmical throb of a motor idling in a stationary vehicle. Wutsdorf guessed that it could not be more than a hundred metres away. Was it Kalewski? Was he, at this moment, limping through the dark towards the hospital? If so, it would be best to be ready. Wutsdorf pulled himself into a sitting position and strained his

ears to catch the sound of uneven, rubber-soled footsteps. Nothing . . .
yet. He must be ready to move at once; there would be no time to
lose. Carefully he got out of bed; a stab of pain shot through his
shoulder but he disregarded it and, groping his way slowly to the door,
opened it and stood listening. Faintly he heard the engine idling and
triumph swelled within him. Vanya had done it. He had found a truck
and come back for him. Wutsdorf shuffled quickly down the dark
corridor in the direction he believed Kalewski to have taken. The
windows with undrawn blinds which lined one side showed as
lighter squares in the pitchy darkness. 'Vanya!' he whispered. 'Vanya!'
—but there was no answer.

Perhaps Kalewski dare not re-approach the hospital. Perhaps he
expected his friend to realize this and come to him. Wutsdorf found a
screen door at the end of the corridor, unlatched it and, descending
some steps, stood on a damp earth path. Now the sound of that idling
engine was much clearer. It came from somewhere over to the right.
Of course if he went towards the sound he might miss Kalewski
coming, in perhaps a different direction, towards him. But in any case
Kalewski would return to the truck when he found Wutsdorf's
hospital bed empty. The main thing, surely, was to reach the truck.

Wutsdorf walked quickly along the path, and was brought to a
jarring, agonizing halt as his wounded shoulder collided with something hard and unyielding as rock. Only an immense effort of self-
control stopped him screaming. He clung, sick and gasping, to whatever it was into which he had walked and hung there until the terrible
pain began slowly to ebb. Then, dripping with sweat, trembling and
weak, he edged slowly around what now revealed itself to be a stone
gatepost without a gate and found himself in a narrow, tree-lined lane
floored with soft sand. He had been walking for nearly two minutes
before he realized that the engine noise was diminishing rather than
increasing, for his ears were still ringing with the shock of that collision
with the gatepost and he had not taken sufficient time to judge accurately the direction of that soft, continuous pulsing throb. It had come
—surely—from the right? But now it seemed to be on his left. And at
that moment the trees on each side of him gave place to what appeared
to be regular walls in the left one of which an arch lifted against the
starry sky. There was a low gate and Wutsdorf fumbled at it until he
found the latch. Then he was walking on coarse grass and the engine
noise was distinctly louder, clearer, Encouraged, he moved more
swiftly and found himself in a narrow path between twin wire fences.
There was a curious smell and things moved in the dusk on either side.

Once a bird awoke in a tree and screamed shrilly. Wutsdorf hurried his steps and was brought up abruptly by another wire fence, this time running at right angles directly across his path. Slowly his hands traversed it, feeling for the inevitable gate. A bolt, heavy and large—the slotted flange was fixed to the staple not with a lock but with a twist of wire. Wutsdorf's strong fingers quickly unbent this; he carefully slid out the bolt, opened the gate and passed through. After barely four metres he came up against another fence and this time he could find no gate. He fumbled along the side and then was brought to a sudden halt by a noise which for the last few moments he had assumed to come from the idling vehicle now, he reckoned, scarcely fifteen metres away. Yet this low, grumbling throb came, surely, from behind him, while the engine had sounded—still sounded—from in front. Puzzled, he turned, walked two steps, found himself under a tree, heard the noise, now above him, swell to a sudden roar and was struck screaming to the earth by a heavy weight falling upon him from above.

Mr Singlefield had dropped in that evening to see Dr Zared about his wife, leaving his car idling at the roadside. Patience's nerves seemed to get continually worse and he was becoming more and more worried about her. He had found the doctor at home but Emerald out—apparently at Spencer's house. He knew his wife was fond of the Eurasian doctor's daughter and he often wondered why, for though he could understand Emerald's attraction for the opposite sex he could not imagine what his wife saw in her. Apart from her extraordinary looks he considered the girl uneducated, bad-mannered and—well, 'sharp' was the word he used to himself. He was relieved to find Dr Zared alone.

The doctor was engaged with his bank book and—of all things—an abacus, apparently working out his financial affairs and he was not particularly cordial in his greeting. If the police officer's wife had not encouraged Emerald to establish her zoo Dr Zared reckoned that he would have been sixty-six pounds and ten shillings better off tonight. Looking up sourly at Singlefield, he felt as if the tall, thin, beaky-nosed policeman had in some obscure way actually swindled him out of that sum. He did not, therefore, offer him the customary drink but indicated a chair and said, 'Well—?'

'It's about Patience. I'm not happy about her health . . .' Singlefield had stared gloomily down at the red-tiled floor. 'No, I'm not at all happy about it.' He had gone on to describe, slowly and carefully as if he was giving evidence in court, all the distressing symptoms of his wife's increasing neurosis.

Dr Zared listened irritably. He was not interested in Patience Singlefield who wasted his time and who really needed a psychiatrist rather than a physician. 'Yes,' he said. 'Yes, yes. I know.'

Singlefield droned on and on and Dr Zared looked with impatient longing at his abacus and his bank book. He wanted to check that figure again.

Then, ripping the night apart with a red knife, came a deep roar followed by a high, abruptly cut-off human scream. Doctor and police officer both leapt to their feet; both knew instantly what had happened. 'Someone's in Rose's cage! Quick, Singlefield! Some damn-fool native— Quick!' The doctor seized a long electric flashlight from his desk and together, with Singlefield jerking at the flap of his holster, they ran out into the dark, turned the corner of the house and came to the cages. The long beam flashed out, cut through the blackness and showed Rose hunched upon a prostrate white-clad body, her head bent, her tail lashing to and fro. As the light struck her she lifted a wet scarlet muzzle and her eyes shone like twin topazes in the electric beam.

'Oh, God!' Dr Zared's voice was filled with fury. 'I *knew* something like this would happen one day! I *told* her it would. Now there'll be claims for compensation. God alone knows how much money this is going to cost!'

But Singlefield was intent on rescue if that was still possible. He ran to the wire, levelled his pistol and put a bullet into Rose's head. Rose sprang into the air and collapsed writhing on the dust. The police officer fired three more careful shots into the twisting spotted leopard and only when it lay quite still did he open the cage and enter.

One quick look at the body was enough to tell him that nothing could be done. 'She's torn out his throat. But—' he stared down at the young pale face with the rough tow-coloured hair, above the huge red wound which separated it from the pyjama-clad torso—'who is this?'

Dr Zared was beside him now, dropping to his knees. 'My shoulder case,' he said. 'One of the last three German prisoners. I can't think what—' Then he glanced quickly up at the tall figure of the police officer. 'Tell me, Singlefield, can the dependants of a prisoner-of-war claim financial damages in a case like this?'

Ten

'. . . she'd had enough, she said. She hated Africa and she wished she'd never married him and she wasn't going to leave England again. So she went home to her mother. But she found that her mother had gone home to *her* mother—in Wales or somewhere because of the bombing. So she had to come back—you see?' Emerald sat beside Emil's bed manicuring his fingernails. 'So much for Patience.'

Emil smiled. 'She appears strange.'

'Strange! She's a proper nut-case.'

'Tell me of the others.'

'Do you really understand?' Gently Emerald bent back one thumb. 'Emil, *do* you understand? You say you do and your English is much, much better than it was. But sometimes I think you just say "yes" without understanding. Do you?' Emerald bent the thumb back still farther and Emil said, 'Stop! You hurt me.'

'Do I? Then tell me—do you understand all I say?'

'Yes, yes, yes!'

Grinning, Emerald relaxed the pressure and Emil said, 'You ought to be a questioner—a—a interrogator-officer. You would make prisoners speak quite quick, I think!'

Emerald's breath hissed slightly between her teeth. 'I certainly would—you first!'

'But as I have nothing to tell, you must tell me about the others.'

'Wait. I'll come around and do the other hand. Look how well I've polished your nails, Shall I paint them?'

'No, certainly!' Emil giggled. 'What would Spencer say?'

'I'd like to know. Perhaps I'd better paint them—then we'd find out.'

'Tell me more concerning Spencer.'

Emerald settled herself carefully on the side of the bed, pulled the manicure set—another present from Patience Singlefield—towards her and started carefully to press back the cuticle from the nails of Emil's right hand. Since the death of the German prisoner in Rose's cage a week ago she had disposed of much of her zoo. This was partly due to her father's insistence, for Dr Zared had taken the horrible accident as a magnificent opportunity to demand the end of his daughter's expensive hobby, but also to the fact that in the sole remaining German prisoner she had found a more absorbing interest. She spent several hours each day at the hospital and though Dr Zared disapproved, the fact that this new hobby cost nothing prevented him from open complaint. So Emerald brought books and fruit and flowers and sometimes Mr Spencer and talked for hours, often moving restlessly about the room followed by Emil's dark eyes from the pillow, sometimes sitting beside the tall hospital bed, occasionally on it, swinging her bare brown legs. Sometimes she said she was teaching Emil English, sometimes that she was helping to guard him. Now she said, 'Spencer? Well, he is a shipping agent—you know that.'

'Yes.'

'And we think he smuggles.'

'Smug-gles?'

'That means to bring goods secretly into a country and evade payment of frontier tax.' Emerald had developed a gift for elucidating English idiom easily and quickly in words she knew Emil to understand.

'Ah—*contrebandier*. But why is he allowed?'

'He is too clever, too secret, for the police to discover.'

'So. Then he is rich?'

'No one knows. I asked him once. He told me that he was very poor. I do not believe him. You have nice hands, Emil. I have never seen such nice hands on a boy.'

'I am twenty years. Man—not boy.'

'You are a boy. You are a boy until you are twenty-one. That is the law.'

'As you like. How many years—how old is Spencer?'

'I don't know. He only told me he was old enough to be my father when I asked him.' Emerald took up the polishing pad. 'He insulted the Bishop, you know.'

'How—'

'The Bishop came down from Dar-es-Salaam two years ago. The Shellybeares gave a garden party for him and asked Spencer—and a lot of other people too, of course. The Bishop spoke to him, and I suppose he thought he must be an Indian or something—after all, he does look rather like one—and asked him, "Are you a Christian?" Spencer was very upset because there are a lot of Christian Indians and natives and so forth here and he guessed that the Bishop took him for one of them. "Me, a Christian?" he said indignantly. "No—certainly not! I'm Church of England, just like you!"'

Emil merely looked puzzled. 'I do not understand—' and Emerald, grinning, dropped his hand and putting her thumb on the top of his small nose pressed it flat on his face. 'Rubber nose! You have no sense of humour. No Frenchman has. Yes, well I'll tell you something else. You know why we won't let Spencer talk about his infernal motor-boat?'

'No. Do you not? All you have told me is that it is his great delight and that your harbour-master is much annoyed by the speed with which he drives it. Always he talks of it when you bring him here. Always he says to me "I will take you out—".'

'Yes. And I always say quickly "In the motor launch." Don't I?'

'Yes—yes, you do!'

'All right. Because he calls it a pinnace, which it is not. And he is *always* saying he will take people out in it. When he first had tea with the Shellybeares he said he would take Mrs Shellybeare out if she got bored. In front of everyone he said, "Mrs Shellybeare, if ever you feel like a change my pinnace is always at your disposal." Only he pronounces it "*penis.*" I was not there, but Tony was, and the Singlefields and some visitors. Tony says it was the most embarrassing moment of his whole life.'

This time Emil laughed until he started to cough and the coughing rocked him and hurt his leg. Emerald held him steady. 'You're supposed to lie *still*—for God's sake!'

Emil gasped, 'It is your fault. You tell me these things.' He turned his flushed face on the pillow and Emerald stroked his thick black hair.

'You look sweet like that! And only about fifteen at the most. Are you sure you are telling the truth when you say you are twenty?'

'Why should I say differently?'

'I don't know. You seem so improbable altogether—worse than Spencer.'

'I have told you all you ask. Spencer tells nothing. You know of my home, of my time in the war marine, of what happens during the submarine voyage—of why, therefore, I am here.'

'Yes, yes. I suppose so.' Emerald conceded. 'It is just that—I never thought of meeting anyone like you, I suppose. I always thought of the enemy as great big toughs with guns. I can't see *you* being much of a menace to anybody.'

Emil smiled. 'I am not a menace.'

'And yet you were a U-boat officer—terribly menacing. You may have done dreadful things for all I know.'

Emil moved his head restlessly; his eyes slid sideways. 'No, no. I do only what I have to do. I obey the orders I am given and—and that is all.'

'You sink ships without warning.'

'Well—my God! That is what submarines are for, *n'est ce pas?* You think we should rise to the sea top and call to them and say, "*Guten Morgen, Kameraden,* we wish to sink you, if you do not have too much objections"? They have cannon, these merchant ships—you know that? So. We should perhaps say "*Messieurs les anglais, tirez les premiers*"—as at Fontenoy?'

Emerald laughed down at him, her narrow eyes gleaming. 'All right, all right! Don't get so upset!' She suddenly bent down and kissed him. 'I wish you were well, Emil. Well, no—I suppose not, because then they'd take you away. I have been truly *hideously* bored with the war for years, but at least it has—delivered you into my hands as it were. Now—what more shall I tell you? About our dear Shelly-beares? As a couple they get on so well together that really they might be friends instead of husband and wife. And—'

'No—about Tony.'

'Oh—Tony. Well—' Emerald frowned. 'He's the assistant D.C.'

'That I already know. He is also your friend?'

'In a way—I'm not sure. But he wouldn't be yours because he doesn't like the French. He says that their chief occupation is parting the English from their money.'

Emil giggled. 'I wish it was true! He is rich, then? I mean he has money with which to part?'

'Oh no, not rich. The rich English don't come out here.'

'Then poor?'

'No—not exactly poor, either. At least I must make quite certain that he isn't since he may want to marry me.'

Emil's eyebrows rose. 'He will marry you? You wish it, then—if he has wealth?'

Emerald slowly began to replace her manicure implements in their red morocco case, frowning unseeingly down at them. 'Well—no. No, I don't wish it, exactly. But I would be a fool to refuse him—my father says.'

'You do not like him so much?'

'He's—dull. And annoyingly virtuous. At least it annoys me. And I think he will always be that way.' Emerald considered Tony for a moment in silence. 'He has no god inside him,' she said at last.

'How?'

'Everyone who is—is properly alive has a god inside him. Mr Spencer has one, for instance. It's a very odd god, certainly, but it's there all right. Latif and Rami have gods—small, pretty Indian ones with too many arms and legs, I expect. But very firm and virtuous and strong-minded people don't seem to—perhaps they drive them out early in life. Tony's got nothing inside him but strong-minded principles. He's stuffed with them like the Shellybeares' Christmas turkey is stuffed with canned sausage meat. Dreadfully dull, both of them.'

Emil examined his beautifully polished fingernails. 'And I? Have I a god inside of me, you think?'

'Oh yes, you've got one all right.'

'But no principles, perhaps?'

Emerald grinned down at him. 'I shouldn't *think* so. But in any case they would have the saving grace of not being wildly virtuous ones. You are not at all like Tony, you see. I will tell you one or two things about him and then—'

'Yes. But first I want Latif.'

'What for?'

'Because I have drunk so much lime and water. I need him to help me discharge it. Then you can return.'

Emerald said, 'I expect I can do it myself.'

'Of course you cannot! You do not understand what I say.'

'Yes I do. I asked my father how you managed.'

Emil's face flushed; he grinned uneasily. 'You should not talk of such things, Emerald. It is— What are you doing!' For Emerald had walked over to the white-painted cupboard and taken out the catheter and the bottle. 'No—you must not!'

'Mustn't I? Little man, little man—"must" is not a word to use to princes— Do you know who said that?'

'Emerald! I will call Latif! You have no right—you—'

But Emerald had pulled down the bedclothes and was staring down at his naked thighs. 'Stay still. Stay *still* I said, damn you!'

Desperately Emil tried to raise himself but Emerald put a hand on his chest and easily pushed him back. 'You know the old Chinese proverb, "When rape is inevitable, lie down and enjoy it"?' Carefully, with frowning concentration, she slid the thin tube into his body and felt him shiver and jerk spasmodically. 'Relax, relax—you'll hurt yourself. If you don't stay still *I'll* have to call Latif—and we'll make a proper party of it.' She glanced up at him, noting his crimson face, the tears on his thick eyelashes. He looked younger and more vulnerable than ever and she smiled stiffly, feeling a hot, visceral excitement mounting within her, a sense of power at once gratifying and guilty.

When it was done she said, 'You see? I can do it as well as Latif.' and turning from the cupboard she came back to the bed. Emil's head was turned away from her and his breathing was uneven. Gently she pulled his head around and kissed his wet eyes. 'This is the second time I have made you cry—do you know that?'

Shakily, weakly, he said, 'You should not—you—you— What is it that you *want* from me?'

Emerald sat down close to the bed head, her face suddenly grave. 'What do I want? You, of course.'

'How—me?'

For answer she slid her hand under the bedclothes, under his pyjama jacket, and slowly stroked his small flat stomach, the tips of her fingers moving caressingly downward, brushing through his pubic hair. 'When you are well. Before—' she swallowed quickly—'before they take you away. Only I wish this bed was wider. We shan't be very comfortable, I'm afraid.'

Emil stared up at her wonderingly and then slowly took her unengaged hand in his. 'Why—' his voice was unsteady—'why me?'

Emerald glanced quickly at him. He was smiling up at her with the peculiar, somehow ugly smile she had seen very seldom on his face and then only in the first days of their acquaintanceship. It suddenly struck her that she had known him hardly more than three weeks—and yet for nearly all that time he had filled her thoughts to the exclusion of everything else. Yet she would certainly not answer his question truthfully—not, at any rate, while he smiled like that. Besides, she was not sure of the real answer herself. She said, 'Because I should like it—that's why.'

'Have you done it before?'

'It is my chief hobby. Let me see— Six times with Mr Shellybeare. Twenty with Tony. Twice with Clive Singlefield—and three times a day with Spencer since Easter.'

They burst out laughing. 'And you, Emil—what about you? Come on, tell me! Or else . . .' She slid her hand farther between his legs and Emil gave a quick gasp. 'Wait! I cannot remember. I—'

'Of course you can remember! Tell me—quick!'

'Several times. But only with two women. A housemaid when I am thirteen, fourteen years—and later in Paris with the woman of my military employer. That is all. Truly!'

Emerald removed her hand. 'I see.' She sounded disappointed. 'I wish you'd never done it before—like me. It would have been nicer.'

Emil smiled triumphantly. He would like to have said, truthfully enough, that on each of those occasions it had been the women who had suggested, urged, pleaded. And now it was the same again. 'It does not matter.'

'Then, you will?'

'Of course.'

'You promise?'

'Yes.'

Emerald sighed and rose to her feet. 'Well, I must go now. I'll bring you some more books this evening.' At the door she turned. 'Don't forget you promised!'

Eleven

When Tony Brickler had driven around the Singlefields' house to the veranda side he saw that the garage was empty—the police officer was therefore out. He swore under his breath and slammed the gears trying to put the car into reverse, but it was too late, Patience had heard him, had come out and was waving from the veranda. That was the trouble with the Singlefields' house; it could only be approached by car through the back garden. This meant that one either had to park in the road and come in on foot or else risk being seen and called in by the ever-bored Patience. Tony had some documents and some questions for Clive Singlefield and since the policeman was not in his office he had hoped he was at home. Now, too late, he realized that he was out on some other business.

Reluctantly he left his car in the dark shade of a banyan and walked over to the house. 'Hallo, Patience. Where's Clive?'

'I've no idea. Isn't he in the office?'

'No.'

Patience shrugged indifferently. 'Well, come in, come in. He may be back from wherever it is at any time.'

As usual, she was wearing a loose, flowered housecoat which bore a halfhearted resemblance to a kimono and on her feet were scarlet Turkish slippers, with curved and gilded points. With her heavy ear-rings and multiplicity of gemmed bangles she presented the appearance of a slatternly gipsy and Mrs Shellybeare had told Tony that she always expected to be asked to cross Patience's palm with silver every time she visited the house.

'And how's the world treating you, Tony?' she asked as soon as they were in the long, cool living-room below the two whirring ceiling fans.

'As well as can be expected. The news is excellent, isn't it?'

'Oh yes, I suppose so.' Patience shrugged and sat down in one of the low hammock-chairs. The war, like so much else, had somehow failed to come up to her expectations.

Tony took off his spectacles and polished them with a small piece of wash-leather. 'It can't be long now. It's amazing how they've kept it up, the Germans, when one comes to think of it. Fighting on two fronts and holding down most of Europe and inventing horrible new weapons and everything, all at the same time.'

'Maniacs.'

'I suppose they must be. Like Kalewski.'

Patience said bitterly, 'That's finished *our* chances of promotion. You don't have to tell me that,' and Tony looked away, embarrassed by the angry misery on the woman's face. He had somehow never thought that Patience Singlefield identified herself as passionately with her husband's career as the general run of service wives, but he had apparently been wrong. 'No one *here* blames Clive. The D.C. has taken great pains to point out in his report that Clive was not to blame.'

'Don't be silly, Tony!' Patience's voice was harder, clearer, than he had ever heard it. 'Of course he was to blame! And of course he *will* be blamed—whatever Mr Shellybeare says. The fact is that those prisoners in the hospital were Clive's responsibility.'

'But—'

'Since they were wounded it was not considered necessary to give them a proper military guard—I know, I know. But Clive was asked to be responsible for them until they recovered. And he agreed.'

'Yes, I know all that. But naturally he wasn't to guess that someone with an unusable ankle would make a break for Mozambique. Zared says that Kalewski would have been unable to put his full weight on that foot for nearly another three weeks. You don't expect someone in that condition to—'

'But he did, didn't he? And he got away—crossed the border.'

'We don't know for certain,' said Tony lamely, but Patience, with a brusque movement of one beringed hand, brushed his words aside. 'Well, we haven't found him—so he must have, mustn't he? And the other one was obviously going to do the same if he hadn't mistaken poor dear Rosa's cage for the open bush or something.'

Tony nodded, frowning, twisting his spectacles between his fingers.

'You know. I can't quite understand this overwhelming desire to get into neutral territory. What difference could it make to them at this stage? You remember how their captain complained to the D.C. about being within neutral waters when he was taken? I have no idea of naval etiquette or what a captain is expected to do under certain conditions, of course. It might be some abstruse tradition about flags or retaining one's sword or something—military people get terribly hot under the collar about their swords, I've noticed. But if not—*if* not —then why this passion for the Portuguese? Internment means prison in any case and our camps are likely to be much better run and much more hygienic than Salazar's.' He paused. 'At first we thought it might be the submarine. We thought that Kielbasa's boat might be a new type. Apparently they have some new-style electro-U-boats they're working up in the Danzig Gulf—or so Barragold told me. Anyway the Navy had a good look at U-996 and found nothing in the least out of the ordinary. She's a perfectly normal long-range cruiser. Well—so then one could only assume that Kielbasa had the idea that beaching on Delgado was not surrendering in quite the same way as—as he was actually forced to do. All right. But why should two N.C.O.s—one of them still quite seriously wounded—break out of hospital in order to try to get over the border themselves? And remember, they had neither maps nor arms nor any equipment at all. It was a desperate sort of thing to do. You'd think they'd be only too glad to stay where they were and keep quiet.'

But Patience was not interested. 'They're maniacs—like I said. The fact is that Clive should have insisted on having guards in the hospital. He's too easygoing. Zared didn't want them; he said, of all things, that they brought flies into the place! He said he'd *tell* Clive as soon as any of them were well enough to need guards. But he didn't.'

Tony laughed. 'You can't blame Zared. No one thought for a moment—'

'I blame Clive. He should have overruled Zared. He's got the right to.'

'Of course, but—'

'And even now he won't!'

'Won't what?'

'Put guards in the hospital.'

Tony stared. 'But my good Patience—there's only Kümmerol there now, and he can't get out of bed.'

'That's what Clive says. But I bet he'll be over the border before long.'

Tony grinned. 'Emerald is guarding him—with occasional help from Spencer—or so she says.'

He rose. There was an unspoken agreement in Masondi that no one should ever be unkind to Patience Singlefield, based on the equally unspoken belief that it would take very little to unbalance her vertiginous mind. But Tony had put in more than the regulation twenty minutes which was expected from even the most informal caller; he wanted to go.

Patience saw this and tried to deter him for she hated being left alone. 'But Tony—what if Kümmerol was to bribe Spencer? Bribe him to take him down the coast in his—his—'

' "Motor-powered seagoing craft" is the term you are searching for, Patience.' They both laughed and Tony said, 'Tell me—what would you expect Kümmerol to bribe Spencer with? A promise of the Iron Cross with Oak Leaves and Diamonds? And that's leaving aside the fact that whatever else Spencer is he's certainly part Jew. No, no—out of the question!' He paused at the doorway and the laughter died from his face. 'But still, I suppose Clive ought to put a guard on as soon as Kümmerol is out of his cast—purely for the look of the thing; for his own protection. Whatever happens, and however unlikely it may be, *this* one mustn't get away.'

Twelve

The boat, of course, was the only way; there could be no question of trying to emulate Kalewski. Lying through the hot days waiting for Emerald's visits, for the time when the plaster cast would be removed, Emil thought continually of Mr Spencer's pinnace and of the short dash down the coast to Delgado which could so easily be made in it. Two hours—three, perhaps—and a grimly ominous future might be exchanged for one of hope. For now, with ample time to think at last, with endless leisure to ponder on both the past and the future, Emil had reached a set of conclusions differing widely from those he had believed hitherto. Only now, rising from the depths of fear and exhaustion, at temporary rest in this silent, sun-filled backwater, was he able to recollect, to rethink and to plan for a future—even one in which he knew that he would never walk unaided again, one in which, so the doctor had told him, he must expect a certain amount of pain if he exerted his shattered leg and where he must never entirely discount the possible necessity for amputation at a later date . . .

'When we take off the cast—' Dr Zared had said, standing at the end of his bed, holding the rail in both hands, staring at him—'you will see what was done by the cannon shell from that plane. You will have to prepare yourself for a—a most distressing sight. I have saved your leg—I think. But it will become a question for you, whether you retain it in the future. If it causes you continual pain to use it, you would obviously be wiser to have it off and to walk with a false one. Yes . . . Well, that is something we shall have to deal with in due course.'

That had been his first encounter with the reality of his present situation—the doctor had told him that he was going to be a cripple from now onward. It had taken Emil some time to assimilate this and he had eventually done so only with a resigned bitterness which was new to him. He was twenty. He might easily live another sixty years —three times his present life-span. And in only another five he would have quite forgotten what it was like to walk normally, to run, to sit and to rise without clutching painfully to a stick or to the arm of a friend.

But by then Emerald had begun to bring him newspapers and magazines, generally several weeks, and sometimes several months, out of date—but frighteningly ominous for all that. Through them he made his second encounter with the realities of the present. He learned what the Germans had done in Russia and, with a sickness in his throat, what the Russians were going to do in Germany. Worst of all, he read of the condition of liberated France where 'collaborators'— anyone who had wished for, or assisted at, friendship between the two countries—were being butchered in the streets; hunted down and killed without trial. France had plunged back a hundred and fifty years to the days of the Terror. He realized with a cold shock that now he could never return to Grévilly. They would kill him—as they had perhaps killed his godfather or M. Pécheur whose son had joined the *milice*. Yet neither the elderly soldier nor the respected lawyer—nor he, himself—had ever wished anything but good for France. Neither they, nor he, had ever done her any harm. Or—had he? For a moment the newspaper had rustled dryly as his hands shook. What about that first sinking—the old French ship? The radio operator, Guéroult . . . *'Why are you wearing that uniform?'* And afterwards . . . But that had been inevitable—an operational necessity. The Kommandant had said so and surely it was obvious . . . and anyway nobody knew about it and there had been no survivors and—and it was much best forgotten.

And then, who had actually done it? The Kommandant had given the order—he was responsible. The actual destruction of the rafts and boats had followed upon his order—automatically, one might say. Yes, yes, but guns did not fire *themselves*, did they? Hand-grenades were not thrown without the aid of a human hand. Kalewski—Wutsdorf—himself.

Wutsdorf was dead. Kalewski safe in Mozambique. He lay here in a British hospital—and less than a mile and a half away, in the rusting, partly flooded interior of a broken U-boat, jammed down behind a small tip-up washbasin lay the log book which gave details of the place and time of a sinking to which no one had as yet admitted. In British hands that book would undoubtedly lead to further questions not only of the officers but of the crew. A guess, the mere suspicion that something unusual had happened, would be enough to have every member of the crew carefully interrogated. And they were very young, most of them, and easily scared. Who could tell what they might reveal under pressure?

Kalewski and Wutsdorf had preferred to place a neutral border between themselves and that still undiscovered log book. Understandably. Emil had been suddenly aware that he was holding his breath and sweating. He had let it out in a long, slow, shuddering sigh. And as he had done so the second orderly, Rami, had come in with his lunch on a tray; come in smiling and friendly as he always was, soft-voiced, sympathetic, careful. And later there would be Emerald, and perhaps Spencer. Emil had shaken his head and tried to bury the grim thoughts of a moment before under the resumption of his position as an ordinary hospital invalid whose whole and only occupation was to recover his health under the care and treatment of his nurses and doctors. Yet he knew that for his own sake he could not afford to disregard those earlier speculations, and that somehow he must take account of and make provisions for them. And even while Rami was adjusting his tray, was carefully propping him upon his pillows, the single answer rose to his mind—Spencer's pinnace.

Thirteen

The matter resolved itself extremely simply a week later when Emerald asked him to marry her. Emerald had been considering this possibility for some days; seriously considering it, that is, for she had idled pleasurably with it, dreamed of it, for considerably longer. Emil held for her all the attractions of every animal she had ever owned, and others which she had barely dreamed of. To possess him entirely, to make him her very own, was now her heart's most ardent wish. And marriage was the only means of doing this with a human being who, even if he was a prisoner-of-war, could not be bought in the market like her parrots and monkeys. It was true that Emil was now physically defective, but that would only make him more dependent upon her. She had once bought a hyrax with a missing forepaw and it had responded to her affection both more quickly and more completely than any other of her pets. She wondered briefly whether a crippled Tony would have made a good husband and realized at once that he would not. For Tony, like so many Englishmen, had a stiff, cold, male pride which was totally lacking in Emil. With a crippled leg he would have become irritable, touchy, easily offended . . . 'I can do it. I can manage. For God's sake leave me *alone*!' She could almost hear his voice as he moved clumsily, but rejecting her help, from chair to chair. His injury would be grasped to him to be used as a self-exasperating goad, erected as a barrier between them—whereas with Emil it would be turned into a bond.

Emerald was no fool, as Mr Shellybeare had often remarked to his wife, and she did not fail to take into account both Emil's position at present and his future prospects. But she knew nothing of war and hardly less of what was now occurring in Europe. The newspapers from which Emil himself was able to construct an all-too-accurate and ugly picture of the events in both the countries of his origin meant very little to Emerald, since she had never seen Europe and had looked upon it merely as the source of the manufactured goods which came—or, during the long years of war, failed to come—to Tanganyika. Emerald knew that had there been no war Emil was to have studied law, and since she was unaware of the continental bourgeoisie's passion for acquiring worthless law diplomas she took this to mean that he had been destined for as respected and well-paid a

193

professional career as that of the British judges in Tanganyika. Whether he had any private money of his own she did not know and could not inquire since her father had always impressed upon her the English belief that someone's 'private income' was a sacrosanct secret which could never be hinted at except after marriage, and by no means always even then. Why this should be so Emerald could not understand, but it was one of the few conventions she had not as yet found time to question. But even if Emil turned out later to be a rich man he had no money at all at present. Emerald had none either, although she possessed some small pieces of jewellery, the property of her dead mother, which she erroneously believed to be of considerable value.

The war was almost over. Everyone said so and Emerald had taken the unusual step of asking Tony to explain the military and strategic position to her and had actually listened to him when he readily did so. As soon as the war was over Emil would become a civilian again, presumably on the very day the Germans capitulated. And after that— well, one supposed he would be completely free to go and to do where and what he wished, like any other civilian. Tony had told her that he thought it probable that most German prisoners would be made to put in several years of forced labour repairing the destruction they had caused, but a cripple could not be made to do anything like that. No, Emil would merely be told that he was free, probably by Mr Shelly- beare, on the day war ended.

Thereafter the first thing to do would be to find him a job. Emerald decided that Mr Spencer, who was so good at arranging things, would do this for her. He liked Emil and had said that he was very intelligent. He should make Emil his assistant.

With that point settled Emerald looked around for a suitable home. There were two bungalows available in Masondi. One, which had last been occupied by a government surveyor, lay in the town proper. It was government property but Emerald, as the doctor's daughter, thought of herself as 'in the government,' too. They could have that. Or there was a rambling, broken-down old place, originally owned by some Germans who had left the country on a vacation to Europe just before the war and had never returned. This abandoned home was now derelict and rotting after more than five years of emptiness and was not really habitable; but it was isolated by more than a mile from its nearest neighbour, which happened to be the hospital, and best of all, it was down by the sea's edge and surrounded by a large, and now wild, garden. Emerald had often been there to collect the small hybrid fruits from the unpruned trees for her animals and had enjoyed the silent, sunlit air of desolation with only the drone of beetles and the murmur of the sea on the far-off reef to break the calm stillness. It was undoubtedly the right place to commence her married life with Emil, once the roof was repaired and the termite-ridden supports of the verandas replaced with iron poles.

A job and a house—the two main requisites before marriage were thus settled. The next thing to consider, thought Emerald, was her father. Dr Zared wanted her to marry Tony; he looked with great favour upon the assistant D.C. and had asked querulously why his daughter seldom now played tennis with her former friend. He would not approve of Emil as a prospective son-in-law since, like so many adults, he was strongly prejudiced against Germans—although of course Emerald could stress the fact that Emil was really French—and in his view the position of assistant to Mr Spencer would be very different indeed from that of assistant to Mr Shellybeare. Still, Emil was a naval officer, even if an enemy one, and, as Emerald knew, officers were considered the social equals of even the highest government officials. Dr Zared would complain bitterly, repetitively and at great length, but his daughter was accustomed to this and seldom let it influence her actions.

So there was nothing more to be done save to ask Emil for his consent. Emerald chose a calm evening and dressed with care. She fed her monkeys, slapping Montgomery who as usual stole most of Alexander's dinner when the less acute monkey was not looking, and, taking the last three Beatrix Potters and a small anthology of English verse designed for fourth-form standards, she set off to make her proposal.

She was accepted by a puzzled but very pleased Emil. He could not entirely comprehend why she should want to marry him in his present condition—a prisoner, penniless, crippled, with no foreseeable future prospects—but he was delighted that she did. For as his strength had increased, the sexual excitement which he evoked in Emerald had become reciprocal and the fact that his ruined and heavily encased leg prevented them from satisfying their mutual lust for each other was a continually increasing exasperation. And he was genuinely fond of this strange girl who had entered his life so abruptly a month ago. Intelligent but very poorly educated, malicious yet almost impossible to offend, her lewdness and her laughter had excited and amused him for weeks. Like him, she was of mixed parentage, belonging wholly to no nation and living in the between-world he understood so well—although, unlike himself, this seemed to cause her no distress whatever.

Marriage to such a girl would never be dull though it might be short-lived. But in any case that was not the point at all. He now had somebody who would give him all the help that lay within her power, exerting herself to the full on his behalf just as if he was already her husband. And smiling up at her, his hands clasped on the pillow behind his head, Emil felt a quick surge of triumphant defiance—of the world and of the war, of Germany whose subject he still was, of avenging France and her allies, most of all of the ugly fate which had done so much to destroy him. In that moment he was filled with a genuine love for Emerald which transcended anything he had felt before. Unmolested, unimpeded by others, it seemed more than likely that they could be very happy together.

And listening to Emerald's chatter about a job with Spencer, about living in the old bungalow near the sea of which she seemed so fond, he realized that she at least believed that they would be unmolested and unimpeded, that no obstacles now stood in the way of her plans save for his physical recovery and the end of the war—both of which she appeared to have arranged to take place simultaneously. Her assumptions were breathtaking in their sweep and assurance—and yet were they not perfectly valid? Why could they not do the simple things which she suggested with such naive certainty? What was more natural, after all, than that a wounded, shipwrecked sailor, cast up far away upon a foreign coast, should marry a local girl and settle down with her to earn a modest living on the shore? It must have happened so many times in the past. A hundred and fifty, two hundred years ago, it would have been entirely unremarkable. As a young French sailor, bronzed, pigtailed and stumping peg-legged from a primitive hospital, he would have been treated with the unthinking charity of the days when men believed in God rather than in bloodstained totemistic ideologies. The British governor would have given him a few gold guineas and the colonists would have watched with amiable indulgence as he built himself a wooden house and settled down with his new wife to fish or trade for skins and feathers with the natives.

'. . . and I'm sure Mr Shellybeare will help us. He's always liked me . . .'

Emerald still thought in those far-off terms. She belonged to the modern world only in appearance, he saw that clearly now. She had never acquired enough civilization to learn the art of abstract hate at which Europeans, after nearly half a century of constant practice, were so adept.

If only things were really like that. If only . . . His heart seemed to swell with despairing sorrow and his eyes pricked with tears at the bitter injustice, the stupid, obstinate evil of the present day.

'Emil—what is it? You're holding your breath, aren't you? I've noticed you always do that when you're upset.'

Surprised, Emil breathed out in a quick exhalation. It was perfectly true, though he had never realized it himself.

'No. I—I was thinking that it would be so good, so very good if we —if all was as you said.'

'But it is—since you want to marry me.'

'I mean the other things you say. For me a position with Spencer. For us a house near the sea. To live here as the others do. To be free.'

'Well—of course we willl. Just as soon as the war's over. It can't be long now, Tony says. And todays's news—'

Emil sighed, moved his head wearily on the pillow and caught her small strong bronzed hand in his. 'Listen, Emerald. You—you do not understand. No, no—truly you do not! I shall not be permitted to remain here. When I am able to walk I will be sent to England, to a camp for prisoners. That is how it will be. The officer-interrogator who questioned me informed me of this when I asked. For how long I must remain there cannot be known. Nothing of the future for me can be known. Churchill, Roosevelt, Stalin—these will make decision. It has been said that all officer prisoners will be killed. No—I do not quite believe. Perhaps only officer prisoners of the Russians. But prison— yes. Prison for some years, I think. Then I think they will send me to Germany.' He paused, filled with a mixture of despair and self-pity at his own words—for he was saying only what he believed to be true— and a careful calculation of their effect upon Emerald.

'But—but *why?*'

'Because it has been so bad—this war. And because of the first war. So long and so bad and so much damage. They wish to revenge and to punish.'

'Only Hitler and the Nazis.'

Emil sighed. 'You do not comprehend the newspapers, Emerald— if you read them. Yes, yes, Hitler and the Nazis—the Party, yes, but also the German people, and most important of them the officers. It is so—you will see.' He stared up at her. 'You know we—the submarine —have tried to arrive in Mozambique? You know we try everything to go there? You know why? Because of what I have already said. The Portuguese are neutral. They imprison us all—for this they must correctly do. But only until the end of the war. As soon as the war ends they give us freedom. Why not? They do not desire to revenge or to punish. Perhaps they allow us to remain—certainly, I think in Mozambique. Or else they allow that we go to other neutral nations—South America, I think. That is why Kalewski went to Mozambique—why Wutsdorf wanted it also. You do not think they run away from this hospital, still so hurt, still unhealed, for only diversion? No—for freedom.'

He reached out unsteadily for the glass of lime juice and water which was always on the bedside table and Emerald quickly handed it to him and took it back when he had drunk. She said slowly, 'Then you—if you could have gone with Kalewski—?'

Emil nodded yes, and Emerald turned abruptly and began to wander restlessly up and down the room, her hands thrust into the pockets of her white shorts. From the bed Emil watched her silently, wondering how long she would take. His gold watch had been ruined by salt water but he guessed later that it had been less than two minutes before she turned and, holding to the rail at the bed's foot, said questioningly, 'Spencer's boat?'

Very quietly he said, 'Yes,' and for a long moment they held each other's glance across the length of the white bed. Then Emerald turned and, walking slowly to the window, raised the blind so that the dying light of sunset filled the room. Turning back she said slowly, 'And—and when we got there—to Mozambique? Wouldn't they intern you? Like you said?'

'Int—'

'Put you in a prison camp?'

'I do not think. No. For I will be only one. And not wearing uniform or with arms. Also my leg. No, I do not think.'

'What—how would we live?'

Emil's voice was stronger now; tinged with a controlled excitement. 'We would—you know *débrouiller*? No. We would—would do what we are able to find ourselves. I can speak French, German, now also some English. Very soon I am able to speak Portuguese, I am certain, too. For persons who comprehend languages there is generally work.'

'They'd let us stay?'

'I am certain, yes. We have done them no wrong. And, Emerald—it is so near. It cannot be different—the manner of living. Also after some time we are able to return here, perhaps. In Mozambique it is not possible for Churchill, Roosevelt, Stalin, to make decisions to imprison or to kill me. When all this is finished after two, three—perhaps five—years we are able to return.'

Emerald nodded. The idea accepted, she was beginning to find it not unattractive. After all, she had never left British territory in her life. 'Or we might stay. It might easily be much nicer—beyond Delgado. Oh Emil—' She came quickly around to the other side of the bed and, sitting gently beside him slipped her hand into his pyjama jacket and began to stroke his chest. 'We will enjoy it there! It will be *foreign*— quite different, but nicer. I'll learn Portuguese, too. Spencer will find me a book and—'

Emil laughed. 'Yes. I, too, think we shall be happy there—beyond Delgado. But you must be careful with Spencer. He is your friend, I know, but he must be told nothing.'

'But—the penis?'

'The penis—yes.' Emil grinned. 'That we must steal. I am sorry, but we must steal it. We can return it. We will do so—naturally. And listen, Emerald. You must learn to—to make it go forward.'

'To drive it?'

'To drive it onward. Because I am unable—here. When I am in this boat, yes—I comprehend the machinery. I also navigate—naturally. But you must learn to commence it. Then, when we are ready, we move quickly by night. Two hours—less, I think.'

Emerald said thoughtfully, 'It is the fastest launch on the whole coast up to Dar-es-Salaam—Spencer says. He's always boasting how fast it is. The police launch could never catch it—at least on a calm sea. The police launch is much bigger but nothing like so fast. The sub- chasers might, perhaps—though Spencer says it's faster than them. But they're usually up the coast or somewhere off Madagascar, I think.' She paused. 'Spencer's always inviting me out in it. I'll get him to show me how it works—at least the starting and the steering. Then, as soon as your cast is off— How long does my father say?'

'Two weeks.'

'Two weeks. And in three—in three we may be there. Emil, in three more weeks we will be together in Mozambique—free!' The solemnness of the thought, the almost unimaginable prospect of such a huge, open, sunlit expanse of future happiness, struck them still and silent. They sat unmoving in the quickly darkening room, staring into each other's flushed faces, while the word *free* seemed to echo back softly from the evening breeze amongst the leaves in the garden and the gentle rustle of the sea's ripples along the beach beyond.

Fourteen

'Do not enrage yourself—you will only shorten your life.' The small glazed china plaque with the Gothic print hung above Mr Spencer's desk flanked on one side by a carved African tribal mask and on the other by an old and spotted steel engraving of Grace Darling and her father setting out from their lighthouse in a terrific sea and clouds of blowing hair and beard to rescue the passengers of the *Forfarshire*. Somebody had once claimed to have heard Mr Spencer state categorically that Grace Darling was his maternal great-grandmother, but if so he had never repeated this before witnesses.

Mr Spencer sat below these decorations at his small neat desk, smiling kindly across at Emerald who stood on its other side fidgeting with a First World War German shell cap which its owner used as a paperweight. 'Yes, dear Emerald,' he was saying in his soft, singsong voice, 'your father told me when I called in this morning. It is to be tomorrow. Is Emil excited about it?'

'Yes, he is.'

'To be able to walk again after all these weeks. Poor boy, I am afraid he will find it difficult and painful at first. It is so dreadful that war should do these things to such young people whose fault it cannot be—even Germans.'

'Emil's really French, though.'

'Mmm. He says so. You know, Emerald, I cannot help thinking that he is unwise to *insist* so much upon that. *Nolens volens*, he had been fighting against the French. If they were to take him at his word they might demand his extrication as a columnist—a traitor. *Then* where would he be?'

'In the Bastille, probably. But—'

'No, no. It was pulled down on the fourteenth of July. But certainly in dangerous trouble. I know the French, you see. They are completely unforgiving and very vengeful. It is their nature—most unpleasant.'

'Are they? Emil's the only Frenchman I've ever met. I suppose they might be.'

'They are—they are indeed.' Mr Spencer examined his fingernails which were a shade darker than was usual among persons of Caucasian ancestry, and said, 'I like Emil. He is a nice boy. But I think I must tell him to say a little less about being French. He is legally a German national. And a German naval officer, too. He will not be released any sooner from a prison camp by pretending otherwise. He would be wiser to resign himself to fate—to accept the inedible, as we say.'

'Do you suppose he'll be kept long? After the war, I mean?'

Mr Spencer shrugged. 'I hope not, but who can say? I expect officers will be kept longer than other ranks. But with his leg . . . Probably he will be back in Germany within a year of the war's end.'

'But he lives in France.'

'That certainly makes it more difficult.' Mr Spencer glanced at his watch. 'Dear Emerald, I have to go now and pack. I leave this afternoon for Dar-es-Salaam.'

'Oh—you didn't tell me! How long will you be away?'

'A week or ten days. Ten days, I hope, because I have arranged for a new treatment for my sciatica—a course of daily hypothetic injections at the hospital there. Your father advised it.'

'Can I use the—the launch while you're away? To go fishing?'

'Of course! I am delighted that you have taken up fishing, Emerald. I was so sad for you about the zoo. But fishing is more fun and much less work. While I am away I will buy some really good tackle and when I come back we will have ever such a fine time using it. But you will take either Ahmed or Khaled with you when you want to go out, won't you? Khaled is best with the engine if it gives trouble. You do not want to get into difficulties.'

Fifteen

On the next morning Dr Zared removed the cast from Emil's left leg, slicing it carefully from hip to ankle with shears. Emil lay on the operating table sweating with the heat and anticipatory dread and wincing every time the cool blade of the shears touched his newly healed flesh. When the cast was removed he waited, breath held, for Dr Zared's opinion of his own work—and it was a long time in coming.

'Yes—yes. Well, yes . . . Well—it's not so bad. Not so bad at all.' In Dr Zared's voice a note of complacency sounded through his habitual tone of irritation. 'It's knitted up very well indeed—considering that I had to put it together from a mere assortment of *fragments*. You can look at it and see for yourself. Lift him up, Latif.'

Emil looked, turned green and sank back in Latif's arms, his eyes shut. '*Scheiss!*'

'No, no. You don't have to worry about the colour. That'll disappear in time—mostly, at any rate.'

'But—but there is no—no—' Emil's voice was a hollow whisper. 'Nothing of—of the—'

'There is very little calf left. That's what you mean? Yes. Most of it was shot away. Yes, yes—but that's just the point.' Dr Zared's voice became still more irritable. 'I tell you, young man, that if it had been any other doctor in this territory—*any* other doctor—you'd be looking at an amputated stump—Oh God! Latif—a basin, quick!'

Later that morning Emerald said, 'What's this?' She held up a set of four metal rods joined with straps above a leather stirrup which hung at the foot of the bed. 'With that—' said Emil a little shakily—'I will walk—soon.'

'A brace— Oh, poor Emil! Will you have to wear it always?'

'No. Your father think only for five or six months. Then there will be another, smaller—then, probably, nothing.'

'When are you to start walking?'

'Tomorrow. Between Latif and Rami. This evening I am to do exercises—but in bed only. And a man comes to make a shoe for me. We—we commence progress, you see.' But his voice was shaky and Emerald, glancing up quickly from the steel and leather brace, saw that his round face was flushed, his eyes sparkling with tears. She came quickly around the bed and took his head in her arms, kissing him, stroking his hair. 'What is it, Emil? Does it hurt *still*? Was it—so dreadful to look at? You're holding your breath again!'

'It was bad—yes. Horrible! But your father is satisfied. So, too, must I be, therefore. I comprehend that I am fortunate. He tells me *always* that I am fortunate to retain my leg!' He gulped suddenly, choking with a mixture of furious frustration, anger, self-pity. 'This happened because of Mozambique. The aircraft attacked us on the journey. We could not submerge. We would not surrender because of Mozambique—so near. We—I and Wutsdorf—we fought the aircraft in order that we might still go on there. And my leg was shot. And then all was for nothing in the end. I am so badly hurt—for nothing at all.'

Urgently Emerald said, 'But we will go there, Emil. We will, we *will*! It will not have been for nothing, either. If you hadn't been wounded you would have been taken away with the others. As it is—

Oh, they've given you some clothes!' She turned to look at a khaki shirt, a pair of khaki drill trousers and a leather belt which lay on a chair near the bed.

'Prison clothes!' said Emil bitterly. He knew he was behaving badly but he had been unnerved by the sight of his mutilated leg, so for the present he had abandoned himself to irrational and almost childish anger and despair.

Emerald said, 'It's quite good cloth—considering. And we can easily get the black diamonds off as soon as we're beyond Delgado.' She came back quickly to the bed. 'Emil—Spencer went to Dar-es-Salaam yesterday afternoon. He's given me permission to use the boat when I like, though I'm supposed to take one of the boatmen and not go out alone. He'll be away for a week or ten days. We'll be gone before he comes back. Soon we'll be gone. You'll be free very, very soon now. Don't be unhappy—not now!' She leaned over him, kissing him, smiling down tenderly at his flushed and strained face.

'Can you yet commence the engine yourself?'

'Oh yes—and steer.'

Emil lay silent a moment, his face turned sideways on the pillow, staring at the opposite wall. Then he said slowly, 'There is something you can do for me—perhaps.'

'What?'

'There is something in the submarine that—I would like.'

'We aren't supposed to go there. It's off limits. I wanted Spencer to take me there the other day, but he wouldn't. He said he'd get into trouble with Clive Singlefield. We went very near it, though. It's getting rusty all over. They *say* it's dangerous.' Emerald paused. 'I could try, of course.' But her voice was dubious. 'What is it you want?'

'My diary.'

'Oh—is that really important? I mean, if I was seen on the submarine by someone and they told—'

'It is important to me.' Still he would not look at her and Emerald grinned suddenly and pulled his head around by one ear. 'Dear, dearest Emil! If you want it so much I'll try to get it. But how am I to find it? And it may have been taken away already. The Navy sent people who went all over your submarine, you know. They took away all sorts of things. I saw them coming ashore.'

'My diary I hid. I do not think they have it. Look—give me a paper and a pencil and I will design a picture to show you . . .'

Sixteen

Emerald, with the native boatman Khaled in the stern, had fished for an hour out beyond the reef, manœuvring closer and closer to the long, partly submerged hulk of the U-boat which lay, canted and bows under, across the southern edge of the harbour entrance. It was nearly six o'clock and the sun was almost down, the sea calm green and tranquil, flat as a pond within the reef but on the outside heaving with the deep slow swell of the Indian Ocean. This swell caused Emerald some doubt as she swung the launch carefully under the rust-streaked weather side of the abandoned submarine. From the stern Khaled, thinking of scratched paint, eyed her disapprovingly as for the tenth time she examined the tangle of ropes and hawsers which drooped from the casing and washed, thick with green and slimy weed, about the low waterline.

With sudden determination she swung the launch across the top of one slow swell, into the succeeding trough; then, with a shout to Khaled to take the helm, she jumped to the foredeck and, as the launch rose up the submarine's side, creaking against the weedy ropes and probably rubbing off some paint, she got one foot into a decaying scrambling net and was away.

Below her the launch sank into another trough and Khaled, muttering to himself, fended off with a boathook, but Emerald, monkeylike, had already scurried up the careened hull and was climbing the conning-tower ladder.

Then she was on the bridge. Rust, and gull droppings—brass cartridge cases greening in the scuppers, torn metal, splintered woodwork. It was here that Emil had tried to fight off the diving aircraft, perhaps with those very guns which pointed blindly up at the sky. She tried to picture the scene but could not, suddenly realizing that she had never seen Emil on his feet or dressed in anything save a white pyjama jacket. And yet—it was really such a short time ago—barely two months. She had been playing with the newly arrived pangolin on the very morning that the U-boat had been limping desperately towards Delgado . . . The hatch was open and she climbed down a long ladder into oily, salt-smelling darkness.

Dark. After the brightness above it was very dark down here; a gloomy dusk filled with the tiny noises of water chuckling and gurg-

ling beneath her feet and forward towards the smashed bows. Emerald
had brought a small flashlight and now she swung the beam about her.
This was the control-room—a mass of machinery, wheels, valves,
dials, levers, and a fantastic spider-web of tubes and wiring. Emerald
marvelled at the ability of anyone who could understand and operate
anything so incredibly complex. Outside, the swell lifted and sank
with a slow muted boom that echoed hollowly through the abandoned hull. She shivered slightly and swung the flashlight to the forward bulkhead. Portside, a heavy door half open. Starboard, a small
projection screened by green curtains. That was it—the captain's
cabin where Emil had hidden his diary.

Emerald quickly crossed the sloping iron deck and parted the
curtains, disclosing a tiny space with fittings of almost doll's house
dimensions and neatness. There was the metal washbasin. She felt
gingerly behind it with one hand. Nothing. Down a little farther . . .
Ah—the sharp edge of a book. She grasped it and pulled. It was
jammed tight, or perhaps water and humidity had swollen the paper,
for it took Emerald several minutes and the whole of her strength to
work and prise it loose. But in the end she got it out, bent and battered
and with its thick black cover scratched and dented. She glanced
quickly at one open page, noting to her surprise that it was full of short
entries and figures and seemingly written by different hands. Was it
Emil's diary after all? It would be a great nuisance if it turned out to
be something else—all this trouble for nothing. But she had gone to
the exact place he had told her and the book had been exactly where
he had said she would find it. It must be the diary. She thrust it under
her arm and pushed through the green curtains which fell softly into
place behind her.

Once more she flashed her torch around the deserted control-room,
noting the great double periscopes in their wells, the seats of the
hydroplane operators, the heavy bulkhead doors. Emil had told her
something of the events which had led up to the U-boat's surrender
and she had listened with interest. But his English was not sufficient to
paint a fully comprehensible picture and she only knew that the boat
had lain damaged for hours at an extreme depth and 'no one of us
knows if we are able once again to rise.' Now, standing in that cylin-
drical claustrophobic shell of massed machinery, an utterly inhuman
jumble of various metals, Emerald genuinely felt something of the
trapped terror those others must have suffered two months ago. She
shivered and turned quickly away towards the ladder. But before she
reached it her foot skidded on a patch of oil and she fell, sliding down

the sloping deck to end up within the gap of the forward bulkhead doorway. Shaken, breathing hard, she clambered to her feet, thankful that she still retained her flashlight. She turned it momentarily into the darkness beyond the door, saw a small compartment lined with pipe-cots and full of tousled bedding and then, farther forward, beyond another wide-open door, the beam gleamed dully from the sides of a great canted torpedo and on something white and round . . . From below that curved metal flank a human skull was grinning at her over the rotting collar of crumpled blue overalls. Emerald gasped, frozen with horror, and a small crab crawled out of one of the empty eye-sockets and paused upon the upper rim like a horny eyebrow to stare at her, its own stalked eyes glinting like phosphorescent green beads in the light of her torch.

Then Emerald was away and up the ladder like one of her own monkeys with a fire under its tail. Up into the glorious calm evening, unfollowed, untouched by something cold and bony, weedy and wet which she felt shudderingly certain had slid agilely from beneath that torpedo to make sure that this new victim did not escape.

And climbing down among the ropes that lay matted over the curve of the saddle tanks, calling to Khaled to bring the launch closer, Emerald could not help glancing back fearfully to the tower which loomed above her, waiting for that bald white head to lift slowly above its rim.

She had not recovered from the shock of her first encounter with a corpse when Khaled brought the launch to its mooring against the harbour wall. Then, still trembling a little, her skin tingling and pimpling with gooseflesh, she picked up the diary—holding it with a certain revulsion for had it not been for weeks in close proximity to that *thing*?—and climbed the stone steps to the jetty.

And there, outlined tall and broad-shouldered against the fading sky, stood Tony Brickler. He smiled down at her, his spectacles gleaming, his blond hair flopping sideways over his forehead. 'Well, well—so you've been out in the—motor-driven, sea-going vessel—have you?'

'Oh, hallo Tony!' Emerald grinned at him uneasily. She had neglected Tony for weeks and now she felt that he must guess the reason. 'Yes. Spencer said I could so long as I took a boatman.'

'Fishing?'

'Well—trying to. Spencer's gone up the coast. He's going to bring some new fishing gear back, he says.' They had fallen into step beside each other and were walking back towards the roadway where Tony's car was parked under two dusty palm trees. 'I'm fairly sure—' Emerald said a little too conversationally—'that Spencer's Spanish. He ought to spell his name S P E N Z A.'

'That would make him Italian. S P E N C I A would be more Spanish. What have you got there?'

'What—?'

'That book.'

'Oh—this.' Uneasily Emerald took the thick black book from under her arm. 'It's a diary, really.' Then, catastrophically—she turned it over in her hands and upon its front cover, tarnished and scratched but glinting in the evening light, the stiff-winged, stylized, swastika-clutching eagle of the Third Reich shone unmistakably upon the imitation black leather. In her rush from the submarine, in her startled shock at what she had seen there, Emerald had not had time to notice that she had been holding the book upside down.

They both stopped. Tony was staring down at the book and when at last he lifted his eyes to hers they held amusement, but also suspicion and something else—a calculating appraisal. He grinned slowly. 'A diary? Do you normally record the events of your daily life in the official stationery of the German Navy?'

'Well—I—I didn't say it was *my* diary, did I?'

'You mean—it is Kümmerol's?'

'Yes.' Emerald's voice was amused, too, but also defensive. 'He said he'd left it in the U-boat and I thought—well, as I was going fishing anyway I'd drop in and get it for him.'

Tony chuckled. 'Ah, I see. Just "drop in and get it for him." And you did, too. Did you happen to meet any of Leutnant Kümmerol's ex-shipmates while you were aboard? There are still some there, you— Ah! I see you did. He didn't tell you about *them*—or did he?'

Emerald swallowed. 'No—no. If he had I wouldn't have gone.'

'Wouldn't you?'

'Tony—what are you hinting? You—you Tony Brickler! What you think you—Leave this alone! It's not yours!'

But Tony's strong hand forced the black book from her grasp. 'You are *not* supposed to board that wreck. It is very dangerous. It could slip off the reef at any moment. Do you want to join the remains of the crew who are still on board in Davy Jones's locker?' While he was speaking Tony had been flipping over the leaves of the book and when he raised his head he was grinning again. 'Poor Emerald! You've had all that trouble for nothing.'

'Why—how?' Emerald looked startled. 'I mean, I only went to—'

'This—' Tony tapped the book with one finger—'isn't a diary, you clot! It's the submarine's log. The Navy searched her all over for it but they couldn't find it. They assumed it had been chucked overboard with all the ciphers and secret papers. Where'd you find it?'

Emerald stammered, 'In—in a small cabin in front. I—I thought—'

'Did Kümmerol tell you where to look?'

'Yes—no! That is I must have mistaken what he said.'

'Oh, yes? Perhaps. And then again—perhaps not.'

Foolishly Emerald tried to wrest the book from him. 'Give it here, Tony, please! He wants it, whatever it is. He's been looking forward all day to having it. His leg's just out of plaster and he's seen it and it's upset him a lot. And—'

'And don't let's be beastly to the Germans, eh?' Tony held the book well out of her reach. 'No, Emerald, you can't have it—nor can he. This is an important find and we'll have to get it straightaway to Naval Intelligence. You know, you *ought* to be given a severe rocket from the D.C. for disobeying a police order. But instead you'll probably get a congratulatory letter from the S.N.O. at Dar-es-Salaam.' They were at the car now and he paused. 'I'd offer you a lift back to town, but—' he was staring down at her and behind his glasses she saw that his eyes were watchful and intent—'I imagine that you're going in a different direction, aren't you?'

Emerald felt herself colouring. 'How do you mean?'

But Tony only grinned once more and climbed into the driver's seat.

'Give him my compliments—and the anticipatory thanks of Naval Intelligence. *Auf Wiedersehen*, Emerald!' He left her standing in the dusty road, empty-handed, staring after him.

Seventeen

At Flores in the Azores, Sir Richard Grenville lay,
When a pinnace like a flutter'd bird . . .

Emil smiled to himself; that, at least, was a word which he did not need to check in Mr Spencer's English dictionary which lay among the Beatrix Potters on his bedside table. Emerald was somewhere out there beyond the reef in the 'pinnace' now. She might at this very moment be boarding the submarine. He hoped that the door leading from the under-officers' mess space into the fore ends was closed and clamped. The British, as he knew, had not shifted the wrecked torpedoes which trapped the bodies of the dead crewmen. It would have been dangerous work in any case and almost impossible to perform in the submarine's present position. He himself had not felt inclined to tell Emerald that there were corpses—skeletons, probably, by now; after two months' exposure to tropical heat, sea-water and crabs—in the boat since that might have prevented her attempt to retrieve the log. He wondered how much longer he must wait before she returned. Then he tried to force his mind back to the poem.

> . . . *Spanish ships of war at sea! We have sighted fifty-three* . . .

Once he had the log in his hands he would have to find some way of destroying it.

> . . . *Then sware Lord Thomas Howard: "Fore God I am no coward* . . .

Of course there was only one page which it was essential to destroy. If necessary he would tear it to tiny pieces and eat them. He had heard of people doing that. And once that page was destroyed there would be no material evidence of any sort to connect U-996 with the *Maréchal Oudinot*. Even the lifebelt which he had taken from Guéroult had been weighted and sunk—by Kalewski on the Kommandant's order—on the morning after the sinking.

> '. . . *I should count myself the coward if I left them, my Lord Howard,*
> *To these Inquisition dogs and the devildoms of Spain.*'

But what of the rest? If he could keep it hidden until they were ready to escape—take it with him to the pinnace—slip it over the side somewhere off Delgado . . .

> *And the sun went down and the stars came out far over the summer sea* . . .

What had this bygone English captain done with *his* log? Had he jettisoned it in time with his secret papers? Did they have logs and secret papers in those far-off days? Emil tried to picture the sea fight of 'the one and the fifty-three'; it must have been a bloody business, but at least the *Revenge* did not have to suffer murderous air attacks at the same time, and at least Sir Richard and his crew had recently been rested ashore rather than risen exhausted from entombment in the depths . . .

> '*Sink me the ship, Master Gunner—sink her, split her in twain!*
> *Fall into the hands of God, not into the hands of Spain!*'

It was difficult to picture Eugen Kielbasa turning to him with that command. And yet . . . Supposing they had been fighting Russians—attacked by Russian aircraft and sub-chasers off Russian-held territory? Yes, it might have been the best way out then. Emil shuddered and put down the poetry book as he recognized Emerald's light step in the corridor outside.

Then she was in the room—empty-handed—and the smile slowly died from Emil's face. 'You—you could not find it?'

'I found the wrong book.' She shrugged. 'You must have told me wrong. Where to look, I mean. And—and there are skeletons there. Oh, Emil, it's a horrible place! You might have warned me. Well—' she smiled down at him and brushed the dark hair from his forehead—'you'll just have to start another diary, that's all. Nothing would induce me to go back to that wreck again—horrible! Tell me, Emil—did you do your exercises—the ones you said Latif was going to help you with?'

Swallowing, Emil said, 'The book you—you found. What was it?'

'The log. You must have got confused. I don't blame you, I must say. I've never seen such—'

'What—what— Where is it?'

'Tony took it. He was waiting on the jetty when I came back. He asked me what it was, but when he found it wasn't your diary but only the log he took it. He said it had to go to Naval Intelligence and that I'll probably get a congratulatory letter from the Senior Naval Officer, though I don't suppose we'll be— Emil! What's wrong? Why are you looking like that . . .?'

Eighteen

And four days later he was walking. It was painful and slow and he needed two sticks with thick rubber ferrules, but there was no longer any necessity for Latif or Rami to be beside him ready at any moment to take his arm, to half carry him back to the low chair in his room. Dr Zared, surprised and pleased at the speed of his progress, kept warning him not to do too much . . . 'A little every day is quite sufficient. You mustn't overdo things or you'll only hurt yourself.'

And Emil was indeed hurting himself. After three or four slow journeys up and down the long hospital corridors he would return to his room pale-faced and breathless with the fierce pain that shot up and down his maimed left leg. Yet the more work the remains of his muscles were made to do the stronger they would become. And he must acquire the fullest possible mobility of which he was capable within the short few days that remained before Mr Spencer was due back in Masondi. For go now he and Emerald must—and quickly. The loss of the log to the British authorities had only been the first blow. The second had followed swiftly upon it. When, on the morning after Emerald's bungled visit to the U-boat, he had been dressed by the orderlies and had left the room supported on each side for his first attempt to walk, a black policeman had risen from a seat outside the door and had followed some half-dozen paces behind. Just two journeys that first morning—down one corridor and up another— and always the slow heavy footfalls of the silent guard, the clink as his loosely held rifle touched the scabbarded bayonet at his side.

That the guard was permanent he now knew. It was changed every four hours, and listening from his bed, or the low chair in which he now spent most of the day, Emil could hear the spoken question and answer, the thud of a grounded rifle and the heavy, fading footsteps beyond the door. And on these occasions Emil sweated with a fear more real than any he had known since the U-996 had regained the surface and he had realized that he was not, after all, doomed to die slowly by asphyxiation in a steel coffin on some dark volcanic jut of the Indian Ocean bed.

What did that guard outside imply? Emerald had been equally upset, but only because it made their escape plan more difficult to put into practice. 'I won't visit Patience Singlefield ever again!' she had said angrily. 'And I hope that when we do get away they fire her husband!'

Since there was only one guard and since he never entered the room it had been obvious from the first that Emil would have to leave by one of the windows. Had he possessed sound legs this would have presented no difficulty at all; for the windows were only four feet above the floor and five and a half above the flower-beds outside in the garden. But with one leg encased in a metal brace which clinked as he walked, unable to stand up without the aid of two sticks, the situation was very different. Even with Emerald outside to help him the effort, let alone the pain, of such an attempt might prove intolerable. Yet they could not wait long, for Emil guessed that as soon as he was known to be able to walk more easily, to do away with one of the twin sticks, there was every likelihood of a second guard being posted below the windows.

Yet his own sense of urgency was based more upon the captured log than upon the guard. He and Emerald together could certainly manage to outwit two of Mr Singlefield's blockheaded black police-men, though the start they would have to get to the motor-launch and leave the harbour might be a dangerously short one. But if the British Naval Intelligence wished to question him over the contents of the U-boat's log they might have him taken to Dar-es-Salaam at any moment. Kielbasa and the rest of the crew had probably been shipped to Britain long ago, unless it was to India where many prisoners were said to be interned and he himself was almost certainly the only re-maining crew member at hand. It was normal procedure to question captains and officers over the contents of captured logs, and he was sufficiently recovered to make the journey to the colonial capital. They might come for him at any time.

But equally, as he told himself continually, they might not give him a thought. The U-boat was out of action and in their hands. Germany was reeling in her death-throes and could last only a few more weeks at most. From a military viewpoint there was no value to be got from the further questioning of a very inexperienced junior officer; it would be a waste of their time. Everything that he could tell them they knew already—technically speaking. If they came for him at all it could only be to make him explain why the oral statements of himself and the others had admitted only one sinking while the log book recorded two.

And what answer would he be able to give to such a question? Could he say that it was a false entry, made in order to claim un-deserved credit from *Seekriegsleitung* on the U-boat's return? No—because, if so, then where *was* the *Maréchal Oudinot*? The British would know that she had been lost somewhere between Conakry and Bahia and the date and place of the sinking as recorded in the log of U-996 would fit in too well with that knowledge to admit of much doubt as to who had sunk her. He might say that he had forgotten the sinking, claiming partial amnesia due to his wounding. It would be a most unlikely story and completely ridiculous when it was found that the Kommandant and the rest of the crew were apparently suffering from the same loss of memory. Very well then—admit that she was sunk. Sunk with all hands. There was nobody to deny this since there

had been no survivors. 'But in that case—' he heard the relentless
questions almost as clearly as if they were being asked in this room—
'why did you conceal it at first? Why did you admit the sinking of
the *Empire Advance*—also with all hands, it appears—but not that of the
Maréchal Oudinot? You sank the tanker, did you not? And you admitted that at once, did you not? Then *why* . . .'

Restlessly Emil grasped the handles of his two sticks, levered himself to his feet and started his slow thudding limp up and down the
room. Up and down; thud and clink of metal; careful not to slip on
the polished tiles. The built-up shoe on his left foot was clumsy and
heavy. Up and down . . .

The footsteps of several people sounded in the corridor, the scrape
of a chair as the guard outside rose to his feet, the click and rattle as he
shouldered his rifle preparatory to saluting. Emil swung around pale-
faced, breath caught, as the door opened and Dr Zared entered followed by a large elderly man in plain clothes—and Emerald.

No uniform. Emil breathed out again.

'Ah—on your feet!' Dr Zared looked pleased and turned to the
man behind him. 'You see, sir. He's already walking by himself. If you
had seen his leg when he was brought in two months ago . . .'

But the other was not attending. He was looking at Emil with a
mixture of pity and, it almost seemed, guilty embarrassment. Emerald
moved around his bulk and said, 'Emil, this is the District Commissioner—Mr Shellybeare. He's come to have a look at you.'

The big man smiled. 'To *visit* you. But Emerald had a zoo—or had.'
He held out his hand but was only further embarrassed by Emil's in-
ability to let go of either of his sticks.

Emerald said, 'Can he sit down, sir?'

'Of course, of course.' And as the doctor and his daughter lowered
Emil into his chair: 'You've done a very good job, Zared, I can see that.
I'll make sure to mention it in the right quarters.'

'Thank you very much, sir.' Dr Zared brightened for a moment and
then looked mournful. 'If only it had been a *British* officer it would
have been much more . . . Would you like to see his leg? Then you'll
understand—'

'No, no, I'm quite prepared to take your word for it.' Mr Shellybeare stood looking down at the small, pale-faced figure in the black-
diamonded khaki lying back in the chair below him. He was filled
with an immense pity which he did not know how to express and a
totally irrational guilt. His eyes met the crippled boy's dark ones and
read only fear and doubt. Good God—he thought—he's frightened of

me. But why? Quickly he said, 'I was calling at the hospital—privately, not in any official way—so I came to see you. Emerald has told us all about you, of course. She says she has taught you English. Is that so?'

'She has teached—taught—me to speak it, yes monsieur—sir.'

'Good. It is always a useful thing to speak another language. And how do *you* find your leg now?'

'It is—' Emil hesitated, thinking quickly '—much better. But it gives me pain if I am to walk far. I am able only to walk a little way—and very slow.'

'It hurts, does it?'

Dr Zared interposed at once. 'It's bound to, sir—bound to. No one could prevent that. But it will hurt less and less as time goes by. Emerald—bring up that chair for the D.C. Where are your manners!'

'No, no, don't bother. I can't stay long.' Mr Shellybeare hesitated, frowning a moment, then glanced from the window and said, 'Well—Emil. I take an old man's privilege and use your Christian name—If there's anything I can do for you, you must tell me. While you are here you are just as much one of my—' he smiled briefly—'subjects as Emerald or anyone else. For instance, I might be able to get word through to your parents that you are safe and nearly well again. Of course you are entitled to write home, as you know. But I could probably get the information to them much more quickly.'

Emerald said, 'He lives with two aunts in France and—'

'Let him speak for himself, Emerald. I'm sure he can.'

Emil, looking up into the big, heavy-jowled face below the thick grey hair, read only kindness and commiseration. He said haltingly, 'It is good of you. But I think—at present time—in France . . .' He stumbled and coloured. 'It is best for my aunts that no one talks of me —you comprehend?'

'Yes—yes I see.' Mr Shellybeare sighed. 'Yes. Perhaps you're right. Tell me, though. When you are released will you not go back to France?'

'I do not know. Once—yes I was certain. Now I read the newspapers which Emerald brings for me and—and I think perhaps I cannot. It is better, perhaps, some other country for some years.'

'Yes. I see.' For a moment there was silence and then the D.C. turned abruptly, glancing at his watch. 'Zared, I must go now.' He frowned a moment, then said to Emerald, 'Look—come and have dinner with us on—let me see—Friday. That's the day after tomorrow. Bring Emil, too. I'll send a car. There may be ways I can help him. You'll do that, will you, Emerald?'

'Yes, sir. Thank you very much.'

'Good.' Mr Shellybeare smiled suddenly and took Emil's hand momentarily in his own. 'I'll see you again on Friday evening. Until then—*Au'voir*, Emil.'

'*Au revoir*, monsieur.'

Nineteen

An hour later, at lunch in his own house, Mr Shellybeare was saying 'Poor little brute! I felt sorrier for him than I can remember feeling for anyone for a long time. Only twenty—and absolutely no future, I suppose. He can't even go home to his aunts when eventually we release him.'

'That—'said his wife sepulchrally from the other end of the table —'is the fault of the French, and they are not so much to blame as the Germans. And he's a German—at least legally—after all.'

'I know, I know.'

'*And* a U-boat officer.'

'We have submarines too, my dear. They are presumably very much like U-boats and do the same work. The only difference is that ours are manned by heroes and theirs by villains—or so one is asked to believe. We are supposed to hate them for their ruthlessness, but the truth is that from Britain's point of view—being an overcrowded island approached by very vulnerable seaways—the U-boats are far the most dangerous weapon that Germany possesses. And since they are the most dangerous they are also the most feared. And since one hates most what one fears most, they are the most hated. That is what it really amounts to. We've built up a picture of the average U-boat officer which is little different from the one we have of a concentration camp guard. When you meet Emil Kümmerol you will see how far off the mark that picture is.'

'And when am I to meet him?'

'I've asked Emerald to come to dinner on Friday and to bring him, too.'

Mrs Shellybeare did not pause in helping herself to potatoes proffered by a table waiter, but said in her deep, calm voice, 'Is that altogether wise?'

'I should hope I can ask anyone I like to dinner in my own district.'

'Undoubtedly.'

'I am distressed for him.' The D.C. was frowning down at his un-touched plate. 'This morning I felt guilty. I felt somehow responsible for what had happened— No, no, I don't mean that, exactly. I cannot stop people firing guns at each other in wartime and tearing each other's legs to pieces with them. No— But when I came into the room he was standing by his chair, supporting himself on two sticks. I was rather taken with him—or would have been but for one thing. He's very small—young for his age, I'd say—and good-looking in a dark immature kind of way, like young French boys often are. But . . .'

'But—what?'

'He was very frightened. Frightened of me. I saw it at once. He tried to smile; he's obviously one of those people who do that when they're frightened. It is not a nice expression.'

'Mmm—no. I suppose not.'

'I tried to reassure him as far as I could. But there was little I could say. I asked him if he would go back to his aunts—they live near Besançon, I understand—when he was eventually released. He did not think he would be able to—and he's probably right, judging by the newspapers.'

'He sees them?'

'Ours—yes. Emerald has taken to collecting them when we have finished with them. I thought at first that old Zared had suddenly come out of his shell and begun to take an interest in something other than himself. But I was too optimistic—she only wants them for this boy.'

'Emerald does?'

'Yes.'

Across the table they glanced at each other. Then Mr Shellybeare said, as if following out a personal train of thought, 'That's another reason, of course . . .'

'What is a reason for what?'

'I'm going too fast, I'm afraid. Let me see—I was saying that I felt I ought to do something for Emil Kümmerol. I do. I feel it most strongly. Here is someone, obviously completely innocent of any harm at all, who has been very badly frightened and horribly hurt. He is now faced with what, I suppose, could be at least a year, possibly considerably more, of imprisonment under fairly harsh conditions. Even when he is released he thinks he will have to go to some foreign country rather than to his home. It is all intolerably unjust.'

Mrs Shellybeare looked down her long nose for a moment and then, raising her eyebrows, stared at her husband. But all she said was, 'Well—?'

'Three days ago I had a confidential letter from Azeredo. As you know, I have always made a point of being on the best possible terms with him; we help each other where we can. His letter was to tell me privately that the Portuguese authorities are becoming a little—well, restive over this affair of the U-boat. I think they may have guessed that it had reached their own waters when it was taken but up till now they have been reluctant to make trouble since no official complaint was lodged at the time. After all, there was no proof . . . But it seems that Kalewski has gone to the German Consul and lodged an official complaint. The Consul himself is reluctant to take action. In the present state of the war he probably feels that the less conspicuous he makes himself the better. Yet he may have to do so. In which case the Portuguese will have to take official notice, of course. Now this could all be very troublesome for everybody—particularly since our friends over the border have that peculiar continental passion for paper work which we do not share. Once the thing gets off the ground, as it were, I can envisage many months of the most tiresome and litigious correspondence between Lourenço Marques and Dar-es-Salaam— largely in order to placate Portuguese *amour-propre*.

'Now the fact is that U-996 almost certainly was in neutral waters when she was taken—albeit only just over the edge of the three-mile limit. Barragold more or less admitted it himself. He seemed to think that all we had to do if the Portuguese complained was to tell them to go to hell, and leave it at that. Since he's an extremely obtuse and pig-headed man I did not take the trouble to point out that—diplomatic usages quite apart—countries on friendly terms do not behave in that way towards one another. But now, if the Portuguese take this matter up, Barragold may find himself in a very awkward position. Our headquarters will have some extremely rude things to say to the S.N.O. —and from what I know of that officer he will have no hesitation in passing them on to Barragold, with compound interest. Yet I'm indebted to the fellow since he did not make trouble for Gopal when he might have. I should like to help him, therefore. And I think I have found a way in which I can, at the same time, be of considerable assistance to H.M.G.—which is my duty—and to Emil Kümmerol— which is not my duty, but my desire.'

Mr Shellybeare paused a moment. 'When this boy comes here on Friday night I will take him into my study after dinner and put this proposition to him. I will ask him if he would like to be sent over the border—'

'But really, Geoffrey! You can't—'

'One moment, my dear, please. He will certainly say yes. They all wanted to get into Portuguese territory—every one of them. For young Kümmerol, at any rate, it will mean immediate release as soon as the war's over. And considering his physical condition, even his internment until then will mean no more than giving his parole not to leave Mozambique and reporting to the police from time to time. He'll leap at the chance—naturally. I will tell him that I can probably arrange this quite quickly provided—*provided*—that he will undertake to go to the authorities immediately he arrives and contradict Kalewski—that he will tell them the U-996 was outside territorial waters—only just outside but, nevertheless, beyond the three-mile limit when she was taken. He is an officer. His word will overrule Kalewski's. The Portuguese authorities will accept it with relief; there will be no long, drawn-out and futile diplomatic wrangle over the affair; Barragold will not be reprimanded for violating Portuguese neutrality—and Kümmerol will be able to settle down to a life of married bliss in Mozambique.'

'*Married bl—*'

'Emerald will be over the border after him within twenty-four hours. But that's Zared's worry—not mine, I'm thankful to say.'

Twenty

When they were a little more than a mile from the hospital Emerald swung her father's car off the road without any warning and into a narrow, overgrown lane. From behind came an angry hoot as another car, driven by an Indian, narrowly missed collision and shot past and down the road. From the seat beside Emerald Emil said, 'Should you not make a sign when you turn the car?'

'I generally forget to. Anyway, it reminds the man behind that his brakes probably need adjusting. Look, Emil—this is the place. It is one of the oldest houses.' The small Austin swung right again and drew up in front of a low bungalow set in a jungle of a garden above whose tangled greenery old date palms soared skyward, their thin grey-shafted boles topped by long fretted leaves gilded in the falling sun and swaying in the breeze from the sea.

Emerald turned off the engine. Birds called to one another in the deep brown dusk under banyans and wild fig trees, a monkey chattered —only these sounds and the perpetual soft rustle of the sea broke the hot silence. 'This is where I wanted us to live—if we could have stayed.'

Emil gazed at the leaning, broken roof of the veranda sagging below the weight of enveloping creepers. The front door hung askew from its termite-rotten frame, broken glass glinted here and there below gaping windows opening into darkness. 'It is in need of much restoring,' he said doubtfully at last. 'It is in great neglect. We could not have inhabited here, I think.'

'Yes, we could! It's a *lovely* place. Nobody comes here and we would never have been disturbed.' Emerald, clambering out of the driver's seat, came round the car and opened Emil's door. 'Come on—I'll help you out.'

Emil shook his head. He had experienced considerable difficulty and pain in getting into the car. 'Why? I am able to see from here.'

'No you can't—not properly. Besides— Come on, Emil!' She put one hand under his arm and pulled him and, biting his lip with the pain, leaning on her heavily, he extracted his body slowly from the cramped little car to stand panting and sweating beside her, leaning on his sticks and gazing around him without interest. In his view the object of this excursion had already been achieved. For it had been to test Emerald's theory that if she was with him the police guard would not interfere with any attempt to leave the hospital. She had been proved right since, like all Africans, the black policeman knew that whatever formal orders he might be given, the one error he must never commit was to frustrate or thwart a white woman. The women were much worse than the men—they were completely unforgiving and unscrupulous and a black man would be made to suffer sooner or later if he failed in proper respect towards one of them. He had let them go with no more than a dubious glance.

Emerald said, 'Perhaps we can find one like this over the border.' She liked deserted houses and had little idea of domesticity—as Dr Zared continually complained. 'Let's go in.'

'But—those steps. I am not able to ascend.'

'You can if I help you.'

Emil's face set mutinously. 'No.' As Dr Zared had prophesied, he had tried to do too much and was consequently suffering severe pain. He had not wanted to come on this expedition, had agreed only in order to test out the guard's reactions. Now he wanted, more than anything else, to return to the hospital, to lie on his bed and take at least one of his pain-killing pills.

'No?' Emerald let go his arm with a suddenness which nearly made him fall. She swung around in front of him, lifting an accusing forefinger towards his face. 'Hi—you! You Emil Kümmerol! You do what I say!' Her eyes and mouth were hard and she was ready, if necessary, to quarrel. Emil had disappointed her deeply by not admiring the old bungalow, She had confidently expected him to be delighted, particularly as this was the first time he had been outside the hospital. Like many strong-willed but immature people, Emerald needed others to admire what she admired, though she was never prepared to reciprocate in like manner. Emil stared at her wordlessly. He, too, was disappointed. He was in more pain than he had been for the past six weeks and he wanted sympathy and understanding and condolence. Now he realized suddenly that Emerald had never been lavish with any of these; he had received infinitely more of all of them from Latif and Rami. Over the past month he had been fascinated and amused by Emerald, had believed that she was deeply in love with him and had felt a continual glow of pleasure at this belief. Now that belief shook and began to totter. But he was not prepared to quarrel— he dare not. He smiled, the peculiar unreal smile which Emerald called ugly, and lowered his eyes. 'All right. We go in—since my pain is not important to you.'

'You've got to get used to it. You talk about it all the time. You think about it more than anything else. If Tony had been wounded I bet he wouldn't make so much of it.'

Moving slowly towards the weed-covered steps leading to the veranda, Emil eyed her bleakly. 'So? Tony is nothing to me.'

'Or me. Not after he stole that book. There you are, you see! You got up them perfectly well—and I wasn't helping you at all.'

It was dark in the old bungalow, dark and cool and very dirty. The cracked tiled floors were covered in a thick layer of dust, and dead leaves from the garden lay in draught-curved swathes or little piles in corners. The air smelled of dry rotten wood, of dust and yet also of the sea breeze outside.

They entered a long room which still contained several pieces of furniture and Emerald walked over to one side and pointed down to something which lay on the floor below a half-shuttered window. Limping slowly after her, Emil saw that it was an enormous dead rat. 'It's been here for a year. I killed it with a stone when I first came here. I left it—I thought the ants would eat it. And it dried up. Nothing ate it. Now it is petrified.'

'*Petrefak?* No. It is not stone. Dry like you say, yes. Not stoned.'

Emil spoke with an effort and only in an attempt to keep up appearances. For the first time the easy contact he had taken for granted with Emerald was broken and he needed to disguise this. Like most such attempts, it failed. Emerald turned grinning from the dead rat and, taking his arm, led him towards a low sagging bed. 'There. You can sit down—or lie down if you want.'

'We should return, I think. The guard will perhaps think we have escaped.'

'No he won't. Even if he does he will wait for a long time before raising an alarm. *He* let us go—didn't he?'

Emil began to lower himself to the bed but Emerald stopped him. 'Emil, do you remember something I said to you more than a month back?'

He smiled uneasily. 'We say so many things—talk so much. I am not able . . .'

'I said that when you were well enough we would—you know. And you agreed. You promised you would.'

Emil swallowed, licked his lips and grinned weakly. 'Yes, I remember. But I am not yet well enough—for that. Not yet.'

'Why not? It doesn't affect your leg?'

'Yes. Because I have pain. One cannot do—that, when one is pained. You think a man takes a woman when he has bad pain in the teeth, for example?'

'You said you couldn't climb those steps—until I made you.'

'When we are in Mozambique—then, yes. When I am stronger. When we are married.'

'Now,' said Emerald sullenly. She would not look at him; standing beside him, not touching him, staring across at the dead rat below the window. It was now, not then, that she wanted him, but she could not explain this; could hardly put it into words to herself. Over the border things would be different. They would be married and—and everything would be achieved, safe, secure. She believed that she truly loved Emil; but she loved him best now, while they were in danger, while every moment together was heightened in suspense and magnified in meaning by that fact. She loved him best now because they were *not* married and very far from being safe or secure, because she was flouting every law and convention by even being with him here— secretly in this silent, empty house. She loved him best now, just because he was in pain, weaker, more vulnerable than she. None of these things would ever be the same afterwards, whatever happened; and his obvious unwillingness only strengthened her own desire.

Emil himself was darkly aware of at least a part of this. He remembered the petulance and indignation of Renée, his aunts' maid at Grévilly, when, one afternoon, he had announced that he was going boating on the Doubs with two school friends instead of climbing quickly to her attic bedroom as soon as his aunts had left the house for their weekly attendance at the *Ligue des Bonnes Oeuvres*. Renée's face had held just that look of sullen, angry frustration. Then she had caught hold of him and, unclipping his belt, had tried to pull down his trousers. But he had fought back, torn her dress, and run out of the back door leaving her crying in the kitchen. He remembered the colder anger of Josephine Salvini, Waldenkolk's mistress, when he told her that he had found a new restaurant and would be away all the evening . . . 'You are still a child! You think more of your stomach than of your—!' He had offended both these women uncaringly, indeed with a certain malicious amusement. For Renée could hardly complain to his aunts nor Josephine to the Admiral. But it was a different matter with Emerald . . . 'All right,' he said, and Emerald raised her face, grinning widely in the gloom. 'But—' his voice was strained—'it may not be—be possible.'

'We'll see.' Her fingers were already unbuckling his stiff new leather belt. 'When rape is inevitable—'

'Lie down and enjoy it,' he completed, smiling wanly. Then he quickly thrust his good leg farther from his maimed one so that his falling trousers were caught at the knee. 'No—you must not look at that leg! You will become—become like me when I first see it.'

'All right.' She helped him lower himself to the dirty bed and then, quickly slipping out of her white shorts, she lay down beside him. Now slowly and intently they handled each other's bodies and Emil, with his weight off his leg, at last set to work single-mindedly to give his strange companion all the sensual pleasure which her unsatisfied instincts craved. His small firm hands moved delicately over her hardening breasts, her taut stomach, in the way Josephine had taught him in the Admiral's apartment on the Boulevard Raspail. He had scarcely thought of women for almost a year, and though a moment ago he had doubted his present ability he need not have worried; his youth, the long weeks of rest in bed had, despite his wound, strengthened him and restored his battered nervous system to a normality he had not suspected. And in the relief of this knowledge his recently abandoned adolescent desire to show off, to pretend to more of anything than he had, in some measure returned. At last it was his turn to demonstrate to Emerald something of which she herself still had no real comprehension. And as his flesh hardened beneath him and began to penetrate the girl's body he experienced a growing realization that here, for him, might well be the perfect partner. He raised himself slightly, looked down at Emerald's flushed face and read the same dawning knowledge, amazed, delighted, in her dark eyes. '*Alors?*' he grinned, holding himself back, and Emerald whispered, 'Oh, Emil—it is, it is!'

'Yes? What?'

She swallowed, shaking her head, unable to speak, and he thrust again with his hips, gently, firmly, watching her eyes widen, her breath hiss between her bared teeth. 'You like?'

'Oh God! Oh God—yes! Emil—go on!'

'*Jawohl!*' He kissed her, pressing his tongue between her clenched teeth which opened to receive it, aware that for the first time he was the master, that it was her body, not his, that was now the suppliant, the beseecher. He moved faster, harder, feeling her shuddering and responding beneath him—and then once more gently slackened, watching her carefully through half-closed eyes. Her fingers slid down his back and then were hard and urgent on the flesh of his buttocks, pressing him forward while her own hips lifted, pressing upward in an attempt to force him into her to the fullest depth. '*Du calme,* Emerald!' He laughed gently 'Be more slow. It is better—*vraiment!*'

'No: no! Oh, Emil, I do love you! I do! I do!'

Again and again. And now he, too, who had restrained himself so long, was carried away on the flood tide of his desire. Momentarily he forgot everything, all that Josephine had taught him and had made him perform ('You are not a little hog, Emil, rutting for truffles. You are a Frenchman and you must learn, also, the ways of giving pleasure') and responding wholly to the demands of his nerves and tissues he broke within her, hearing her sudden quick, animal cry, feeling through the fierce voiding surge the pelvic bone of her lower body sharp against his own, and then fell back breathless, sweating, his hands automatically stroking her as their bodies came gently apart. For a long moment there was silence save for their harsh breathing, the slight rustle of dead leaves stirred by the sea breeze and the creak of a swaying shutter. Slowly, through an overpowering, nerveless lassitude, Emil sensed the dull pain in his leg returning. Then he felt his closed eyelids delicately pulled apart and Emerald was leaning over him with an expression on her face which he had never seen before or believed it could wear. She kissed him gently on the lips and smilingly he mumbled, 'Then—now you know? Now you are satisfied—for the present?'

'Emil—is it always like that?'

'Perhaps. It is depending. With us—yes, I hope.'

Emerald gave a long contented sigh and rose from the bed. 'With us,' she repeated. 'Yes, with us it will be. I know.' Then, glancing at her watch, she said, 'Oh God, Emil, we must hurry! Even that black idiot outside your door won't wait much longer. Oh Christ! Oh God—make him wait! We can't have trouble *now*.'

She pulled on her clothes with frantic speed and then eased Emil to his feet. As he stood, clutching one stick and groping for the other beside the bed, his unbelted, unbuttoned khaki trousers fell to his ankles and Emerald looked for the first time at the stick-thin, discoloured and mangled limb within the steel brace. She caught her breath sharply, bent and, pulling up his trousers, belted them around his waist. 'You can button them in the car.' Then, pausing, she caught him to her and kissed him with a loving tenderness, a deep compassion which she had never shown before.

On the way back to the hospital she said suddenly, 'We ought to go tomorrow,' and Emil, startled, glanced quickly at her. 'But are we not to visit your friend, the District Commissioner?'

'Yes. I mean afterwards. It's the ideal time. Everyone in the hospital will know we are at the Shellybeares'. They won't know how long we'll be and they'll never dare telephone—oh, for ages. It would be taking a diabolical liberty, you see. We'll leave very early, saying your leg hurts, and drive right around outside the town and leave the car as far away as possible. I'll have the launch fuelled and ready and we'll have to row her out of the harbour as quietly as we can. If Ahmed and Khaled together can row her, so can we. And then—and then . . . Ah, I can't wait to be gone!'

The car swung out on a curve which for a moment brought the whole sunset panorama of the harbour into view. 'Look—there's the launch! Down at there the harbour wall.'

'Oh—yes!' Emil gazed with interest. Two flags, one white and red, one blue and yellow, fluttered at the launch's short mast. 'Why is it flying "H.L."?'

'What?'

'Those flags.'

'Oh, Gopal gave them to Spencer soon after he got the launch. He always flies them. They're pretty, aren't they?'

'He does not—' Emil giggled—'know the International Code?'

'No. Why?'

'H.L. It means "It is dangerous to go so fast".'

They laughed delightedly and Emerald said, 'Dear Gopal! Perhaps, in a way, I shall be sorry to leave here after all.'

'I, too. I wish that—'

'But we must. We have no choice.'

The car drew up beside the poinsettia hedge on the hospital's deserted parking lot. 'Now I'd better go home, Emil. I'll get the launch ready tomorrow morning and I'll call in here with some books and things, about midday—just as if everything was ordinary.'

For a short moment they sat silently in the twilit interior of the car, their hands clasped together. And then, impulsively they were in each other's arms—lovers now, fully, completely, for ever.

Twenty-one

That evening Latif took Emil to the bathroom and assisted him into the bath. And for the first time for weeks Emil was embarrassed at the gentle Indian's presence. For so long he had been used to the continual handling of his body by the two orderlies that this had seemed no stranger than Dr Zared's impersonal clinical examinations. But tonight, as Latif undressed him, eased him carefully over the white enamel side and lowered him into the tepid water, he felt oddly uncomfortable. Could there be any sign on his body by which the dark eyes above him might guess who had last stroked so lingeringly his naked flesh? Tonight he tried to take the rubber sponge and wash himself. but Latif, smiling, shaking his head, said, 'No—not yet,' and pulled it gently from his grasp.

He was glad when he was dressed once more in pyjamas and back in his room—the room that tomorrow evening he would be leaving for ever. From his high bed he looked around at the undecorated white walls, the windows which, when unshuttered at early morning and at sunset, gave a wide view over the neat green hospital garden; the twin tables, the long chair upholstered in startlingly floral cotton—the cupboard against the wall from which Emerald had taken the catheter on that memorable morning which now seemed so long ago. He smiled at the recollection and picked up the leather-bound illustrated copy of *Alice in Wonderland* which Emerald said was her own favourite book.

It was not, he thought, a particularly easy one for a foreigner to understand, despite its simple English. There were double meanings, surely, odd convolutions of speech, which only those to whom the language was their own could perhaps appreciate. And yet how easy it was to understand that such a book, full of oddities and inconsequencies, spoken by animals of the most eccentric natures, should appeal to Emerald. Despite the illustrations, it was not the gentle, fair-haired little Alice in her blue Victorian frock and virginal stockings but another very different girl, ebony-haired, bare-legged, grinning, that he seemed to see, wandering with her hands in the pockets of her white shorts, through the pages . . . *'It is a long tail, certainly,' said Emerald, looking down with wonder at the Mouse's tail; 'but why do you call it sad?' And she kept on puzzling about it while the Mouse was speaking, so that her idea of the tale was something like this*—'Fury said to

                                a mouse, That
                                  he met in the
                                    house, "Let
                                      us both go
                                      to law: *I*
                                      will prose-
                                      cute *you*.—
                                      Come, I'll
                                      take no de-
                                      nial: We
                                      must have
                                      the trial;
                                      For really
                                    this morn-
                                  ing I've
                                nothing
                                to do."
                                  Said the
                                    mouse to
                                      the cur
                                      "Such a
                                      trial, dear
                                    Sir, With
                                    no jury
                                      or judge,
                                      would
                                      be wast-
                                    ing our
                                    breath."
                                    "I'll be
                                  judge,
                                  I'll be
                                  jury,"
                                said
                              cun-
                              ning
                              old
                                Fury:
                                "I'll
                                try
                                  the
                                    whole
                                    cause,
                                    and
                                  con-
                                  demn
                                  you to
                                  death.' "

Twenty-two

Next morning at ten-thirty Emerald strolled casually down to the harbour. She had four East African twenty-shilling notes in her pocket, money with which tomorrow she was supposed to pay the household servants' fortnightly wages but which she intended to give to one of Mr Spencer's boatmen to buy a full load of fuel. She had decided that this could only safely be done at the last moment. Yet as she wandered with careful slowness down the long jetty she caught sight of Tony Brickler's small grey car, and her heart jolted when she realized that it was parked above the mooring normally reserved for Mr Spencer's launch. Tony—she wished suddenly that she had paid him more attention in the past few weeks, had not neglected him quite so obviously. He would not have become jealous for that, she guessed instinctively, was not his nature, but suspicious—yes. He was no fool, and after Kalewski's escape . . . his own knowledge of her continual visits to the hospital . . . the episode of the U-boat's log, '*Auf Wiedersehen*, Emerald . . .' What was he *doing* there by the launch?

She hurried her steps and passing the small car she came to the jetty's edge, hearing his voice below and Khaled's deeper one in monosyllabic reply. They had lifted the engine hatch and were doing something to the machinery. Emerald felt herself begin to tremble, but her voice was quite normal as she called, 'Hi, Tony—what are you doing with Spencer's *pinnace*?'

He turned at once, smiling up at her, cleaning his oily hands on a piece of cotton waste. 'Hallo, Emerald. You want to take it out?'

'Later.'

'Fishing?'

'Yes.'

'Oh—well, it'll be ready in another five minutes; if you're not in a hurry.'

Emerald felt the trembling of her legs begin to subside a little. Nothing was wrong, then. But what was Tony doing here at all?

'Since when have you become one of Spencer's boatmen?'

'Me?' He was laughing now, soundlessly, his shoulders twitching. 'Well, only about a week ago. Khaled thought the magneto was faulty so we took it out and we checked it in my garage. I've had it there since last week—since the time you visited the U-boat, actually.'

227

Emerald swallowed, feeling her mouth drying, her heart thudding. 'What—what are you trying to say, you bastard?'

Tony went on carefully, unconcernedly, cleaning his hands on the cotton waste. Behind him Khaled clinked amongst the machinery with a small spanner. 'Only that I've put it back now and the boat's in perfect order again. You can go fishing in it—or anything you want. You could make the longest trip you liked in it—now.'

Emerald could not speak. She stared wordlessly down at him and then, throwing the soiled waste into the water, he looked up, his eyes expressionless behind his spectacles. 'Been to the hospital, Emerald? No—obviously not. They took him away at seven-thirty this morning.'

'THE HANDS OF SPAIN'

One

Endlessly, ceaselessly, the grey autumn rain poured down over the ruined city, desolate and fire-scarred under the weeping sky. The periphery alone was properly habitable. Here, in the dull suburban roads, a great quiet reigned, the quiet of peace; the peace of desolation. Peace had fallen six months ago like a heavy blanket under which all sounds were muted, all actions slowed to the unsteady, faltering heartbeat of a German city more than half dead.

From the window of the ground-floor room which served as an office Corporal Post stared out through the dripping glass, over a gleaming laurel hedge towards an identical window partly screened by an identical hedge on the other side of the street. That house was empty, so was the one on its right. In the one on the left lived a coal-less coal merchant to whom, from time to time, Post furtively took a pailful of coal from their own rations. If Captain Kaye knew of this, and Post thought that he probably did, nothing had as yet been said about it. The Captain might disapprove, though not to the point of ordering the cessation of his clerk's illegal activity. But even during the recent war Kaye had never known cold or hunger, whereas Post had known plenty of both since well before it—he was able to sympathize. Post had been working for the Captain for nearly seven months—since one lucky April night when, returning tired, lonely and penniless to a crowded Paris Y.M.C.A. hostel, he had found Kaye slumped in the stertorous sleep of the very drunk in the arch of a narrow street leading off the Butte of Montmartre. Post had automatically gone through his pockets but someone had been before him and there was nothing left but a crumpled envelope bearing the address of a quiet but expensive hotel some streets away. Out of nostalgia more than anything else—he had done it so many countless times for his father—Post got the Captain to his feet and, eyes and ears wary for the military police, manœuvred him home. He had hoped for a small financial reward for this service but Kaye was too drunk, the hotel staff too swiftly competent in taking over, to allow of this. Post left his own name and the address of the hostel and then, without much hope, returned to it.

Yet next day at the early hour of eight in the morning he had been called to the telephone, called half-way across Paris, to receive twenty dollars and the explanation that the Captain had not, as might have been assumed from appearances, been under the influence of alchohol but taken suddenly with postprandial fish poisoning. Post, young, pale, narrow-eyed, smart and polished, had let no flicker of amusement appear on his face but had accepted the story with correctly deferential respect and, a few moments afterwards, an invitation to dinner that night. The upshot of the dinner had been his present job and with it promotion to corporal's rank. 'Discretion—' Captain Kaye had said—'is a most necessary attribute in our department. It seems to me that you are discreet.'

Discretion was one of twenty-two-year-old Post's virtues—the others being good manners and a personal neatness and cleanliness which had always predisposed his army superiors in his favour, marking him out for early promotion which somehow never materialized, the idea being at first postponed and then abandoned as Post's defects came to light. For Post seemed instinctively to possess all the old soldier's ability to malinger and shirk every sort of unpleasant duty. He had a particular dislike of manual work and would go to astonishing lengths to avoid it; yet on the occasion when his superiors had attempted to accommodate him in this foible by giving him clerical jobs in store-rooms and offices the fast-growing list of missing articles made it imperative to shift him back to a position where he was no longer able to lay his quick clean fingers on disposable items of U.S. Army property. He had been thrown from unit to unit, arriving at each with a black report of his past, a neatly pressed uniform and a snapping salute. 'This boy's been misunderstood. Probably his last C.O. was a sonofabitch,' was the instinctive reaction of each new commander and each in turn did everything he could to 'help' Post—and each in turn was sadly disillusioned. Except Captain Kaye.

Post had always been unpopular in the U.S. Army, but his unpopularity was nothing compared to that of his wealthy, erudite and talented patron—Kaye was universally loathed, although he had some haughty, sneering friends in the desk-bound rear echelons of the British and French forces. Like his young clerk, he also took an inimical view of the Army and its institutions, though he took it from a different angle; while Post stared up with cold, polite hatred, Kaye looked down in scorpionic ridicule. They suited each other very well, were happy in each other's company, and lived and worked in mutually untrusting friendship.

At first Post had suspected and hoped that Captain Kaye was a practising homosexual. Since he himself was almost sexless he would have acceded to any requests of the Captain's and later exploited the position in terms of firm yet delicate blackmail. But though Post had hinted that he was open to any suggestions Kaye had never responded. They both lived lives chaste as monks.

And now, on this wet autumn afternoon as the Captain's small car at last appeared around the curve of the long road and drew up beyond the laurel hedge, its tyres hissing on the wet macadam, Post thought, not for the first time, that there was something distinctly monkish about Captain Kaye. That burly figure now clambering from the too-small driving seat, the massive head, bulbous nose and thick brown beard pied with grey—all would have suited to perfection the Christ-mas-card portrait of the merry monk, cellarer to the abbot, jovial, brown-capuchined, white-corded, sandalled.

Post moved swiftly into the vestibule and had the front door open before the Captain—shoulders hunched under turned-up collar, hands thrust deep in pockets—had reached it. Valet-like he took the Captain's hat, the Captain's stick, the Captain's gloves, and helped him smoothly from his dripping raincoat.

'Anything come in, Mr P?' Kaye's voice was light, surprisingly weak for such a broad-chested, burly man, and despite his American uniform he spoke an English which could not have been faulted by the most Oxford-educated B.B.C. announcer—Oxford, in any case, being Kaye's old university.

'No, sir, nothing at all.'

'Leaving us well alone, are they? Well—we can't have Reynolds after all.'

'No?' Surprise raised Post's pale eyebrows. He hung the Captain's coat on one of six ornate unpolished brass hooks and followed his superior from the ugly little hall into the still uglier little sitting-room —now used as their office. Straddling before the fire, Kaye blew out his bearded cheeks and eased his shoulders under his well-cut tunic. 'No. The Cowboy got to hear of it. He's taking a specially vindictive interest in Reynolds.'

'But if Reynolds *asked* . . . Surely—?'

'Reynolds was told to ask again—to have second thoughts, as it were.'

'The dirty bastard!'

'You refer, I take it, to the Cowboy rather than Reynolds?'

'Yes.'

'Quite so. I'm sorry, of course. Not for Reynolds—he's a moron— but for myself. A last chance to give the Cowboy another gastric ulcer or it might have been a cerebral hæmorrhage this time, who can say?' Kaye examined his fingernails, then turned and spread his hands before the fire. Over his shoulder he said, 'Ah well, there it is. When I am disappointed in my expectations I do not, you will note, Mr P, start screaming and smashing the furniture and assaulting my subordinates. But then of course I'm not a backwoods Texas general—merely a captain, and a noncombatant one at that, I'm thankful to say.' He turned back to the room, took off his gold pince-nez, polished them with a silk handkerchief he drew from his cuff, replaced them. 'You remember Major Harkhurst?'

'Yes, sir.'

'He's been arrested and flown back to London. Illegal currency deals. Yes, thousands of pounds involved, I understand. I had always thought Harkhurst was a rich man in his own right. Apparently not, however. Major Glenberyll was in headquarters and he told me. A great loss—I refer to the Major, not the money—to the British. Glenberyll was distressed—naturally. It happened three days ago. That's the trouble about having our own little place out here—we don't hear of these things promptly as one does nearer headquarters.' For a moment Kaye's head sank towards his chest, he brooded silently. Behind him the fire whispered, answering the soft whisper of the rain in the silent street beyond the window.

Post stood quietly waiting and in a minute the Captain looked up, blinked and said, 'Mr P—tell me this. If you were a submarine commander and you believed that it was vital to the safety of your boat and crew to destroy the survivors of an enemy ship which you had just sunk—if you believed that unless you did this your boat would inevitably be tracked and destroyed within twenty-four hours—what would you do?'

'Kill the survivors—surely,' said Post promptly. 'I mean, what else . . .'

'Exactly.'

'I mean I'd— Well, I'd *have* to, wouldn't I?'

'You could leave them—and accept the consequences.'

'Hell, no!'

'Exactly,' said the Captain again. He sighed briefly. 'Well—that is what we are on to now instead of Reynolds. Glenberyll's the J.A. He was looking for someone to take the defence in place of Harkhurst and was only too pleased when I told him that I was temporarily free and would take it on if he liked. He's sending the papers round this evening.'

'I don't quite see—' began Post cautiously, but the Captain cut him short. 'At present the position is not much clearer to me, either. I've told you the nub of the matter, though. A German U-boat torpedoed and sank an old freighter—nearly a year ago, I think Glenberyll said. Owing to the ship's position at the time the Captain believed—or says he believed—that only the immediate elimination of the few sur-vivors could save his boat from early discovery by Allied aircraft. He therefore machine-gunned them and destroyed their lifeboats and made off. But he failed to kill them all and in the event there was one who lived. Then the U-boat was damaged and forced to surrender. Its log was checked and it was found that the sinking of the freighter corresponded in time and place to the deposition of the said survivor. Hence the U-boat captain and another officer are now on a war crimes charge. At least that's the outline Glenberyll gave me. The court con-venes next Thursday—or would have done so until this unfortunate business of Harkhurst. I told Glenberyll I'd probably need more time if I was to prepare the brief properly. So—' the Captain, warmed now, left the fire and, taking a bottle of whisky and a small glass from a cup-board near his desk, poured himself a shot and swallowed it at one gulp—'instead of defending an illiterate ex-farm hand on a charge of rape I shall be defending a probably very literate pair of Huns on what I think technically is a charge of piracy upon the high seas.'

Two

'. . . and therefore fully qualified as a British barrister as well, you see. And since he spent the last five years before the war living in Paris and attending all the more salacious and scandalous French court cases I imagine he's pretty well up in the Code Napoléon, too.'

The short, bald captain leaned forward to knock out his pipe into the brass ashtray on the low table at which he sat with two other officers of the British Judge Advocate General's staff, and continued, 'The fact is, my dear Glenberyll, that he's never had to practise for a living. His father died a week after he was called to the Bar and left him a very fine fortune. A great waste of talent—or so it was said at the time. He started writing novels. I can't think why—they were very bad ones. Anyhow he had a theory that any novel could be sold in thousands of copies irrespective of all literary merit so long as it re-ceived enough publicity. His first one had failed completely and it appeared most unlikely that his second would do any better. It was a dreadful piece of nonsense called *Where Is Thy Sting?* and dealing with the adventures of a man employed to lay out the corpses of Paris suicides dragged from the Seine. If I recall it correctly, one of the corpses is that of a beautiful girl who turns out not to be completely moribund after all and is brought back to life by the mortuary attendant and subsequently falls for him—only to find that he is already unhappily married. So she pushes his wife into the river and in due course the wife appears on the mortuary slab, too—Oh, it goes on and on— most improbably. Well, anyway, he had written this horror-comic under the pen name of Harvey Prentice, and as soon as the book was published he wrote a letter to *The Times*—above his proper name— stating that although the book was extremely good—brilliant, even— its author, Harvey Prentice, was a liar, a plagiarist and a thief. He then, in the name of Harvey Prentice, sued himself for criminal libel and carried on a flaming correspondence with himself under both names in the columns of *The Times* for a fortnight. He achieved his publicity all right, and of course he was careful to have the thing settled out of court. Even so it was quite scandalous. Most of us thought he should have been disbarred.'

From his place beside the speaker Major Glenberyll, a lean, balding man with a narrow face and quick, intelligent grey eyes, sipped his gin and bitters and said curiously, 'Wasn't there some trouble between him and Patton—earlier this year?— Look, it's my turn. What are you having? The same again?'

'There's *always* trouble between him and any superior officer he meets. As I say, he's never needed to earn his living and therefore he's not used to taking orders from anyone. As for the Patton business—I suppose he had a certain amount of justification. Well, we all know enough about Patton, don't we? There's always justification. It started when they met in London. Patton looked him up and down and said, "Why the beaver, brother?"'

'Kaye was furious. "My beard, sir?" he said coldly. "To hide a war wound, actually. I have permission, of course."

' "Where were you wounded, Captain?"

' "Here, sir, in London. Flying glass from a bomb explosion."

' "Christ-on-a-crutch!" shouted Patton. "And you have the goddam nerve to call *that* a war wound! I don't know what our officers are coming to nowadays! If you cut your thumb opening a can of army bully I suppose you'll put in for a Purple Heart, eh?" and he stormed off. As a matter of fact the scar on Kaye's chin was caused when someone bashed him with a bottle in a pub. He's generally quite a moderate drinker, but every so often he breaks out and indulges in the most horrifying drunks. It's his only vice as far as is known. Otherwise he's a most respectable man . . . Well, anyway, later on one of Patton's men came up on this rape charge. Patton was keen to have the thing over and done with quickly and quietly for the sake of Third Army's reputation. Kaye was defending officer. He knew what Patton wanted and he determined to thwart him. He did. He made that court-martial as sensationally lurid as any pre-war *cause célèbre* and kept it going for a full week. He even got the man off in the end by proving that he was a raging homosexual with no interest in women—and implying in a dozen different ways that most of the officers of Third Army were of the same inclination. He actually used the term "rotten to the core with unnatural vice"—and was strongly rebuked by the court for doing so. Since then he's credited—or credits himself—with having given Patton a gastric ulcer. He says it is his sole and most valuable contribution to the Allied war effort . . .'

Three

The rain fell interminably from the low grey autumn sky over the city, over the burned and broken docks, over the flat grey North Sea . . . 'But they called it the German Ocean, didn't they?' said Colonel Whaley-Wren, turning from the window of his temporary office in one of the very few habitable buildings remaining near the harbour. 'What a mess they made of things—what a really appalling mess.' His voice, like his movements, was soft and slow and careful. To Major Yatchett and Commander Gordon-Bryce, sitting in the visitors' chairs before the desk, he seemed the epitome of a lawyer, perhaps a judge, for a full horsehair wig above a scarlet fur-trimmed robe would set off that lined, parchment-coloured old face to perfection. Yet the Colonel was not a lawyer but a regular soldier of wide, even vast, experience as the rows of medal ribbons above his left breast pocket proclaimed. These included the Victoria Cross, earned as an eighteen-year-old volunteer at Spion Kop—from which death-trap he had escaped with the loss of most of the toes on his right foot. In ordinary circumstances he would have been invalided out of the service upon dismissal from the hospital, but he did not wish to leave the Army and pleaded strongly to be allowed to remain. His V.C. pleaded still more strongly and he was retained. Since then Colonel Whaley-Wren had lived, as it were, upon the moral earnings of his medal. It, and the fact that he came from a satisfactorily upper middle-class family, had ensured his rapid commissioning and subsequent slow but steady promotion in military administrative circles. For without the requisite number of toes he could not, of course, fight again.

Partially toeless, he had sat through the First World War in military railway depots at Reading, South Shields and Market Bosworth. Later, in a variety of hot, whitewashed offices in India he had sat through long, confused campaigns on the North-West Frontier. Genial, bald and very slow, he had sat through the Second World War in offices at Aldershot, Caterham and Bury St Edmunds—and only in late August, nearly four months after the cessation of hostilities, had he leisurely packed his bags and crossed the North Sea—or the German Ocean—to help administer the occupied enemy.

Though the last time Colonel Whaley-Wren had heard a shot fired in anger was while he crouched in the corpse-filled trench below Aloe Knoll under the murderously accurate enfilading fire of Commandant Oppermann's burghers, he had gained, through forty-five sedentary years, an almost unparalleled knowledge of the interior working of every department of the British Army. He could not possibly recall the number of courts-martial upon which he had sat—and for the last fifteen years it had generally been as president—but his knowledge of military law, procedure and precedent were unequalled by anyone outside, and perhaps by most within, the Judge Advocate General's Office itself. And it was for a short briefing on the background of the military tribunal upon which they were shortly to sit, under Colonel Whaley-Wren's presidency, that the two junior officers had been requested to call at his office this morning.

Now the Colonel sighed slowly, and slowly turned from the window to crumple lumpily into the padded chair behind his desk. 'Well—' he said, adjusting a pair of reading spectacles on his red-veined nose—'well, well, well. Hmmm. Yes—this forthcoming trial.' He glanced up over his spectacles at the two younger men. 'I've been asked, as you know, to give you both an idea of the procedure we are adopting. The J.A. in the case asked me to do that. You've both sat on courts-martial before, I imagine?'

'Yes, sir,' from Commander Gordon-Bryce.

'No, sir—only courts of inquiry,' from Major Yatchett.

'Hmmm. Well, it doesn't really matter. The present trial will, in the main, follow the procedure of the ordinary Field General Court-

Martial. The position is this: early in nineteen forty-three Britain initiated a body termed the United Nations War Crimes Commission. It was regrettably very evident by then that the enemy were behaving so frequently with a disregard of the Laws and Usages of War that punitive measures would have to be taken against them at the conclusion of hostilities. Each country sends this Commission the particulars of any war crime of which it acquires information, and after examining the report the Commission then decides if there is a prima facie case. If it is decided that this is so the papers are then passed to the legal authorities of the country concerned—which, generally speaking, means the country against whom the alleged crime has been committed. In our case such documents are examined a second time by the Attorney-General. If he also believes that there is a case to answer, the papers go to the Judge Advocate General's Office for the initiation and preparation of a trial. All right?'

'Yes, sir' from both officers although neither appeared anything but mildly perplexed, and Yatchett looked frankly bored. He had been detailed for this job simply because someone had to go and his company had suffered an early-morning inspection by the battalion commander when that officer had a hangover. It was Major Yatchett's colonel's drinking habits which were responsible for Major Yatchett's presence here today.

'Well—' continued Colonel Whaley-Wren with the mild enjoyment of one imparting abstruse knowledge to novices—'the Court itself is convened under royal warrant which empowers a military court to try foreign nationals for specific crimes committed in any war subsequent to that commencing on the second of September nineteen thirty-nine.'

'Meaning this last one, I suppose, sir?'

'No. Meaning *any* war in which H.M. has been engaged after that date.'

'But—' Commander Gordon-Bryce looked puzzled—'there has only been this one, hasn't there? Since then, I mean?'

'I myself am not aware of any other, I must admit.'

'Then it *does* mean this war.'

'No,' said Colonel Whaley-Wren comfortably. 'It means what it says. Do not forget the operative words "any" and "subsequent to".'

Gordon-Bryce looked baffled and momentarily indignant. Major Yatchett was gazing glazedly out of the window at the rain. 'But—' the Colonel added kindly as if handing out a charitable though unmerited encouragement to a stupid student—'it naturally *includes* this last war. Yes. Well now, the position with the case we are dealing with is slightly complicated by the fact that the alleged offence has been committed against two countries.'

'Two?' echoed Major Yatchett, who felt it was time he spoke, yet as briefly as possible, to indicate, untruthfully, that he was listening.

'In actual fact seven are involved.'

'Oh, God!'

'Do not worry—only two are taking part. Seven are involved in so far as the nationalities of the crew of the sunken ship included British, French, Belgian, Dutch, Danish, Chinese and Brazilian. At least one national of each of these countries died as a result of the incident and consequently each country has the right to call for proceedings against the accused. However, only two have done so—Britain and France. The ship involved was originally French but was taken over by the British and was steaming under the Red Ensign and commanded by a British captain. None the less the chief officer and a majority of the crew were French—as is the single survivor upon whose testimony the most important evidence may well rest. Consequently the French are being represented, and there will be three French officers—two naval and one military—sitting with you as members of the court. I can assure you—' Colonel Whaley-Wren's voice held a note of wearily remembered exasperation—'that to find three French officers who spoke even passable English, to acquire their services from their superiors and to collect them in one place at the same time, has been a —a not inconsiderable achievement upon the part of those responsible for the organization of this trial.' For a moment he pondered gloomily upon the expenditure of time, toil and temper which that achievement had involved. Then he continued more equably, 'Now the main differences—the rain, Yatchett, will not, I fear, cease despite your fixed regard of it through the window—as I was saying, the main differences between this trial and an ordinary court-martial are firstly, that the court is not administering British military law, or, for that matter, British Statute Law, or what, in other countries, is termed Municipal Law. It is administering, basically and with amendations, the complex and rather vague set of rules and regulations known as the Laws and Usages of War which in themselves are largely based upon International Law and those parts of it incorporated in the Hague Conventions. Another difference is that I, as President of the Court, will be in no more than nominal charge of the proceedings. We shall be directed by a properly qualified lawyer, a member of the D.J.A.G.'s staff, who will, I expect, assume the full duties of the role normally un-

dertaken by the judge in a British criminal trial at home. I will be--
hmm—little more than a Master of Ceremonies. You and your
French colleagues will really be what is known on the Continent as
"Assessors"—which means, in effect, the jury; although unlike members of a British jury you will have the right to question witnesses
directly. I advise you, however—' Colonel Whaley-Wren glanced
pointedly over his spectacles at each officer in turn—'to exercise that
right with the very greatest discretion—if, indeed, at all. An improper
question from a court member can earn him a severe rebuke from the
J.A. I only hope that someone has told the French that.'

He paused. 'Well then, it only remains for me to say that counsel
for the prosecution and for the defence will be, of course, fully qualified legal men.' He glanced down at a paper before him. 'Lieutenant-
Colonel Rostwood from the D.J.A.G.'s office is prosecuting and
—hmm—since there was some difficulty about the proposed British
defence counsel I see we have an American—Captain Matthew G. Kaye
of the U.S. Judge Advocate General's staff, assisted by German counsel
—Dr Adalbert Stusser. Yes. Well, I think that's all. Well, gentlemen, I
needn't keep you any longer, I believe. Thursday morning, nine
o'clock—and don't, please, be late. You've no questions, I take it?'

Major Yatchett really had no questions since he had listened to very
little of the Colonel's speech, and that little had seemed to him intolerable gibberish. But it had gone on for a long time, and glancing
at his watch he was angrily aware that he was going to be very late for
a luncheon party to which he had been looking forward. So he said,
rather rudely, 'Yes, sir. Wouldn't it be better to cut out all these preliminaries and shoot them out of hand?'

'Shoot whom out of hand, my dear Yatchett? Captain Kaye? Dr
Stusser? The Deputy Judge Advocate General?'

'No—the men who did it.'

'Ah! I take it you mean, by that expression, the accused. Yes,
certainly it would. Very much better. You, Commander? Any
questions?'

Commander Gordon-Bryce looked slightly shocked. He was a
painstaking, conscientious and godly man who intended, upon his
release from the Royal Navy, to enter the Church. 'Well sir, I follow
what you've said about procedure. At least—' he added cautiously—
'I *think* I do. But I don't know—not really—what this trial's about. I
was only roped in—detailed, I mean—yesterday evening. What are
these men—the accused, that is—supposed to have done?'

But Colonel Whaley-Wren had lost interest. He, too, had suddenly remembered that he was late for a luncheon engagement. 'You'll hear all about that at the trial itself, I daresay,' he said, shovelling papers quickly into a drawer. 'Anyway, it's no use asking me. I've absolutely no idea—none whatever. Good morning to you both. Good morning, good morning.'

Four

Capitaine-de-vaisseau Roger Meilhac woke in the night, hot, damp and shivering. On the low slate gable below his bedroom window he heard the drip and splash of rain—this European rain which went on and on, so unlike the torrential but quickly terminated downpours of the West African coast. He was uncertain whether he was about to start another attack of malaria but the possibility both frightened and obscurely pleased him. The fear was for his safety—to lie here, ill and alone, in an obscure German hotel in a town he had never before visited. The pleasure was only in the thought that, after all, he would avoid this embarrassing trial to which, angry and resentful, he had been ordered by an almost equally angry and resentful superior. If, upon his arrival two days ago, he had lodged as was his right at the Allied Officers Club, or even at the British Transit Camp, he would have been perfectly safe from a medical point of view—even a doltish British medical officer could take care of a malaria case. But Capitaine Meilhac had refused to do this since he could trust himself in neither of those places.

Meilhac was, he believed, a rational man, and at forty he considered that he was an experienced one. He knew perfectly well that the individual English officers he would have met either at the club or at the camp were no more to blame for the happenings of the last six years than he was himself. Also, if they ran true to form they would probably keep themselves to themselves, eating their meals silently or with the minimum of monosyllabic conversation before screening themselves once more in the lounge behind their newspapers. One had only to keep well away from the bar and those voluble Americans.

But one could never be certain that it would be quite like that. No one ever ran exactly true to type. He might be accosted, spoken to. And then, almost certainly, he would be extremely rude and—God forbid—he might even get into a fight. Anything was better than that, even this down-at-heel hotel with its servile patron and its lack of everything—soap, heating, hot water.

He shuddered in a sudden spasm and reaching, for his flash-light, clicked it on—naturally the bedside lamp did not work. Now the quinine bottle. How his hands shook! And this water—dangerous? Defiantly he took a long gulp and lay back sweating.

Tomorrow, if he was not down with fever, which seemed satisfactorily likely, he was to sit in judgment upon two naval officers of the nation which had conquered and occupied France five years ago. The ancient enemy . . . Eighteen-seventy and that altered telegram; von Moltke and the Crown Prince trapping the French armies at Sedan and Metz . . . Nineteen-fourteen and von Kluck's terrible thrust into the heart of France—the 'sacrificial road' to Verdun . . . And then the finality of May nineteen-forty. But surely the *natural* enemy of France was England—through hundreds of years of warfare while swords and bows gave way to arquebuses and matchlocks and these to musket and rifle. Century after century. A short period of armed truce interspersed by quickly flaring quarrels as the two countries jostled jealously over their expanding colonial empires; then that fat, lecherous old king who never stopped eating and who liked Paris—the Entente Cordiale epoch. But there had been little cordial about it except the name. The war of 1914 had seen nothing but endless bickering and feuding between the two General Staffs and extreme mistrust among their respective politicians—even the very troops had disliked and despised each other and it was well known that the common English soldier had returned to his country with a detestation of all things French and only admiration for his German adversary.

Capitaine Meilhac groaned and, half sunk in a feverish doze, flung one weary fire-scarred arm upwards across his head. During the recent war he had fought in two savage battles, both against the English. They were the only actions in which he had ever taken part.

Mers-el-Kebir in the long, hot stillness of a July afternoon with the best part of the French fleet at anchor in the great harbour, the crews still dazed with the shock and bitterness of a lost war in which their great guns had not fired one single shot . . . The entrance of a fast motor torpedo boat with gold-braided English officers in the stern while the Mediterranean Fleet steamed ominously over the horizon. The terms put to Admiral Gensoul that baking afternoon had been unbelievable. The fleet must either scuttle itself immediately, surrender to the English and steam under English guns to a British port, or suffer a full-scale attack where it lay. Gensoul, having no authority to take such actions, prevaricated and demanded time.

The first most of the French crews knew of what was happening was when the guns opened up on them from out to sea. Since their furnaces were out the French ships could not manœuvre and they presented sitting targets. Meilhac had spent that afternoon under heavy shellfire tearing about the harbour in a motor launch frantically trying to deliver orders and counter orders which became ever more unrealistic as ship after ship, struck by full salvoes, blew up, capsized or blazed like torches. It was while approaching the *Bretagne* that Meilhac's boat had been shattered by a near miss intended for the cruiser. He himself had been thrown, burned, bleeding and unconscious into the harbour to float there, supported by his life-jacket, until rescued more than an hour later.

And when, a fortnight afterwards, Meilhac left the hospital it was to see the great base empty but for charred and canted wrecks whose broken superstructures protruded here and there above the calm sea.

In France there was fury and demands for war against Britain, but to Meilhac, still weak from loss of blood, a declaration of war was merely academic—France *was* at war with Britain. What else was the meaning of those shattered hulks and the thousands of new sailors' graves in the Oran cemeteries?

In September he was at Dakar, posted there with many other ship-less survivors to man the shore batteries. There was only one possible enemy against whom they could fire and on the twentieth of the month he came. But this time the French were ready. Menacing radio messages from De Gaulle were answered by menacing replies from Pierre Boisson, the High Commissioner: '*La France m'a confié Dakar. Je défendrai Dakar jusqu'au bout*,' and Meilhac, staring through the slitted casemates of his battery on Gorée Island, saw once more the loom of British battleships upon the sea.

That battle lasted two days and ended in as complete a French victory as Mers-el-Kebir had been a French defeat. When at last the thunder of guns from sea and shore fell silent and the battered British fleet trailed away westward Meilhac knew triumph and revenge for the first time. And on the fifth of October he had attended the splendid memorial service for those who had fallen. Watching the victorious commanders mounting the cathedral steps between the rigid ranks of Senegalese—Barreau, the Commander-in-Chief, Vice-Admiral La-croix, Air Force General Gama, Marzin, commanding the *Richelieu*, finally Boisson himself with the gold chain of office over his white uniform; hearing the bells tolling *Aux Champs* and the Salute to the Dead sounding from vault to vault—Meilhac had been certain that now France would—France *must*—fight with Germany for the destruction of their common enemy.

He wanted nothing more, and through the long torrid months of office work that followed at naval headquarters, work interspersed with bouts of malaria which left him yellow, shaky, thinner than ever and ageing perceptibly, he thought only of the war against England which mysteriously did not come. Deskbound, in his imagination he sailed with the Kriegsmarine and his heroes were the dauntless Kommandanten of the U-boats, fighting their terrible, lonely war under the waters of the world's oceans, remorselessly seeking and sinking the British flag on all the seven seas.

Meilhac had never been a communicative man and he kept his thoughts and opinions largely to himself, confiding them only within the small circle of friends whom he knew fully shared his views. It was as well for him that he did so; and although his disbelieving rage when at last all French Africa joined the Allies was almost unbearable, he controlled it between thin grim lips and went coldly to work on the new and most unappetizing plans of co-operation with the nation he had so long thought of as the enemy. He was employed for a whole hateful year in a headquarters largely staffed by English naval officers and he even learned their language; more, he often thought, to avoid the excruciating discomfort of hearing them trying to speak French than for any other purpose. He made no friends among them and guessed that his dislike was reciprocated. Cold, formal, sardonic, he did his work, shrugged his shoulders, and retired at night to his ascetic quarters.

And the war ended. France was 'liberated' and he returned, was promoted to his present rank and employed first in Paris, then in occupied Germany, where his job had been to assist in tracing and repossessing the large assortment of naval documents taken from France by various German Intelligence organizations during the occupation. Then, suddenly, there had come this request from the British for a senior French naval officer and two juniors, all of whom must be English-speaking, to sit upon a case in which it appeared French interests were involved. Meilhac had protested curtly that he was too busy; had been overruled and, shrugging his narrow shoulders, had obeyed.

The quinine cooled his heated blood and he slept—to wake early and exhausted in the shabby worn room across whose window the grey rain slanted. His head felt heavy and drowsy but he knew he had no temperature. If he had been going to have one of his recurrent bouts of malaria he had killed it in time. He would have to take his place in court after all.

Five

Commandant Henri Lautig and Lieutenant-de-vaisseau Hervé Marlignon sat together in the Allied Officers Club eating breakfast. Lautig, a blond, short, red-faced Breton was eating American soybean sausages, American canned bacon and a leathery omelette of reconstituted eggs. He had already consumed a plate of cornflakes with reconstituted milk and he was looking forward to some American pancakes with maple syrup which he intended to eat next. He was enjoying his breakfast immensely; it was worth coming all the way from Antwerp to get a meal like this. Between mouthfuls he said, 'I doubt that it will last long. Two days, perhaps three.'

'It depends.' Lieutenant Marlignon, young, dark, spectacled, watched the soldier eating with interest. He himself drank only tea. 'The prosecution have, it seems, mislaid their most important witness. They are naturally somewhat unwilling to commence until he is available.'

'*Quel dommage*,' remarked Lautig contentedly. 'For myself, I am most content to remain here while the Americans feed me. Do you know what is my favourite food? *Le beurre d'arachide*. It is an American speciality. No one else knows it. One day I think I must introduce it to France. I could undoubtedly make much money. Tell me, Marlignon, have you friends here? Americans?'

'No.'

'A pity. I had desired if possible to become acquainted with a friendly American in the hope of procuring a few cans of that butter to take back with me.'

'The defending officer is an American. I was introduced last night.'

'So?' Lautig wiped his mouth and grinned. 'Well, perhaps I can make a bargain—"*M'sieur le Défenseur*, I will acquit the accused for a consideration—say three cans of your magnificent peanut butter. For six I will award them substantial damages into the bargain. For twelve I will also recommend them for the Grand Cross of the Légion d'Honneur".'

Marlignon laughed. 'And for twenty-four?'

'Ah, for twenty-four I will offer them a new submarine and the right to sink all craft found between the Pont de la Concorde and the Pont d'Austerlitz. Also—'

Marlignon cut him short. 'Look—over there by the window. You see the tall English Lieutenant-Colonel who stoops?'

'Yes.'

'That, *mon cher Commandant*, is the military advocate for the prosecution—he who has mislaid the chief *témoin à charge*. His name is Colonel Rostwood. I spoke to him yesterday evening.'

A mess waiter approached with Lautig's pancakes and syrup and the Commandant glanced over them at his younger companion. 'So? We have been here, you and I, for less than twenty-four hours and you have already met the two advocates and spoken with them. I, upon the contrary, have spoken to no one but your Capitaine Meilhac, a most unsympathetic personality, Marlignon; his manner of speech seems designed to be used only for ordering mutineers to be hanged at the yardarm. One feels some sympathy for the accused with such a man upon the court.' He wrinkled his snub nose, poured dark golden syrup on to the cakes. 'Probably you can tell me more about this whole affair. As a sailor you will doubtless understand it better than a poor devil of an infantryman.'

'But you already know the outline?'

'I know only that two German officers are indicted for killing the survivors of a ship which they sank. And I assume that we are to attempt to discover whether there is truth in this. Knowing what one does of the Boche, I imagine that it is extremely probable. We are well used to examples of *Deutsche Starrheit* by now.'

Marlignon smiled. 'It is not only probable. It is quite certain. They admit it.'

Lautig stopped eating and stared across the table. 'They admit it! Then—then why all this trouble? No, no, I am not complaining. I do not object to being here in the least. I approve the English—unlike your Capitaine Meilhac—and I approve still more the Americans. I have, as you see, a great liking, too, for American food. But to take us all from our duties in order to listen for five minutes to a formal plea of "Guilty"—'

'But I do not believe they are going to plead guilty.'

'But you said, did you not, *mon cher*, that they admitted their guilt? I do not comprehend—'

Marlignon grinned, his face suddenly animated and boyish. 'You know, M'sieur le Commandant, I was once nearly a lawyer. My father particularly wished it so. But no—I objected most strongly. I was sixteen at the time and I could imagine nothing duller, more *ennuyeux*, than to sit in stuffy offices and airless court-rooms and to develop a potbelly and be called "*Maître.*" No, no, not for me. Well I chose the Navy—and here I am. Yet now I sometimes wonder if my father was not right. I find the law in many respects most fascinating. Yes, I assure you—and particularly this case. But I have not answered your question. The accused admit the action with which they are charged but they are to plead "not guilty" since they maintain they acted within legal rights.'

Six

The court-room was small and dark, sombre with mahogany and dull bronze and the commingled smells of dust, old paper, ink and gas. It was burrowed somewhere in the centre of an ancient block of buildings which had escaped all damage during the raids and which for the past two years had been shut up, disused and empty. On this dank morning in late October, lit by weak gas-mantles set in ornate wall-sconces and one low-slung gaselier, it was a room unchanged for a hundred years, redolent of age, of beards and stovepipe hats, of long dull speeches and the dry rustle and whisper of desiccated documents. It had existed since time began and it would last for ever. Those who passed through it were flickering shadows, less substantial, because less enduring, than the shadows of its own fittings thrown by the dim gas-light. Its tombstone atmosphere of gloom and heavy restraint flatly contradicted the existence of youth or sunlight or freedom or human happiness. Only law and doom and darkness existed here. It was a life-denying place.

Two men, pale from long imprisonment, thin and sickly from months of poor and inadequate food, sat in the panelled, bronze-barred dock, their dark blue uniforms merging with the general drabness around them. Both were listening expressionlessly to the calm voice of the elderly British lieutenant-colonel, standing behind the table in the well of the court, as he opened the case for the Prosecution . . . 'to try enemy nationals for war crimes committed in any war commencing after the second of September nineteen thirty-nine, as has been fully confirmed by the highest authorities.

'In this case we find the court composed of both French and British officers since both countries are concerned. And since the two accused are naval personnel three members of the court are themselves naval officers.' He paused to clear his throat, glanced down at the pile of papers before him and continued, 'I understand that the facts of the case in their general outline are known to you all. A few minutes before half past seven o'clock on the evening of the fifth of January of this year the steamship *Maréchal Oudinot*, a freighter of seven thousand five hundred tons, the property of the Niort Steam Navigation Company of Rouen and at the aforementioned date under charter to the British War Transport Ministry, was steaming alone in the South Atlantic bound from Conakry to Bahia. At that moment two torpedoes fired from close range struck the ship's starboard side, one forward in the proximity of the Number One cargo hold and the other amidships directly under the bridge. The ship was blown apart and sank in two pieces, the bow very quickly indeed and the stern section some three or four minutes later. Owing to the extreme force of the explosions, the great damage caused, and the consequent rapidity of the sinking, the majority of the crew, who were below decks at the time, were either killed outright or trapped and drowned. It can safely be said that by twenty-five minutes to eight o'clock the *Maréchal Oudinot* had disappeared below the surface, taking with her to the bottom a large majority of her crew.

'This sinking was so far in every way typical of the unrestricted sea warfare waged by the Germans since the beginning of the recent war; initiated, indeed, in the previous one. An unarmed and completely defenceless merchantman was blown apart without any warning, nor were the crew given even the slightest chance to take any action to save themselves. On the contrary, as I shall shortly show, it was the predetermined intention of the first accused—Kielbasa—to send this ship to the bottom with all—'

But the heavy, hirsute figure of Captain Kaye was suddenly on its feet and his quick, high voice interrupted that of the Prosecutor. 'Please the Court, I object. This trial is concerned with the events *subsequent* to the sinking of the steamship *Maréchal Oudinot*. That is clearly stated in the indictment which the Court has before it. Learned Counsel for the Prosecution has, I submit, no right to include the sinking and the manner of the sinking as part of the case against the accused. It is both irrelevant and inadmissible.'

From his place, wigged and black-gowned, on the right of the pudgy, uniformed figure of the President, Major Glenberyll glanced from the defending counsel to the Prosecutor. 'Colonel Rostwood, while of course you must open in your own way, and while you are perfectly entitled to commence by drawing a general picture of the circumstances in which the incidents giving rise to this trial took place, animadversions upon the conduct of the accused prior to those incidents are undesirable. Defence Counsel is quite right in stating that the sinking itself is not upon the indictment.'

The Prosecutor was unmoved. 'Yes, sir. I am aware of that. But I submit that my remarks on the sinking bear considerable relevance to the charges upon the indictment—at least in so far as they concern the first accused.'

'In that case Defence Counsel's objection is overruled. You may carry on.'

Colonel Rostwood shifted his papers again, rubbed one side of his nose with a thin, tobacco-stained forefinger, and continued. 'The steamer did not, however, carry its entire crew with it to the bottom. About a dozen men—men who had been on deck or who had made their way there very rapidly after the explosion—were able to leap overboard. In fact one or two, with commendable courage and foresight, were able to release a lifeboat from its lashings and to throw into the sea various smaller pieces of equipment before leaping for their lives from the foundering vessel. Thus, when the German U-996 surfaced close at hand it was to find approximately a dozen survivors— among whom were the ship's captain, his second officer and his wireless operator—in the water or climbing up on life-rafts or floating beams and spars. The submarine moved in among this floating wreckage, life-rafts and survivors, but made no effort to assist them in any way.'

Behind the Defence table Captain Kaye rustled papers ominously and glanced pointedly at the Judge Advocate. Colonel Rostwood disregarded him and continued. 'Upon one piece of wreckage were three crew members: the wireless officer, a Negro stoker and a Brazilian galley-boy. This wreckage was approached by the submarine and hailed. The wireless officer was ordered to climb to the submarine's deck where he was briefly interrogated by the second accused— Kümmerol. Then a lifebelt with the ship's name upon it was taken from him and he was ordered back to his improvised raft. Before leaving the submarine he was told by Kümmerol that he and the others were sure to be rescued in a short time—probably next day. Still no efforts of any sort were made to assist these survivors struggling for their lives in the water. No one on board the U-996 inquired if any were hurt or wounded. No help was offered to right capsized rafts or—'

'Please the Court—' Captain Kaye was again upon his feet—'I must once more object to my learned friend's remarks upon the accused's conduct prior to the facts upon the indictment and—'

'Captain Kaye, I really do not think that these interruptions are necessary.' Glenberyll's voice held a note of restrained impatience. 'Are you disputing what Prosecuting Counsel has just said?'

'No, sir. I would, however, like to state in fairness to the accused that there was a B.D.U. order in existence which explicitly demanded that U-boat crews must make no attempt to rescue survivors of sunken ships. I have a copy of the order here—if I may quote from it . . .' Kaye adjusted his pince-nez and read: 'Issued from the Headquarters of Grand Admiral Doenitz, seventeenth of September nineteen forty-two: "No attempt of any kind must be made at rescuing crew members of ships sunk, and this includes picking up persons in the water and putting them in lifeboats, righting capsized lifeboats and handing over food and water".' He glanced up at the Court and his voice took on a mildly apologetic note. 'A harsh order, but an order, none the less. Orders are there to be obeyed. The accused were doing no more than their duty in the matter and, as I have said, it is not upon the indictment.' He paused a second and then added gravely, 'Gentlemen, the accused, my clients, are facing a most serious charge. They are on trial here for nothing less than their lives. In these circumstances I feel that they should not be stigmatized for obeying their service orders; particularly when such obedience is not upon the indictment.'

'Yes, I think the Court must agree to that.' Glenberyll turned to the tall, stooped figure of the Prosecutor, bent over his table studying a paper. 'Colonel Rostwood, I think it would be best if you kept as strictly as you can to the indictment. The accused are charged with a specific offence which has nothing to do with any failure to render assistance to the survivors. I am sure, of course, that you had no intention of purposely censuring the accused over this matter.'

Colonel Rostwood bowed. 'None whatever, I assure you, sir.'

Glenberyll turned his head, eyebrows raised inquiringly, to the Defence table. Captain Kaye bowed. 'I accept my learned friend's assurance.'

Once more the Court settled back to listen, first to the soft hiss of the gas and the rustle of papers, and then to the Prosecutor's slow voice once more taking up the story of the sinking of the *Maréchal Oudinot* almost ten months ago.

Seven

Motionless, leaning forward a little, with his crossed forearms resting on his knees and the two and a half gold rings on his cuffs glinting in the soft light, Eugen Kielbasa listened to the story of those events which seemed to have taken place so long ago; listened expressionlessly to the description of his own part in them and saw no longer the dark court-room but the twilight sea, heard no longer the dry voice of this English colonel but the whistles and calls of the men in the water, the excited voice of Emil—beside him then as he was now. So it had happened—as somehow, ever since he had stood shouting with rage in the rocking rubber dinghy off Cape Delgado, threatening with useless clenched fists those diving planes, he had known that it would. The decision which he had taken on that calm January evening amid the debris of the old freighter was one which he had known even then must haunt him for the rest of his life. And even then he had darkly guessed that one day he might have to justify it before an audience other than his own crew.

It would certainly have been much better if the matter had not come out; better for both the reputation of the German Navy in general and the U-boat service in particular. But for that matter it would have been infinitely better if those British planes had been fifteen minutes or so later upon the U-996's track so that she would have been within the very loom of Delgado . . . In that case he would now be living secure and safe in São Paulo. But he had always been a stranger to self-pity and it did no good to think of that lost hope now; it was merely a sharp pain in the heart. Nine months of imprisonment in various camps in South Africa and England had passed since then— slow days, slower weeks of discomfort, boredom and hunger, and with the shadow of this trial looming ever closer.

It had been in May that he had been flown to England and taken to London, to a big quiet house in Kensington, for questioning. A bare room, trestle tables, men in civilian clothes who, he found out later, were legal officials and their interpreters from the British Admiralty. They had shown him an affidavit—'I, Leutnant-zur-See Christl Johann Huberein, of Klagenfurt, Austria, do hereby make oath and say as follows . . .' And there, in carefully typed German, with an

English translation, had been Huberein's own account of the story now being retold in this stilled court-room.

He had been shown affidavits by Sehlte and several other members of the crew. There was no doubt as to their genuineness. He had read them in silence, guessing, before the men at the table had told him, that the whole affair had come out, though how exactly he could not know, and that its consequences would mean some sort of a trial. They had suggested that he should make a statement himself but he had refused to do so. He would justify his fateful decision only in open court or not at all. He had wondered, at that time, whether Emil would be confused or tricked into making a sworn statement and had hoped sincerely that he would not. In this at least he now knew that his hope had been fulfilled. Emil had refused to say anything until three days ago when they had met again at last in a small guarded room in the presence of Captain Kaye, Dr Stusser and Captain Kaye's young clerk.

It had been a shock to see the change which his wound and nine months of imprisonment had wrought in Emil. All the life and energy, the bright self-assurance of a year ago, had drained away. His face was grey and hollow under the cheekbones, his eyes dark-circled and fearful, and he licked his dry lips continually. He walked haltingly and with a heavy stick and his blue uniform hung loosely upon him. Eugen knew that he himself had changed but not—surely not—to the same extent. The last time he had seen Emil had been as he rose from his knees beside the stretcher on the dock at Masondi. Under the vivid sunlight Emil had been sprawled below him in bloodstained overalls, his black hair falling across a face white and dripping with sweat, lying motionless and less than half-conscious, the pupils of his eyes reduced to pinpoints by morphine. Yet in the long months between then and now that picture had faded, to be replaced by Emil as he had been on the earlier part of the cruise. Somehow Eugen had expected him to be like that when they met once more; he had forgotten the gravity of that wound and the effects, particularly on someone of Emil's temperament, of prison life.

So that meeting, to which he had long looked forward, had been difficult and embarrassed; and soon it had come home to Eugen that Emil was very frightened indeed of the forthcoming trial. This had been a considerable surprise to Eugen, who himself was not frightened at all. He had tried, during the subsequent conversation with the two counsel, to encourage his young comrade, but he did not feel he had succeeded. And in this he had certainly not been aided by the assistant

Defence Counsel, Dr Stusser, whose work it had been to prepare the material brief for Captain Kaye. Stusser was a gloomy man who tut-tutted and shook his head and kept repeating, 'A bad business . . . a bad business, I'm afraid,' until Eugen had asked him pointedly why, if he felt that way, he had accepted the brief in the first place. Stusser had glanced up quickly, coldly. 'Herr Kapitänleutnant, I accepted it because, like you, I am a German and I must consider it my duty to do what I can for you in your present difficulty. But please do not imagine that this means that I either approve or condone your admitted action in this matter.'

Eugen had been taken aback. 'So? Yet I have just been at consider-able pains to explain exactly why I took that action.'

'Explain, explain! Yes, indeed! And today Germany is full of people like you explaining things like that!' The lawyer's face had reddened. 'To me, at any rate, it is a shameful thing that so many of my countrymen are now having so volubly to explain so many hateful actions.' He had turned and spoken in harsh, halting French to the American captain who had, Eugen was pleased to remember, answered him tersely enough. After that much of the translation was done by Emil while Stusser had sat sulkily silent.

If Eugen had taken a quick dislike to Stusser his heart had warmed immediately to Captain Kaye. The American lawyer's questions had been acute and to the point and had lacked any trace of hostility. Despite the inconvenient necessity of Dr Stusser's presence at that first conference, they had made quick and easy contact with each other's minds. Things had gone still better at the second meeting, conducted mostly in English yesterday evening, in which Stusser's aid had been dispensed with and only Emil had, when necessary, interpreted in French—a language Captain Kaye spoke almost as well as his own.

At its close the Captain had sat tugging gently at his beard and frowning down at the papers on the scrubbed deal table before him. 'There can be no doubt about the pleas, of course—operational necessity. And for you, Kümmerol, superior orders. In the circum-stances in which the incident took place those pleas are exceptionally strong ones.'

'Then—you think it will be all right?' Emil had asked hopefully, but the Captain had been cautious in his reply. 'Frankly, that must depend largely on the members of the Court; depend, that is to say, on how open to logic and reason their minds may be. This trial is coming on at a most unfortunate time. Every day the papers are full of new discoveries of Nazi barbarities. Legally untrained minds—particularly in the aftermath of the recent war—may not find it easy to grasp the fact that there is a very great difference, at least in intent, between this atrocity and those others.'

Eugen had followed the gist of this speech and was hardly surprised when Emil had protested, wide-eyed with shocked distress. '*Atrocity!* But—but, M'sieur le Capitaine, it was *not* an atrocity! I mean—'

'It was—' the American officer's voice was calmly neutral—'something which I most certainly would class under that heading. So will you, young man, if you are honest with yourself. Your captain ordered, and you carried out, the killing of unarmed and defenceless men struggling for their lives in the sea. It was an atrocious thing to do.'

'But—I—we—it seemed you understood. Now you say—'

'I do understand. If I did not, I should not have accepted this brief. *What* you did is one thing. *Why* you did it is quite another. Do you imagine that I am going to approve your action, as such, in court? For that matter, do you imagine that I approve it now? Of course I do not! But that is not the point. When I first heard of this case and was asked to take on the defence I went back to my office and put the circumstances of the incident very simply and hypothetically to Corporal Post here. I asked him what he would have done had he been, in effect, in Kielbasa's position. He replied immediately that he would have done as Kielbasa did. That decided me, subject to future investigation, to take the case. Listen; it is my contention that the average intelligent, rational and dutiful naval officer of any country in the world would, when placed in Kielbasa's position, have acted as Kielbasa did. You yourself merely did your duty by obeying your captain's order. But that does not mean to say that an atrocity was not committed—as the Prosecution will certainly point out. Do you understand me now, Kümmerol?'

'Yes—' Emil's voice had been hesitant—'I think so.'

'I don't.' The Captain had suddenly leaned forward, peering closely at Emil through his incongruous pince-nez. 'What you wish is to be *forgiven* for what you did—is it not?'

'Well—'

'Ah! But one is *forgiven*, surely, for committing a crime or a sin or whatever you like to term it. You therefore admit, inwardly at any rate, that you did something wrong. Don't you?'

'But we had to!' Emil's face had flushed and he had spoken on a rising note which had made Kaye flap both big hands at him. 'Calm down, my boy. Calm down. Yes, yes—you had to. Very well. We won't go into that side of the matter any more—at least, here. As I have said, you have very strong cases to plead. But . . . Well, we shall see.'

Eight

Colonel Rostwood, like Captain Kaye and the Judge Advocate himself, was a professional lawyer. He was neither an eminent King's Counsel like Major Glenberyll nor a wealthy cosmopolitan dilettante like the Defence Counsel, but he was a competent, middle-of-the-road, provincial barrister who, before the war, had specialized in impersonal civil lawsuits involving the financial affairs of litigious business companies. He was happiest and most at home when immersed in the dubious and complicated details of cases in which United Trust Syndicates sued Commercial Banks with Amalgamated Finance Corporations intervening. The present case, let alone the novel procedure under which it was being conducted, was something as far outside his experience as it was outside Captain Kaye's. They were both able men but both realized that they would have to rely upon, and accept direction in most respects from, the Judge Advocate, who had the *de facto* responsibility for the proper interpretation of this newly designed form of trial. It was best, thought Colonel Rostwood, to proceed with caution for he was, after all, treading on unexplored ground. And there was the question of the delayed witness. Fortunately the Defence were having the same trouble and a bargain had been struck. As soon as he had concluded his opening speech, therefore, he put the matter to the Judge Advocate.

'Now we come to the witnesses, and here I must ask the Court's indulgence. As it is known, there was, in the event, only one survivor from the *Maréchal Oudinot*'s crew—the wireless operator. This man is, I need hardly say, the Prosecution's chief witness, but owing to unexpected difficulties and the delays due to the present dislocation of communications it has—most regrettably—been found impossible to achieve his presence here in court today. I am therefore constrained to call secondary witnesses—members of the U-boat's crew. But before doing so I should like to ask the Court's permission to call my chief witness, Guéroult, at a later date.'

Major Glenberyll looked mildly dubious and a little irritated. This was the sort of irregularity he had hoped to avoid; and one, too, which he felt should be avoidable. 'When, exactly, does the Prosecution think that this witness will be available?'

'It is hoped by the day after tomorrow.' Colonel Rostwood glanced over at Captain Kaye. 'I understand that m'learned friend for the Defence is in a similar position and will request a similar indulgence.'

Major Glenberyll, eyebrows raised, turned to Kaye. 'Is that the case?'

'It is so, sir. As my learned friend has said, the Defence has an important witness whom we would wish to call. We know where he is and we are making every effort to get him into court as soon as possible. The fact remains, however, that we will probably have to crave the Court's indulgence to allow that he be heard at the end of the case.'

'Who is this witness, Captain Kaye?'

'A certain Korvettenkapitän Gericht. He is an eminent U-boat Kommandant and was for some time attached to the headquarters of the U-boat service—B.D.U. It *may* be possible for him to be here tomorrow in time for the main defence case. Otherwise—'

'Otherwise you are in the same position as Colonel Rostwood, are you not? In the circumstances, then, I may take it that a bargain has, as it were, been struck, in this matter between counsel?'

Both Colonel Rostwood and Captain Kaye bowed assent. 'Very well. In that case the Court will, of course, accede to your joint request. And now, Colonel Rostwood, we are ready to hear the first witness you wish to call.'

'Thank you, sir. My first witness is Leutnant-zur-See Christl Huberein.'

And there, suddenly, in the dark polished witness-box was Huberein, looking exactly the same, except that he was very much cleaner and smarter in his best blue uniform, than he had appeared during the last dreadful day of the U-996's cruise. Red-haired, red-faced, grinning nervously, he stood fidgeting in the box, waiting to take the oath. Once he looked across at the dock, but his kind brown eyes faltered and turned away.

Colonel Rostwood took him slowly through the preliminaries— his age and background, service record and various dates. He then drew from him a somewhat confused account of the opening stages of the U-996's cruise, the first air attack and the death of Oberleutnant Chirol . . .

'So then the Kommandant promoted you to the position of acting First Officer of the Watch?'

'Yes. After Franz—Oberleutnant Chirol, I mean—I was the next most senior executive officer on board.'

'Did you feel yourself competent to undertake this assignment?'

'No. Not really—no.'

'Why not?'

'Well, I had only been on one previous patrol of any length. I did not consider I had enough experience.'

'Had you seen any ships sunk before?'

'Three—yes. During my first patrol.'

'And at these sinkings were there any survivors?'

'Yes. In two cases there were survivors.'

'And in the third case?'

Huberien licked his lips. 'That was a sinking in convoy. We were unable to see. We saw only the ship was sinking and then we were forced to take evasive action from the escorts. We—we were depth-charged and damaged.'

'Let us return to the first two cases you mentioned; those in which there were survivors. Was any attempt made to kill them?'

'No.'

'Was the possibility of doing so considered?'

'No.'

'Were there—to your knowledge, at that time—any orders concerned with the killing of shipwrecked survivors?'

'No.'

'Since then have you ever heard of any such orders?'

'No.'

Colonel Rostwood changed the papers in his hands and continued, 'Now we come to the sinking of the *Maréchal Oudinot*—as far as you, Huberein, were concerned, the fourth sinking in which you took part. Please describe the time and navigational position of this encounter.' Huberein did so and the Colonel nodded. 'Very well. Now, did the Kommandant, Kapitänleutnant Kielbasa, discuss the question of sinking this ship with you before he took action?'

'No.'

'Did he just give the order to sink her?'

Huberein's face convulsed into the contorted lines which, to the two accused in the dock, meant plainly that he was trying desperately to work out an answer which would be favourable to them, and Eugen, at least, felt an irritated foreboding. Christl ought to have the sense to

see that the unvarnished truth was the best defence. But it was unlikely that he would.

'Well—well, the Kommandant took a long time to decide—I mean
after we'd sighted the ship. I don't think—' Huberein looked unhappily towards the dock, met Eugen's cold stare and dropped his
eyes— 'I had the impression, that is, that he did not want to sink her.'

'You had that impression?'

'Yes.'

'Why?'

'He was a—a humane man. I mean he—well, he never punished the
crew if he could possibly help it. He just gave verbal reprimands, and
he—I don't think he liked sinking ships.' Huberein's face was redder
than ever, but he stumbled on. 'Once—I can't remember exactly—he
said something about it being a pity at this stage of the war—I think.'

'What did you think he meant by that remark?'

'Well—I suppose he meant that Germany was losing the war and—
well, it was a pity to sink ships for nothing—since it couldn't help us
win the war by then.'

'Hmmm,' grunted Colonel Rostwood unbelievingly. 'Hmmm—I
see. Well, did he, on this occasion we are discussing, say anything of
that sort?'

'No.'

'He said nothing—nothing at all? Think carefully, please.'

Huberein bit his lower lip, rolled his eyes and said, 'No, I don't
think— Oh, yes! I think he said something about her being a coal-
burner, or something. Yes. He said, "Since she's not an oil-burner
we'll sink her".'

'Ah, I see.' Colonel Rostwood repeated slowly. 'Since she's not an
oil-burner, we'll sink her. I see. Yes. And what did those words mean
to you?'

'Mean to me? That—that she did not burn oil,' said Huberein with
the complacent relief of a schoolboy answering an unexpectedly easy
question.

Beside Captain Kaye at the Defence table Corporal Post giggled,
receiving for this indiscretion a long cold stare from the Judge Advocate and a terrifying frown from his chief. Scarlet-faced, he shrank as
far as possible into a corner.

Colonel Rostwood sighed and continued, 'I mean, what significance—other than that if the *Maréchal Oudinot* did not burn oil she
presumably burned coal—did you place upon the Kommandant's
words?'

'Well—only what he said, I didn't think.'

'Huberein, at this date you had been in the Navy for over four years as a rating and as an officer. You had attended submarine training school in both those capacities. You had been on several short training patrols as well as one long war cruise. You can give me a better answer than that.'

'I don't know what you mean—'

'Then I will repeat my question. What significance did you, as acting First Officer of the Watch, place upon the Kommandant's words "As she is not an oil-burner we'll sink her"?'

Huberein swallowed. 'I'm not sure what you mean. I don't think I placed any significance upon them.'

Colonel Rostwood turned to the Judge Advocate. 'Please the Court. This witness is purposely prevaricating. He appears to forget that he is under oath.'

The Judge Advocate glanced down at his papers a moment to hide a quick smile. 'After all he is *your* witness, is he not?' Then he glanced sternly at the unfortunate lieutenant. 'Huberein, you can do better than this. You have sworn to tell the whole truth. Failure in this respect is perjury and is heavily punished. Come now—think if you cannot answer Counsel's question a little more intelligently.'

But Huberein remained stubbornly silent. He knew nothing of law or of courts. He was unaware of any difference in testifying for the prosecution or the defence. He only knew that in assenting to give evidence he had meant to do everything he could to help his comrades, and now he guessed that it was intended to force from him a damaging admission. After a minute Colonel Rostwood said, 'Very well. Let me be more particular. Would you agree that an oil-burning ship, when sunk by torpedoes, leaves a very large area of oil upon the sea's surface in comparison to that left by a coal-burning ship?'

Before Huberein could answer Captain Kaye was on his feet. 'Please the Court, I object. That is a very leading question. I submit that it is out of order for the witness to be forced to answer it.'

The Judge Advocate drummed lightly on the bench with a pencil. 'It is phrased in that way, certainly . . . But as the witness is being obdurate— Colonel Rostwood, can you rephrase that question?'

'Yes, sir.'

'Then the objection is overruled.'

'Huberein, can you tell me the difference between the size of the area of water likely to be covered in oil when an oil-burning ship is sunk by torpedoes, compared to that in which the ship is a coal-burning one?'

Huberein hesitated and the Judge Advocate said sharply, 'You will answer Counsel's question.'

And now there was nothing for it. 'The area of oil left by a sunk coal-burner is the smaller.'

'A great deal smaller?'

'Yes.'

'Thank you very much,' said Colonel Rostwood sardonically.

There was a short pause in which, though he had taken no part in the proceedings so far, Colonel Whaley-Wren decided to drink some water. He poured it from the jug before him into a tumbler as slowly and carefully as if he had been measuring medicine. All eyes were upon him as he drank it, replaced the glass, and, taking a silk handkerchief from his sleeve, patted his white moustache with great deliberation. He replaced the handkerchief with movements so slow as to be almost farcical and then cleared his throat gently to signal that the hypnotized court might resume its business.

Captain Kaye had watched this performance at first with surprise, then with quickly increasing admiration. The President was not a lawyer and it had seemed to everyone that he must remain a mere figurehead dominated entirely by the Judge Advocate—as silent a spectator as the most junior and inexperienced of the assessors. But he had just demonstrated that this was by no means the case and Kaye realized at once that Colonel Whaley-Wren intended, when the time came, to make up his own mind on the guilt or innocence of the accused unswayed by any legal argument—and he would probably make up the minds of the other officers who sat with him, as well. The President was suddenly metamorphosed, in the eyes of the Defence Counsel, from a pudgy old man in drab military uniform into a scarlet-robed judge in bands and full-bottomed wig. He wished he had taken more pains to learn about Colonel Whaley-Wren before the trial began.

Colonel Rostwood had probably received the same impression. At any rate he waited respectfully until the President's silk handkerchief was safely tucked away before turning once more to his witness. 'Now, Huberein, I want you to tell the Court in your own words all that happened between the time that the Kommandant said "Since she is not an oil-burner we'll sink her" until the actual torpedo attack and the sinking.'

'But Herr—Herr Oberst, it was an ordinary routine affair. It was a question of manœuvring the boat and readying the torpedoes and so forth.'

'I have no doubt of that. You may none the less describe it. Use what technical terms you please—the naval officers present will understand them.'

Stumbling Huberein went over the normal routine of a submarine attack. Nervously pausing from time to time to lick his lips, he described the alterations of course and speed, the swift yet unhurried orders and replies, the automatic responses of a submarine's captain and crew as they moved in for the kill. And despite the slowing down of his narrative due to translation, the dark court-room seemed to give place to the tense, hot atmosphere of the brightly lit control-room of a U-boat and the members of the Court glanced from time to time curiously at the dock, as if finding it strange that the pale-faced, spectacled young man listening so emotionlessly had once held such lethal power in his hands and had ordered it with such calmly ruthless efficiency.

'. . . one torpedo struck amidships and one forward. She broke apart and sank very rapidly.'

'You say the range at which the torpedoes were fired was three hundred metres?'

'About that. A little less, I think.'

'Is not that a very short range indeed?'

'Yes.'

'Could not the explosions, at such a short range, have damaged the submarine itself?'

'Not a boat as large as ours. But we received a considerable shock wave from the explosion.'

'Was it necessary to approach so closely to the ship before the torpedoes were fired?'

'It is always preferable if possible—yes. Because it gives the ship's look-outs less time to catch sight of the tracks and to take avoiding action.'

'The *Maréchal Oudinot* was proceeding very slowly, was she not?'

'Yes.'

'She was unarmed and unescorted?'

'Yes.'

'In effect, then, she was a sitting target?'

'Well—yes.'

'How many torpedoes did you carry?'

'Twenty-one.'

'And you were progressing on a very long-range cruise in which your target area, close to the straits of Aden, was still a long way

away. Yet the captain deliberately used two torpedoes—two irreplaceable torpedoes—to dispatch one very old freighter. Could the
Maréchal Oudinot not have been sunk with one?'

'Well, it depends on—' began Huberein unhappily, but was cut
short by the repeated question. 'Could the ship have been sunk by
one torpedo? Answer Yes or No.'

'Yes.'

'Since it was unescorted and unarmed could it not equally well have
been sunk by surface gunfire? Yes or No.'

'Yes.'

'Yet two torpedoes, at a range so close as to be virtually point-blank
—as to severely jar the U-boat—were fired at her. Both, naturally
enough, hit her. And the result—remember, she was a small ship by
most standards, only seven thousand tons—was that she was torn in
two and sank immediately.' Colonel Rostwood paused. 'Very well.
The U-boat then surfaced and approached the area of the sinking.
What happened then, Huberein?'

'I was left in charge in the control-room. The Kommandant went
to the bridge.'

'How long did the submarine remain on the surface in the vicinity
of the sinking?'

'It is a long time ago. I can only remember roughly—about fifteen
or twenty minutes, perhaps.'

'And during this time you remained below in the control-room?'
'Yes.'

'Then what happened?'

'We resumed our former course upon the surface.'

'In other words—you left the site of the sinking?'
'Yes.'

'And then?'

Huberein's eyebrows contracted, then raised straining into his forehead. He took a deep breath and under his neatly pressed blue uniform
his shoulders seemed to straighten as if for a physical struggle. 'The
Kommandant called me to the bridge. I went up. The Kommandant
was there with the Gunnery Officer.'

'Do you recognize the Kommandant here today?'
'Yes.'

'Do you recognize the Gunnery Officer here today?'
'Yes.'

'What happened then?'

'The Kommandant explained to me that the sinking had left a lot of wreckage on the surface and that he intended to destroy this. He said that there were some survivors on these pieces of wreckage but that he thought most had life-jackets. They would be told to jump off before the destruction began.'

'What did you reply?'

'Well—' Huberein gulped—'I was very surprised and—and—horrified. I said that we knew that mercantile life-jackets could only support the wearers for about eight hours. Therefore those in the water would die before dawn—before any real chance of being rescued. I—I asked him not to do this thing.'

'Once . . . or several times?'

'Several times, I think. I said I could not agree that it should be done. I did not think it was necessary.'

'What did he say to that?'

'He said it was a case of choosing between our lives and theirs—and that it was his duty, as Kommandant, to choose ours. I said it was a terrible decision, and that they were humans, too. He—' Huberein looked miserably down at his hands gripping the bronze rail of the box—'he said he wished that they were fish—then the problem would not arise. I could see he was determined to carry out his intention. He ordered me below once more and to tell the Chief Engineer and some under-officers what must be done.'

'He wished they were fish—' Colonel Rostwood gave the dock a slow bleak stare—' so that the problem would not arise.' He paused for a long moment, then bowed to the President—not the Judge Advocate this time—and said, 'No more questions, sir.'

Colonel Whaley-Wren remained as impassive as a Buddha and the Judge Advocate turned to the Defence table. 'Do you wish to cross-examine, Captain Kaye?'

'If it please the Court.' Kaye rose to his feet, straightened his tunic, adjusted his pince-nez, and without looking down held out a hand. Post at once put a small scribbling-pad into it and, armed with this, the Captain walked slowly to the witness-box.

'Now, Lieutenant Huberein,' he began pleasantly, 'you have told the Court that at the date and time of the sinking your submarine, U-996, had reached the position of zero two degrees, thirty-five minutes south, by nineteen degrees, ten minutes west. That is to say you were some miles south of the Equator and to the west of, but between, the port of Freetown and Ascension Island. Is that correct?'

'Yes, that is so.'

'I see. Good. The U-boat was between these two British bases and somewhat closer to Ascension. Now what do you know about this particular area of the South Atlantic at that time?'

'It was a dangerous area for German submarines.'

'Very dangerous?'

'Yes.'

'Why, particularly?'

'Because there were constant enemy air patrols between Freetown and Ascension, and very often there was an aircraft carrier in the vicinity.'

'I see. Now I want you to tell the Court in what circumstances a U-boat would consider itself in very serious danger of discovery and attack from the air.'

'Well—' Huberein hesitated—'if it was surfaced in daylight anywhere within the known radius of enemy air patrols. Then it would be in grave danger.'

'Yes, yes—obviously. But that was not normal procedure, was it?'

'No. We only surfaced at night—and preferably when there was either none or very little moonlight. Only in very exceptional cases— damage of some sort, as later happened to us—would a U-boat think of running on the surface in broad daylight. It would be a most dangerous thing.'

'What other dangers of discovery from the air were there?'

Confident now, Huberein said, 'The oil and wreckage from a sunken ship could lead to the discovery and destruction of a U-boat if they were found sufficiently soon after the sinking.'

'How soon would that have to be?'

'Well—it depends on several things. If it was discovered in anything under twelve hours the danger would be extremely grave indeed. After that the danger would lessen as the area of search increased.'

Kaye nodded. 'What you are saying is, is it not, that a modern aircraft sighting an obvious sinking within some twelve hours or so of the occurrence can easily search the entire area in which the submarine must still be?'

'Yes.'

'Would such a searching aircraft have difficulty—we are speaking of this time last year, remember; that is to say close to the war's end—in locating a submerged submarine—given the aforementioned circumstances?'

'No; very little difficulty. By that time the enemy possessed extremely efficient detection devices.'

'And if detected in this way what chances would a submarine have of escaping destruction?'

'Very few. The enemy aircraft no longer relied upon bombs. Most of them carried special quick-sinking depth charges. Once detected, a submarine would be continually followed. Other aircraft would be homed on to it and it would be attacked until it was destroyed. If there was a carrier in the vicinity the chances of the submarine's survival would be virtually none at all.'

'Thank you.' Captain Kaye looked carefully around the court, readjusted his pince-nez and continued equably, 'Now, one last question, Huberein. You told Colonel Rostwood a little time ago that when the Kommandant informed you that he intended to destroy the wreckage upon the surface, and when you understood that this must almost inevitably mean the deaths of those survivors who clung to it, you protested several times.' Kaye looked down at his scribbling-pad. 'Your words were—"I said I could not agree that it should be done. I did not think it was necessary." But you have just told the Court that evidence of a sinking found within twelve hours placed a submarine in acute danger of destruction. You have told us of the particular danger, due to constant air patrols, of the geographical position of U-996, and have said that if carrier-based aircraft were at hand the boat's chances of survival were nil. You have made it quite plain that the U-996 found itself in that very situation at the time of the incident. How do you reconcile these two statements?'

It took some time to translate this question into German and while it was being done Huberein's rubbery features were continually contorting into new masks of anguished doubt. When the translator's voice had ceased there was a long silence. Captain Kaye waited patiently, glanced at his watch, looked up at the dark ceiling, and at last said, 'Well?'

'I—I was not the Kommandant.'

'The Court is aware of that fact. Also, you are not in the dock to-day.'

'I could not agree with the order, because—'

'Orders are not given to be agreed with or disagreed with, are they? Orders are given to be obeyed, are they not?'

'Yes.'

'Were you *given* an order about this matter by the Kommandant?'

'No.'

'In that case the matter of your agreement does not arise, does it? Did you do anything to prevent the carrying out of this order—

beyond your gratuitous remark—' Kaye's voice was coldly sarcastic—
'that you did not *agree* with it?'

'No.'

'Why did you tell the Court that in your opinion the order was not necessary?'

Huberein swallowed twice. 'I believed that there was an alternative.'

'Ah! This is most interesting. And what was this alternative?'

'Well—we could have left the scene of the skinking immediately and as fast as possible.'

'And if you had done so—if you had done that—how far from the scene of the sinking would you have been when dawn broke and the first daylight patrols flew?'

'About one hundred and fifty sea miles, roughly.'

'Well within the radius of air search, in other words?'

'Yes. But—'

'If you had been the Kommandant is that the course you would have adopted?'

'Yes—yes, I think so.'

'You do not seem very certain—' Kaye's voice was sardonic—
'and with reason, since by your own admission you would have been condemning yourself and your crew to certain death.'

Colonel Rostwood was quickly on his feet. 'Please the Court, I object. Defence Counsel is putting words into the witness's mouth which he never uttered. The witness has said—has admitted—only that in the circumstances a submarine's chances of a safe escape would be very few, and only if an aircraft carrier was present—which in this case was not so—would those chances be *virtually* none at all. He has said nothing at all about "certain death".'

Major Glenberyll nodded. 'That objection is sustained. The witness has said nothing of certain death. Please be more careful in your examinatory methods, Captain Kaye. The Court wishes to allow the Defence all the latitude possible but that does not, and will not, include the distortion of witnesses' testimony.' He glanced down at the clerk's table below him 'That last remark—it is hardly a question—of Defence Counsel will be struck out of the record.'

Captain Kaye sighed gently and turned once more to the witness-box. 'What you are saying, Huberein, is that if you had been Kommandant you would have taken a very grave risk, a risk which I think you have admitted would have been so grave as to be virtually courting the destruction of your boat and your crew, rather than adopt the course taken by Kapitänleutnant Kielbasa. I am prepared to believe that you would have acted in that way, but I suggest to you that it was not one in which any responsible, dutiful or rational submarine commander would have acted. I suggest to you that, by acting in that way, by deliberately placing the vessel and the crew which your country had confided to you at a most desperate time of war in such a terrible and *avoidable* danger, you would have shown yourself totally unfitted for command. I suggest that no captain of a war vessel with the smallest sense of duty either to his country or to his own men—'

'I object!' Once more Colonel Rostwood rose to his feet. 'Defence Counsel is needlessly bullying this witness. Simply because he said that he did not agree with a particularly cold-blooded order—'

'I am not speaking of his disagreement. I am speaking of his remark that it was—'

'You are putting a false construction upon—'

'I assure you that I am not in any way attempting—'

Crack, Crack, Crack! From somewhere underneath the bench Colonel Whaley-Wren had found a gavel and was using it smartly. The noise of his blows echoed like pistol shots through the court-room. All voices were stilled. 'Both Counsel may consider themselves rebuked for unseemly wrangling,' he said mildly. 'Counsel for the Defence is, I think, attempting to refute the witness's remark that the order from the first accused—the order which, in the event, is the cause of this trial—was unnecessary. It is well within Counsel's rights to do this. At the same time Defence Counsel must understand quite clearly that the Court will not tolerate the browbeating of this or any other witness. Subject to this correction, the cross-examination may proceed.'

Both Colonel Rostwood and Captain Kaye inclined their heads gravely towards the President and the former resumed his seat.

'Huberein—' Kaye's voice was wearily gentle—'do you still say, now and after so long a time for reflection, that Kapitänleutnant Kielbasa's order was unnecessary? You are standing, alive and well, in the witness-box today. Most of the crew of U-996 are alive and well. If the Kommandant had taken the alternative course which you say you yourself would have taken, you and the two accused and the rest of the crew would very probably have been nothing but decaying bones in a shattered wreck in the depths of the South Atlantic. You have—I ask the Court to note this well—stated quite plainly and in your own words that very fact. Now, do you, or do you not, say that the Kommandant's order was unnecessary?'

The Court was so silent that the sound of rain drumming on some distant skylight of the old building could be heard clearly. Every eye was on Huberein's anguished face. At last he gulped, tried to say something, stopped quickly and then in a dull, tired voice said, 'No. It was a —a necessary order.'

Captain Kaye waited motionless for a long minute. Then he said, 'No more questions,' and walked slowly back to his place. No sign of any emotion showed on his bearded face, but when he had at last sat down he felt under the oak table for Corporal Post's hand and gave it a jubilantly triumphant squeeze.

Colonel Rostwood was immediately on his feet for re-examination, and his voice had lost much of its original calm as for over half an hour he strove to make Huberein take back his statement that the elimination order had been necessary. But the Austrian lieutenant would not do this. The most he would say was that he himself would not have given the order, a remark out of which the Colonel strove to make as much as possible but which, in view of the witness's earlier admissions, was not of any particular value to the Prosecution's case. In the end a pallid and exhausted Huberein was stood down from the witness-box and the Court adjourned for lunch.

Nine

Colonel Whaley-Wren had lunch by himself. By virtue of his rank he had a small table, laid for one, in the dining-room of the Senior Officers Club. He ate smoked salmon with thin brown bread and butter, jugged hare with red currant jelly, brussels sprouts and roast potatoes; and then he had some Stilton cheese. He complained gently that the cheese was not Stilton but Danish Blue, and though he was assured fervently that this was not so he refused, equally gently, to accept the assurance. Then he ordered a glass of port and sat reading last week's *Punch*. He did not think about the trial at all.

Major Glenberyll had lunch at the Deputy Judge Advocate General's requisitioned apartment. There were two other legal officers present as well as the D.J.A.G. himself. They had mulligatawny soup followed by roast pheasant. There was not really quite enough pheasant for everybody but there was an excellent salad to go with it and plenty of claret. They spoke of the trial with interest and considerable technical knowledge. The story of Captain Kaye's libel action against himself was retold since one of the legal officers had not heard it before. It was received with much merriment.

Commandant Lautig and Lieutenant Marlignon went to the Allied Junior Officers Club and ate canned chile con carne with soda bread and peanut butter, followed by lemon meringue pie topped with reconstituted cream. Commandant Lautig had second helpings of both. They drank Coca-Cola with rum. Around them several gay and noisy parties were in progress—at one of them they saw Major Yatchett— and much beer and wine was being consumed in the celebration of alleged birthdays. It was a great relief to be out of that dismal court-room and the Commandant's spirits, which had sunk to a low level during the morning, soon revived. They did not discuss the trial since they were quite unversed in British legal procedure and had understood extremely little of what had been going on. Commandant Lautig had, in fact, believed for most of the morning that Huberein was one of the accused.

> *O drapeau de Wagram! O pays de Voltaire!*
> *Puissance, liberté, veil honneur militaire,*
> *Principes, droits, pensées, ils font en ce moment*
> *De toute cette gloire un vaste abaissement.*

Capitaine Meilhac sat in his hotel bedroom reading *Les Chatiments*. He took his battered little edition of Hugo's poems with him every-where and received much consolation from it. Before him on the table stood a glass of mineral water, his bottle of quinine pills and the empty shell of a boiled egg. He was feeling more tired, iller, older than ever before and his head ached badly. He abominated this trial and wished that he could go to bed and forget it. The two accused Germans were obviously not guilty—that much must be plain surely, even to the abysmally low Anglo-Saxon intelligence. If young Kielbasa had been one quarter the cold-blooded savage the Prosecution would probably make him out to be he would have had that damned red-haired Austrian shot on the fore casing with his own pistol for mutinous insubordination.

The English were upset because warfare by submarine blockade was the most deadly weapon that could be used against them—until the invention of the new bomb. They invariably turned the full force of their propaganda machine against it, and since they believed their own propaganda . . . They thought that a submarine should warn a ship before it sank her and allow the crew to escape in boats. Did they not realize that the crew, like any other combatants, were legitimate targets? Did they, in their turn, think of giving a U-boat warning before they dropped their depth charges upon it? They had ruled the sea so long that they believed that they should be allowed to dictate the rules of sea warfare—rules which they would naturally bias heavily against the submarine. Capitaine Meilhac narrowed his eyes against the pain behind them, glanced at his watch; saw that he still had half an hour to spare before the court began its afternoon hearing, and returned to his Hugo.

Captain Kaye and Corporal Post drove back to their suburban house for lunch—which they prepared themselves in the kitchen. The grateful coal merchant on the other side of the road had given Post half a dozen eggs, so they scrambled these and at the same time fried a pound of English pork sausages which Post told his chief he had bought from a friend in the British NAAFI but which in fact he had taken, together with two packets of soap and a pair of gloves, from the unattended car of a British officer two days before.

They worked in their shirtsleeves and Captain Kaye, who like many bachelors often enjoyed cooking, was very genial over the stove. He felt he had had a good morning, and when they took their plates of eggs and sausages into the sitting-room and drew the table up to the bright fire he became expansive and reverted, as was his custom in such moments, to reviling his old enemy.

' . . . as an officer and a gentleman—or some hooey like that. Why, I really cannot imagine, Mr P, because of course he's not a gentleman himself. He couldn't be since they don't have gentlemen in the Lone Star State—only mock-gentlemen, which bear as much resemblance to the genuine product as mock-turtle soup bears to the proper thing. I've only visited Texas once, but that was *quite* sufficient. I can now fully sympathize with General Sherman when he said, "If I owned both Hell and Texas I'd rent Texas and live in Hell"— And if that dime-store cowboy with the pearl-handled pistols thinks I care about missing the Reynolds case he is very much mistaken. I despise him'—said Captain Kaye grandiloquently—'from the bottom of my expatriate Yankee heart. And anyway I've had enough of Third Army rape cases. They all belong to the same old firm, "Man, Rogers & Grieves." This present business is much more fun—though, admittedly, it's much more difficult, too. Rape's rape, but in this case I've had to do a considerable amount of research into the rules of sea warfare, a highly abstruse subject, I can assure you.'

'I didn't know there were any.'

272 An Operational Necessity

'Oh yes, indeed. But none of them are very clear—except the Rule Britannia, otherwise known as the Freedom of the Seas. And that has been severely flouted, which, I think is really what this trial is all about. Are you enjoying it, Mr P?'

Post grinned at his chief over his large glass of milk—milk was another gift from his coalman. 'Sure I am, sir. But—'

'But you must *not* giggle in court! Probably you could do that back in the States. I've no doubt, for instance, that you could scream with laughter like a demented hyena in a Texas court-room without occasioning the slightest surprise. But in a British court you must behave with becoming *gravitas*. You don't want our two clients to get their exit visas just because you can't control a misplaced sense of humour, do you?'

'No, sir! But that guy—he does look awful funny in that wig, doesn't he?'

'No, I do not think he does. A barrister's wig becomes Major Glenberyll exceedingly well. I have one, too, and I flatter myself that when *I* am properly accoutred for court I look—distinctly awe-inspiring. It is a great pity that I and Colonel Rostwood must appear in uniform; the Court would pay much more attention to us both if we were properly wigged and gowned. What's more, it is prejudicial to the Defence. The Court is composed of military personnel and Colonel Rostwood's rank gives him the edge over me. They'll probably think a colonel must know more about everything than a mere captain. But come, Mr P—if we don't clear away and wash up now we'll be late for the postprandial session.'

Ten

But the afternoon sitting brought little new information to light. The Prosecution was intent on firmly nailing the lid upon its box of material proof and member after member of the U-boat's crew was called to the witness-box to testify to having heard the Kommandant's order or to having seen the machine-gunning, grenade-throwing or ramming. A succession of very young men—scared, pale, hungry faces above shabby uniforms, still marked with P.O.W. diamonds, or even shabbier civilian suits—appeared in the dark, polished box, cast frightened glances from the bench to the dock and gave uncertain, hesitant answers to Counsels' questions. They were truthful enough;

but even so the dominating motif of their evidence was 'I cannot remember,' and in time this began to harass Colonel Rostwood. The Prosecutor's tone grew sharper as the hours wore on and this had the natural effect of alarming the witnesses and confusing them. By contrast Captain Kaye became more and more friendly. At first avuncular, he ended the afternoon in a positively paternal glow, doing almost everything save pat the surprised and grateful youths upon the head. In this way, and with a minimum of effort, he induced the witnesses to retract most of what they had said in the examination-in-chief, thus necessitating re-examination by the Prosecution. In the end it was apparent that none of the sailors remembered accurately what had been said or what had happened on the evening of the fifth of January.

To anyone with a legal background this was hardly surprising— few but the most self-confident witnesses can give accurate and unshaken statements of violent events which have taken place several months previously. But, as both counsels were well aware, a confused witness who contradicts himself will give a lay jury the impression of untruthfulness and unreliability even though these very confusions and misstatements are often an obvious proof of honesty. It is the controlled and unshakable witness who, more often than not, should be regarded with some dubiety.

By the time the Court adjourned until the next day the position had hardly changed since the morning, and it was a jubilant Corporal Post who accompanied his captain through the long, poorly lit corridors and the cavernous hallways out into the dank darkness of the autumn night. 'We're winning all right! We're going to win for sure, sir.'

But—'Don't be so certain of that, Mr P,' said Kaye as he stood in the shelter of the gloomy portico, buttoning his gloves, turning up his coat collar and unfurling his umbrella with the fussy care of a middle-aged bachelor acccustomed to guard his health above all else. 'It hasn't started yet, I can assure you. What you have seen so far are largely preliminaries.'

Eleven

There was no darkness within the walls of the great prison five miles outside the city. Electric lights blazed in cold brightness behind grids in white-painted ceilings, glaring unshaded, unmuted, over scrubbed stone, bare boards, steel bars. Emil, sitting on the narrow cot in his cell, shivered and pressed his cold hands between his knees. The prison was poorly heated through lack of fuel and despite the vivid lights there was a graveyard chill in the air, which smelled always of wet stone and disinfectant.

He was in prison and on trial for his life—stark and plain, the facts were those. They were the most terrible of all, but there were others, too. He was alone in the world now, for the death of his father among the flames and crashing masonry of the first great raids had been followed less than a year later by the deaths of both his aunts. Their deaths could, he supposed with a numb despair, be indirectly attributable to him.

The Mlles Coucy had never been particularly popular in Grévilly-le-Gros-Moulin. They were old-fashioned, snobbish and apt to be tight-fisted. Their part-German nephew had never, except during the short and shameful period of defeat and collaboration, the month or two after Mers-el-Kebir, made them any more acceptable; and since they were adamant and haughty old ladies this very fact had hardened them in their preference for Franco-German collaboration, their unqualified acceptance of Pétain and Vichy.

With their old friends Colonel Amoret-Labonde, Maître Pecheur and a few other more or less wealthy minor landholders, they had formed a nucleus of extreme right-wing sympathizers—anti-Socialist, anti-British, anti-Gaullist. The immoral and restless France of the nineteen-twenties and -thirties of which they had always deeply disapproved had been brought down in the well-merited disaster of nineteen-forty, and now a sterner, more traditional France, a France in which the workers would be made to know their place, in which decent and respectful behaviour towards the upper classes would be enforced from above—a France which under these conditions and in due course of time might hope to return to the virtuous happiness of *La Belle Epoque*—was to be refashioned. Many others all over France

274

had felt the same way, but most had been intelligent enough or young enough to turn with the turning tide of war. By the time that Emil was recalled from Paris to Germany the Mlles Coucy and their few friends were disastrously isolated among an ominously hostile population engaged in helping the Resistance and suffering the terrible reprisals of the German Security forces. Four days after the liberation of Paris the Coucys' old friend and family lawyer, Me. Pecheur, was shot in the back as he walked home from his office. With a son serving as an officer in Darnand's hated *milice*, it was not, thought the townfolk of Grévilly, very surprising. His funeral was hurried and furtive and the only mourners were the old Coucys and Colonel Amoret-Labonde.

One night a week later a boy from neighbouring Roulans, a partisan wounded in a mismanaged ambush, tried to obtain a refuge and hiding-place in the Coucy home. He failed. Bigoted, blinded to the reality of events, the old ladies could think only of two things, and it was to their unacknowledged credit that neither of these concerned their own safety. If a wounded partisan had been found in their house by the Germans they would, of course, have been summarily hanged from their own garden trees; but knowing this, they also knew enough to realize that there could be almost equally disastrous consequences for Emil. To possess relations who harboured partisans was quite enough to have any German—and more particularly half German—officer stripped of his rank and sent to a penal battalion on the East Front. And in all probability it was just such a one as this exhausted bleeding youth panting in their back porch who had shot their old friend Théophile Pecheur a week ago. They sent him away. He was taken by the Germans twenty minutes later and next day his mutilated remains were on show at a cross-roads.

Vengeance came equally swiftly four nights later. The Resistance fighters ringed the house before dawn and fired it. Since it was very old and largely made of wood it flared quickly into great pillars of flame in which both Mlles Coucy, their equally old cook, Célestine, their Pekingese, Poufette, and four cats all perished together.

Though this had taken place in late September of the previous year, a time when Emil was ending his hurried and concentrated training with the U-boat Lehr Division in the Gulf of Danzig, he had heard nothing of it until the following July when at last a letter from Colonel Amoret-Labonde dated more than two months earlier had reached him in the grim austerity of an English prison camp.

As an *ancien militaire* the Colonel had suffered less than his old friend for his unpopular views, though he had been deprived of his civil rights and his ration cards and dared not enter the village but lived a half-starved existence shut in his house half a kilometre outside. His letter had been dark and sombre and despairing. Both the Mlles Coucy had been posthumously deprived of their civil rights and what remained of their property had been confiscated—whether permanently or temporarily it was impossible to tell. Whatever happened, Emil should not come back to Grévilly. The Colonel had written nostalgically of the Coucys and of the days of his godson's childhood; then stating that he was sure that they would never meet again in this world, he had taken a sad farewell of 'one for whom he had always felt a very deep, indeed, a fatherly affection.'

Emil had wept over this letter—but not for long. He knew, by then, that the full facts concerning the sinking of the *Maréchal Oudinot* were known to the British. He had been taken to London, cautioned by an Admiralty lawyer, shown statements by various members of the U-boat's crew and asked by a British Intelligence officer to make one himself. He had been led to a small room containing only a table and a chair. On the table were half a dozen sharpened pencils and a thick pile of lined foolscap. 'Now sit down and write out, in your own words, what happened on the evening of January the fifth. You can take as long as you like. Just let us have *your* version of events—what you saw and heard and did yourself. Put down everything you can remember. When you've finished, ring the bell.' Then he had been left alone.

It had been the first time he had been alone since—he had struggled to think back—since he had been in the Masondi hospital. It was unbelievable that it was only three months ago; it seemed a lifetime. He had limped over to the barred window. Outside in the wide garden chestnut trees lifted their dark-green foliage to the grey London sky; there was a distant, curiously muted hum of traffic. At Masondi there had been the birds, and the splash of hoses during the daily waterings of the shrubs in which they lived. Masondi—Latif, Rami, Mr Spencer, Emerald—a vanished world. Or perhaps one which had never really existed except in a dream. But the uneven thud of his surgical boot on the bare boards was proof enough to the contrary.

He had turned back to the table. All that paper. He could sit down and write. He could explain everything on that paper and do it carefully, taking as long as he liked. No one would interrupt or question him. There was a big piece of india-rubber so that if he wanted to change something he had written he could do so without anyone being the wiser. Here, in this small room, he had power of a sort at last; the power to explain fully, coherently and in his own words exactly what

had happened on that evening seven months ago in the South Atlantic
—and why it had been done. Later his words would be read and understood and accepted. To refuse—to write nothing—was surely to
deprive himself of this power. And a refusal would make him appear
guilty, too. How else could such a silence be interpreted? An innocent
man had no reason to conceal anything, and he was innocent. It was
just a question of explaining why . . . He had sat down, pulled the big
block of paper towards him and taken up a newly sharpened pencil.
And then, suddenly, he had had a quick vision of this room as it had
been yesterday and would be tomorrow. Just as empty, just as quiet,
but with a figure at the table, a figure in field grey or blue, or perhaps
in shabby civilian clothes, crouched pencil in hand scribbling, scribbling in self-justification—desperate, evasive, anguished . . .

He had sat still for a long minute staring at the blank paper before
him. Then he had risen and limped back to the window; and he had
still been there, looking out at the chestnut trees, when they had come
for him an hour later. They had been surprised, then coldly threatening. 'Nothing to say? You don't want to give your version? Have you
thought about the value of a little co-operation with us? You realize,
of course, that there is going to be a court process over this affair?
You will have to justify yourself in court. Surely that would be easier
if we could get together a little first?'

'If I am to be tried, I shall be permitted an advocate?'

'Yes. But—'

'Then until I can talk with him I shall say nothing—and write
nothing.'

So—back to the prison camp and more months of empty waiting, of
uncertainty and of growing fear as the dull grey English summer
shaded imperceptibly into autumn. The first chill penetrating the
bleak iron huts, the falling leaves and closing evenings; and then the
abrupt order to make ready for transfer to Germany.

And now at last here he was—no longer merely a number on a long
list of prisoners but 'the second accused.' He was on trial for his life.
The bearded American Advocate-Captain who spoke such good
French had explained that at their last conference yesterday evening.

'I take it you have both realized what a verdict of "Guilty" could
mean to you? Of course the Court has no obligation to award such
a penalty. This is not by any means an ordinary English murder trial
in which the accused is either found guilty and hanged or not guilty
and acquitted. You are not even being nominally charged with murder
as such. The indictment is "in violation of the Laws and Usages of

War, being concerned in the killing of members of the crew of the said steamship." Note the word *concerned*. That allows a lot of latitude —though perhaps rather more for the Prosecution than the Defence, I fear. None the less, I shall probably bring up the fact that death sentences upon you are a possibility at an early stage of the trial. I shall do this in order to impress members of the Court with the serious consequences of a "Guilty" verdict. It is the experience of most lawyers that a jury is very much less willing to bring in such a verdict if the result can be a death sentence than if it can only be one of im-prisonment.'

As a defending counsel Emil found Captain Kaye extremely re-assuring. True, he had refused to give any opinion on the outcome of the trial . . . 'It is my job, aided by Dr Stusser here, to do everything that can be done and to say everything that can be said, for you both. And that I shall certainly do. But it is *not* my job to guess the Court's reaction to my own or the Prosecution's plea. That I will not do.' Yet even this very refusal somehow inspired confidence.

Emil guessed correctly that Captain Kaye preferred his first to his second client. Eugen Kielbasa was firm, calm, unshakable in his belief in the rightness of what he had done. Kaye had agreed at once that Eugen should testify in the witness-box but had hesitated over Emil. 'You do not *have* to testify, Kümmerol; please understand that. It is entirely optional. Kielbasa equally does not have to, though in his case he would be ill-advised not to do so. But if his plea of operational necessity is accepted, then you are, of course, automatically exonerated since you merely obeyed his order. And you are very much his junior, in age as well as rank . . . The Court might think it natural enough should you decide not to enter the witness-box . . .' He had frowned, Emil remembered, and shaken his great head. 'Yet since we cannot know their reaction at this stage . . . Yes, I suppose I cannot advise against it.'

So tomorrow—Kaye thought it would almost certainly be to-morrow—he would have to stand where Huberein had stood today and explain to that row of silent men why he had acted as he had on that faraway evening which now seemed so far away as to be an event in somebody else's life—nothing to do with him at all. It had seemed easy enough until he had watched Huberein under cross-examination today. But now he was not so sure. . . .

He shivered again, rubbing his cold hands together, feeling the increasing ache in his left leg which pained him so much more now in the cold weather than it had in the summer months. There was still talk of a possible amputation. The doctors at the English prison camp had been divided in their opinions but had, upon the whole, considered that amputation just below the knee might be best . . . 'It would mean a complete ending of the pain, and you might even find walking a good deal easier with an artificial limb.' But—'Anyway, don't let us decide in a hurry. We'll think more about it after this trial, shall we? It may not be necessary, after all.' No, under certain circumstances it clearly would not be necessary. Emil shivered once more. Tomorrow . . . tomorrow . . .

Twelve

'May it please you, sir. Members of the Court . . .' Captain Kaye, rising on the second morning of the trial to open for the Defence, was more than ever aware of his lack of wig and gown. It distressed him unduly, for he was a man who placed considerable value upon ceremonial and traditional trappings and he had a somewhat theatrical cast of mind. His was a distinctly European rather than American mentality and, allusive, cynical, dilettante, touchy and snobbish, it contained a great deal of what was best in the peculiar London-Paris intellectual axis of the early nineteen-hundreds. Wealthy himself, he affected a certain mild disdain for riches and a biting contempt for the overt American admiration of them. But he was miserly with his money and spent long hours worrying over his investments. A careful and intelligent barrister, he had, nevertheless, seldom practised in civil life since the time needed would have had to be deducted from the necessary sessions of investment-worrying; but he had taken an energetic interest in the law and had attended all the more startling cases on both sides of the Channel during the inter-war years. In the same way that his money gave him freedom, his legal training and qualifications provided both professional status and an absorbing hobby, and attended by a series of young and generally handsome valet-secretaries—of whom Corporal Post was the most recent—he had led a comfortable, studious and useless life for more than forty years. He was a happy man, though he was not aware of his happiness since it was so often marred by some small but upsetting imperfection—today it was his lack of wig and gown.

'. . . in opening this defence I do not consider it my task to traverse once more the ground which was covered—painstakingly covered, one may say—by Prosecuting Counsel yesterday. The Court is now thoroughly acquainted with the events which have given rise to this trial. The sighting, following and sinking of the steamship *Maréchal Oudinot*, and the events subsequent to that sinking, have all been repeated by witness after witness in almost tedious procession. There may have been—indeed there *have* been—many discrepancies in the testimonies of those witnesses; discrepancies and omissions due, doubtless, to the atmosphere of strain, excitement and danger of that time, to the extreme youth of the German sailors themselves and to the comparatively long period which has passed since the sinking. It is no part of the case for the Defence to challenge any of these witnesses on the more important material facts. The floating wreckage left after the sinking of the *Maréchal Oudinot was* attacked by gunfire and grenades as ordered by the U-boat Kommandant and the result of this was—as the Kommandant knew it would be—the death of many of the survivors.

'No. The Defence plea is one of operational necessity. To put the matter in simple non-technical words, it is that Kapitänleutnant Kielbasa gave the order to destroy that wreckage because the only— the *only*—alternative open to him was to accept the extreme probability of the destruction of his boat and her crew. Please note the words "extreme probability." The Defence cannot, of course, claim that refusal to destroy the floating wreckage would have certainly and automatically sealed the U-boat's doom. In war, with all its chances and hazards, nothing is ever quite certain or completely automatic. It is possible that the air patrols so feared by U-boats in that area might not have flown on the following day—all the pilots might have suddenly been taken ill or all the machines developed engine trouble. Perhaps even if they had flown, all the observers might have been reading newspapers as they passed over the wreckage, or lost in reveries of their early childhood and happy schooldays. Those things are possibilities—though you may think them highly unlikely ones, as indeed they are. But the *probability*—the *extreme probability*—was that the patrols would be flown as usual and the incriminatory wreckage discovered soon after dawn—with fatal results for U-996. And a commanding officer—every member of the Court will unhesitatingly accept this, I am certain—has to take his decisions and give his orders on probabilities, not on far-fetched possibilities.

'Captain Kielbasa was in sole command of a large submarine and a crew of fifty-five men engaged on a perilous but important mission for his country at a desperate period of the war. Those naval officers who sit here today will be able to assess, better than those of us who are soldiers, just how remote and lonely and cut off such a command could be. And if it could be remote and lonely for an Allied submarine commander, how much more so must it be for the Kommandant of a U-boat with no friendly ports and bases scattered liberally all over the globe, with no possibility of help from the moment he left Germany until the moment he returned—a hated and ruthlessly hunted quarry in all the seven seas.

'It was in these conditions that Kielbasa had to take his decision on that evening of the fifth of January. And remember that he already knew that four sister boats of U-996 had disappeared with all hands and without trace in these very waters during the past nine months. That the decision he took was a hard one cannot be doubted, but that it was the right one—the one that any sane, conscientious commander of *any* submarine in *any* navy would have taken in those same circumstances—that—it—was—the—*only* one—' Kaye's voice, which had risen and slowed as he slammed emphasis into each word, suddenly dropped and quickened to its normal, dry matter-of-factness—'is something which the Defence respectfully submits that the Court can do no other than accept.'

Up on the bench the members of the Court, sensing a pause, eased themselves in their chairs, shifted their feet. In the small press gallery reporters scribbled quickly and rustled papers. The Judge Advocate was busy making notes and at the Prosecution table Colonel Rostwood expressionlessly examined his fingernails. From the dock the cold, pale faces of the accused regarded their counsel, who was pleading in a language which they could only follow with some difficulty, in patient hope.

Captain Kaye cleared his throat, glanced at his notes and recommenced. 'Now that is the plea for the first accused, Kapitänleutnant Kielbasa, and in due course evidence will be called in support of it. The plea of the second accused, Leutnant-zur-See Kümmerol, is, quite simply, that of superior orders. He was Gunnery Officer on board the U-996 and was therefore the officer to whom the captain turned when giving orders to destroy the wreckage. As a junior officer Lieutenant Kümmerol had to obey the orders of his captain. He is here in the dock today for that reason and for that reason only. Kapitänleutnant Kielbasa does not dispute the giving of that order and Kümmerol does not dispute that he carried it out to the best of his ability. We must remember that the order was given in what, in land warfare, is termed "the face of the enemy"—that is, in action. I do not, I think, have to remind the Court of the universal military penalty for refusing to obey an order given by a lawful superior in the face of the enemy.' In dealing so briefly with his second client Captain Kaye's voice had been almost toneless in its disinterest, plainly implying that as there was no case to answer it was ridiculous to waste words upon it.

He paused once more and then continued carefully. 'As I have, I hope, made plain, it is no part of the Defence's case to question the major material facts giving rise to this trial as these have already been made known to the Court, but to show that what was done was done out of no lesser motive than the sheer blank necessity of self-preservation. I do not think that anyone can make this plainer to the Court than the first accused, Kapitänleutnant Kielbasa, the man who had to make the decision, give the order and take the actions which have brought him and his subordinate here today. Kielbasa will tell you that he takes full responsibility for that decision, that order, those actions. He is perfectly prepared to justify all these things today in court and to explain clearly and in the plain words of a sailor exactly why the events of the evening of January the fifth of this year took place.'

Captain Kaye noticed with satisfaction that there was an undoubted stir of attentive curiosity as the U-boat Kommandant left the dock and, walking to the witness-box, turned and faced the Court. A great deal must depend on the impression Kielbasa made, particularly upon the lay members, and in this respect at least Captain Kaye had few doubts of success. He had taken considerable pains to see that both Kielbasa and Kümmerol should appear before the Court to their best advantage. Their uniforms, shabby and threadbare from long usage, had been cleaned and pressed, their white shirts carefully laundered. Kaye had managed to find each a new black tie and had arranged for a civilian rather than a prison barber to cut their hair. Despite their pallor and a certain gauntness neither, today, looked different from any other pair of young officers in any other western navy.

Captain Kaye felt his confidence increase as he carefully took Kielbasa through the preliminary questions of his naval past and the early weeks of the cruise. 'Now, Kapitänleutnant, will you tell the Court what course you took when you left Kiel?'

'I went through the Sound to Kristiansand south, and from there into the middle of the North Atlantic, passing between Iceland and the Faeroes. From there I turned south into mid-Atlantic west of the Azores and then south-south-east which took me to a position between Freetown and Natal and then between Freetown and Ascension.'

'Were you travelling upon the surface or submerged?'

'We submerged by day and ran upon the surface most of the night.'

'How did this affect your crew?'

'It was extremely trying for them. They were very young and in-experienced and for fully three weeks none of them ever saw daylight. It was something they were unused to and it was bad for their health and worse for their spirits. I was surprised and impressed by the way they stood up to it.'

'Did you expect to carry out your whole cruise in this manner?'

'No. I do not think that it could have been done in any case. But as soon as I was out of the Freetown-Ascension area, that is to say as soon as the boat began to enter the great expanses of the South Atlan-tic, I estimated that I should be able to run on the surface for some hours each day—so long as a careful lookout was kept.'

'I see.' Kaye glanced at the Court and then turned once more to the spectacled, scarred young man in the box above him. 'Now we have heard something of this Freetown-Ascension area in the course of this trial—properly, I believe, since it is a matter of the greatest relevance. Please tell the Court what you know of it.'

'At that time it was considered an area of great danger to our sub-marines by reason of constant Allied air patrols between these two points. It was known to all U-boat Kommandanten as a most perilous passage and it was also known that four submarines had recently been lost there without trace.'

'Four other U-boats lost there without trace,' repeated Captain Kaye as if to himself but loudly enough for the Court to hear. He paused, took a green notebook from his pocket and consulted it for a few moments. It contained the start of an anthology of detrimental remarks made by various persons upon the appearance, capabilities and behaviour of General Patton. Shortly he replaced it, locked his hands together behind his back and took a deep breath. 'Now, Kapitänleutnant Kielbasa, you were a long way from your designated area of operations when you sighted the *Maréchal Oudinot*. You were also, by your own admission, in a zone of particular danger. Did it not appear to you that in the circumstances it might be the wiser course to disregard this ship and carry on with your cruise?'

'No.'

'Why not?'

'For two reasons. The first was that all Kommandanten had over-riding orders to sink all enemy shipping wherever they found them if at all possible. The second was that my crew needed, above all else, a victory after the exhausting and hazardous weeks they had just passed.'

'I see. Yes. And you approached to very close range and fired two torpedoes. I think that the Prosecution brought out also, in the examination of Lieutenant Huberein, that you knew the *Maréchal Oudinot* to be a coal-burner?'

'Yes, I was fairly certain of that.'

'Very well. You attacked the ship at close range. You used two torpedoes when one would, according to your First Officer of the Watch, have done the work adequately—and you believed the ship to be a coal-burner. Will you tell the Court frankly what these three points add up to?'

In the dock Eugen sniffed, raised his eyebrows above his heavy spectacles and then said firmly, 'They added up to this—that I wanted to destroy the ship completely and to sink her as quickly as possible. I closed the range as far as was safely possible in order to be sure of certain hits and I used two torpedoes in order to be sure of maximum damage. My reasoning was that in this way she would take everything with her to the bottom, which was what I wanted. A ship that is only holed and sinks slowly naturally leaves much more wreckage upon the surface. The fact that she was a coal-burner meant that, particularly if she foundered quickly, the area of oil left on the surface would be negligible.'

'You realized that by carrying out this intention it was probable that the *Maréchal Oudinot* would go down with all hands?'

'Yes.'

'That did not worry you?'

'No. They were, after all, enemy sailors.'

'You did not consider them as in any sense noncombatant?'

'No, I did not.' Eugen's tone was decisive. 'On the contrary I considered them very much combatants. They were performing war service for their countries—which is to say they were performing hostile war action against Germany—of a nature no less effective than any enemy soldiers in action on the fronts. I regarded them in that light. Nor do I see how they can be regarded in any other.'

Captain Kaye looked grave but inwardly he was extremely pleased. What Kielbasa had said might give considerable offence since the myth that merchant seamen were noncombatants was one dear to the British heart. But the hypocrisy of this attitude was simple to expose and it was important that it should be made plain. 'I see. In effect, then, you are saying, are you not, that a merchant ship flying an enemy flag in wartime is as much a military objective as an army truck, and her crew as much military personnel as the driver and assistant driver of such a truck, whether that vehicle is empty or loaded?'

Before Eugen could answer the Judge Advocate intervened. 'That won't do, I'm afraid. You are putting the words into his mouth. You know better than that, Captain Kaye.' But his voice was not unfriendly and held a slightly amused note. He knew, as well as the Defence Counsel, what the latter was doing. But once would have to be enough.

Kaye bowed. 'I must apologize. I withdraw the question.'

'Very well. But please do not repeat the error.'

Turning back to Eugen the Captain said, 'What did you do when you surfaced?'

'Firstly it was my intention to see more clearly the result of my torpedoes. I wished also to ascertain that I had succeeded in sinking the ship without leaving too much floating wreckage.'

'And what did you find?'

Carefully Eugen said, 'That there was a great deal of floating— remains. This was mainly due to the unfortunate fact that the ship was carrying a deck cargo of wood which had not been visible to me through my periscope.'

'There were some survivors also, were there not?'

'Yes.'

'How many?'

'It was growing rapidly dark and I can only give a rough idea —perhaps some twelve or fifteen.'

'Did you interrogate any of these?'

'I ordered the Gunnery Officer, Leutnant Kümmerol, to try to locate an officer and ask the usual questions—the ship's course, destination, cargo and so forth—and he succeeded in doing this.'

'Very well.' Once more Kaye braced himself. 'You had, up till now, carried out a routine sinking in every way. The ship was gone and you had interrogated a surviving member of the crew. This—' he was addressing the Court now, though still looking towards the pale, spectacled figure in the witness-box—'was a perfectly normal and in no way illegitimate occurrence of the recent war at sea. Thousands of ships were sunk by hundreds of submarines in exactly that way. What did you do then?'

'It was quite dark by now. I continued my course on the surface at slow speed for about a thousand metres. During this time I was assessing the situation and trying to decide what to do. I was extremely worried about the wreckage left on the surface and the certain discovery of it next morning by air patrols. In the end, to my great reluctance, I decided that there was no other course open to me but to sink all the wreckage that could be sunk and to try and break up and disperse as much as possible of the rest.'

Kaye nodded. 'You say you were reluctant. Why?'

Eugen hesitated a brief moment, then said slowly. 'Because I knew that if I did so most, if not all, of the survivors would die. They were clinging to the wreckage and even at that moment were probably attempting to bind together the logs and floating crates and drums which I must disperse and destroy if I was to save my own boat and crew. There was no other course open to me, but it was a decision I took with intense unwillingness and distress.'

'That is very understandable. You were placed in a most terrible dilemma. What did you do after you had taken this decision?'

'I called the First Officer of the Watch, Leutnant Huberein, to the bridge and explained to him and to the Gunnery Officer what I had decided must be done. Then I ordered machine-guns brought to the bridge and set up and I reversed course. I also ordered the signal lamp to be brought up and to be used as a searchlight to find the larger pieces of wreckage. I ordered the Gunnery Officer to take a megaphone and shout to any survivors who might be on the wreckage, ordering them to abandon it.'

'You had no intention, then, of machine-gunning the survivors? Only the actual wreckage?'

'That is so. I had no wish to fire on human beings, and no intention of doing so if at all possible.'

'You intended, you say, to order them off the wreckage before it was destroyed. But supposing they did not obey you?'

"I would still have to destroy the wreckage. But I expected that they would obey me."

'And drown?'

'Not necessarily. They had life-jackets. They would have, therefore, eight hours at least. They would not drown immediately.' As if aware of the inadequacy of this answer Eugen added, 'It was quite impossible for me to do anything more for them. I could not save them, but I would not kill them.'

'And did they obey you and abandon the wreckage?'

'In most cases, yes. I do not think that any wreckage containing human beings was fired upon, although in one case when some survivors—I think only two—remained on a small raft of logs the raft was broken up by ramming and the two men were thrown into the water.'

'Who carried out the firing?'

'The Gunnery Officer and two under-officers.'

'Was the result successful?'

'In the event it must have been.'

Captain Kaye frowned. 'I don't quite understand that answer. Please clarify it.'

'I mean that had I failed to destroy or disperse the wreckage I should not be here in court today. I should be dead somewhere on the bottom of the South Atlantic. My presence here is therefore proof that the wreckage was satisfactorily disposed of.'

'I see. Thank you.' Once more Captain Kaye paused to remove, examine and replace his pince-nez. 'Now Kapitänleutnant Kielbasa, you have told the Court with extreme frankness and clarity of your own decisions and actions and your reasons for taking them. One further question and I have done. The events of which you have been speaking took place after a strenuous and extremely tiring patrol, during which you had upon your shoulders, and for the first time, the full and entire responsibility for a large submarine, its crew and its mission, at a very desperate stage of the war at sea. You had already endured three full weeks of extreme strain and you knew that you must endure many more. That was the position when you took the decisions and actions for which you are now answering to this Court. But since that time ten months have passed, during the greater part of which you have been a prisoner—which is to say that you have had ample leisure to reconsider and reassess all those decisions and actions in peace and quiet. Do you now—after this long period—still consider your decisions were the correct ones?'

'I do.'

'And that they were inevitable under the then circumstances?'

'Yes.'

'And that you acted as you did in want of any rational alternative?'

'Yes.'

'And that should you, in some quite unimaginable way, find yourself in exactly those circumstances again, you would take exactly those same decisions?'

'I should have to; since once again there would be no rational alternative open to me.'

'Thank you.' Captain Kaye turned to the bench, inclined his head to the Judge Advocate and walked back to the Defence table.

Colonel Rostwood did not waste any time over preliminaries. 'You have told the Court that you decided to destroy and disperse the wreckage. What did that wreckage consist of?'

'There were, as far as I could see, a great many baulks of timber. There were also a few metal drums—empty oil drums, I imagine—and wooden boxes and so forth—the usual flotsam which sunken ships leave on the surface.'

'And life-rafts?'

'There was something that looked like one—only upside down.'

'I suggest to you that there were at least two life-rafts, and that both were floating the right way up.'

Eugen's eyebrows rose. 'That is not *my* recollection.' He emphasized the 'my' as if to add point that he, unlike the Prosecutor, had been on the scene of action.

Colonel Rostwood did not like this, and he was equal to it. 'You cannot recollect the life-rafts which were comparatively large and high out of the water, but you *can* recollect the baulks of wood which were smaller and lower in the water. I see. Well then, do you recollect the lifeboat—tell me that?'

Briefly Eugen's tongue flickered over his lips and one hand moved up to the long scar across his left cheek. 'I do not think there was a lifeboat.'

'You do not *think* there was a lifeboat.' The Prosecutor's voice was dryly sceptical. 'I will produce a witness who remembers that lifeboat very well; a witness who will tell the Court how two young crewmen of the *Maréchal Oudinot* managed to cut the lashings which held this eighteen-foot fully equipped lifeboat—boat, not raft—to the roof of the steamship's stern deckhouse, so that when that section of the ship sank the boat floated off. This witness will also tell the Court that the U-996 found the unharmed and buoyant lifeboat with its searchlight and deliberately machine-gunned and then rammed it. It was by far the largest piece of what you have termed "floating wreckage" which you destroyed. Do you still say you do not remember it?'

'If there was such a lifeboat then I did destroy it, I suppose.'

'Answer the question, please! Do you remember that lifeboat?'

Eugen swallowed. His eyebrows were raised to a degree that corrugated his forehead in deep lines. 'I have said that I do not remember a lifeboat. I have said that it was very dark. I have said that I destroyed all floating wreckage. I cannot remember destroying a lifeboat but I may have done so.'

'You may have seen a large white lifeboat and, if so, you did destroy it. Your recollection or non-recollection of what you destroyed is not particularly clear, is it? And if you cannot remember gunning and ramming such a large object how is it that you are so certain that you did not fire upon living survivors? You have told the Court that you did not do this, have you not?'

'I did everything I could to avoid it.'

'And if you were told that after your submarine finally left the scene, after more than two hours of intermittent machine-gunning and grenade-throwing, three dead bodies riddled with bullets still lay across bits of wreckage and that one man, gravely injured by machine-gun bullets, was dying in a water-logged raft—would you still say that you did not fire upon the survivors?'

Eugen's shoulders lifted in a mixture of irritation and helplessness. 'Yes, I would still say so. The firing was performed by the light of the signal lamp, but naturally many of the bullets must have travelled outside and beyond the lamp's illumination. What the bullets may have hit in the darkness is not necessarily what they were aimed at. They were not aimed at human beings.'

'And bullets travel a long way and very fast. A submarine on the surface is also a fairly fast mover by comparison with a life-raft or someone clinging to wreckage. You circled in and out and round and round what you are pleased to term "the wreckage" for *over two whole hours*. Are you seriously asking the Court to believe that large, unwieldy pieces of flotsam—let alone unpowered rafts—could have drifted beyond your area of search in that time and on a calm, windless sea?'

'No.'

'Then I suggest that you saw all your targets. You also ordered the use of grenades, did you not?'

'Yes.'

'How far can a man throw a grenade?'

'I am not sure. About twenty or twenty-five metres, perhaps.'

'Were grenades thrown at rafts or wreckage with people on them?'

'No.'

'Are you certain of this?'

'Yes.'

'Then how do you account for the fact that at least two survivors were wounded by grenade fragments—one so badly that he subsequently died from his wounds?'

'I cannot account for such a thing.'

'Yet it occurred—as I shall bring evidence to show. Do you think, perhaps, that the survivors of the steamship threw grenades at each other just to pass the time?'

Eugen sniffed. 'That is a ridiculous question.'

At once Colonel Whaley-Wren's gavel cracked out its wooden remonstrance. He leaned forward and fixed the U-boat Kommandant with a long cold stare, but his voice was quiet and almost toneless as he said, 'Kindly remember that you are, by your own choice, giving evidence in court. It is not for you to comment on Counsel's questions but to answer them. I warn you that remarks of the sort you have just made can do your case nothing but harm. Now answer the question properly.'

Sulkily Eugen said, 'No.' Then he added, 'For all I know they may have had grenades in one of the rafts and have tried to throw one at the submarine. It may have exploded prematurely.'

Quickly Colonel Rostwood snapped, 'What rafts?'

'What—'

'I asked *what rafts?*'

'The—the ones they were in.'

'But you said you only saw what might have been *one* raft—and that was upside down. Now, apparently, you say that there may have been grenades in this capsized raft and that some of the *Maréchal Oudinot*'s crew—presumably underwater, too—may have prepared them and tried to throw them at your submarine.'

Captain Kaye rose quickly. 'Please the Court, I object. My learned friend is twisting the witness's words. What my client is actually trying to say is that if survivors were wounded by grenades he can think of no possible way in which this could have been done by grenades from his boat. The hypothesis of grenades in the possession of survivors themselves is not his but that of my learned friend.'

The Judge Advocate nodded. 'I think that must be accepted by the Court. The objection is sustained.'

Colonel Rostwood inclined his head and turned back to the box. 'Kielbasa—I am shortly to bring evidence to the effect that survivors were hit by, and in some cases killed by, machine-gun fire and grenades. You have stated plainly that you gave orders for machine-gun fire and grenade-throwing in an area in which you knew these survivors to be. Do you seriously say that these men were hit, wounded and killed by machine-gun fire and grenades emanating from a source other than U-996?'

'No, I cannot say that.'

For a second the Prosecutor paused. Then he said politely 'No. I agree, you cannot say that.'

There was a short wait while Colonel Rostwood referred, in turn, to a small notebook. Then he said, 'There has been considerable mention of mercantile life-jackets during both the examination-in-chief of Lieutenant Huberein and yourself. This has centred around the length of time which such life-jackets are capable of supporting a human being in the water. You, for instance, stated that even when ordered to jump from what you have continually and misleadingly called "the wreckage" into the sea, the survivors would not drown immediately because of their life-jackets. But how many survivors were, in fact, wearing life-jackets?'

'I do not know. I have always understood that it was customary for all British maritime personnel above decks to wear life-jackets at all times.'

'What you have always understood is not an answer to my question. Did you see any survivors wearing life-jackets?'

'I cannot remember.'

'I will bring evidence to show that very few indeed of the survivors were wearing life-jackets. The majority of those whom you ordered to leap into the sea and whom with your searchlight you must have seen perfectly clearly, were not equipped with them. That, however, made no difference to you, I suppose?'

'I have said already that I had no choice in what I did. Therefore it could make no difference.'

Colonel Rostwood turned a page in his notebook. 'Now, Kielbasa, you have admitted freely that you spent at least two hours cruising about the area of the sinking attempting, in your own words, "to destroy and disperse the floating wreckage." At the end of that time you say that you believed that you had succeeded in this project. Is that so?'

'As I have said, I should not be here otherwise.'

'That is not an answer to my question. I want to know whether you believed, at the time when you resumed your course, that you had succeeded?'

Eugen frowned thoughtfully for a moment. 'No. I was not sure then. I could not be certain, in the darkness, of how far I had succeeded. I doubted if I had dispersed enough wreckage. But the lack of any enemy air action next day proved I had done so.'

'In other words there was still a good deal of wreckage on the surface when you left the scene of the sinking. Wreckage which you were unable to sink?'

'Yes.'

'But no sign of survivors?'

'I do not think so. I cannot remember.'

Colonel Rostwood paused a moment. 'I suggest that you left the area when you did, not, as you have stated, because you were unable to sink the rest of the wreckage, but because you believed that you had killed all the survivors?'

'No.'

'I suggest that what actually happened was this. At first you wished to destroy the floating wreckage, including at least two rafts and a lifeboat, and at the same time to drown the survivors before dawn by making them jump into the sea, knowing as you did that even those few who had life-jackets could only survive for a maximum of eight hours. But when you realized that much of the wreckage was un-sinkable—which you must have done quite quickly—you also realized that living survivors would manage to collect enough of it to construct some sort of makeshift rafts once your submarine had gone. This would have defeated your purpose, since living men standing and waving upon rafts, however makeshift, would have been much more easily seen by air patrols than dispersed and lifeless wreckage. You therefore deliberately turned your weapons upon such survivors as still remained alive in the water and did not leave the area until you believed that you had killed them all. That is correct, is it not?'

There was a strong hint of weariness in Eugen's voice as he replied, 'No, it is not. I have already said that I did not order fire upon the survivors—only upon the wreckage.'

Imperturbably Colonel Rostwood turned a few pages of his note-book. 'Now when you left the scene of the sinking you went below and spoke to the boat's company over the loudspeaker system, did you not?'

'Yes.'

'Telling them of what you had done, and that you had taken the decision to do so with—' the Prosecutor glanced at his notebook—'with a very heavy heart.'

'That is so.'

'And you went on to say that the crew should remember the thousands of German women and children killed in Allied air raids?'

'Something like that. I cannot remember the exact words.'

'The exact words are not important. Why did you say that?'

'Why? In order to—to demonstrate—to ask the men to remember that war was harsh. To say that the men whom we had—had been forced to leave to drown were members of the same nation who were killing our civilian population every night.'

'Had you yourself lost relations in the bombing raids?'

'Only a few distant ones. Cousins—relations by marriage.'

'You had lost relations. And it is not impossible, perhaps, that you were grieved and angered by this—even if they *were* only cousins and relations by marriage. I suggest that your killing of the survivors of the sunken ship might, in part at least, have been motivated by a sense of revenge. You had lost innocent and defenceless relations in the air raids of the Allies. Here were some equally innocent and defenceless Allied personnel who might be made to pay with their own lives and in their own turn for your loss. Later, a sense of guilt caused you to make an exculpatory speech to the crew. Is that not close to the truth?'

In the witness-box Eugen took a deep breath. 'No, it is *not!* Firstly, I had lost no relations close enough to me to cause such feelings. Secondly I did not look upon the surviving sailors of the *Maréchal Oudinot* as innocent in the sense which you imply—that is, as non-combatants. I looked upon them as naval personnel who must accept the dangers and risks of war as much as my own crew. Thirdly, I was acting under one motive only—to safeguard my boat and my men. I was very distressed at what I had had to do, but I did not feel guilty about it.'

'You saw no reason to feel guilty?'

'No. I had no choice, as I have said. But I felt saddened and distressed and I thought that the crew might feel the same way.'

'We are not discussing the crew. You have stood up in court today and said—on more than one occasion—that you firmly believe that what you did was right. You even told defence counsel that in similar circumstances you would again act in the same way, did you not?'

'Yes.'

'And therefore, you say, you neither felt then, nor feel now, any guilt. Not sadness or distress—we are not talking of those—but *guilt* at what you did on the evening of January the fifth of this year?'

'Again—*no*.' Eugen's voice was exaggeratedly tired, but as if to indicate that he was in full control of himself he smiled slightly as he spoke. Kaye, at the Defence table, wished uneasily that he had refrained from doing so. Both his clients were handsome, or at least of striking appearance in somewhat unusual ways, yet neither was able to smile attractively or sincerely. They had faces which despite their youth seemed somehow made for repose. But Eugen was not to smile again.

'Why then—'the Prosecutor's voice was deliberate—'did you most carefully instruct all your crew that nothing whatever was to be said about this particular sinking? Why did you and your officers, under preliminary interrogation shortly after your capture, admit to sinking *only* the tanker *Empire Advance*, the *second* ship you destroyed—and remain completely silent about the first, the *Maréchal Oudinot*?'

'Why—' Eugen swallowed and again came the quick movement of one hand to the long scar on his face. 'Why—? Well, it is, for a prisoner, only necessary to give his name, his rank and his service number—'

'We are all aware of that regulation. Answer the question, please. Why, if you felt no guilt at all, did you go to such lengths to cover the traces of your action?'

'I did not . . . I am not sure how this question . . . I cannot say that—'

'*Why?*' The Prosecutor's voice was raised for the first time. 'Why, if you felt no guilt did you try to hide the fact of the sinking?'

Eugen breathed deeply. 'It was my duty to mislead the enemy, and—'

'Why did you try to hide the sinking of the *Maréchal Oudinot* by giving that order to your crew?'

'I—I saw no reason to inform the enemy of our operations. I—'

'You sank two ships. The tanker, *Empire Advance*, was the bigger and much the most important. It was sunk in an area in which the sinking might well have gone undiscovered. Yet you chose to tell the interrogator of that and to most carefully attempt to hide the relatively unimportant sinking of the *Maréchal Oudinot*. I ask you again—*why?*'

'I have told you.'

'You have *not* told me.'

Captain Kaye was appalled. Here was something about which he knew nothing whatever—at which he had not even guessed. Instinct more than reason, a knowledge that somehow the shaken Kielbasa must be given time to collect his wits, drove him to his feet. 'I object. Witness is being browbeaten by—'

'The objection is overruled.' The Judge Advocate's voice was cold. 'The witness, far from being browbeaten, is being thoroughly evasive.' He turned to Eugen. 'You will answer the question of Prosecuting

Counsel. Why, if you felt no guilt over your action concerning the survivors, did you go to the lengths you did to hide the fact of the entire sinking?'

Eugen's normally pallid face was flushed, his breathing rapid. 'It—it had been a very unpleasant thing. I have *said* that. It could, perhaps, have been twisted into use for propaganda purposes against Germany, and particularly against the Navy. I did not feel guilty about it—no. But I felt that it was better not alluded to. I—we—all prisoners have a right to mislead and to misstate under enemy interrogation. That is well known, I think.'

It had been a good recovery but, as Kaye realized with angry frustration, it had not been in time. Why, oh why had not Kielbasa told him of that compromising order to the crew, that so-guilty-seeming silence, before the trial?

Now Colonel Rostwood was saying quietly, 'I suggest to you that your reasons for that order and your subsequent silence were quite different. I suggest that you knew perfectly well—both at the time and afterwards—that what you were doing was both very wrong and entirely illegal. That it was—and that you knew it to be so—a flagrant contravention of the Laws and Usages of War. That it was—and that you knew it to be so—nothing less than the most horrible and cold-blooded murder.' Without waiting for a reply, he turned, bowed quickly to the Court, and resumed his seat.

After a short moment the Judge Advocate turned to the Defence table. 'Do you wish to re-examine, Captain Kaye?'

But all Captain Kaye could do was to shake his head silently and Major Glenberyll glanced at his watch, then at the President, and receiving a nod said, 'In that case the Court will adjourn for lunch.'

Thirteen

'Now, Kümmerol, what training have you received with regard to disobedience and its consequences in the Navy?'

From the witness-box Emil looked down into the encouraging bearded face of his counsel and spoke the words that he had been told to learn by heart. 'I have been taught that in the face of the enemy there could be no such thing as disobedience, and that it would always be punished by death.'

'What was your age at the time of the sinking of the *Maréchal Oudinot*?'

'Twenty.'

'How long were you in the Navy until the time of your capture?'

'Three years.'

'Had you, during that time, ever heard of a naval officer refusing to obey an order when in action against the enemy?'

'No.'

'Very well. Now I want you to be very careful how you answer this next question. Can you clearly remember receiving orders from the Kommandant at the time of the sinking of the *Maréchal Oudinot* regarding both the ordering of guns to the bridge and the actual order to use them?'

'Yes, I remember those orders.'

'Please repeat them to the Court.'

Emil cleared his throat nervously, glanced at the row of faces along the bench all grave, all turned to him, all waiting . . . 'The Kommandant said this. "You are the Gunnery Officer. Order up the two M.G. 15s and ammunition—and have grenades and Schmeissers up, too. You are to destroy the *Überrest* by gunfire. Shout at them first to jump in the sea—then destroy all the larger pieces of wreckage".'

'Those orders were given to you directly by your captain, Kapitän-leutnant Kielbasa?'

'They were.'

'Was it known to you that by carrying out those orders you might commit a punishable offence?'

'No.'

'Did the Kommandant give you the reason for his order?'

'Yes. He always did this if it was possible. He told me that we must eliminate all traces of the sinking if we were to avoid discovery and destruction from the air during the next day.'

'So you had no option but to carry out this order?'

'No.'

'But let us for a moment make a hypothesis. Let us assume that you had refused to obey—that you had said, "Herr Kommandant, I am not in agreement with this order and I will not obey you." If you had said that, what do you think would have happened?'

For a moment Emil paused, grasped the rail of the box, all eyes upon him. 'Either he would have shot me at once with a pistol, or he would have arrested me and court-martialled me later that night and had me shot on the after casing before submerging at dawn. Those are the most likely things. Or he might have kept me under arrest until we returned, when I would have been tried and then shot—or perhaps hanged—in public. But for the sake of the boat, and for my sake too, I think he would have shot me at once.'

Kaye nodded. 'Thank you. That is a very full answer. Now one more question—again a hypothetical one—and I have done. You have told the Court that you had no knowledge that by carrying out this order you were committing an offence. That I am sure the Court can well believe since—other considerations such as the strain, the danger, the immediacy of the whole thing, quite apart—you had no reason to think otherwise. You had been given an order, and an obvious, sound and logical reason for it had been supplied. But let us assume that instead of being a twenty-year-old boy who had joined the Navy straight from school you had been a mature man of thirty who had studied law and had practised it. Let us assume that as such a man, a properly qualified lawyer of some experience, you had doubts as to the legality of this order. Would you then, do you think, have been able to refuse to obey it with impunity?'

'No. It would have been exactly the same.' Emil licked his lips and glanced once more along the ranged faces of the Court members. 'In a submarine, more than anywhere else, the lives of the crew are in the captain's hands—all the time. They must place complete trust in him and he must demand that trust. They must give him unhesitating obedience in everything he orders—and that, too, he must demand. Only in that way can a submarine function at all. There is not—there never can be—any alternative to that.'

Captain Kaye nodded gently, tapping his palm with a pencil; then he walked back to his chair.

As Colonel Rostwood rose to cross-examine, Emil felt the sweat break out on his forehead. He knew that this man, this tall, elderly, rather desiccated officer with the watery grey eyes and the clipped moustache, was going to try to kill him. That was what he was here for and it would be towards that object that every one of his questions would be asked. He swallowed, watching the Colonel walk slowly towards him —a man who wanted to tie him to a post and put twelve bullets in his chest.

'Now, Lieutenant, I want firstly to remind you of two things.' The Prosecutor's voice was calm, almost gentle. Emil stared down hypnotized. 'One is that you are under oath to tell the truth: the other is that you are giving evidence by your own choice and of your own free will. This means that you are expected to answer my questions just as fully and as truthfully as those of Captain Kaye. And—I understand that you have never been in a law court before—do not assume that the Prosecution is bound to try and trip you up with trick questions or to confuse you into making damaging admissions. All I want from you is the truth: nothing more, but equally nothing less.'

Emil nodded. He was more frightened than ever because this man had seen his fear and noted it. And yet it was true that he was here on his own initiative. Captain Kaye had not requested him to testify; had, indeed, seemed doubtful if he should do so. But he had wanted to since he believed that he had nothing to fear from the truth. From the Court—a Court composed of the victorious enemy—yes, much to fear; but from the truth nothing. If this English colonel only wanted to know what had really happened . . . But Colonel Rostwood was already speaking. 'Who actually performed the firing at the rafts and wreckage, Kümmerol?'

'I and two under-officers.'

'Obersteuermann Kalewski and Matrosen-Obergefreiter Wutsdorf?'

'Yes.'

'Where, to the best of your knowledge, are these two men today?'

'Wutsdorf is dead. Kalewski is in Mozambique, unless he has gone somewhere else.'

'Were they in the same hospital as you in Tanganyika?'

'Yes, they were.'

'You were badly wounded in the leg, were you not?'

'Yes.'

'That was when the submarine was trying to reach Portuguese African territorial waters in an attempt to beach itself in neutral hands?'

'We *were* within territorial waters when we were attacked by British planes.'

'That is immaterial at present. The U-boat tried to intern itself by beaching on the Mozambique coast but failed very narrowly. You and several other wounded were taken to a Tanganyika hospital not far from the Mozambique border. Is that correct?'

'Except that we *were* within neutral waters at the time of the attack.'

'That was not part of my question.'

'But you asked me to tell the truth—and that *is* the truth.'

'Very well. But please answer the rest of my question.'

'Yes—the rest of what you ask is what happened.'

'How many wounded were retained in the hospital with you?'

'Seven, I think.'

'Of whom all, save Kalewski and Wutsdorf, subsequently recovered and were taken to a prisoner-of-war camp?'

'I believe so.'

'But these two petty officers escaped from the hospital, even though their wounds were by no means healed. Both attempted to escape across the border into Portuguese African territory. Kalewski succeeded and has not been heard of since, but Wutsdorf was shot while resisting recapture. That, as far as you know, is the truth, is it not?'

'No.'

Colonel Rostwood glanced up surprised. 'You mean that you deny any knowledge of this happening?'

'No. I mean that Wutsdorf was not shot. He was eaten by the doctor's daughter's tame leopard.'

The entire court stirred and rustled. For the first time Colonel Rostwood looked flushed and at a loss. 'But—but—I had naturally assumed—I understood that this man escaped and—'

From the witness-box Emil glanced worriedly at Kaye, received an amused, approving nod and said, 'Wutsdorf got out of the hospital, probably to try to follow Kalewski. It was a dark night and it seems he lost his way. He walked into Rose's cage—Rose was the leopard, you see. And—and Rose was up her tree—and she jumped on him and killed him. When Dr Zared and the police officer arrived she was beginning to eat him. So you see—'

But Colonel Rostwood had recovered himself now and was thoroughly annoyed. The witness was taking things entirely in his own hands. It wouldn't do at all. 'That's enough, Kümmerol! You are here to answer my questions, not to make irrelevant statements to the Court.'

'But you—you *asked* for the truth.'

Before the Colonel could speak again the Judge Advocate said, 'That is correct. Colonel Rostwood, you impressed—very rightly, I'm sure—the witness with the necessity of telling the whole truth. This story about the leopard is only an attempt to tell the truth as he recalls it over the death of one of the petty officers. Are you certain that the man in question was shot?'

'No, sir. I—I admit that I had assumed that. I knew that both petty officers had escaped from the hospital but that one had died before reaching the Mozambique border—before, in fact, getting far from the hospital.'

'Then you do not question the witness's veracity—this story of the leopard?'

'No, sir. But I respectfully submit that it is an irrelevant interpolation in my cross-examination.'

'But Colonel Rostwood, you yourself told us—it was in your opening statement to the witness—that Kümmerol had never been in a court of law before. You cannot expect him to know what is relevant and what is not.'

'Quite so, sir.' With an effort Colonel Rostwood managed to resume his former air of calm. 'I do not think that the witness had any conscious intention of being irrelevant. With permission, therefore, I will continue to cross-examine.'

'Please do so.'

Once more the Prosecutor turned to Emil, but this time his face was slightly flushed and there was an angry gleam in his eyes. 'Both Kalewski and Wutsdorf broke out of the hospital in an attempt to flee across the border into neutral territory. Considering that the distance was at least forty miles and that both were still suffering from unhealed wounds, the dangers of such an attempt were obviously extreme. One man succeeded; one died. Now Kümmerol, can you think of any reason which might have induced these two men to take the action they did?'

Emil thought for a moment. 'Yes. Yes, I can.'

'Ah! Then please tell the Court.'

'Well, Kalewski was—was the strongest and most determined man of our crew. He was a—a remarkable person. He was not a German but a Baltic Danziger, and with the war so nearly lost I think he ceased to think of himself as connected with Germany. He was an excellent under-officer while in the Navy, but after capture I think he felt his duty was over. He wanted to escape and start a new life. As for Wutsdorf—he had always been a close friend of Kalewski's and was much under his influence. That is why they escaped from the hospital, I think.'

But this answer was not at all the one which Colonel Rostwood wanted.

'That is merely *your* version, is it not?'

'That is what Kalewski told me.'

'He *told* you?'

'He visited me in my room before he left. He could walk then, though not easily. He told the orderly he was going to the lavatory, but he visited me instead.'

Once more Emil had the full attention of the Court and this time he was aware of it and seized his chance. He had realized, after the Prosecutor's mistake over the death of Wutsdorf, that Colonel Rostwood really knew nothing of what had happened at Masondi and that therefore he himself might produce what fabrications he wished. He was not yet certain how he might use this knowledge to his advantage but at least it allowed him to attract the Court's attention to himself as a person rather than as a witness. 'And I would have gone, too, had I been able. For I am hardly more a German than Kalewski. I am three-quarters French and I was forced into the German Navy after the occupation of France. I, too, therefore—'

But from the Defence table Captain Kaye was rolling his eyes up to heaven and shaking his huge hirsute head in despair. Emil's voice stumbled and halted momentarily and Colonel Rostwood's cut in quickly, 'So you, too, would have gone if you could? Yes, I can well believe it. Now Kümmerol—did any other prisoner in the hospital attempt to escape?'

'Not as far as I know.' Emil's voice was sulky. He had so often wanted to make that speech concerning his French origin, and he had actually seemed to find an opportunity. Then Kaye . . .

'No. But the two men who did—and you have admitted that had you been well enough to have accompanied them it would have been three—were those who had performed the actual shooting and grenade-throwing against the survivors of the *Maréchal Oudinot*. I suggest that all three of you knew that what you had done on that evening of the fifth of January was a monstrous thing and that, should it be discovered, you would all three be in a very difficult position. I suggest that that was the real reason why Kalewski and Wutsdorf broke out of the hospital and why you would, had you been able, have gone with them.'

'No, it is not.'

'You did not think it wrong to machine-gun helpless men struggling in the sea?'

'I did not do that. I fired only at the wreckage after the men had jumped off.'

'You knew, at any rate, that they would die as a result of the firing. Did you think that wrong?'

'I had to obey orders.'

'That is not an answer to my question. Did you think it *wrong*?'

'I think all killing is wrong, and as war is largely killing war is wrong. But I did not start the war.'

'We are not talking of the war but of this particular incident when you knowingly caused the deaths of unarmed and defenceless men struggling for their lives in the middle of an ocean. Did you think that wrong—answer yes or no.'

'No.'

'You stand by that opinion?'

'Yes. It was not—'

'Very well. Then why did you, under interrogation, lie about the sinking of the *Maréchal Oudinot* and pretend that it had not occurred?'

'Because I had been ordered to do so by the Kommandant. It was our duty to mislead the enemy interrogators if we could. It is well known that such is the duty of captured personnel.'

'But why the *Maréchal Oudinot*? Why not the *Empire Advance*?'

But Emil had been briefed on how to answer this question during the lunch interval, and now he gave the answer which Eugen should have given that morning. 'Because I could understand that the admission of the destruction of a ship in the Freetown-Ascension area might make the passage of other U-boats in that area still more hazardous.'

'I see.' Colonel Rostwood frowned and Emil almost smiled. The cross-examination was proving much simpler than he had at first supposed. He realized with surprise that he was almost enjoying it.

Baffled, Colonel Rostwood appeared to have taken refuge in a notebook. Emil glanced again at the Court members and saw that now they were watching him with expressions which, though more restrained, bore indications of the same indulgently amused admiration as he had been wont to evoke on the faces of his elderly friends at Grévilly or on those of Konteradmiral Waldenkolk's equally elderly colleagues. And Emil knew that in their eyes he was no longer an unknown but rather disgraceful figure—'the second accused' —but a personality in his own right; a human being at last. And because of this he knew he was safe; because of this they would not kill him. They were more than half way to understanding him and perhaps soon they would do so fully. *To understand all is to forgive all* . . . If only now, at this moment, he could turn and talk to them unrestrainedly, could tell them all about himself as he had told the British naval interrogator at the Masondi hospital—about his life at Grévilly, his Aunts Coucy, his complicated nationality and the difficulties with which he had to cope in dealing with it; about . . . But the Prosecutor had lifted his face from his notebook and was speaking again. 'Very well—you wished to mislead the enemy. That is, one may say, understandable. But why did you wish to mislead your own side?'

'Mislead—? I—I didn't.'

'You did not wish to?'

'No—of course not.'

'Then why did you make this entry in the log of U-996 concerning the sinking of the *Maréchal Oudinot*—"*Sunk with all hands. A short search was made for survivors. None was found*"?'

Emil swallowed and gripped the bronze rail before him more tightly. He had not expected to be questioned on that entry in the log; he had not even thought that the Prosecution knew about it—or if they did that they were interested. It was—or had seemed to be—something which had lost its relevance once Guéroult's survival had made certain that the story of the sinking of the *Maréchal Oudinot* must come out in full. He was being tried for obeying his captain's orders—not for making false entries in the submarine's log book. And yet somehow he guessed instinctively that this question was a dangerous one and tried to play for time. 'I don't understand. I—'

'That is what you wrote, is it not?'

'I cannot remember clearly. I made many entries in the log, naturally. It is impossible for me to remember everything I wrote.' But there had been a quiet menace in the Prosecutor's voice which began to panic Emil into a disastrous reaction of evasive prevarication. 'All watch officers must make continual entries, as is well known. I cannot remember making that one. I do not think I did. I do not think it was my watch, or that—'

Coldly Colonel Rostwood cut him short. 'We have the log book accessible. Do you want me to send for it in order to stimulate your memory?'

'No! I mean, if I *did* have the watch—'

'You did.'

'Then—then I must have written something. I—'

'You wrote those words I have just quoted. And you signed your initials to them. Do you, or do you not, dispute that?'

Swallowing, seeing Captain Kaye's bowed head shaking in despairing frustration, Emil said distractedly, 'No—no, I do not—in that case.'

'Very well. Then you admit that you deliberately recorded a lying —an entirely false—entry in the submarine's log book. Why?'

Emil stared down helplessly and Colonel Rostwood, without waiting for an answer, continued, 'I suggest that you *knew* that you had performed a criminal action and were not prepared to admit this.'

'No—no. It was not—'

'That you were so certain that it *was* a criminal action that you were not prepared to record it officially even for your superiors in B.D.U.'

'No! It was not that. It was—'

'No—' Colonel Rostwood's voice, interrupting him, was suddenly loud—'no, you are right. It was not! You are no fool, Kümmerol, as you have adequately demonstrated in your testimony before the Court. On the contrary, and despite your age, you are an intelligent and quick-witted man. You made that false entry in the log *not* in order to mislead your superiors but to safeguard yourself in the event which became a reality—of your capture. You foresaw that capture. With the war obviously nearing its close you may have even envisaged surrender. And you believed that you, Kalewski and Wutsdorf had between you killed all the survivors. You were determined that there should be nothing—*nothing whatever*—to implicate you in that killing. That is the real truth, is it not?' He paused, reversed pencil pointed upwards in accusing interrogation.

But all Emil could do was to shake his head dumbly. For he knew that what the Prosecutor had just said was not only completely true but completely unanswerable in his terms. Colonel Rostwood had never, in his wildest moment, conceived of being placed in the position in which he himself and Eugen had found themselves on that evening last January; he could not, or would not, understand it—after all, it was not his job to do so.

And now all the fight drained out of Emil. He had been hours, surely, in this small, high, narrow box. He felt exhausted and weak and through his left leg fiery pains stabbed regularly up into his body. He dared not look at the Court and still less at Captain Kaye. He wanted only to be allowed to sit down; at all costs to take the weight off his leg—to sit down and shut his eyes and be left alone. But relentlessly Colonel Rostwood's voice beat up at him from below. 'You knew you were doing wrong, did you not? Can you deny that now? You knew that you were committing a criminal and atrocious murder, did you not?'

'No.' Emil's voice was little more than a mutter between numb lips. 'I was ordered to do it. I had no time to think—'

'Very well! Very well, then. Now answer this— Do you think *now* that what you did was wrong?'

From his seat at the Defence table Kaye half started to his feet, and then sank back. His eyes fixed on Kümmerol in the box, he willed him with all his might to make just one more defiant effort and to say 'No.' If only Kümmerol would look across at him again just for a second surely he could get that message through . . . But when Kümmerol did look up his eyes, glinting with despairing tears, met only those of Colonel Rostwood, and tiredly he nodded yes.

Fourteen

It was getting late now and outside the court the autumn dusk must be falling over the drab streets, but Corporal Post had informed his chief at the commencement of Emil's cross-examination that the Defence's most important witness had arrived, and Captain Kaye decided, despite the advanced hour, to put him in the box at once. Whatever happened, the members of the Court must not go home tonight before the soundness of the 'operational necessity' plea had been made manifest to them. Within two minutes of Emil's exhausted limp back to the dock his place was taken by a burly, red-faced man in a surprisingly smart light grey check civilian suit and a loud tie. He looked like a youngish but prosperous bookmaker—vulgarly genial, aggressively alert.

Captain Kaye's voice was suitably brisk and businesslike as he addressed him. 'Your name is Bruno Gericht?'

'It is.'

'What rank did you hold in the former German Navy at the end of the war?'

'Korvettenkapitän.'

'What decorations do you possess?'

'I hold the General Service Cross, the Iron Cross First and Second Class—also the *Ritterkreuz* with Oak Leaves.'

'You have, I understand, commanded several U-boats during the war?'

'I have been Kommandant of five U-boats and have performed seventeen war patrols.'

'I see. Now, Captain Gericht, will you tell the Court how many Allied ships you sank during this time?'

'During my commands I sank thirty-four Allied ships.'

'Later, I believe, you were transferred to the U-boat Command—*Befehlshaber der Unterseeboote*?'

'That is correct. I was attached to B.D.U. from the seventeenth of November nineteen forty-three.'

'What were your duties, Captain?'

'I had many. The most important were to brief outgoing Kommandanten and to correlate their reports on return.'

'Did you brief Kapitänleutnant Kielbasa before he set out in U-996?'

'I did.'

'Do you recognize him here today?'

'I do.'

'What did you tell him about the situation in the South Atlantic zone?'

'I told Kielbasa that the position in this particular zone was becoming extremely difficult. I told him that four boats had recently been lost in this zone—almost certainly in the area of Freetown-Ascension Island. I told him that we believed the destruction of the boats to be due to two causes. Firstly that, like U-996, they were the biggest in the U-boat fleet—heavy, somewhat slow, long-range cruisers which were therefore the easiest to hit, the most vulnerable. Secondly that we knew that there were constant air patrols in the Freetown-Ascension area, expressly flown to prevent our U-boats from breaking into the South Atlantic; and that these air bases were operated in connection with aircraft carriers which could chase submarines until they could destroy them. I told Kielbasa that he should exercise extreme caution in this region. I told him that he must take every precaution not to be discovered in this region since otherwise the enemy air force would pursue him with all available planes and destroy him.'

Kaye nodded, paused and adjusted his glasses. 'Now, Captain Gericht, how do you suppose—in view of what you told him in your briefing—Kielbasa would regard the traces of any ship he might sink in the Freetown-Ascension area?'

'He would undoubtedly regard them as very highly dangerous for himself. As an acute danger to his boat.'

'What could he do to eliminate that danger?'

'He could destroy all the large pieces of wreckage—those which might most easily be detected from the air.'

'We know that the S.S. *Maréchal Oudinot* was a coal-burning, rather than an oil-burning, ship. Would her sinking leave an area of oil upon the sea's surface large enough, by itself, to betray that sinking?'

'No, not in my opinion. A small patch of oil might have been left, but there are many such patches on the sea—they can occur from the cleaning of a ship's bilges, for example.'

'Now, Captain Gericht, it has been suggested in Court that Kielbasa would have been better advised to have taken advantage of the hours of darkness before him to leave the scene of the sinking as rapidly as possible rather than waste time in destroying the wreckage of the sunken ship. As a thoroughly experienced submarine commander, will you give the Court your opinion on that point?'

For the first time the U-boat ace lifted his head and looked at the Court. 'In my opinion that would have been the wrong thing to do. In the best possible conditions his boat could only have covered a distance of approximately one hundred and fifty sea miles before dawn. To air reconnaissance that would have been of no importance at all and the boat would still have been well within the area of enemy air operations next day.'

Kaye waited, letting the echoes of that firm, hard, decisive voice—the voice of a most forceful and determined sea captain—have their full effect upon the Court. Then he said, 'I see. Thank you very much,' inclined his head briefly to the President and returned to the Defence table.

Colonel Rostwood, as was his custom, came to the point with brevity. 'Captain Gericht, you say that you have sunk more than thirty Allied ships during the war. Were these sunk while you were in what I think is termed a "wolf-pack" with other U-boats—or when you were alone?'

'Most were sunk when I was with a wolf-pack. But some I sank alone.'

'What was your procedure after a sinking in the latter case?'

'To get away as quickly as possible.'

'Is that better than destroying the floating wreckage?'

'In the North Atlantic—yes. There were so many sinkings and so much floating wreckage that it no longer mattered, since in that area the presence of U-boats was well known to the enemy. In the zone where Kapitänleutnant Kielbasa's sinking took place this was not so.'

'I see. Now, Captain, what would you, as an experienced U-boat Kommandant, have done if you had been in Kielbasa's position?'

Before Gericht could answer this question Captain Kaye had risen to his feet. 'Please the Court—in my submission the witness should be warned that he need not answer this question since it might incriminate him.' The Defence Counsel had achieved the oblique answer to Colonel Rostwood's question in his own last one, since it was inconceivable that a man like Korvettenkapitän Gericht, having affirmed that the course taken by the U-996's Kommandant was the right one, would himself have taken any other. But instead of telling the witness that he might disregard the question if he chose the Judge Advocate paused, and then said carefully:

'I am not so sure that this witness does enjoy that privilege.' Then, apparently thinking better of this, he turned to Gericht and said, 'You can refuse to answer a question if you think it might expose you to prosecution for a war crime.'

They were ominous words and their effect on the witness was marked. The burly man in the box hesitated and muttered something to himself; he looked dubious and unhappy. Like Captain Kaye, he knew that he had already substantially answered the question in the affirmative sense and he was wondering uneasily if he had gone too far. Taking into consideration his own admission of thirty-four Allied sinkings as well as the well-known British attitude towards submarine warfare, he felt it better to hedge—a blunt refusal to answer might all too easily be taken as indicative that he had something to hide in his own war record. After a short pause he said uncertainly, 'I really do not know the case sufficiently well to give an answer.'

But Major Glenberyll did not like hedging. 'Come, I'm sure you can do better than that. You know the circumstances, do you not? After all, you have been giving evidence about them.' He paused, but as Gericht remained obstinately mute added more sharply, 'You were asked what you would have done had you been the Kommandant to U-996 and had just sunk the *Maréchal Oudinot*.'

'It is very difficult—now that the war is over, you understand . . . I cannot really be expected to put myself in the enormously difficult position of Kapitänleutnant Kielbasa at that time. I do not think that . . .'

Coldly the Judge Advocate cut short this worried, uncompleted sentence with the austerity of a schoolmaster refusing excuses from a guilty but evasive boy. 'Has the fact that the war is over deprived you of your imagination? I ask you again—what would you have done had you been in Kielbasa's position?'

Gericht swallowed, his florid face was deeply flushed and one beringed hand beat a rapid nervous tattoo upon the rail of the witness-box. 'I—I would have done everything possible to save life, of course. That goes without saying, I hope, since it was a measure that was taken by all U-boat Kommandanten. But as to what happened—I—I can only think that owing to the long period of strain he had undergone and the danger he was in that—that Kapitänleutnant Kielbasa lost his nerve.'

'Do you mean, then, that you would *not* have done what Kielbasa did had you kept your nerve?'

And despite his Iron Cross First Class, despite his Knight's Cross with Oak Leaves, Korvettenkapitän Gericht, eyes lowered, muttered sullenly, 'I would not have done it.'

Fifteen

Corporal Post placed the plates of fried chicken and potatoes in their places and the big wooden bowl of salad in the middle of the table. Then he stood back and said in his best English accent, 'Dinner is served, sir!'

Captain Kaye swung round from his writing table smiling broadly. 'Well done, Mr P! You are becoming a most competent Jeeves. So much so that once we are out of uniform I expect you'll want to leave my service and enter a ducal household. I'll have to see what I can do for you in that direction.' He rose, pushing aside his papers, taking off his glasses, blinking his slightly reddened eyes, and Post asked interestedly,

'Do you know any dukes, sir?'

'Not intimately, Mr P, I must confess. Shall we say that I have met two—one royal, one not. Neither possessed the slightest intelligence, good manners, nor, as far as I could judge, common sense. Whether they possessed money I have no idea—but probably not. Most dukes are destitute today. You'd do better financially to barbecue steaks for the Cowboy—on a spit with a built-in record player which sings "Home on the Range" when they are done. Yes. Well now—where did you get this chicken? Your coalman?'

'Yes, sir.'

'You didn't give away our entire stock of fuel for it, I hope?'

'No. Only a pair of Army boots. I had—' Post's voice was a little uncertain; one never knew quite how far one could go with Captain Kaye—'meant it for tomorrow so we could celebrate our victory. But—'

'Ah yes, but—!' Kaye shook out a paper napkin. 'But, indeed!' His pince-nez glinted in the electric light from above. 'We didn't have a very good day, I'm afraid. I wish our clients had told us about that damn-fool order of silence and that crass entry in the log book. That's the trouble with most clients, though. They believe that their counsel is bound to do better for them if he *believes* that they are innocent, and in order that he should they hide any incriminating details from him. If only they'd realize that we don't give a damn for their guilt or innocence. When we defend we are on their side unconditionally, and when we prosecute we are equally against them. Whether they've actually committed the offence as charged is entirely beside the point. Mr P, you have cooked this chicken to perfection! If I paid them, I would raise your wages. Fortunately I don't; so that, too, is beside the point.'

But Corporal Post had put down his knife and fork and was staring at his chief across the table. In a strained voice he asked, 'Sir, are they —are they dead ducks, then?'

'Ducks? I thought we were talking of chicken.'

'I mean tomorrow—will they be goners?'

But as usual Captain Kaye would not commit himself. Instead, he wiped his mouth, took a drink of whisky and said with irrelevant piety, 'The Lord giveth and the Lord taketh away.' Then he went on eating with enjoyment, yet every so often casting quick glances at Post's pale, troubled young face at the other side of the small oval table. He did not speak again until he had finished, when he belched gently, sat back, stroked his beard and said, 'You appear to be taking our young friends' fate very much to heart, Mr P. But, after all, what are they? Jerries, Krauts, Square-head bastards, Huns, *les sales Boches, salauds Allemands*—and so on and so forth, doubtless, in a great many other languages, which I am more than glad to admit I cannot speak. "But"—you would say—"they are still human beings, even if they have been defeated in war." In the words of a poet, celebrating, appropriately enough, another sea battle: "*Out spoke the victor then, As he hailed them o'er the wave: 'Ye are brothers! ye are men! And we conquer but to save:—So peace instead of death let us bring*".' That, of course, was written in a civilized age. No use today, Mr P—no use at all. We don't think like that now. You can hardly imagine the Cowboy enunciating such incorrect sentiments, can you? Nor, I am afraid, are they the terms in which our clients considered addressing the poor wretches on that peculiarly ubiquitous detritus continually termed "the floating wreckage".'

Post nodded. 'I know. Only they were in a goddam awful position.' He leaned forward suddenly. 'Sir—what would *you* have done in their place?'

Captain Kaye's eyebrows lifted almost as high as Kapitänleutnant Kielbasa's. 'Good God, Post—don't ask me! I'm not a tough and highly decorated U-boat Kommandant with thirty-four ships to my credit.

I'm only a middle-aged lawyer in uniform, a man of somewhat esoteric, but, I hope, suitably sublimated, tastes, who has neither heard nor desired to hear a shot fired in anger throughout the war. What is more, I am despised and covered with obloquy by one of the greatest, most courteous and knightly generals who has ever added gilded laurels to our gloriously star-spangled banner. No, don't ask me. All I will say is that if *I* was testifying before an ex-enemy court in defence of a junior officer of my own service I think I would be prepared to run a certain amount of risk to help him—particularly if I believed that he had taken the only possible course of action.'

Post nodded grimly. 'I know. That guy—'

'Never mind. We shall see if we cannot retrieve the situation to-morrow. First there's this witness whom the Prosecution have at long last found—the sole survivor. I can't see what good he'll be to Rost-wood now, I must say. He can only confirm what has already been admitted—the facts of the sinking and shooting. Of course Rostwood subpœnaed him before he knew what our pleas were going to be. Probably at the time he thought we'd dispute the material facts. And now he's landed with this fellow and has to put him in the box for form's sake. I don't imagine that will take very long. I'm sure *I've* got nothing to ask him. Well, then we'll both make our closing speeches and I have the right to make mine last. That's going to be the real battle, Mr P, you can take it from me. And now—' Captain Kaye yawned widely—'another whisky for me and then bed. Tomorrow I must have all my wits about me—such as they are.'

Sixteen

Emil had hardly slept all night and was brought behind Eugen into the dock, drawn and pale, his eyes dark-circled. Wordlessly they glanced at each other and took their seats, while behind them their escort of red-capped military police did the same. It was the third, and in all probability the last, day of the trial, but to Emil it seemed as if he had spent weeks—months—an eon of timeless time in this dark room whose panelled walls and sombre railed-in compartments—dock, witness-box, curved raised bench, press gallery—all had a deadly eternal air like the furnishings of some anteroom in Hell.

The trial had tired him even more than he had realized and today he longed for it to be over, a longing which almost overcame his fear of what that end might be. Yet this morning both that longing and that fear were overlayed by emotions still more powerful. For today he knew that he would see Guéroult again. Somewhere within this very building Guéroult was waiting at this moment, and very soon he would be standing in that witness-box, only six metres away from the dock. They would be almost as close together as they had been for a few brief minutes ten months ago upon the fore casing of U-996.

So often during the last months Emil had thought of the *Maréchal Oudinot's* radio officer—a man whom, until he had reached England from Tanganyika, he had firmly believed to be dead. Even before that, lying on his bunk in the U-boat as she edged her way into the Indian Ocean still bound on her long war cruise, he had held desultory imaginary conversations with Guéroult's ghost, explaining, apologizing, attempting to put matters right between them. Finding that Guéroult still lived had been a jarring shock; yet surely that shock had been preceded by a stab of wild delight and relief. Guéroult alive—not killed, after all. No need any longer for those guilty explanations with an accusing spectre. A burden had fallen abruptly from his shoulders.

But not for long. For Guéroult alive meant that the full story of the sinking would come out. Guéroult and the log book together could probably encompass his death. And soon the knowledge that Guéroult was alive had become more of a burden than the earlier belief that his bones lay fathoms deep in the South Atlantic. For if a dead Guéroult was a fit subject for sorrow, guilt and remorseful nocturnal dialogue, Guéroult alive was a source of apprehension and, above all, of acute embarrassment. For that evening on the casing there had been made, surely, one of those rare contacts when two human beings hitherto unknown to each other and finding themselves suddenly face to face, realize simultaneously a spiritual kinship closer than any blood tie—a mirror-meeting, confusing, alarming, wholly delightful. Yet fifteen minutes later . . .

And that, of course, was what he had wanted so badly to explain— but at the end of a reasonably long life when he, too, was a disembodied ghost. He did not at all like the idea of doing it in the flesh —particularly in the present circumstances. Not that he was going to be allowed to explain personally to Guéroult. Had Germany won the war he would have sought out the *Maréchal Oudinot's* sole survivor and tried, as persuasively as he knew how, to put things right between them. Since Guéroult was also a Frenchman he was presumably open to logic, and realizing revenge was impossible, he would also have realized that Emil's remorse and distress were sincere. He would have accepted his explanations even though they might never have become friends. But now . . . Emil shuddered despite the stuffy warmth of the specially heated court-room . . . Guéroult's presence today would be an unbearable distress.

A nudge from one of the guards behind him made him grasp his thick, rubber-shod stick and struggle to his feet. The Court members were filing into their places. He looked across at them as he had done yesterday and, more curiously, the day before. Now on this third morning their well-known faces were as wearisome as the dutifully displayed photographs of defunct and unloved relations adorning the drab walls of a petite-bourgeoise parlour. Emil even knew their names. Yatchett, the English major—gingery hair, gingery moustache, gingery eyebrows, heavy square chin, bored, unintelligent eyes. Lautig— fat, jovial, blond, and sleepy in the afternoons. Marlignon—neat and attentive. Gordon-Bryce—balding, worried, fidgeting with his pencil, the only one who ever made notes. Meilhac—a gaunt, yellow face expressing the epitome of disinterest and contempt, a hollow, re- peated cough . . . They sat, then rose formally as the President, fol- lowed by the black-robed, wigged figure of the Judge Advocate, entered and took his seat. These last two were ominous figures, al- though at first the pudgy President had been a complete enigma. Emil had thought of his face as essentially a benign one, of his gentle voice as the expression of a mild and kindly spirit. Now he knew he had been wrong. He had studied the President for long hours and had come to the peculiarly prescient conclusion that Colonel Whaley-Wren was by far the most inhuman man he had ever set eyes upon. And in- human in the correct sense of the word; neither savage nor cruel, for savagery and cruelty were highly human attributes, but with most if not all of the ordinary sentiments of man for his fellow men non- existent or atrophied. Colonel Whaley-Wren, alone of the members of the Court, would decide the verdict completely impartially since either way the fate of the accused meant absolutely nothing to him at all.

As for Major Glenberyll—Emil looked upon him with unmixed dread. Unlike the President, the Judge Advocate retained his full range of sentiments and emotions in excellent working order, and Emil had a strongly instinctive belief that they were ones very different from, and very antipathetic to, his own. And he represented the Law. It was he who fashioned for the members of the Court the framework within which this case must be judged. In the last resort it was he who would decide—not upon the abstract justice, the actual logic of the Defence pleas, for that was for the Court—but upon their validity in law. And since, as Captain Kaye had explained, this trial was being conducted under a largely unprecedented form of procedure, that left Major Glenberyll with an extremely wide latitude of interpretation.

They were all sitting down again, rustling their papers into place before them. Below Emil at the Defence table young Corporal Post had started his endless experiments with the circulation of the human blood by cutting off its supply to one of his fingers with an india-rubber band. Somewhere by the Prosecution table Colonel Rostwood was rising to his feet, clearing his throat. Any minute now . . . It would not be so bad for Eugen. He had never spoken to Guéroult and could only have seen him at a distance from the bridge—a white blur in the dusk on the fore casing. But for himself . . . Emil looked down at his own hands below the blue cuffs with their single gold rings and small gold stars and resolutely determined not to look up. He would not look at Guéroult—not from here, not as a prisoner . . . And they could not make him. And he would not listen, either. He would say things over to himself, an inward voice raised and drowning all other sounds —'*Fury said to a mouse, That he met in the house, "Let us both go to law: I will prosecute you . . ."* '

Seventeen

Dryness. A peculiar, unreal atmosphere haunted by the allusive scents of dry wood, dry paper, dry dust; an intimidating smell of sanctified, ordered age. Gaston, like Emil two days ago, stood for the first time in the unpitying precincts of an old court-room, a place in which no one had ever smoked or eaten or drunk or laughed or even, save in a strictly legal sense, sworn aloud. A place which in these respects resembled a church, but a church which dealt only in man-made doom rather than in hopeful salvation. Gaston had looked forward to just such a place and it did not disappoint him now. But he, too, would not look towards the dock—not yet.

It was nine months since he had awakened in the sick-bay of the *Hipòlito Irigoyen* and nearly seven since he had been released from the hospital in Pernambuco and sailed for England. They were months which, like those of early childhood, he was only able to recall in a disjointed and hazy fashion, so out of focus and proportion that he was even now uncertain what was dream and what reality.

He had been very ill, hovering on the edge of death for weeks and recovering so slowly, so weakly, that the puzzled doctors were for ever examining him in the belief that he must be suffering from something far more lethal than the exhaustion and starvation of that thirty-five-day ordeal on the raft. But they had found nothing except an apparent lack of any will to live, a haunted, listless despair which time and again took him back through tears to flushed restlessness, to fever and to a delirium from which, in a weary cycle, drugs lulled him slowly back to weakened, empty calm. Yet his constitution was too strong for a spirit no longer interested in life and his determined heart beat on, his small, tough body insisted on living and he, perforce, must remain its prisoner.

And once this peculiar dichotomy was resolved he recovered rapidly enough—nor, now, could he remember why it had ever existed. For of course he must live—how else could he pursue his overriding aim to find and bring to justice the crew of the U-boat? As soon as he realized this his strength had increased daily and he had clamoured for a British consular official. The Argentinian doctors were dubious. What the patient needed, they felt, was a psychiatrist rather than a diplomat; but he insisted so desperately that, frightened of a further relapse, they let him have his way. Gaston talked solidly for nearly two hours, slept for sixteen and awoke practically as good as new. The doctors kept him, against his will, a week longer and then released him, shaking their heads in wonderment. Two of them spent most of their spare time for weeks afterwards in writing an elaborate thesis, based on the case history of their patient, which was subsequently turned down by every learned medical journal to which it was submitted. But Gaston, the war over, was in Dieppe by then on a long holiday at home. He had not returned at once. A brief note to his parents that he was alive had sufficed until he had gone to London to make statements both oral and written, to sign affidavits and to answer, eagerly, carefully and fully, all questions put to him. He had asked continually for news of the destruction, capture or surrender of any U-boat that might have been the destroyer of the *Maréchal Oudinot* and though later, to his fury, he discovered that the British had had the entire crew in their hands long before he reached England, he had not been told of this until Colonel Rostwood had run him to earth in Belfast, where his newest ship was loading cargo, less than a week before the trial.

And even then there had been difficulties. 'Leave the ship and fly to Germany?' the captain had asked with angry incomprehension. 'But, good God, can't you sign an affidavit, or something? You *have*! Well then . . . And what am I supposed to do, eh? Do you think I'm going to wait here until you've finished testifying in Germany? D'you think you're the only sailor as has been sunk by a bloody Jerry? All right, all right—if you want to sign off you can, I suppose. But don't think I'll give you your job back in a hurry, young fellow! Radio officers are ten a penny today, let me tell you!'

The captain was right. In the great postwar shipping shortage there were far more officers of all sorts than there were berths for them. By throwing over his present job he was probably consigning himself to an indefinite period on the beach. But that did not matter. Only one thing mattered—to be present in court when the man he still knew only as 'Emil' sat in the dock. And later, to be present when . . . But he would not tempt Fate by progressing too far in his demands. Not yet.

As Captain Kaye had surmised, the Prosecution had become slightly dubious of the value to be extracted from a personal appearance of the *Maréchal Oudinot*'s radio officer soon after the pleas of the Defence were made plain. After all, his full and detailed affidavit was in Colonel Rostwood's hands and when it came down to the material facts of the case surely the testimony of the actual subordinates of the accused was far more damaging than that of an adversary and a victim whose evidence must obviously be heavily coloured by his personal feelings. Colonel Rostwood had almost cabled a cancellation of the subpœna on the eve of the trial and had only been prevented by the lucky arrival of an urgent letter from Guéroult in which the writer's passionate desire to testify had been so evident that the Prosecutor's curiosity had been aroused. And last night he had sent a car to the airport for Guéroult, had taken him out for a late supper and listened with continually growing interest to his story. Long before it was finished he had determined to put him in the box and let him tell it again to the Court.

And now he bowed to the President, then to the Judge Advocate, and addressing his words to the latter, said, 'I want to request that this witness be heard in his mother-tongue, that is, in French. I have, of course, made a translator available for such members of the Court whose knowledge of that language may necessitate one. I hope that, since all previous witnesses have testified in their own languages, this may be considered permissible.'

Major Glenberyll nodded. 'I do not see why the Court should object to that—providing, of course, that the Defence does not. Captain Kaye, I believe I am right in saying that you speak fluent

French and one of your clients, at least, has stated in so many words that he does also. What are your feelings about this?'

'The Defence has no objection, sir.'

'Very well then. Please carry on, Colonel Rostwood.'

But the Colonel, whose own French, though reasonable, was not fluent, had not made his point entirely clear. 'Thank you, sir. It is my intention firstly to establish certain basic facts, and for this I think it will be more convenient to use the English language. Then I intend to ask the witness to tell the Court in his own words what occurred after the U-boat left the scene of the sinking—I assure the Court that this is extremely relevant to the Prosecution's case—and it is then that I would wish him to be heard in French.'

The Judge Advocate nodded; the Prosecutor bowed and turned to Gaston, small, neat and in his blue uniform surprisingly similar in appearance to the crippled young German lieutenant who had given evidence yesterday afternoon—and took him quickly through the necessary formalities of identification, and then the actual torpedoing of the old freighter. Gaston answered carefully, accurately and without impatience. He could wait. He had waited ten months already. He kept his eyes on the Prosecutor's face, glancing only once at those of the Court members.

'Now, Guéroult, when you were floating on the hatch cover directly after the sinking, you were approached by the German submarine and ordered on to the foredeck for interrogation, were you not?'

'Yes, that is so.'

'And there you were asked various questions by a German officer?'

'Yes.'

'Do you see that officer here in court today?'

Gaston took a quick breath and looked. A thin, pale-faced youth hunched over a heavy stick, head bent, eyes resolutely averted. For a moment doubt flared horribly. *That* wasn't 'Emil.' No, it couldn't be! The small smiling dandy, the round face above the open collar of the tailored overalls, the cockily slanted white-covered cap . . . No, no. This ill, shabby, battered creature was somebody quite different. They —Oh Christ!—they'd got the wrong man. But no—they *couldn't* have. Or—or 'Emil' had died and this was another officer—one who had been below decks or out of sight up on the bridge or . . . Or perhaps, just perhaps, his 'Emil' had not been the killer after all! Perhaps he had gone below—protested the order even—and left it to this other man to carry out the butchery. If that was so—Gaston's heart leapt with wild delight—'Emil,' the Frenchman, was guiltless. The true murderer was only this broken German in the dock. But—could it be? He swallowed, hearing through his confusion of hope and doubt the Prosecutor's prompting, 'Well—?'

'I—I am not . . . Is he— His first name is Emil?'

Sharp and immediate came the Judge Advocate's voice. 'You must answer Counsel's question. Do you, or do you not, recognize in Court today the officer who interrogated you on the deck of the U-boat?'

And now, quickly, Colonel Rostwood said, 'I think it might help if the second accused was requested to stand up and face the witness-box.'

'Very well. Kümmerol—stand up and turn towards the witness.'

Slowly, somnambulistically, as if under the influence of some will-trancing drug Emil rose, levering himself with one hand on his stick, the other clutching the dock's dark rail. Slowly he turned to the left and, raising his head, looked across the six metres of space which separated him from the witness-box. For one long agonized moment his own dark eyes met Gaston's. No one in the court could fail to sense the taut electric contact which flared suddenly across that narrow space. In his seat beside Capitaine Meilhac Commander Gordon-Bryce shivered; the scene reminded him of a tiny sand arena at Antananarivo and the sudden confrontation of two male scorpions, pincers high and trembling in the first surprised glare of suicidal enmity, which in a few minutes must kill them both.

Then, snapping that tension, came the radio officer's voice, shaky, sick, barely controlled: 'Yes.'

'All right. Kümmerol, you may sit down. Colonel Rostwood, please continue your examination.'

But now, to the Prosecutor's surprise and irritation, Guéroult seemed distrait. His answers were bungled, badly phrased and un-convincing. He forgot details which had been completely clear last night and once or twice, particularly in the precedence of events, he contradicted himself. Colonel Rostwood wondered if, after all, he had been wise to put him in the box. Nevertheless, certain points at least were made clear.

'The lifeboat was, in fact, floating free and right side up?'
'Yes.'

'You saw it clearly?'

'I did. Because the U-boat held it in its searchlight until it was rammed and sunk.'

'It has been alleged that members of the U-boat's crew shouted to survivors to leave the rafts and larger pieces of wreckage before they were attacked. Is that your recollection?'

'I think they shouted at us when they came back. But afterwards they fired without warning.'

'Did they fire at wreckage with survivors still upon it?'

'Yes.'

'Could they have known that survivors were on that wreckage?'

'They must have seen them since they illuminated each piece with their searchlight before firing. I saw several men on one raft. They were held in the light and machine-gunned, then rammed. The U-boat went on and then turned back. When its light found the raft again it was upside down but two men were crawling on to it. The U-boat came at it again firing all the time. Both men let go and threw up their hands and sank.'

'Did you see grenades thrown?'

'I heard the explosions and I saw the flashes.'

'At what were they thrown?'

'At a capsized raft with several men on it.'

'Did you, later, find dead or wounded men struck by grenade splinters?'

'I and the Captain found two men dead of grenade wounds on some logs of wood. The Second Officer had severe grenade wounds—later he died of them. The—the galley-boy also had a wound from a grenade.'

'How long did this firing and ramming last?'

'About two hours, I think.'

'There was then no question—no doubt at all—that machine-gun fire and grenades were *deliberately* directed at human targets—not merely at empty wreckage?'

'No. They fired at us—and it was deliberate. And also the ramming. They rammed the logs which had been our deck cargo and upon which some survivors were trying to support themselves. These logs were very heavy and the ramming threw them about; several men were badly hurt because of that.'

'The U-boat used the searchlight for all these attacks?'

'Yes. The light was used all the time.'

'So that the U-boat crew on the bridge must have seen men on the wreckage?'

'Yes. It is impossible that they could not have seen them.'

'Why, in your opinion, did they cease firing and leave the scene after two hours?'

'Because they believed they had killed us all.'

'Thank you.' The Prosecutor paused. Guéroult seemed to have recovered himself sufficiently after that odd confrontation with Kümmerol. No doubt it had been a shock of sorts to see again the man who had first given him brandy and promised that help would come soon and then, a few minutes later, had tried to kill him—but equally, it should surely have been an encounter for which he should have been prepared. But now . . .

'Now Guéroult, I want you to tell the Court what occurred between the time the U-boat left the scene and the time you were rescued by the Argentine steamer. And, as you know, you may do this in your own language.'

Gaston nodded. He cleared his throat. '*Messieurs*—' he began uncertainly, then glanced along the row of faces above the bench and commenced, slowly, seemingly unemotionally, to tell of the first days of the long martyrdom on the raft.

He told of the painful collection of the wounded men, of old Captain Crawshaw's calm competence, of that first night spent flashing S.O.S.'s into the blackness with the big torch. The dawn and the wreckage still scattered over the sea under a dull, low, grey sky; the hot fitful breeze . . . '*It'll rain before noon; Gaston*' . . . The realization that a sighting by aircraft was now unlikely until the weather changed . . . He told of the men on the raft; the dying Chinese boy, Lin Hsiang, Roldan with his shattered thigh, Slater with his mangled feet, and the great Negro Rayner, crouched bloody-faced in the stern. Then the worsening weather and the attempts to find anything of value among the wreckage . . . The rising sea at noon and the commencement of the first squall. . . .

High up in its carved pediment above Colonel Whaley-Wren's head the court clock ticked gently on, its hands moving imperceptibly across the old-fashioned Roman numerals on its time-yellowed dial; and below in the still court-room Gaston's voice lifted and fell, now firmer and more confident as, slowly at first and then quite suddenly and completely, the dark court-room fell away and he was back once more on the life-raft in the middle of the South Atlantic.

The hurrying squall and the rising wind dispersing the wreckage over a wave-covered sea so that soon the raft was alone under rain and wind, lifting and falling with its sodden, blood-stained cargo over the high, rolling swells. Lin Hsiang's mercifully quick death—drowned by the rain in a few inches of water—and the groaning and crying of the young Spanish lamp trimmer. The Captain, old and bulky in the

bow under the rain, watching through that night and the next . . .
watching Rayner.

Four days of rain and wind and then the sudden re-emergence of the
sun—how gratefully welcomed at first, how bitterly hated later.
Torpor and heat and Slater's decaying legs and the spoonfuls of water
twice a day. The red-eyed Captain Crawshaw still crouched, ragged
and silver-jowled, in the bow, still watching the crumpled black giant
in the stern . . . Glaring, drumming sun, an eye-searing expanse of salt
water. Day following day in silent, hopeless, burning succession and
the fear, piercing its way through pain and lethargy, that the Captain's
sanity was going . . .

The court clock ticked on. Along the bench every face was turned
towards the witness-box below which Colonel Rostwood stood
immobile, slightly stooped, holding his notebook. Then—and Gaston's
voice stumbled momentarily—the Captain's furtive nocturnal stealing
of food and water, the empty boxes and drums that should not have
been empty . . .

From the gallery came the rustle of the reporters' pencils and the
occasional flap of a turning page. And now Gaston told of the death of
Slater and at last, after so long, the coming of a light breeze from the
east. Then the Captain's sudden attack on Rayner, forcing him into
the tiny life-float before he himself had fallen into the sea. The fight
for the float and its capsizing, as the raft drifted impotently away . . .
A nightmare was being recounted now and, gripped in its vicarious
terror, the Court sat like images, unblinking eyes fixed upon the
speaker in the witness-box. Forgotten now, completely out of mind,
the two dark-blue uniformed figures in the dock sat as silent as the rest,
but with eyes cast down, and from the gallery one reporter, more
curious than his fellows, glanced at them briefly and wondered what
they could be thinking. On and on went Gaston's voice and now it
took, to at least some of the listeners, an odd quality. For if what he
had been telling was a tale of brutal suffering and horror, the story
seemed to lighten perceptibly after the Captain's death. A bright sea—
the coast of Brazil not far off—and for the young man and the small
boy who had miraculously survived so much, a knowledge of almost
certain salvation. The flying-fish, the first sight of a steamer, the little
red-sailed raft and its two remaining occupants gliding on into the
evening with a belief—almost, it seemed, a certainty—that the next
day would see the end of their long ordeal . . . 'And then I slept. He
did not wake me, and I slept all night and far into the next morning, I
think. When I awoke he was gone. The raft was empty except for my-

self. I cannot account for it. In the night—in the darkness—he had disappeared without a cry or a splash—nothing. I was alone. For me that was the end. I do not remember much more except that from that moment I believed that I, too, was certainly to die. Nor did I care, for with the child's death I seemed to have lost all motives, all reason, to hold any longer to life. I do not think there were any ships to be seen, but I did not look carefully. I no longer cared, you see. I cannot tell you more, for I no longer remembered. I do not think I ate or drank again while upon the raft. I did not try to sail or steer. Once I woke to find myself lying on the boards and I called for Philippe to help me sit up, for no longer could I do so by myself. Then I remembered and I wept and soon I must have lost consciousness. The next thing I remember is the sick-bay of the Argentine ship and the ship's doctor lifting my head off the pillow. It is thought that I was probably between four and six days alone on the raft. All told, I had been upon it thirty-five days.'

Gaston's voice stopped at last. He blinked confusedly for a moment and then, as the Court began to stir and to stretch its cramped limbs, he looked down at the Prosecutor. He had spoken for nearly an hour and a half.

Turning to the Court Colonel Rostwood said, 'I would like to ask permission for a short adjournment before cross-examination of the witness commences. I do so because, as I am sure the Court will appreciate, he has spoken at great length and, understandably, under considerable strain. If he could be permitted a short rest—say, fifteen minutes, perhaps—by himself . . . Naturally the Prosecution would have no access to him during this time.'

From the bench the Judge Advocate frowned dubiously. 'That is unusual procedure. But in the circumstances I think the Court would be inclined to look favourably upon the request—unless the Defence objects?'

Captain Kaye rose slowly. 'With respect, sir, I do not think the question arises. The Defence does not wish to cross-examine this witness.'

The Judge Advocate lifted his eyebrows in quick surprise. 'You are quite certain of that, Captain Kaye?'

'Yes, sir. We do not feel that there is anything arising out of the testimony of this witness which can usefully be disputed at this stage. I will, of course, be touching upon many of the points raised in my closing address.'

'Very well. Then, since no more witnesses are to be called on either side the time has come for these closing speeches. Are you ready to make that for the prosecution, Colonel Rostwood?'

'Yes, sir.'

'Very well. Then—' the Judge Advocate glanced quickly at his watch—'the Court will hear you now and then adjourn for lunch. This afternoon it will be the turn of the Defence.'

Eighteen

Colonel Rostwood, returning to the Prosecution table, leafed quickly through a folder of papers, selected three sheets, rejected with quick expert flips of his fingers several others, and advanced, with his almost apologetic stoop, to the well of the Court.

'May it please you, sir—Members of the Court. I feel that I should commence by trying as far as possible to clarify the meaning of the term "war crime" and the position in which we in this Court are placed with regard to trying such crime.

'Basically I think it may be said that the whole conception of war crime stems from the early codes of chivalry as understood during the fourteenth and fifteenth centuries. Before this there had been little which could in any way be called standard practice in the rules of war. Battles were fought in a manner which differed little from the days of the savage Goths, Norsemen and Tartars, prisoners and wounded being despoiled, slaughtered, sold as slaves or ransomed according only to the individual caprice of the victors.

'But by the end of the two centuries of which I speak a definite code comprising rules of warfare had come into being under the name of "chivalry." As bows and arrows gave place to muskets and cannon there were some alterations to this code, but the code itself remained. For by the fourteenth and fifteenth centuries it had come to be realized that warfare of the old, unregulated and savage kind could no longer be tolerated by civilized societies. I would emphasize the words "civilized societies" because even today it is realized that in wars against savages the Laws and Usages cannot apply and a savage tribesman who may kill the wounded or prisoners of a European power is not entitled to any protection by the rules of warfare as understood in International Law.

'And in the same way that an illiterate savage is treated as such under these rules, so must those members of a civilized country's armed forces who break them be punished for so doing.

'The accused are German nationals. That is to say, they are members of a civilized western nation which voluntarily and of its own free will has subscribed to the International rules of war. They stand before this Court arraigned for breaking one of the most important—that unarmed enemies may not be wantonly killed. More than this, their own country's courts, in a well-known judgment after the war of 1914-18, gave explicit expression to the illegality of the very act of which these two men stand accused. I refer to the judgment of the Supreme Court of the German Reich in the case of the *Llandovery Castle*, when two U-boat officers were found guilty of machine-gunning the lifeboats of a sunken hospital ship, and I will read the actual words from page fifty-five of Command Papers of 1921, Number 1450.' Colonel Rostwood took a heavy pair of horn-rimmed glasses from his pocket, adjusted them and read slowly from one of the papers in his hand. '*The firing on boats was an offence against the Law of Nations. In war on land the killing of unarmed enemies is forbidden: similarly in war at sea the killing of shipwrecked persons who have taken refuge in lifeboats is forbidden.*' Carefully he removed his specatcles and put them away. 'Thus the very nation to whom the accused belong decided, in its highest court of law, that it was a war crime to kill survivors from sunken ships. I submit therefore, that there can be no question but that the crime alleged is indeed a war crime, and that this Court has the complete right to try the accused upon that charge.'

The Colonel paused, then shifted his papers and continued. 'The Prosecution must, and does, accept that it carries upon itself the burden of proof that the accused did actually commit this crime. But in fact there does not appear to be any doubt about this. The first accused fully admits that he gave the order to destroy the wreckage and, though he avers that he gave the order to fire upon the wreckage only and not upon the survivors, he admits equally fully that by his actions the survivors were meant to die—as indeed most of them did. The Court may well think that it is immaterial whether a man is shot or killed by drowning—it is still murder, and for the accused to pretend otherwise is nothing but peculiarly cold-blooded hypocrisy. The Court has also heard testimony very much at variance with that of the accused with regard to the targets of the firing. Whether Guéroult, or the accused Kielbasa, is speaking the truth on this matter is something which, of course, the Court will decide for itself—and will doubtless bear in mind the question as to which of the two has the more to gain by lying. But—it is said by the Defence—the accused has fully accepted the responsibility for killing the survivors of the sunken ship. The killing is not in question. The killing was, indeed, most regrettable, and was undertaken—I use the accused's own words—"with a very heavy heart"; but none the less accepted as an absolute necessity—something termed, in fact, an "operational necessity".'

Colonel Rostwood paused again. 'Now, what the accused is saying, in fact, is this. "I had to choose between the lives of those men struggling in the sea or the lives of my own crew—and it was my duty to choose the latter. In this dreadful predicament I had no real choice at all." But, Members of the Court, is that true? It is, perhaps, conceivable that such a situation might genuinely arise in wartime, though I myself find it difficult to imagine one. But can the position of the Kommandant of U-996 on the evening of January the fifth be truly said to be of that sort? He himself has said that his boat would certainly have been destroyed had he not acted as he did, and that the proof of this is in his own present existence and that of the various crew members who have testified before this Court. Had he taken any other course, he says, he would have been dead upon the bottom of the sea. But we know that upon the day after the sinking the so-dreaded air patrols did *not* fly because of bad weather conditions. Nor did they fly the day after that. We have heard from the Prosecution's last witness, Guéroult, that it was not the U-boat which broke up and dispersed the wreckage—on the contrary, there was a great deal of wreckage still in a small sea area at dawn—but the rising wind and sea at about noon of that day. In other words, not only did the U-996 fail to destroy the traces of the sinking, but it need never have attempted to do so. Its action was useless and it was saved from danger of air detection, not by that action, as the Kommandant has claimed—but simply by the deterioration of the weather. The destroying of the survivors' rafts and boat and the callous machine-gunning of the men themselves was, in other words, not only useless but *unnecessary*. That, Members of the Court, is the Prosecution's case with regard to the plea of "operational necessity."

'Now we turn to the plea of the second accused, Kümmerol. He, it will be noted, bases his defence upon superior orders. "I was the Gunnery Officer," he says. "It was my duty to control and order all gunfire. In this capacity I received a direct order from my captain to fire at the rafts and wreckage and to destroy them, both with machine-guns and later with grenades. The submarine was in action. I, as one of the officers, was absolutely and imperatively bound to obey my captain. I did so. Had I refused to obey him he would have shot me or had me shot. I had no choice, therefore, but to obey."

'But let us again look at the aforementioned case of the *Llandovery Castle*. There, the German court decided that two members of the U-boat's crew who, in the same way as Kümmerol, were acting under the direct orders of their captain, committed a war crime in firing at the lifeboats since they were doing something which, in fact, was illegal. The Supreme Court of the German Reich stated that if an order is given which is itself illegal, there can be no defence of "superior orders." In the Prosecution's submission the order given by Kielbasa was illegal and therefore Kümmerol cannot plead the defence of "superior orders" in obeying it.

'Those, in the main, are the Prosecution's refutations of the two pleas of "operational necessity" and "superior orders." But I want to make three more points.' The Colonel opened his notebook, examined it briefly, and said, 'The first arises from the cross-examination of Korvettenkapitän Gericht—the expert witness called by the Defence to substantiate Kielbasa's plea. This officer was, indeed, a most eminent U-boat Kommandant. He had commanded five U-boats, performed seventeen war patrols, sunk more than thirty ships and been very highly decorated. Such a man, the Court may well think, is one who may speak with authority on the circumstances of the present case. Yet, when he was asked the direct question of whether he would, in like circumstances, have taken the same action as the accused, Korvettenkapitän Gericht stated that he would not have done so. My second point is more circumstantial but, the Court may well think, more rather than less indicative of the accused's guilt. I refer to two things. Firstly the extreme efforts made by Kielbasa to get his badly damaged boat into neutral waters and to beach it there. He spared nothing to do this. Even with his boat unable to dive and partially filled with gas as the result of an earlier air attack—even with his wounded lying exposed on his deck—he fought to the last to reach the Mozambique coast. And he very nearly succeeded. Why did he do this? Why, under machine-gun and cannon fire from British aircraft, did he insist on risking the lives of his crew and himself when he was in hopeless case, and his value as a combatant was obviously finished? There was no longer any reason to prevent him from surrendering with honour. Why, then, this urgent anxiety not to fall into Allied hands?

'Again why, from the Tanganyika hospital where at least ten of the crew were being treated for wounds sustained in their last adventures, did the two men—the only two men other than the second accused—

who had machine-gunned the *Maréchal Oudinot*'s survivors make their desperate attempt to flee into neutral territory with their wounds still unhealed? And I would remind Members of the Court that the second accused, Kümmerol, stated in the witness-box that had he been less gravely wounded he would have gone with them. Again, gentlemen, why this intense hatred—or perhaps fear—of remaining in Allied hands?

'Thirdly, and this is undoubtedly the most significant piece of evidence as to the guilty knowledge of the accused which has come to light during this trial; why the orders to the crew to refrain from any mention of the sinking of the *Maréchal Oudinot*? Why, above all, the false entry in the log book stating that the ship was sunk with all hands and that there were no survivors?

'Members of the Court: in the estimation of the Prosecution there is one answer, and one answer only, to all these questions. It is that the admitted killing of the survivors from this sunken steamship was, in fact, an act of murderous revenge. You will recall that immediately after the U-boat left the scene of the sinking the Kommandant went below and spoke to the crew over the loudspeaker system. He admits this. He told the crew that he had ordered the destruction of the "*Überrest*"—a term which, translated, means "the remains" and *not* merely "the wreckage"—with a "very heavy heart," but that the crew should recall the deaths of civilians in the air raids which the Allies were now carrying out deep in the heart of Germany. We know, too, that Kielbasa had lost relatives in these raids.

'Members of the Court: we know that the actual wreckage of the *Maréchal Oudinot* was *not* dispersed or destroyed by the U-boat but by the sudden change in the weather. Indeed, it is difficult to see how any sailor in his senses could have imagined that floating wood could ever be sunk by machine-gun fire. We know, on the other hand, that most of the survivors were killed by that fire and by grenades. The Prosecution believes that it was first and foremost at the men struggling in the water that the U-boat opened fire, and that this was done mainly out of motives of revenge and hatred. Once begun it had to be finished if only in order to leave no witness to the bloody deed. "Stone dead—" to quote Cromwell's famous—or infamous—dictum—"hath no fellow." It took two hours, apparently, before Kielbasa and Kümmerol believed their crime to be fully accomplished. For can one really suppose that otherwise the U-boat would have cruised aimlessly around in circles, idly ramming its way through floating logs and spraying barrels and packing-cases and such flotsam with machine-gun bullets while men threw grenades at floating bottles? No Kommandant in his right mind would order such procedure.'

For the last time Colonel Rostwood paused. Then he lifted one long arm and pointed towards the dock. 'Sir. Members of the Court. The accused, having sunk the steamship *Maréchal Oudinot*, did then wantonly and with guilty intent fire machine-guns and throw grenades at the survivors, thus killing many and wounding several, of whom we have first-hand evidence that three at least—an Englishman, a Chinese and a Spaniard—died later as a direct result of their wounds. I suggest to you that this was nothing but cold-blooded murder and that the indictment against both accused is proved beyond any reasonable doubt.'

Nineteen

There was an air of grimly determined pugnacity about Captain Kaye, as he rose that afternoon, which Corporal Post had never seen before. Ever since the two of them had inhabited their present quarters it had been the Captain's genial habit to share his somewhat informal meals in the sitting-room beside the fire with his military factotum. But at lunch today Post had been brusquely relegated to the kitchen —the Captain needed to think. And he must, reflected Post, have plenty to think about. Colonel Rostwood had proved a very much more formidable opponent than he had at first seemed. What was more, Gericht, upon whose expert evidence the Defence had placed much value, had proved a broken reed, whereas Guéroult, whose evidence the Captain had discounted in advance, had obviously made a heavy impact on the Court—and especially, one might suppose, upon the French officers.

Washing up at the kitchen sink, while in the next room Captain Kaye's curved calabash billowed clouds of almost railway-engine smoke into the darkening air, Post thought that he, too, might consider taking up the law as a profession. Since his early youth in the back streets of a large city he had looked upon the law as a tyranny to be attacked subversively and broken—if one was clever enough or lucky enough—with impunity. He had never looked upon it before as a sinister but exciting competitive game—a sort of vocal bullfight, except that the black-clad matadors very sensibly juggled with other men's lives rather than their own.

For a brief time he wondered how Kielbasa and Kümmerol were

feeling at present. What had they been given for lunch? Were they managing to eat it? He was on their side still because, after all, he was on Captain Kaye's. But since Guéroult's testimony he did not feel quite the same passionate identification with them as he had done at first. If they had caused that appalling saga of agony and despair and death out of any motive save sheer blank necessity to save themselves, then they deserved the penalty which the Prosecutor had obliquely demanded. But had they? Did Captain Kaye still believe in their innocence? Had he ever believed in it? Did it make any difference to him if he did or did not? There was perhaps much more skill, Post realized with a humility most unusual to him, in manipulating the law than even the cleverest criminal could show in breaking it.

Captain Kaye was indeed aware that the Defence was now in a perilous condition. Rostwood's last witness had done the accused an immense amount of damage by his story of the raft—completely irrelevant though it was. Whatever excuses or reasons he might expound in defence of Kielbasa's actions or Kümmerol's predicament, the fact remained that the men in the dock were responsible for that long-drawn agony, and the chances were that the Court had every intention of exacting a bloody retribution from them. There were two things alone which might—just might—alter that intention. The two most important attributes of Homo sapiens—logic and reason. For law itself, as the Prosecutor had shown, was unstable ground; and emotion—used all too well by Guéroult—must be kept in reserve—a last desperate shot in an otherwise empty locker.

Well then, thought the Captain as he rose, holding out one hand for the papers Post at once placed in it, he would just have to do his best this afternoon—and it had better be a good best if two young men were not to face the rifles of a military police squad in the very near future.

He fitted the pincers of his glasses into the small depressions on each side of his thick nose and glanced thoughtfully at the President and then at the blue and khaki figures ranged along the bench. 'May it please you, sir—Members of the Court. We have heard this morning a story which must have filled each of us with horror and pity. We have heard from the only survivor of the *Maréchal Oudinot* the terrible story of the events between the sinking of his ship and his rescue thirty-five days afterwards. It is appalling to think that experiences of that sort—some, perhaps, not quite so prolonged and dreadful, others perhaps even worse if they may be—must have been the fate of very many sailors of many nations during the six years of the war at sea.

Yet so it almost certainly has been. For year after year, in summer and in winter, ships were sinking, crewmen were struggling for their lives in the water or slowly dying of exposure and thirst and hunger cast away on tiny rafts. Some—one must hope many—were rescued. But undeniably many were not and must have perished as miserably as the poor men in Guéroult's raft. Terrible indeed must have been their end—yet I think perhaps equally terrible must have been the deaths which overtook so many submarine sailors during the past war. Many, admittedly, must have died much more quickly; but many, too, must have been trapped in undamaged compartments of their sunken craft on the sea bed where, unlike the poor castaways on the life-rafts, they must wait for death without the slightest or faintest hope of rescue. How many of the twenty-eight thousand German U-boat men who perished during the war died in this ghastly way we shall never know; but it was an ever-present likelihood for every officer and rating of the German submarine fleet. The accused, my clients, had to face that death in the same way as all the others—and in fact it was one from which they escaped by the narrowest possible margin.'

Captain Kaye paused, brooding sombrely at the floor. Then he lifted his big head and grasped the lapels of his tunic in sudden decision. 'But, Members of the Court, that is war. That *is* war. And the countries of each one of us here in this court-room today have been engaged in war for six years. Neither you, sir—' a bow towards the President —'nor you, gentlemen—' a series of bows towards the bench—'nor, I may say with equal certainly, my young clients the accused, were responsible for that war. We were none of us consulted about it nor asked our opinion. If we were, as some of us were, well advanced into adult life we were requested, or perhaps we volunteered, to give our services to our countries. If, like the second accused, or for that matter Guéroult, we were minors—boys in our teens—we were rounded up, told to get into whatever uniforms were thrown to us, and to obey orders without argument. One way or another, once in the service of our countries, we were involved in fighting a war for which individually—and if this goes for men in the prime of life, how much more does it go for the young—we had no responsibility at all. And war is at all times a murderous business. We talk now of "war crimes," but the real crime is war itself and the war criminals are those who commence it or who, having the power to do so, fail to prevent it. The Prosecution has told us that the fourteenth and fifteenth centuries were chivalrous in their mode of warfare. Not being myself a student of that period of history I must bow to my learned friend's superior knowledge. But I must assert my personal belief that even in the most knightly times the dire position in which my clients found themselves —that of "kill or be killed"—must have had upon occasion to be faced. And I am most dubious if it was resolved in any other way, however chivalrous the age, than that in which my clients resolved it last January in that deadly dangerous area of the South Atlantic. For all human beings, like most animals, possess an immensely strong instinctive sense of self-preservation; an instinct which is profound, fundamental from the days of our earliest evolution millions of years ago. It was there in the fourteenth and the fifteenth centuries quite as strongly as it is here today and it will be there until mankind has so radically altered his nature as to be something quite different from anything we know now. We can no more make laws against it than we can make laws against love or fear or hate, for it is as much a part of all ordinary men as they are.

'And, Members of the Court, we are dealing with this ordinary instinct in ordinary men of today. Ordinary young men brought up to ordinary standards of decent behaviour in ordinary homes such as most of us have known ourselves, I trust. Ordinary young men, yes— but forced into very unordinary difficulties. Very tired young men, very overstrained, frightened and exhausted by the danger and the grim conditions of life in a hunted submarine which may never surface except for a few short nocturnal hours. And upon these ordinary young men is suddenly thrust this question—"Will you kill the enemy, helpless as he is, and save your own lives and perform the duties you owe your country—or will you let him live, thus abandoning both life and duty?" For that was the plain question which the accused had to decide on that evening of the fifth of January this year.'

Captain Kaye turned for a moment to glance at Colonel Rostwood and then swung back. 'My learned friend has pointed out that it was the weather which prevented the air patrols from flying over the wreckage next day and this may be, indeed almost certainly is, true. But on the evening of the sinking of the *Maréchal Oudinot* there was no hint of a change from the calm, cloudless weather then prevailing in the area of Freetown-Ascension Island. No hint, at least, to the Kommandant of U-996. Sir—Members of the Court, Kapitänleutnant Kielbasa is not a clairvoyant. He could not know that a sudden, quite unusual and unexpected weather change was about to take place. He had to act on the evidence before his eyes—a clear sky, a calm sea. And certainty of air patrols at dawn. He did so act, and I submit that it makes *not one slightest jot of difference* to his plea of operational necessity that a totally unexpected change of weather conditions grounded the air patrols next day. To take a contrary view is to deny both logic and the processes of the human reason. There have been no doubts cast upon the sanity of the first accused, and in fact he acted like a sane man. Had he taken, and acted upon the view that there was a one-in-a-thousand chance of a change in the weather which would ground the hostile aircraft he would not have been sane. Not, at any rate, by standards of sanity acceptable in any navy of the world.'

The Captain paused to reshuffle his papers. 'My learned friend has made great play with the direction of the machine-gun fire and the grenades. Were they aimed at empty wreckage or at human beings? Now the accused have stated that they called on the men clinging to the wreckage to abandon it *before* they fired. Guéroult, in his testimony, agreed that they did this. The accused have also stated that after their warning they fired at the wreckage whether or not men were upon it though they did not see any men and if men were hit by bullets it was unintentionally. Now, I put it individually to members of the Court. If you were called upon to leave a spar or a raft or some piece of flotsam before fire was opened upon it—what would you do? Would you remain and await the bullets? Or would you slip into the dark sea and hope to avoid them and, perhaps, regain the wreckage once the submarine had passed by? I, most certainly, would have adopted the latter course and Guéroult tells us that that is exactly what he, Captain Crawshaw, and other members of the steamer's crew did. But, one may say, "The question is immaterial. Some men undoubtedly were hit and died as a result." That is so. The Defence admits it. The accused have stated that they well knew that by their actions the survivors would die. And this is in no way inconsistent since it is no part of the accused's plea that they did not cause the deaths of the survivors but—and I cannot repeat this enough—that they did so believing that they had no choice if they were to save themselves. Thus the fact that it is now ascertained that some men died as a result of the machine-gun fire and the grenades does in no way affect the plea of operational necessity. At this point I wish to say a few words concerning the well-known German Supreme Court judgment on the *Llandovery Castle* case. The Prosecution has, by implication at least, compared that case with the present one, and I must crave the Court's indulgence to allow me to refute a comparison which is as invidious as it is inaccurate. On the twenty-seventh of June nineteen-eighteen the British hospital ship *Llandovery Castle* was sunk in the Atlantic Ocean about one hundred and sixteen miles south-west of Ireland by U-86 whose commander, Oberleutnant-zur-See Patzig, erroneously believed her to be illegally transporting American airmen. On questioning some of the survivors in the ship's lifeboats Patzig discovered his mistake and in order, as he thought, to conceal it, he destroyed the boats and their occupants by gunfire, intending to leave no living witness to his crime. Not only, therefore, was the torpedoing of the *Llandovery Castle* a war crime in itself but it was aggravated by the second crime of murdering the survivors. Neither the *Llandovery Castle* itself nor the survivors offered any sort of threat at all to U-86 and the killing of the latter was murder of the most wanton and useless sort. I submit that the present case differs wholly from that one. In the present case it was the floating wreckage rather than the survivors which the accused wished to destroy. The wreckage, as has been fully shown, was an immense potential danger to U-996 and had to be destroyed for that reason, and that reason only. There was no question, as in the case of Patzig, of attempting to cover the traces of a crime, since no crime had been committed. The celebrated judgment of the German Supreme Court on the sixteenth of July nineteen twenty-one was one which would never have been pronounced upon the present case which, in all essentials, is totally different from that of the *Llandovery Castle*.'

Captain Kaye paused to remove and readjust his glasses. 'The prosecution has stated that Korvettenkapitän Gericht made it plain that he would not have done as Kielbasa did if in the latter's place. It is true that Gericht did say that in evidence. But what he did *not* say was what he would have done—because he knew full well that Kielbasa took the only course a Kommandant could have taken.'

Again Captain Kaye paused and shuffled his papers. 'Now, Members of the Court, I want to turn expressly to the case of Kümmerol, the second accused. It bears a great similarity to that of Kapitänleutnant Kielbasa since he too, like his captain, found himself facing the question—kill or be killed? He was twenty years old at the time of the incident; he was, that is to say, still a minor—a boy. He had had no legal training. He had been, as all naval personnel are, deeply indoctrinated with the implicit belief that a superior's orders must be obeyed at all times and without question. He knew, too, that his captain could, and indeed would have to, shoot him if he disobeyed the order to fire upon the wreckage. On the one hand—obedience to his service orders, to his duty as a naval officer, to a captain he admired, trusted and liked. On the other—dereliction of duty, disobedience, and a disgraceful death at that captain's hands. Members of the Court, I ask you once more and in all sincerity—what would each of you have done had you been in Kümmerol's place?

'And now I must deal with a point which the learned Prosecutor—for reasons which I really cannot comprehend—brought up in his closing speech. I refer to his suggestion that the survivors of the sunken ship were killed for no other reason than some sort of aimless revenge for the bombing of Germany in general and the decease of a few cousins or in-laws of the first accused in particular. I must admit that I hardly feel it necessary to waste much time in refuting what I can only term this quite ludicrous suggestion. The *Maréchal Oudinot* was sunk in an area highly dangerous for U-boats; that, by now, is something of which we are well aware. Now would any sane commander spend two precious hours of darkness, which might otherwise be used for getting as far as possible from the sinking, in cruising around the area using his signal lamp—a distinctly dangerous thing to do in itself—to search for and kill a few pathetic swimmers in order to take a ridiculously vicarious "revenge" for the deaths of one or two distant relatives thousands of miles away. Really, gentlemen! You have heard Kielbasa give evidence; you have listened to him speak; you have watched his demeanour before the Court. You have therefore seen that he is a man of intelligence, calmness and reason. The action he took was to lessen the danger to his boat—not to senselessly augment it. Why, then, did he mention the raids over Germany in his speech to the crew? Quite simply to demonstrate that the killing of unarmed and defenceless persons—which he admitted, as he admits now, that he had been forced to order—was also undertaken on a vastly larger scale by the enemy! There was no question of exultation over blood spilled in revenge; on the contrary, he said—and I myself sincerely believe him—that what he had done, he had done with a very heavy heart.

'Now, Members of the Court, we come to another aspect of this case with which my learned friend has made great play—I refer to the order of silence imposed upon the crew by Kielbasa and the false entry in the boat's log made by Kümmerol. The Prosecution points to these two things as immensely damaging proof of the accused's knowledge of the illegality of their actions. In effect my learned friend is citing them as undoubted demonstrations of *mens rea*—guilty intent.

'Now here we are indeed treading upon difficult ground. But the ground is difficult only because it is uncharted. If war crime is not an entirely new conception, war crime trials are. To the vast lay public civil justice, if not entirely understood in its detail, is none the less a very well-understood conception in itself. But almost nobody, until very recently, had any but the vaguest idea of criminality and the administration of justice as it affected acts committed in war. Kielbasa and Kümmerol knew well that what they had done—I refer to the act itself and not the reasons for it—was something which could only be looked upon as a brutally unpleasant thing. Under none but the terrible circumstances in which they found themselves would they have dreamt for a moment of committing it. But they *had* committed it—unwillingly, undoubtedly with intense distaste—but there it was. Very well. And what if they were captured, or forced to capitulate to the enemy? How would that enemy—an enemy exasperated by six years of furious warfare—look upon their act? Could they be sure of a fair trial? Could they be sure of a trial at all, or even a chance to explain themselves? No, they could not. They would have no rights to such things. There was nothing whatever to prevent the enemy from executing them summarily, unheard, untried. Neither of the accused was to know that he would be accorded the sort of trial which is progressing today; a trial in which each of them enjoys every right and all the legal safeguards to which civilized man is, or ought to be, entitled. If they had known this they would not have feared to admit their actions. But they could not know it—any more than they could know of the imminent change in the weather conditions of which we have heard so much. And since they are reasonable men they took reasonable precautions. The silence order and the false entry are *not* infallible indications of guilty consciences, but indications of an ordinary attempt at self-preservation in circumstances in which no legal safeguards to this end could possibly have been foreseen.'

Captain Kaye turned to the Defence table and handed his papers to Corporal Post. Then he turned back to the bench. 'Sir—Members of the Court. I have done. I ask you to consider very carefully all I have said. I do not need to ask you, for I know that the Judge Advocate will do so, to remember, as you consider your verdict, that the accused must be given the benefit of all reasonable doubt should such doubt arise in your minds. More than anything else, however, I would ask you to place yourselves in the position of each of the accused separately and to ask yourselves, with truth and sincerity, both how you would have acted in their positions and what sort of understanding you would have hoped for when called upon to justify it.'

Captain Kaye bowed to the President, the Judge Advocate and the Court; then turned and sat down wearily between Corporal Post and

Dr Stusser. He took a handkerchief from his sleeve and dabbed at his forehead with a hand which trembled slightly. It was over. He had done all he could; had said all—he thought with satisfaction—that any defending counsel could possibly have said for the accused. Now it was only a question of the summing-up and the verdict. He wanted to win, but for the moment he wanted whisky very much more. That speech had taken a lot out of him. Old—he thought moodily—getting old, that was the trouble. Well, he needed a rest. At his age . . . Forty-four wasn't really old at all, of course. Still—one tired more easily . . . If only he could slip out with Post and send him to the car for the whisky. One could not, of course, be seen drinking on the premises, but one could take it into the lavatory. It would make all the difference . . . His legs ached, too; he'd been standing too long. Varicose veins? Incipient, at any rate. No wonder Patton had said he'd never seen anybody who looked less like a soldier. Patton!—the very thought of him acted like whisky. Captain Kaye's beard bristled and he sat up straighter in his chair. His one daydream was of prosecuting Patton—preferably for indecent assault upon a minor—before a full court at the Old Bailey in London . . . But the Judge Advocate was speaking—

'. . . and therefore you are, as Members of this Court, concerned to decide whether or not there has been a violation of the Laws and Usages of War. Now it is a fundamental usage of war that the killing of unarmed enemies is banned as an outrage against humanity. It has been banned for centuries as the result of the experience in warfare of all societies which have become civilized. To fire in such a manner as to kill or cause to die the unarmed survivors of sunken ships is an extremely grave breach of these laws. And that it is right to punish such breaches has been recognized for a long time. I do not think that there are any doubts or difficulties about that.

'Now I must remind you of points to which reference has already been made, quite correctly, by both counsel. Firstly, it is not the duty of the accused to prove themselves innocent. It is the other way about. It is the duty of the Prosecution to prove their guilt beyond reasonable doubt. And I would stress the term "reasonable." You are not to consider this term to include unrealistic or hypothetical excuses. "Reasonable" in this case must be taken to mean sensible and well-based. Secondly, it has again rightly been said that if there should arise in your minds, as you weigh and consider the evidence that you have heard, such a reasonable doubt, then it is your duty to give its benefit to the accused. That is to say that in any genuine dubiety, when the scales are evenly balanced in your minds between guilt and innocence, you should adopt the more charitable course and settle for innocence.

'Now let me touch briefly on the facts. I wish to be brief because both counsel have, in the course of their opening and closing speeches, drawn very full, able and accurate pictures of the facts as they are known, and because the facts in themselves are hardly in dispute at all. The *Maréchal Oudinot* was sunk at very close range and with the admitted intention of destroying her so completely and quickly that she would sink at once and take, if possible, all hands to the bottom with her. She sank quickly but she did not take all hands to the bottom and several survivors—one figure given is about a dozen, and that seems as close as we shall get—were left floating in the water and holding to various pieces of buoyant wreckage, among which were beams or logs of wood and at least two life-rafts. Meanwhile the submarine surfaced, moved in among these men and those pieces of wreckage and rafts, and called to one of them—the witness, Guéroult —to come aboard and answer questions. He did so, was interrogated by the accused Kümmerol, and returned with the assurance that the survivors would be rescued by their own friends next day. The submarine then left the scene and the survivors continued with their efforts to right rafts, collect the wounded and generally to organize their attempts at self-preservation. Shortly upon this scene the U-boat, which all in the water believed to have departed, returned at full speed, and turning its signal lamp upon the surprised survivors of the steamship, shouted orders to them to abandon their pieces of wreckage and their rafts on pain of being fired upon. As far as can be known some obeyed this order and some did not. Then for a space of two hours the U-boat cruised in and out among the floating wreckage firing machine-guns upon it and later throwing grenades. During these two hours several members of the sunken steamship's crew appear to have been killed and several more, of whom some subsequently died, to have been wounded. Then the submarine left the scene once more—this time finally.

'If those facts are reasonably clear it would certainly seem that the accused had a grave case to answer. Let us see how they answer it. The first accused, Kielbasa, the captain of the submarine, admits broadly the facts I have related, but says that he had no option but to act as he did in order to save his boat and crew from detection and destruction by Allied aircraft in the very near future. He regretted what he had to do, he says, but nevertheless he made up his mind that it must be done and he did it.

'Do you think that this is true? Do you think that those really were his motives for the action he took? If you think that this is so, you must consider carefully whether this so-called operational necessity could in any circumstances afford a defence for a war crime such as Kielbasa is charged with.

'Now it may be that circumstances—it is not necessary to envisage them—might arise in which the killing of an unarmed enemy for the purpose of saving a belligerent's life might be justified. I cannot say. But I suggest to you that you carefully consider the facts which have emerged from Kielbasa's own testimony. He cruised about the scene of the sinking for at least two hours without attempting to make use of his full surface speed of eighteen knots to get away as fast and as far as possible. He thought it better, he says, to go around firing at wreckage with his machine-guns. Do you, or do you not, believe that machine-gun fire could be considered an effective way of destroying large pieces of mainly wooden wreckage floating on the sea? And do you not think it likely that a patch of oil would have been left at least sufficiently large to indicate a sinking from the air and to result in a search for the offending submarine?

'Do you, or do you not, think that the most obvious manner in which a submarine commander might have attempted to save his boat and his crew would have been to have left the scene of the sinking as fast as he was able and to have put the greatest possible distance between himself and that sinking's traces in the hours of darkness which stretched before him? The naval officers among you, at least, will doubtless be able to come to a fairly expert conclusion upon that point.

'There is, too, the possibility of another view which the Prosecution has suggested—namely, that here was a U-boat captain tired and over-strained after a long and exacting voyage who suddenly had the opportunity to destroy several Allied nationals whom he regarded as members of the nations responsible for the air raids over Germany. The Prosecution suggests that he may have taken this opportunity to exact some sort of revenge upon the persons of the unfortunate sailors struggling in the water.

'All these are matters which you must decide yourselves. Kielbasa has admitted that he gave the orders to fire and to throw grenades; he takes the sole responsibility for these orders openly upon himself.

'Now let me turn to the second accused, Lieutenant Kümmerol. It is once more quite plain that this officer did fire and did throw grenades at the wreckage. He openly admits this. He says, in effect, "I was ordered to do this by my captain. I had to obey this order, and I did obey it." And under cross-examination he made what you may think to be a somewhat significant assent when he agreed that now—here today—he thought that what he had done was wrong.

'This brings us to a point already raised by the Prosecution—namely, that of superior orders. And this proposition is quite clear. The duty of a subordinate with regard to obeying orders from above is definitely limited to legal orders, and to legal orders only. There is no duty to obey an illegal order. You have to decide, therefore, and in view of what has been said earlier, whether the order Kümmerol received was a legal one or an illegal one. For the fact that a law of warfare has been broken by obedience to an illegal order from a superior does not alter the illegal nature of the act itself nor confer impunity from punishment upon the subordinate who has obeyed that order. Now the objection may well arise in your minds that Kümmerol was not to know this. Here, you may think, was a very young man without any previous experience of sea warfare, and, in fact, upon his first war patrol in a submarine. He cannot be expected to weigh and judge the legality or otherwise of his captain's order. And indeed if this were a case which necessitated a careful examination of problems arising out of International Law you might well come to the conclusion that it would be less than just to hold someone like Kümmerol responsible for what he has admitted that he did. But is it not obvious to you, and should it not have been obvious to Kümmerol, that to order the deliberate killing of men struggling in the sea, as these survivors were, could not possibly be a lawful command? Do you not think that this would have been obvious to the most rudimentary intelligence? Kümmerol was twenty years old at this time—not a child—and his intelligence was not in the least rudimentary. He speaks at least two languages fluently and by his own admission he held a staff position in a Naval Intelligence office before joining the U-boat arm. Do you see before you an uncouth peasant lad, semi-literate and able only to obey, clumsily and unthinkingly, any and every order given to him, if explained patiently in words of one syllable? If so, you may have to take his obvious natural defects as at least a partial excuse for his actions. But if you see only a well-educated, rather cosmopolitan, quick-witted young ex-staff officer, you may think that such a person could not fail to realize that the order to kill helpless survivors from a sunken ship could be anything but illegal. You alone are the judges in this case and you alone must make up your minds about that.

'And now I must draw your careful attention to the wording of the indictment—"in that they, in the Atlantic Ocean on the night of the fifth of January nineteen forty-five, when Captain and Second Officer of the Watch of the Unterseeboot 996 which had sunk the steamship *Maréchal Oudinot*, were, in violation of the Laws and Usages of War, concerned in the killing of members of the crew of the said steamship, Allied nationals, by firing and throwing hand grenades at them." You are not required to decide whether the accused are guilty either of murder or of manslaughter—neither of these terms finds a place in the indictment. You are asked to bring in a judgment of whether the accused are, or are not, guilty of being concerned in the killing of survivors of this sunken ship in violation of the Laws and Usages of War.

'Let me say this, too, about my own position in this trial. I am here to give you advice and nothing else. If anything I have just said leads you to think I have formed an opinion upon the matter, you are perfectly free to disregard that opinion completely. You have to decide this case—I cannot emphasize this enough—upon your own judgments.

'Finally, let me say that I am sure it will have been of satisfaction to you that both the accused have been defended by such very able and resourceful counsel. Everything that could properly be put forward on their behalf has been said, and extremely well said, by Captain Kaye. I must urge you to pay all the attention you think right to his words. Now you will retire and consider your verdict.'

Twenty

The old court building was a warren of dim corridors, alcoves and unexpected, asymmetrical little rooms. In one of the latter, a bare cramped place with a peculiar window set at an angle and looking over a tiny brick-paved courtyard empty except for a dead, anonymous shrub in a green-stained stone urn, Captain Kaye and his associates awaited the verdict.

Corporal Post and Dr Stusser, who had early taken a strong mutual dislike to each other, sat in two heavy chairs upholstered in slippery black horsehair, while the Defence Counsel himself stood in the narrow window bay staring out at the dank and darkening courtyard and fingering his beard. There was little to say and the silence, unbroken for almost ten minutes save for the ticking of Dr Stusser's heavy old-

fashioned pocket watch, at last grew intolerable to Corporal Post.
'How long do you figure they'll be, sir?' he asked with an unintentional abruptness which made the German lawyer start and frown disapprovingly. In Dr Stusser's world young men, particularly junior
non-coms, did not address their elders and superiors unless themselves
spoken to first. But though Captain Kaye, a martinet where legal
etiquette was concerned, would have responded to such an interrup-
tion from a civilian clerk with a basilisk stare, he practically never
reproved a soldier. It was one of his ways of demonstrating indifference
for things military—discipline most of all. Now he answered mildly,
'Some time yet, Mr P. Some time yet, I imagine. The longer the
better, from our point of view. If you're hungry, why don't you go
out and buy yourself a bun or something? Or there's some chocolate
in the car, I think.'

Post grinned uneasily. 'I'm not hungry, sir, thanks. I'm—I'm just
worried. I didn't like what the Major said.'

'Ah,' said Captain Kaye. 'Ah, I see,' and he turned back once more
to the gloomy prospect from the narrow window.

Twenty-one

In another part of the building, in a brightly lit room below ground
level the two accused sat silently between two silent guards. Captain
Kaye had visited them for a brief ten minutes as soon as they had been
brought down from the dock. He had been calm and businesslike with
no slightest sign of elation or dejection visible upon his bearded face.
'Well—there we are. Now I'm afraid there's going to be a wait—
probably a long one. This case is not easy and it's the first of its kind.
I think the Court will take quite a long time to reach a verdict. You'll
just have to be patient, although I know that's not easy.' He had
glanced from one to the other of his clients, expecting the inevitable
question as to his opinion on the probable verdict. It had not come. The
two grave, pale-faced young men had nodded understanding and then
Kümmerol had said, '*M'sieur le Capitaine*, we wish, both of us, to thank
you very much for your help. It is true, what the—the *Avocat-
militaire* said. You have given us the most extreme assistance. You
have said for us all we would have said for ourselves—and much more.
And—' he had smiled briefly, wanly—'very much better.'

Kaye was both moved and distressed. Kümmerol's voice had been heavy with foreboding. The summing-up had been unfavourable and he knew it. What was more, there was now something the Captain himself had to say, and which he would rather not have said. He smiled and for the first time patted Kümmerol's shoulder. 'Do not worry too much. You both have a very good chance, I am sure of that. But I have to say this. If the verdict goes against us I am entitled to ask for mitigation of sentences before those sentences are determined. I want you to understand that I can and will do this. So that if—'

'*Non*,' said Kielbasa suddenly. Captain Kaye glanced quickly at him in surprise. 'How do you mean? You mean that you do not want me to plead mitigating circumstances?'

Eugen's French was poor and he generally spoke directly to Kaye in English, but he was embarrassed by the near-by presence of the English guards so now he used the former language. 'Monsieur, please attend. I—like my friend here—am most grateful for your great help. You have said what I would have said—only better. But, with per-mission—without offence—did you *believe* it?'

'Believe what, exactly?'

'Believe that I ordered the destruction of the *Überrest* for the reasons I gave you—and which you gave the Court.'

Kaye looked gravely at that broad-browed face, the big glasses, the small firm chin below the wide-lipped mouth. 'Yes,' he said at last. 'I have always believed that.'

'And that I took the right decision?'

'That you took the only one that seemed possible—that was rational.'

'But—you do not think, even so—'

Carefully Captain Kaye said, 'That, Kielbasa, is largely what this whole trial has been about. Despite what the Prosecutor said, despite the gallant Korvettenkapitän Gericht—I think that the members of the Court will find it very hard to do anything but accept that you took the only rational course. But whether or not it was the right one—'

'I can find no difference.'

'No.' Kaye nodded. 'No, I do not think you can. I can understand that, too.' His voice took on a gentle, almost an intimate, tone. 'Listen, Kielbasa. There *is* a difference—most unfortunately—between acting rationally and acting rightly. You were perfectly justified in taking the action you did. In such a position any sane, responsible officer would have done the same. But on another plane the matter becomes more difficult. To be brief, there are people who, while understanding and sympathizing with your reasons, might say that to take any risk, however grave, was preferable to doing what you did. Because what you did was an outrage against humanity. The Judge Advocate used those words. Let me try to explain them, for their significance is not easy to understand. What they mean in the present context is that by your action you attacked something very basic and important and quite outside any considerations of nationality or duty or—or anything else at all. You attacked the whole concept of what makes the difference between a civilized human being and a savage animal—that is to say, the human soul or, in words that are regrettably banal, "the spirit of humanity".'

Patiently, eyebrows raised, Kielbasa said, 'I am afraid I do not understand. You must believe me very stupid, I think.'

'No.' Kaye shook his head firmly. 'I do not. The more intelligent one is, the more one knows, the less easy it is to accept the proposition that man has a soul at all, or that there *is* such a thing as a spirit of humanity. I strongly doubt it myself, more often than not. I can only hope.'

Kielbasa smiled, slowly, uncertainly. '*Alors*—I only want to say that I see my position like this: I did what I believed to be correct at the time and I am more than ever certain that it was correct now. I was trying to save the lives of my crew—more than fifty men, monsieur, as against some twelve or so of the others. If men have souls—and *I* think they do—then I have saved, in the end, some fifty of these at the expense of a dozen. Is that an outrage against humanity? I was *right*. And whatever the Court may decide I shall still be right. And if they say that I was wrong, that will not change anything. If they find me guilty, I am still right. If they shoot me, I am still right. Nothing— while men can think and have the power to reason—will ever alter that fact! And so I must ask you, in my case, not to plead for any mitigation since that might be thought to be an admission that I was wrong.'

'I do not think—'

'Yes, yes! It might be. And that I will never, never admit—because it is untrue! Anything else I will say, but not that. If the Court are reasonable and just men—then they will acquit me. If they are neither —then I am not prepared to ask such fools for mercy. You understand me?'

Slowly Kaye nodded yes. 'Very well, I must, of course, do as you ask.'

'Thank you. But for Emil here, it is different. He only did what I ordered. If—if the verdict goes against us, then please do all you can to help him.'

That had been more than half an hour ago. And now they sat together silently between their silent guards—waiting.

Twenty-two

In a much larger chamber, directly behind the court-room itself, the members of the Court sat around a massive mahogany table under the light of two bronze gaseliers. At the head of the table, slumped in a carved and thronelike armchair, Colonel Whaley-Wren listened patiently to the arguments which went back and forth most unproductively between his five juniors. He alone had not as yet given an opinion upon anything at all.

But the others had all given theirs. Capitaine Meilhac, supported firmly by Major Yatchett, was for a verdict of 'not guilty:' Commander Gordon-Bryce and Commandant Lautig were for 'guilty', and Lieutenant Marlignon was dubiously in agreement with them—though more out of his detestation of Capitaine Meilhac than anything else.

It was Yatchett who was speaking now. 'No one can say I like Huns—I don't. I loathe them. But that's not the point. The point is, surely, that—well, what else could Kielbasa have bloody well *done*? And the same goes for the young fellow—only more so. What else could either of them *do*? I mean—'

Commander Gordon-Bryce cut in. 'That's not entirely true, Yatchett; really it isn't. Surely the J.A. indicated that plainly enough. He could have run for it. Very dangerous, perhaps, but he *could* have. He chose not to—but he *could* have. And according to that Captain Gericht—who was much more experienced—he *should* have. Now as a sailor myself, though I admit not a submariner, I'm fully convinced—'

'But one must use some imagination, Bryce! Common sense, after all, is the least one might expect—'

Commandant Lautig said, 'Major, we are not lawyers. That is why we are here. But we must, I think, try to follow the law as it is explained to us. That, surely, is our sole duty.'

Capitaine Meilhac coughed harshly, looked down his long yellow nose like a disgusted camel, and said, 'It was a bitter decision. That we must all accept. But it was the one a truly conscientious captain had no option but to take. I would have expected a French officer to have mastered his emotions, his own feelings; remembered his duty to France, his service and his men—and to have done the same. I would have done so.'

'Then—*pardon, mon Capitaine*—' said Marlignon quickly—'you would have been facing a court, too. And if the Germans had won, a German court. Do you think you would have been acquitted?'

'That is irrelevant.'

'I do not think so.'

'Surely, my dear Yatchett, the Judge Advocate made it sufficiently plain—at least to anyone with a minimum of intelligence—'

'Whatever he may have said I *still* can't see how, in the name of bloody common sense—'

'Messieurs, we are here this evening to administer the law as it—'

'I'm not at all sure, really, that the whole thing—'

'The Judge Advocate *said*—'

Colonel Whaley-Wren glanced covertly at his watch, sighed very softly and fell to pondering what he might have for dinner.

Twenty-three

Corporal Post had found a piece of chewing-gum in his pocket. He took it out and looked at it but did not quite dare to put it in his mouth —not yet, anyway. If he could find out how much longer they were to sit in this dreary room it might be different. 'Sir—if the verdict is "guilty," will they be—'

'Not necessarily—but probably.'

'Why "probably"?'

'To encourage the others, one must suppose.'

'What others, sir?'

'Mr P, you are not, I'm sure, going to tell me that you have never heard of Voltaire?'

'What's that, sir?'

'A Frenchman of some distinction.'

'Oh—it sounded kind of like a game.'

'If you have a desire to chew gum, my dear Mr P, pray do so. You will not discommode me, and as for Dr Stusser—well, that is one of the penalties of losing a war. But—' added Captain Kaye with sudden ferocity—'you get rid of it before we go back into court—see? Otherwise I'll skin you!'

Twenty-four

After the arguments in the jury room had gone around in ever widen-
ing circles for nearly an hour Colonel Whaley-Wren decided that the
time had come to return to court. The evening was well advanced and
outside darkness must have fallen finally over the drab town. He had
brought his gavel with him and now, with the slightest of movements
he gave the table before him two light taps.

Silence fell abruptly. Faces angry, exasperated, wearily patient,
slowly fell into quieter lines of polite expectation. The members who
had been leaning forward over the table sat back, those who had
slumped in their seats sat up and straightened their shoulders. Major
Yatchett even hurriedly adjusted a pencil on the blotter before him
to that it formed a parallel line with the edge of the table.

Colonel Whaley-Wren alone retained his inelegantly relaxed posture. He smiled benignly around the table, carefully put his gavel into
one of the huge envelope pockets of a tunic still cut on World War I
lines, and said slowly, 'Well now, gentlemen, I think perhaps you had
better listen to me for a little. Pray give me your fullest attention . . .'

Twenty-five

'Kapitänleutnant Eugen Kielbasa, the Court finds you guilty of the
charge. Leutnant-zur-See Emil Kümmerol, the Court finds you guilty
of the charge.' The President's slow, precise voice ceased, and in that
dull, dry, muted air there was neither resonance nor echo. In the silence
the two accused—now the convicted—stared stonily back, refusing,
for the first few seconds, to accept what they had heard; clinging for a
moment longer to the numbness of the hour of waiting.

Then the tension broke and the court seemed suddenly full of furtive
subdued movement. In the cramped gallery the reporters rustled the
leaves of their notebooks, the clerks in the well of the court shifted in
their seats and reached for pens to record the verdict. Those at the
Prosecution table sighed gently and relaxed; their job was over now.
Colonel Rostwood was not a vain man but he could not help inwardly
congratulating himself upon the verdict. To have defeated Kaye was

something to congratulate oneself about, for Kaye, despite—or rather, because of—his oddities was a well-known figure in legal circles and had a formidable reputation.

At the Defence table Dr Stusser looked sulkily resigned. He had had little to do with the trial, but even so his own small repute would be slightly diminished by defeat, whereas if they had won it would have been very advantageously augmented—Adalbert Stusser, the lawyer who had been instrumental in saving a heroic U-boat Kommandant from the vengeance of the victors. In the years to come that would have brought him a lot of defence briefs. But though he had hoped for a favourable verdict he was a pessimist by nature and had not thought one likely. He glanced at Captain Kaye, but the senior counsel had been busily writing what appeared to be a private letter ever since they had been called back to court. Nor had he looked up or stilled his busy pen as the verdict was pronounced. He would have to stop now, though, because the Judge Advocate was speaking to him. 'Captain Kaye, do you wish to address the Court in mitigation on behalf of your clients? As I think you are aware, you have the right to do so under present procedure.'

Captain Kaye put down his pen and rose to his feet. Whatever he might be feeling, he appeared quite as unruffled as if the verdict had been in his favour. He walked slowly round the Defence table and, halting below the dock, he adjusted his spectacles and in lieu of a black gown, seized the lapels of his O.D. tunic. 'May it please the Court. I am instructed to plead mitigation only on behalf of my second client. My first, Kapitänleutnant Kielbasa, has stated several times in the course of this trial, both directly and indirectly, that he and he alone made the decision and gave the orders to destroy the wreckage, well knowing that the survivors upon it must die. He believes firmly that he was right to do this and has said that whatever the verdict his opinion would remain unchanged. He has said—with a logic which I think must be accepted—that if the verdict went against him he could see no reason or, indeed, grounds for pleading mitigating circumstances. I must admit that I would have liked to have asked the Court's forbearance in dealing with him and to have adduced several reasons for doing so; but I have to accept his instructions in this matter. Now, as to my second client—Emil Kümmerol, The Court in its wisdom has decided that this young man obeyed an illegal command and cannot therefore claim immunity on the grounds of superior orders. That is, as we have been informed, the law. The Court may also have considered that he must have been at least partially aware—

sufficiently so, at any rate—that what he was doing was, to say the least, irregular. After all, the First Officer of the Watch, Huberein, complained to the Kommandant in Kümmerol's presence concerning the order and, indeed, begged that it should be rescinded. Kümmerol did not join his voice to Huberein's and when given the order to organize and take part in the destruction of the wreckage he obeyed.

'Now it was, as we have been told, the Kommandant's practice to give reasons for his decisions whenever possible. And a very good practice that is. He gave the reasons for this particular decision and Kümmerol accepted them. Even Huberein, who was in the much safer position of being off watch and in temporary charge below, has agreed in the witness-box that this order was necessary.

'Very well, Kümmerol believed that his own life and the lives of the rest of the crew depended on obeying this order. Death—the horrible undersea death in a depth-charged submarine—would be the consequence of any other course taken by the Kommandant. He believed that. But he also *knew* that death by shooting awaited him if he refused obedience to this particular order. Now he once more faces death by shooting because he did obey that order. Can we—can any Court of any country which claims to administer civilized justice—put a man into the position in which whatever he does—either positive or negative action—must automatically lead to his own death? If so, then obviously Kümmerol is in an impossible position. He refuses to obey —and he is shot for disobedience in the face of the enemy. He obeys—and he is shot for war crime. Sir—Members of the Court. Can we, civilized men of civilized countries, really countenance something like that? I submit that to sentence Kümmerol to death is to make a mockery of justice—a public mockery which can do nothing but the gravest harm to our legal institutions and will redound to our eternal discredit. If this is done, gentlemen, what can one expect future generations to say when they read the records of this trial? Will they not say, "This was not justice. This was nothing but vengeance. Worse—it was judicial murder, still more horrible and cold-blooded than anything which—"'

'Just a minute, Captain Kaye.' Major Glenberyll's voice was calm and even but it held a severely warning note. 'You are supposed to be pleading mitigating circumstances on behalf of Kümmerol, not delivering anticipatory animadversions upon hypothetical actions of the Court. You will serve your client best by holding to your proper brief.'

Captain Kaye bowed acknowledgment. 'I have nearly done, sir.

There is little more that I can say. I would ask the Court in particular to remember Kümmerol's age. He was still a minor when he committed this offence and I think I may safely claim that this is usually considered a cause for mitigation since a minor cannot be expected to possess the same experience, knowledge, and consequent capacity to judge his actions as an adult.

'More than this, Kümmerol has already suffered severely since the destruction of the *Maréchal Oudinot*. The U–996 was sunk by depth charges east of the Mozambique Channel and remained thirteen hours on the sea bed, only surfacing by a miracle. For thirteen hours the crew, including Kümmerol, faced what seemed certain death by slow asphyxiation. Later the U-boat, when upon the surface and unable to dive, was attacked by aircraft and Kümmerol's left leg was so badly damaged in this attack that he has become a cripple for life and it is still very probable that he may have to suffer amputation of the limb. He has lost his home and all close relations during the last eighteen months and, crippled as he is, it would seem that there is no future career open to him. Few persons of his age can have suffered more ruin as a direct cause of the war and I would most earnestly beg the Court, in deliberating sentence, to ask themselves whether this unfortunate boy has not already suffered enough to atone for what he unthinkingly did earlier this year, and to consider whether he may not be allowed to go free to make whatever he can of the rest of his life. The Prosecution has quoted Cromwell. Now let me, in my turn, remind you of the words of Bacon, "The nobler a spirit, the more objects for compassion it hath".'

Captain Kaye bowed and walked back to his place. That was that. From behind him he heard the President's old voice saying quietly, 'The Court will now retire and consider the sentences,' and then came the scrape of pushed-back chairs, the shuffle of feet. Glancing up at the clock above the bench as the members of the Court filed out, he saw that it was already past six. Colonel Whaley-Wren had missed his tea; he would be anxious to return to the comforts of the Senior Officers Mess and a hot bath, a change of uniform and a whisky before dinner. When one was old such things assumed an importance which to younger men seemed laughably disproportionate. Captain Kaye did not think they would have to wait long for the sentences. He turned to Post, who was still gazing round the court at the empty dock, the empty Prosecution table, listening to the subdued movements of the clerks below the bench and to the less subdued ones of the Press in the gallery. Someone coughed; someone stifled a laugh; a heavy book falling to the floor brought a momentary startled silence. 'All right, Mr P. We can pack up now. Dr Stusser, I think we borrowed these two books from you, did we not? They *are* yours? Good. Mr P, put all these notes in the orange folder and put *this* in the brown briefcase. And I think we might help ourselves to this box of paper clips which the Court has so thoughtfully provided. Petty larceny technically, I expect, but all stationery is so difficult to find these days that I consider it fair game. And if there are any free pencils or rubbers about we'll share them equally: half for us, half for Dr Stusser. Or— wait. Let Dr Stusser have them all. Thy need, Dr Stusser, is greater than mine.'

'Sir?'

'Yes, Mr P?'

'Sir—do you think they'll get the hot seat? Both of them? After what you said?'

Captain Kaye regarded his clerk with sudden interest. 'You tell *me* what *you* think.'

'I—I guess they can't do that to Kümmerol. Not after what you said. They can't . . . can they?'

'Why not?'

'Well—because of what you said.' Corporal Post's voice was angry and stubborn and he stared at his chief as if daring him to contradict his words. 'You've forgotten the paper clips,' said Captain Kaye.

Twenty-six

In an alcove off one of the corridors Colonel Rostwood was talking to Major Glenberyll under a dusty gas bracket. The Judge Advocate's work was finished, too. 'Well, well. Old Kaye put up a pretty good show, eh?'

Major Glenberyll nodded, smiling reminiscently. 'Yes, he gave us our money's worth. But—old? He's not forty-five yet, is he? You don't call that old, do you?'

'No, no—' the Prosecutor's voice was testy—'I used the word in its genial connotation. Of course he's not old—a lot younger than me, at any rate. I wonder if he'll take up regular practice once he's out of the army?'

'May have to—if his private income's suffered in any way comparable to my poor savings. But I doubt if it has. The Yanks have done pretty well out of this war financially. They always do, don't they?'

'Oh come, Glenberyll! That's hardly fair, you know. I think you forget what we owe America.'

'I don't forget it,' said the Judge Advocate dryly, 'but I prefer to leave it to the Treasury. It's their worry, not mine, I'm thankful to say. Good lord, there's the bell! Old Whaley-Wren's got them over the last jump bloody quickly. Wants his dinner, I suppose. Well—see you later, then.'

Twenty-seven

And once again the stilled court-room, the ultimate, apologetically hushed cough, the muted scrape of the last chair pulled into place . . . rustle of papers in the gallery . . . silence. The ticking clock stood at twenty-six minutes past six.

Very slowly Colonel Whaley-Wren adjusted his spectacles, leaned forward and clasped his hands together upon his big blotter. A heavy gold ring glinted on one finger and the soft gaslight glowed on his scarlet staff colonel's collar tabs and on the small crimson ribbon of his V.C. 'The findings and sentences of this Court are subject to confirmation. Kapitänleutnant Eugen Kielbasa, the Court sentences you to suffer death by shooting. Leutnant-zur-See Emil Kümmerol, the Court sentences you to suffer death by shooting.'

But he was not to have the last word. Cromwell had been quoted by the Prosecution. Bacon had been quoted by the Defence. Now from the dock, coldly and with bitter sarcasm, Kielbasa quoted Schiller: '*Mit der Dummheit kämpfen die Götter selbst vergebens.*' And since the interpreter in the well of the court heard it clearly, he automatically translated it for the benefit of the Court. 'Against Stupidity the Gods themselves battle in vain.'

WINTERFALL

One

A cold wet autumn was merging imperceptibly into winter—the first winter of haggard, battered Peace. Over the gaunt, fire-stained city, and beyond it above the great prison in its distant suburbs, the low skies wept endlessly as the dark, dwarfed days succeeded each other in slate-grey similarity. Within the prison, lights burned all day except for those periods when the power failed and cells, corridors and offices faded into temporary twilight.

What does one do when awaiting death? How does one pass the time during that severely rationed allowance of days before extinction? Eugen, in his small, insufficiently warmed cell, had asked himself this question on the morning after the trial. He had at first supposed that he should do what was known as 'putting one's affairs in order.' He had heard of people doing that and the phrase pleased him; it sounded calm, sensible and tidy-minded. But then he realized that he had no affairs to put in order. He had heard nothing of his family despite inquiries made through several sources—of which the most recent failure had been that of Dr Stusser—and he had no means of knowing whether they were alive or dead. If they were dead he might be heir to a considerable amount of money, the family business, property and various possessions. But even if such happened to be the case he could not know whether these things still existed. Or rather, he corrected himself with suddenly caught breath, he could not know in time . . . The best thing to do seemed to be to make a short provisional will leaving everything he might, perhaps, possess to his sister Viktoria in São Paulo. He accordingly sent for Dr Stusser, who came the next day.

The meeting took place in a dank unheated room divided into two by a fence of small-mesh chicken wire. Dr Stusser, pinched and cold and shivering in his threadbare overcoat, glanced continually from his young client to the British military policeman beside the door, as if he, too, was a prisoner of the victorious powers. 'That's best—yes, certainly that's best. I will draw up a provisional testament and bring it here tomorrow. It will have to be witnessed, of course. Perhaps the prison authorities will allow . . .' his voice had trailed away dismally and he had stared down at his sodden shoes awaiting, with a distress which was none the less real for being concealed beneath an appearance of irritation, the inevitable next question.

And it was one which Eugen himself was reluctant to ask. Yet ask it he must. 'I suppose there is nothing—now—that can be done?'

'The sentence—' said Stusser carefully—'has not yet been confirmed. It may be commuted.'

'To life imprisonment?'

'That is normal—yes. But of course you would not serve such a term. Three or four years—five at the most, I imagine. The trouble is.' He had hesitated—'that they know that, of course. And so . . .'

'So it will be confirmed—not commuted.'

'We could try some sort of petition, perhaps. But, frankly, I doubt success.'

'I see.' Eugen had pondered a long minute, rubbing one finger idly along the wire mesh in front of him. 'I would do that, or anything else, if I thought there was a reasonable chance of success. You must understand, Herr Doktor, that though I believe, though I *know*, that I was convicted illogically and without proper cause, I would do anything to induce them to—to alter the sentence. I would even, I think now, admit guilt if they would promise me my life. But—' he said slowly— 'I think they always intended to kill me from the start—to kill us both.'

'No, no. I am sure not—not in that way.' Dr Stusser was a lawyer and the trial had been pre-eminently a lawyer's trial. Colonel Rostwood and Major Glenberyll had been—still were—his colleagues as much as Captain Kaye. 'The British would not do that. English lawyers are highly—'

'You forget that I come from a family of lawyers, though I am not one myself. The English put great value upon appearances. They say, do they not, that "Justice must not only be done, but be seen to be done"? Perhaps the seeing is more important than the doing? Our U-boat war was waged harshly—but no more so than their bombing raids. At least we did not kill women and children, did we? But they hated the U-boats, and so . . . No, you are right; a petition would do no good. I will not write one. But—' Eugen had said with sudden decision—'I will write a memorandum instead.'

And so, as the dark indistinguishable days slid by, Eugen sat writing at the small table in his cell, and the pacing guards, peering in through the spy-hole as they passed and repassed the heavy door and seeing the steadily growing pile of manuscript, shook their heads and wondered at such industry. 'Poor bugger never stops except to eat. Goes right on to midnight sometimes, he does. Think he's going cuckoo?'

'Could be. Could've been that way to start with, couldn't he? That'd explain it, eh?'

'Then he'd have got the nut-house—not what he *is* getting. Making his bleeding will, you think? If he is, he must have a fucking lot to leave!'

'No. Did that the second day. I witnessed for him. No. Writing his life story, more like.'

'Christ—what a time to do it!'

'Bloody good time, if you ask me. At least you don't have to bloody guess the last chapter.'

'Christ!'

Two

For Emil, in another distant part of the great prison, there was no such distraction. The strain of the trial, the cramped dock, the penetrating cold and, most of all, the brutal shock of a sentence for which, unlike his captain, he was unprepared, had together brought him to the prison hospital. He lay in a room by himself, a room twice the size of an ordinary cell but less than half the size of his one in the Masondi hospital, and stared out of a high, heavily barred window at the dreary sky against which only one old stone chimney smoked gently into the damp air. His guards were not military police but medical orderlies, sternly efficient, unsmiling, taciturn. He thought with longing of Rami and Latif, most nights he dreamed of them and of Dr Zared and, eternally, of Emerald.

For four days after the trial Emil was feverish, sick and restless. Then, reluctantly and strongly against his will, he began to get better. He tried to disguise this even from himself, for—'They can't do it to me while I'm *ill*. They can't take me out of bed and—and— The doctor wouldn't let them. While I'm here I'm safe. I'm safe in bed.' And later —'The sentence will be reversed. It *must* be. It wasn't my fault, what happened—anybody can see it wasn't my fault.'

But the fever died away and with proper rest and attention the pain in his maimed leg dwindled to nothing more than its usual dull ache; after a week in bed even that ceased. It was then, when he was recovered, when he was sitting up in bed once more and reading *Peter Schlemihls Wunderbare Geschichte* which one of the orderlies had found in a cupboard, that he had his first two visitors—the prison governor and a British major who announced himself as the Deputy Assistant

Provost Marshal. 'I have to tell you that the sentence passed upon you by the Court has been confirmed by higher authority.'

White-faced against the white pillow Emil had stared up, dark eyes wide with dawning horror. 'You mean—that—that . . .' he had stuttered and swallowed, unable to speak further.

'I'm afraid so—yes.'

Emil licked his lips and his glance darted around the room seeking some escape, some way out. 'There—there must be a mistake. I think someone is mistaken. I—'

'No. There has been no mistake, I assure you.'

'But—whoever confirmed it cannot have read the case! Listen—I was forced to fire those guns! I was *ordered* to! Don't you understand?'

The two officers had glanced at one another quickly, their faces expressing distress, irritation, embarrassment. Then the Provost major said, 'I can't discuss the case with you, I'm afraid. That's not part of my job and in any case I don't know the details.' He had paused, then added awkwardly. 'Is there anything you want to know? I mean—' he added hurriedly—'about the—the date. I mean you may have things to arrange or people to see before—before . . .' He had stopped confusedly, but as Emil remained silent and merely continued to stare at him he had at last said abruptly, 'In ten days. On the sixth of November. You will be told the exact time later.' And quickly the two officers had left the room.

Emil had returned at once to his book—the story of the man who had sold his shadow to the Devil—and forced himself to read on and on. Outside, beyond the rain-spattered window, the old chimney smoked steadily against a sky which deepened through the short afternoon until the early darkness closed in, sealing off the outside world in premature night.

Three

The confirmation of the sentence came as no surprise to Brigadier Whaley-Wren, whose promotion had come through the day before. He noted it, as it passed with scores of other small pieces of official information across his desk in the course of his day's work, and reflected momentarily that this time a satisfactory and valuable precedent had been set. It had been necessary to make it plain to all submarine services that the ordinary rules of civilized warfare applied to them just as much as to regular infantry. It was to be hoped that the example about to be made would effectively do this—it would be fully covered by the Press, photographed, filmed and given the widest publicity for this reason.

For, contrary to the impression he had given in court, Whaley-Wren had had strong feelings about the recent trial. These feelings were neither of indignant anger against the accused for what they had done, nor of pity for their victims, but were more abstract sentiments concerning conduct and behaviour. The Brigadier, after all, had been reared in an age in which a very broad range of conventional concepts —so widespread as to appear, at the time, almost instinctive to a certain class of society, but by now mostly abandoned or entirely forgotten— governed the behaviour of everybody—or at least everybody in his own world. That world had been rigid, criss-crossed with steely divisions and subdivisions, puritanical and extremely harsh, yet Whaley-Wren had lived to enter a new one which was amoral but strangely squeamish—at least by his standards. The two accused in the *Maréchal Oudinot* trial had plainly broken the laws of warfare—had behaved like nervous savages rather than properly commissioned officers. Brigadier Whaley-Wren had early come to the conclusion that the Kommandant of U-996 had given his now notorious order in a fit of frightened cowardice and this, in his eyes, was quite as bad— perhaps worse—than if the order had been given out of feelings of sadistic vengeance.

In his day officers had not behaved like that in any circumstances at all—even the Boers had seemed to understand this. For after all, if one obeyed no rules or made up one's own as one went along any game lost its point at once. Though Brigadier Whaley-Wren did not look upon war as exactly a game he did consider it, in common with many of his contemporaries, as a contest in which the opponents matched each other in a wide range of skills and capacities and under a set of regulations which, if not distinctly defined, were none the less clearly understood. And it was these rules which he had determined to see vindicated in the recent trial. To him, though not, apparently, to the junior members of the Court, their vindication was of infinitely more importance than the lives of two undistinguished foreign officers who had broken them.

He initialled the confirmatory order as having been noted, initialled half a dozen others in the same way, shuffled them all into his 'Out' tray and rang for his mid-morning tea.

Four

Capitaine Roger Meilhac never knew whether the death sentences upon the accused had or had not been confirmed. Doubtless the information would have reached him had his own death not preceded it. But the cold damp discomfort of the private hotel he had preferred to the Allied Officers various Messes, the fit of malaria which he had stifled, but had not cured, with a massive dose of quinine; the weather and the long hours in court together brought on a feverish chill which turned to double pneumonia overnight. When, on the afternoon of the day following the trial, Capitaine Meilhac was admitted to hospital, the doctors looked grave; and by the next day's dawn they knew that the thing was hopeless. So Roger Meilhac drowned—not at sea, as he would have wished, but screened on a hospital bed and in the water generated by his own inflamed and heaving lungs.

Five

'. . . The British attitude towards the submarine is at once ambivalent and thoroughly inconsistent with that country's expressed views upon sea-power. The submarine, once accepted as a serious technical achievement, had to be allotted its proper place in sea warfare. Mistakenly, but not perhaps surprisingly, the English attempted to incorporate it into the Fleet and to fit it into the line of battle. Their long-standing traditional and emotional involvement with capital ships made them eager that this entirely new weapon should be subordinated to the dreadnought as an auxiliary with a special protective role—in much the same way as, a little later, they were to attempt to subordinate the aeroplane. Both attempts, based as they were upon false and wishful premises, failed. The submarine was fitted only to act *offensively* rather than as a defensive escort to the heavy battle line, while the aeroplane, far from becoming merely the long-range reconnaissance eye of the capital ship, subordinated the capital ship by removing its main armament, flattening its deck and turning it into a carrier. Thus it fell to the Germans in the First War, and the Americans in the Second, to demonstrate the new—and to the British, hateful—conception of sea-power based on the submarine and the aeroplane. Now one of the greatest weapons of sea-power is blockade, and for more than two centuries this had been the exclusive prerogative of Britain, whose great surface fleet could and did blockade whole continents in time of war, thus giving the Island State a potency out of all proportion to her small population and tiny professional army.

'But during the First World War—and very much more so during the Second—the German Navy struck back with its own, still more deadly form of blockade—blockade by submarine. Britain had long been invulnerable because she was an island. Now that geographical fact made her immensely vulnerable in the face of this newly perfected weapon. It is hardly surprising that this sudden and extremely serious threat not only to her traditional position as supreme ruler of the seas but also to her very life in time of war, should have caused immense commotion in Britain. The country reacted with the production of many skilful anti-submarine devices, yet it is extremely unlikely that these of themselves could have won either war at sea had Germany not bungled both wars on land.

'But one additional manifestation of British reaction to the submarine menace was an emotional hatred of this particular form of sea warfare, based on a deep anger at the loss of her traditional dominance. The frustration and fury of a British admiral at finding his 30,000-ton flagship struck below the waterline and put out of action by an invisible and comparatively diminutive boat at which he was almost powerless to strike back must indeed have been awesome to behold. It was a frustration and fury which was, and still is, shared by the nation as a whole; a nation which, while being in the inconsistent position of being forced to use a considerable number of submarines itself, began by terming the crews of enemy boats "pirates" in the First World War, and naming them "war criminals" in the Second. . . .'

Eugen sniffed, laid down his pencil and rubbed his cold hands together to restore the sluggish circulation. The memorandum was progressing well. It was a pity that he would not have time to revise and polish it, for otherwise it might have made an interesting work. Like another spectacled and studious young man whom he had never met but whose horribly slow and painful death he had caused, he would have liked to leave some published book behind him. Books outlived men. But there were only another six more days left.

Six

The rain ceased at last and was replaced by the first frost. A smoky, frosty fog hung over the city, but somewhere above that pearly opalescence there seemed a hint of light. Captain Kaye rubbed his hands and remarked that 'there was a nip in the weather but that it would do us all good.' Reynolds the rapist had managed to retain his services after all, and the Captain was happily immersed in the salacious details of his case. 'A peculiarly unpleasant affair, Mr P,' he announced over the breakfast table. 'In fact, I might use the word "repellent" without overstating things. The unfortunate female involved was sixty-one years of age and Reynolds had her held down by four stalwart Senegalese working for ten dollars apiece.'

'Where'd he get that dough?'

'Ah! Where, indeed? But the joy of the matter is that he's a Texan himself. No wonder they wanted to keep me out!'

'I don't see how you'll get him off, sir.'

'Well, nor do I,' admitted the Captain judiciously as he buttered a slice of toast. 'I don't think it possible to actually get him *off*. No, the evidence is far too damning. For one thing, each of the Senegalese has become a witness for the prosecution. In order to earn another ten dollars apiece, I suppose.'

'But—they *helped* him!'

'Quite so. But they've turned King's Evidence, as the British call it. You'd never make a lawyer, Mr P, you know. You suffer from a belief in justice and that naturally disqualifies you at once. But, as I was saying, I don't think I can get an acquittal. But I can plead diminished responsibility.'

'He's nuts?'

'No—but he's a Texan. "Lack of all moral sense due to a bestial environment amongst a debased and degenerate society." You smile? You don't think I would dare? You're wrong. Effrontery, Mr P, is to a good lawyer what audacity is to a good soldier. It doesn't always succeed, but it's surprising how often it does.'

'Supposing there's a Texan on the Court?'

'Well, I'd take damn' good care to find that out first, of course. But I doubt it, for they're not fond of the law—and with good reason. Texas was a barefaced theft itself and I sometimes think that the people who now inhabit it are God's punishment upon the United States for breaking the Eighth Commandment. For an allegedly merciful God I must say that the punishment seems unduly severe. And talking of severity—I fear the British are showing themselves implacable over the sentences imposed on our two last clients. Both of them are definitely to get what you so inaccurately and inelegantly term "the hot seat".'

'*Both!* But—'

'I heard it by chance yesterday evening. The sentence was confirmed several days ago. They are both to be shot at the end of this week, I understand.'

Seven

Four days. Four more times the late dawn would break; four more times the early dusk would fall. Grey-faced, Emil sat in his room in the prison hospital, his rubber-shod stick beside him. He had made a complete recovery but the doctors had decided to retain him for 'the time being.' He would return to his cell only on the day before—before . . . Dry-mouthed, he tried to swallow and turned his head hopelessly from locked door to barred window. No escape. He was trapped now much more surely even than he had been when U-996 lay sunk in over two hundred metres of water off the Grand Comoro. He had escaped miraculously then—but now it was different. Now he wished only that the depth charges which had sent the U-boat plunging to the sea bed had succeeded fully in their task of destruction, as they so nearly had. The past year had been nothing but pain and sorrow and growing fear and would culminate in a last agony in some seventy-two hours. Seventy-two hours were all that he had now, while other people lived to seventy-two years. It would have been better to have died in the submarine. '*Sink me the ship, Master Gunner—sink her, split her in twain! Fall into the hands of God, not into the hands of Spain!*'—It would have been far better. As it was, he and Eugen Kielbasa were to be made scapegoats for the U-boat war—the expiatory victims for the thousands of ships sent to the bottom in six years of sinkings. One of the orderlies had even told him that Eugen was writing about it, putting the whole affair on paper so that one day the truth might be known, the Court's irrational decision displayed for the judicial vengeance that he believed it to be.

But he himself had shown little interest and felt less. What did it matter what the world would think in a future he would never see? For him the world existed only for the next seventy-two hours. '*When I shut my eyes the world is not there.*' Did they close the eyes of people after they were shot? Or did they leave them open and staring in the last frightful shock?

He shuddered, feeling sweat break out on his forehead. Surely to be dead was not so dreadful. Everybody had to be dead one day and everybody accepted that. And many people, the unfortunate ones, knew when they were going to die for it was not only courts but also doctors who delivered death sentences. And death before a firing squad was—physically, at any rate—less terrible than the agony of many forms of disease. Man's life was very short by any serious measure of time. Twenty-one years, or seventy-two—was there really so much difference? And—'*Yes!*' screamed a voice within him. '*Yes! Yes! There is!*' The specious comforts of abstract philosophy, of comparing this with that, meant nothing at all when faced with the reality of approaching execution. Tense, frightened, sweating, he grasped his stick and lurched upright: stood trembling a moment and then started limping around the small room. He was moving; he was a living, moving human being with the *right* to live as long as his heart would beat. Death—natural death—however prolonged and painful the dying, was ultimately acceptable. It was unnatural death, the killing of a live body, that was so terrible—and so obscene. *Thud, thud, thud, thud,* went his stick over the shining brown linoleum.—Then what of the *Maréchal Oudinot*? Of those men in the water? But they had not known they were going to die and that had made all the difference. It put their death in the same category as deaths suffered in an auto smash-up or a railway accident or an earthquake. War was horrible, of course. We all said that. We all *said* it. But how many truly believed it? Did regular soldiers believe it? Did generals and admirals and politicians? If so, why all the talk of glory and heroics; drums, flags, medals and white stone monuments? No. War was awesome, often terrible—but not truly horrible, for if it had truly been so mankind would have abandoned it by now in the way that the true horrors of ritual murder and human sacrifice had been abandoned by civilized society.—Not quite abandoned, though, after all, for a mixture of the two was to be acted out in seventy-two hours from now. And he was innocent of any crime in the proper sense of the word. He had been forced into a position in which . . . But would Eugen really have shot him if he had refused to obey that order? It was most unlikely. Perhaps—but only if he had refused mutinously, flatly, summarily. If he had requested apologetically to be excused . . . if he had pleaded not to be made to fire himself because he had talked to Guéroult and promised him safety . . . ? Almost certainly Eugen would have said wearily, 'All right, all right—I suppose I'll have to send for Letzer.' It was partly because he had known this that he had not complained nor objected. He had accepted Eugen's reasoned and logical explanation of the operational necessity of the order, and in accepting it he had accepted, too, his own duty to obey it.

He turned and dropped, panting a little, into his chair. For a moment he stared blankly at the chimney beyond the window. It was not smoking today and dully he wondered why. Then once more he tried to collect his thoughts. For it was useless to go on and on retracing the past. That got one nowhere. He was left, sick and frightened, in his chair with not one constructive notion of saving himself. That was no use. Something must be done; someone must be seen. Some effort, however hopeless, must be made. He would send for Kaye. There was no one else. Kaye had defended him well in court and it was not the American captain's fault that the verdict had gone against him. But still—surely Kaye had a responsibility to his late clients. Perhaps he could do nothing more. But perhaps—if he would go and see someone . . . See the general or whoever it was who had confirmed the sentence. Perhaps if he were to explain once more . . . Yes. Kaye must come. And quickly. Emil's breath hissed between pale lips at the stab of pain as once more he struggled to his feet to shuffle across to the locked door and press the bell.

Eight

Major Yatchett was also thinking of seeing Captain Kaye with regard to the sentence passed upon Kümmerol. He had regretted his agreement to the verdict and the sentences of the Court almost from the moment they had been delivered. In his opinion they contradicted justice—and much worse, plain common sense. That they did not contradict law had been made very clear by Colonel Whaley-Wren in two addresses to the divided and argumentative Court members. —'We are here, gentlemen, to adminster the law. It appears that all of you, to a greater or lesser degree, have forgotten that. The law has been laid down by persons who know a great deal more about these things than any of us here this evening. And the law has been explained to us in clear terms by the Judge Advocate. If—' he had glanced pointedly at Yatchett—'those terms were not clear enough for all of you to grasp I will readily explain them again—if necessary in words of the greatest simplicity. But first let me make one thing very plain. You are not being asked to adjudicate on the behaviour and motives of the accused as such, but whether or not they committed the crime with which they are indicted; that is, were they, or were they not, concerned in the killing of members of the crew of the *Maréchal Oudinot* by firing and throwing grenades at them . . .'

There could of course be only one answer to that. And once the verdict was agreed there had, it seemed, been no other course but to pass sentence of death. Anything less, they had been told, would invalidate what was to be a most valuable precedent for the future . . . 'Perhaps ultimately something of the gravest and greatest importance. For do not forget that a most urgent reason for this and other war crimes trials is to make sure, by a plain deterrent, that barbarities in time of war can and will be punished with the utmost severity. Only thus can we hope that they will never be repeated.—And one further point, gentlemen. You are not finally condemning these men to death. The sentences will be reviewed by higher authority who will take into consideration all mitigating circumstances. The ultimate fate of the accused is up to this confirming authority—a man far more senior and experienced than any of us. What is more, he can, and undoubtedly will, act without any thought for the very important point of precedent of which I have spoken, since this will not be prejudiced once formal sentence is passed by us . . .'

This, to Yatchett, had been perfectly plain reasoning. The Court was there to judge and to sentence the accused strictly according to law, and the severity of the law must be upheld as a future deterrent. Once this was formally done, the actual punishment of the accused might be considered in a freer and more informal atmosphere in which the motives and pressures that had actuated them as individuals might be taken into full account. It had been a somewhat reluctant and dubious acceptance of this reasoning, sound enough as he could see it to be, which had induced Yatchett to agree to both verdict and sentences. He had assumed that both the accused would have their sentences commuted at a higher level.

To learn, therefore, that the contrary had happened came to him as a shock. He was busy at the time and had angrily told himself that he was not to blame for the confirming officer's surprising severity. He himself had passed the responsibility to a higher echelon and what was decided at that rarefied altitude was no affair of his. Yet later he had found himself pondering worriedly over the matter. What had gone wrong? The plea of operational necessity which to himself and the French naval captain had seemed so compelling, the plea of superior orders which had appeared so unanswerable in terms of human reason —had both these failed to have any effect on the confirming authority? For that matter who, or what, *was* the confirming authority? Perhaps just a single overworked man who had felt it his job merely to rubber-stamp the Court's decision. A quick shiver of doubt had passed through Yatchett. Perhaps—surely—the confirming authority had taken exactly the contrary posture to that indicated by Colonel Whaley-Wren. Instead of considering the responsibility for the fate of the accused lay with him, he had assumed that it lay with the Court— the Court which had sat upon the case for three whole days, hearing the back and forth sway of Counsel's arguments, seeing and listening to the two Germans themselves and then, after deliberating the point most carefully, had decided that they should die. Perhaps the confirming authority had been puzzled, perturbed even, at the apparent rigorous harshness of the Court's decisions, but had not felt competent to reverse them. If so, a lethal misunderstanding had been arrived at and, as so often, the fault lay with impersonal procedure rather than with any individual caught up in it. Then—what to do?

It had taken Major Yatchett, who was neither a quick nor an analytical thinker, a considerable time to arrive at the decision that he himself must take some action, and he had arrived at it most reluctantly. He could not be said to be extremely busy since soldiers very seldom are; but he was busier than he ever remembered being before, being fully occupied for five hours a day and partially occupied for another one and a half, so that he had the impression of being indefatigably industrious and desperately pressed for time. And now this . . . At first he had tried to forget it, to shrug it off and to let events take their course. He was not a callous man but he had seen enough of war to take an unsentimental view of violent death—which was one reason why he had been capable of taking a calmer view of Kielbasa's 'operational necessity' than Commander Gordon-Bryce, a shore-based sailor. But it so happened that his office was not far from the prison in which Kielbasa and Kümmerol were confined and every time he looked out of his window he saw, across a gaping waste of bomb rubble, one great blank grey wall. As day followed day it was impossible not to be jolted by that view every time he glanced up from his desk, and to think with ever-growing unease that somewhere behind that forbidding façade two men sat waiting for the death which was reaching out to them across a rapidly decreasing period of time.

And when at last he knew that he must do something and rang the Provost Marshal's office it was to learn that time was very short. The execution was due to take place in three days. Yatchett put back the receiver and, pushing away his chair, rose to his feet. But he could not use them to take him anywhere until he had first thought where to go, so he sat down again and thought hard. What he had to do was to find the 'confirming authority' and explain that he himself had believed . . . that he had assumed . . . that he had been led to think . . . No, no. That wouldn't do. He was only one member of the Court, after all, and not even a naval man. Besides, to go to the confirming authority himself would be to go over the head of the Court President, thus outraging military etiquette. No, he must find at least one other member of the Court who agreed with him in desiring a commutation of sentence and who felt he had been equally misled. Then together they must see Colonel Whaley-Wren and only then—and preferably with the Colonel, though if necessary without—request an audience with the confirming authority. Relieved, and rather proud, to have planned his course of action so quickly, Major Yatchett picked up the telephone again.

Half an hour later he replaced it after the last of nearly a dozen calls, and sat frowning down at his cluttered desk. Colonel—now Brigadier —Whaley-Wren had been recalled to London on urgent business. Capitaine Meilhac was dead. Commandant Lautig had gone back to France on leave and Lieutenant Marlignon was in Berlin and seemingly inaccessible—at least in the short time still left.

The only member of the Court to whom Yatchett had spoken had been Commander Gordon-Bryce, and the naval officer had not agreed with him, had refused to take any action in the matter . . . 'Yes, yes, Yatchett. I know. Yes, I was told of the confirmation—like you, I imagine. Yes. Yes . . . Of course . . . Yes, I *do* see what you mean but I can't agree. Why not? Well, firstly because they were definitely guilty as charged; you can't deny that. And secondly because the whole thing was so horrible, *and* unnecessary as it turned out. The weather change, rather than the submarine, was responsible for— Yes. Yes, but— Yes, I know. Yes, my dear man, I *did* give full weight to *all* that and I *still* say it was a risk he should have taken rather than— No one in his proper senses? I assure you *I* wouldn't have done it, and I consider myself to be reasonably sane. There are certain traditions common to sailors about this sort of thing . . . No, you can't be expected to, obviously, but it is so. The other—the sub-lieutenant? No—no I don't, actually. I had the strong impression that he and the Kommandant were close friends, and I don't think for a moment that Kielbasa would actually have . . . No, of course I don't *like* sentencing people to death! What an odd way you have of expressing yourself. And it's all very well to say I've not given proper weight to their motives—but have *you* given any weight at all to Guéroult's evidence? *Guéroult*—the radio officer—the sole survivor. Good heavens, Yatchett! If you've even forgotten who *he* was you've undoubtedly got your values in this matter very mixed up. Until I heard him I admit I was slightly inclined to your way of thinking. But his evidence changed all that and . . . What's that you say? Irrelevant? How can you possibly say that! What . . .? No, no, I won't. And there's no reason to become offensive, either. *No*—that's definite! Good morning.'

So that was that. Major Yatchett slowly filled and lit his pipe while a new thought formed equally slowly in his mind. Guéroult—he had indeed forgotten that short, ruddy, dark-haired young sailor from Dieppe. Now it all came back clearly. The witness-box with yet another blue-uniformed figure grasping the bronze rail; Rostwood's request that Guéroult might tell his story in French. The tautly grim confrontation with Kümmerol, eyes cast down, turning slowly in the dock . . . Guéroult's account of the raft which even the translator's flat nasal voice could not rob of its terror and tragedy. Guéroult . . .

If Guéroult would agree to go with him to the confirming authority —that Whaley-Wren was in London seemed an advantage now—the sentences might yet be commuted. Guéroult's request for mercy would be bound to have a far greater effect than that of any member of the Court . . . But, Yatchett told himself despairingly, Guéroult must have gone home days ago. Of course he would have done so for he was not a naval man and had no duties in occupied Germany after his evidence was given. Probably by now he was far away on the Atlantic. It was really not worth the waste of time even to try to find out, but—Yatchett, glancing involuntarily out of the window saw that the morning fog was lifting slowly, disclosing that high blank wall—he would make this one last effort and when he drew the inevitable blank there would be nothing more he could do. Wearily now, he lifted the receiver from its bracket . . .

Nine

At six that evening he sat in a bedroom of a small and ugly hotel—the same hotel, though he did not know this, from which Capitaine Meilhac had so recently been taken to the hospital and to death—confronting Guéroult. Somehow the management had received a fuel allowance for the steam heating, and the premises from being icily cold had become preposterously hot. Guéroult sat on the bed, a small, stocky figure dressed in blue uniform trousers and an open-necked white shirt. He listened carefully to Yatchett, who leaned uneasily forward from the one hard chair, and nodded quick understanding to the latter's stumbling explanation of his presence. From time to time he refilled two narrow glasses with brandy from a bottle on the bedside table.

'Yes, yes, I comprehend, m'sieur. I comprehend well.'

Major Yatchett nodded gratefully. 'I thought that probably you were unaware of the full facts since, as a witness, you were only present in court to give your testimony.'

'That is so.' Gaston grinned widely. 'You remember that, then?'

'Very well. It was a—a ghastly experience for you, obviously.'

'Ah—obviously? To you, M'sieur le Major, that was obvious?'

'Of course. But, as I have said, however terrible it was, the full facts of the case have to be taken into consideration.'

'You think, undoubtedly, that I have not considered them.' It was a statement rather than a question, and Yatchett watched as more brandy was poured out even though his own glass was not yet half empty. Guéroult's hand trembled a little and Yatchett wondered if he always drank like this. Probably, considering his high colour—and it would do him no good. 'Yes,' he said at last. 'I don't suppose you've had the time. And after what you've been through perhaps you haven't wanted to—to go into the case all over again. So I thought that . . .'

'I know all the "facts" as you call them, m'sieur. I have studied all the documents. And the authorities—the British authorities—have been to me most kind. They have put all information at my disposal. Tell me—' he had looked up, his eyes gleaming—'what you think of the defending advocate—the American officer?'

'Kaye? Oh, he did a very good job, I thought. In fact I'm sure he believed in his clients' case.' Major Yatchett eased his long legs and sipped his brandy. It was a cheap raw spirit and despite himself the muscles of his mouth twitched in distaste. 'As a matter of fact I'm glad you brought Kaye's name up, because it's to him we'll have to go first. I mean he can present the matter far better than you and I who aren't lawyers. I thought we'd go to him as soon as possible—perhaps this evening. There's no time to lose, because—'

'One moment, m'sieur, I beg!' Gaston was laughing, holding up a small square hand in protest. 'One moment, please!'

'Yes, yes, of course. I'm rushing you, I know. I'm sorry.'

'No, you are not rushing me, m'sieur. You are not rushing me here and you are not rushing me to Monsieur le Capitaine Kaye, either. Now, please—you answer me one thing. I have answered you. Now you answer me—yes?'

'Of course—if I can.'

'You can. Tell me then—were you not surprised to find me here. Still in this city so many days after the trial?'

Major Yatchett looked a little surprised. He could not see the point of the question. Still, it was true; it *had* surprised him.

'Yes. Yes I was, as a matter of fact. I had felt almost certain that—'

'And you do not of course know what I am doing here?'

'No. That's not my affair, naturally. I've no doubt that—'

'I will tell you. Permit that I tell you. But first—a little more *eau-de-vie*?'

'No, no. But certainly tell me if you wish. Only—' Major Yatchett glanced at his watch—'time is a little short, so . . .'

'*Pardon*, m'sieur. Time is not short. There is more than forty-eight hours to wait yet.' Abruptly Gaston rose from the bed and stood, legs stockily apart, hands on hips, staring down at his visitor. 'I am here to wait, you see. I am here to wait until the day after tomorrow when I have permission to attend a small military ceremony which is to be held on an old German rifle range four kilometres outside this city. I have waited nearly a year—a long time, m'sieur. I have been patient. And I will be patient, too, with you for I am truly grateful to you as a member of the Court which gave so just a verdict, so just a sentence. I tell you plainly that I cannot understand why you now wish to reverse that sentence—but I tell you also that it is too late!' Gaston was no longer smiling, his face was hard, his eyes narrow; under the weak yellow electric light sweat gleamed on his forehead and at the base of his throat. 'You are not a sailor, M'sieur le Major, and so I do not think that you can well comprehend what it was like on that raft. It was very slow death for all of us. It was also torture. It continued for a long time. Germans have killed people slowly and by torture in the camps. It is not important why they did it, or for what reasons. Reasons can be found for most things if one tries to find them. What is important is that such men must be put to death.' Gaston suddenly dragged a thin crumpled envelope from his trouser pocket—'This, m'sieur, is a letter which came to me at Belfast, sent forward by my mother from Dieppe. I received it just before I came here to give testimony. It is from an old military man in France who is the—the how do you say? The *parrain* of Kümmerol. Poor man, what a disaster! But what does he say? Does he say that his—his *filleul* must have had a good reason for doing as he did? No—for he knows that there could be no reason. He says that he is sure that his *cher* Emil could never do something of that sort. He believes that there is some terrible mistake and that it was not Emil who fired the guns and threw, also, the grenades, but some German man. You know, one supposes, that Kümmerol is to all intents a Frenchman? Yes, indeed. It is a terrible thing to have to admit, but it is so.—*Alors*, this old colonel thinks that I was mistaken—the explosion, the sinking, the darkness, you see. These things, he thinks, gave me confusion. He thinks that when I see Emil clearly in court I will find that it was someone else whom I spoke to upon the submarine. He asks that I make plain to the Court that this is so—and then to try to find the villain who fired the guns. So I write to him that I should take great care to identify correctly the man who had interrogated me. If it was a mistake I should be sure to make that plain to all. And—oh Jesus!—When I came to the court that day I looked at the prisoner and I thought that old man was right. I thought the man beside the Kommandant was not the Frenchman called Emil whom I remembered. I could not understand. But for one moment I hoped—so greatly hoped, m'sieur, that I cannot tell you how much—that I had been wrong; that the Emil who had spoken to me kindly upon the foredeck was not the same man who had come back to kill me. I felt, for one beautiful moment, "Yes, it is true, what the old colonel say! No Frenchman could do that. I have been mistaken!" *Hélas*—it was a quick illusion. As soon as he stood up and turned towards me I knew him. It was he.' Slowly Gaston pushed the letter back into his pocket. 'I cannot tell him, this poor old man—not yet. I am hoping that I may commiserate later. I do not know. But to you, m'sieur, I can say only that once again I thank you for your just decision in court and that I am sorry for your present confusion, though I cannot understand it. I would suggest that if you think over the matter in good calmness you will soon comprehend that you are suffering from a delusion. And now, I regret I have an engagement. . . .'

Ten

'Thus it can clearly be seen that the terminology of the indictment was so framed that it was possible for the Court to arrive at a verdict of guilty while disregarding the actual facts of the case even though these were explained in full detail by the defending officer. It is not difficult to see in this the hands of men deeply prejudiced against both the whole principle of blockade by submarine and the technical changes which, by perfecting both submarine and aeroplane, have made obsolete the surface battle fleet and changed the entire structure and conception of sea-power. New forms of warfare are invariably resented and calumniated by those whom they place at a disadvantage, and upon being taken prisoner the men who operate them are often treated as fit objects for revenge. That the present case is an excellent example of this truth there can be no doubt. And that it will one day be seen as such cannot be doubted, either.'

Eugen put down the pencil and sat back, easing his cramped fingers. The memorandum was finished. That one day it would speak for him when his own physical voice had long been stilled, of this he was contentedly certain. And to him that mattered more than anything else. Or—he told himself a little shakily—it ought to. For now it was done there was nothing to do but wait. This evening—tonight—tomorrow—tomorrow night—a long time of waiting. He wished that he could have spun the memorandum out until at least noon tomorrow.

He stretched and rose to his feet and as he did so he heard the muffled crash of nailed boots in the stone passage outside, the clink and rattle of a heavy key. Yes, Dr Stusser would have come. And it would probably be his last visit. As the door opened to reveal the red-capped guard Eugen carefully lifted the thick sheaf of manuscript and tucked it under his arm.

In the visiting room Dr Stusser was looking colder and more despondent than ever. He nodded as Eugen, accompanied by the inevitable guard, entered from the door beyond the partitioning wire fence, but he did not rise from his chair. 'Well—' his voice held its usual note of irritable impatience, but under it Eugen sensed, as before, a nervous and unwilling compassion—'I've come, as you see. And—Ah! That is your—your final deposition?'

'Yes. Have you permission to take it?'

'I have. It will have to be examined before I may retain it but that is, I think, a mere formality to be certain that it contains no technical information which might be withheld. If it is merely your views upon the trial and the facts giving rise to it, I do not think any difficulty will be made.' Dr Stusser eyed the thick mass of manuscript with wary distaste. 'What am I to do with it?'

'I want you to keep it until you are quite certain that you can place it safely in the hands of my sister in São Paulo. At present the postal situation is probably still precarious. You must be quite sure that it is going to arrive safely before you part with it.'

'Very well. You must give it to the guard, and when you return to your—your room he will take it to an office from whence I may reclaim it in a few days' time. Now—' if possible Dr Stusser's expression became still more uncomfortable— 'I have some other news for you. I have located your parents.'

'So?' Abruptly Eugen sat down, and taking off his glasses began to polish them with a handkerchief. His hands shook violently and he felt sick. 'Where—?'

'They are in the Russian area of occupation. And I understand that they are in ordinary health. The third address you gave me was correct but they had moved north-east to be with your aunt and uncle upon their farm—that was when the bombing became bad and, of course, the farm was much safer. Then your father became ill and they were unable to leave before our troops were forced to fall back. . . .'

'They—know about me? What has happened?'

'Yes. Yes, they do. They have been trying to get permission to travel in order to come here. It is extremely difficult.' Dr Stusser shifted his feet; his eyes slid quickly away from Eugen's white face behind the wire mesh and fixed themselves upon a distant corner. 'Yes. Well, they may be able to arrive here in four or five days. I believe that if the military authorities were approached they would grant a stay of —of . . . for that period. I believe they would do that, I cannot *promise*, of course, but I think so.' Dr Stusser's voice trailed miserably into silence and from the other side of the wire Eugen said distractedly, 'I don't know, I don't know . . . I was not expecting such news. I think, perhaps . . .'

'I can try,' repeated Dr Stusser tonelessly.

'For me—only?'

'How do you mean?'

'Kümmerol.'

'No, no.'

'He would have to—to go the day after tomorrow?'

Dr Stusser nodded.

'Then, no.' Eugen's voice became steadier at once. 'No, I do not want him to have to go alone. And even if a delay was allowed for me I think such a visit would be—terrible for us all. No; I will write a letter for them and leave it with you.'

'Very well.' There was relief in the lawyer's voice. 'I think you are right to decide so. I will do what you say.'

Abruptly Eugen rose. 'Then that is all.' He paused uncertainly. 'I must thank you for all you have done. I have mentioned this in the letter to my sister which is enclosed in the memorandum. You will not find her ungrateful.'

Dr Stusser shook his head helplessly; his face was painfully flushed. 'No, no, Herr Kapitänleutnant. I did only what I could. I am bitterly grieved that I could do no more. If there should be anything further— you have only to let me know. And so . . .' He swallowed, tried to speak again but failed, shook his head once more and almost ran from the room.

Eleven

Emil also had a visitor that day—that last day but one. Captain Kaye came to the prison in the late afternoon. He came in a mixture of fear, anger and deep resentment, but these feelings were aroused more by Corporal Post than by his recent client.

For when he had received Kümmerol's request for an interview he had at once decided not to accede to it. If Kümmerol had testamentary depositions to make or private affairs to put in order the right person to see about them was Dr Stusser.

'And he knows that,' Kaye had said pettishly as he shovelled more coal on to the office fire. 'I know he knows, because Stusser told them both, as soon as the trial was over, that he would still be in contact with them. My own role in the affair finished with my speech for mitigation. I'm sorry for them both. I must admit I think they are being harshly treated. But the fact is, Mr P, I can't do anything more for them at this late date. In the unforgettable French of Lord Westmorland, "*Je voudrais, si je couldrais, mais je ne cannais pas.*" Only if a review of the proceedings or a retrial had been ordered would I have been involved again. As it is, the matter's closed as far as I'm concerned.'

'Maybe he has something important to say.'

'He can't have anything important to say to *me*.'

'Then why's he want to see you, sir?'

'I can't imagine, I'm sure.'

'Then—hadn't you better go?'

'Why—for God's sake?'

'Because they're killing him, day after tomorrow,' Post had replied dispassionately.

Kaye had replaced the shovel in the brass scuttle and risen, dusting his hands together, eyeing his clerk-valet-cook thoughtfully. 'That case upset you badly, didn't it? Because it is the first one in which you have assisted me which has involved a death sentence? But I don't suppose it will be the last. You know well that I dislike forecasting results, and that I never do so. Today I will break—just this once—that very excellent rule. Reynolds is going to be found guilty and subsequently hanged. There is no doubt in my mind about that, and there never has been. Needless to say it will not prevent me doing everything I possibly can for him at the trial. But *not* afterwards.'

Post shrugged his shoulders morosely. 'Well—sure; if he's guilty. Seems to me they ought to hang the Senegalese, too. But if he's guilty he ought to hang. And he is guilty of course. But these other two weren't.'

'They were guilty as charged. Ah! I understand. You are not worried about the hanging of Reynolds because you cannot conceive yourself in his position. But you *can* conceive yourself in Kümmerol's. That's it, isn't it, Mr P?'

'More or less. And you said yourself that you'd have done the same as Kielbasa—we both would.'

Captain Kaye smiled. 'You and I as submarine commander and gunnery officer, in fact. We'd have made an odd pair, eh? I don't know though—' he turned towards the ugly, oak-framed mirror above the fireplace—'my beard is quite nautical, and you have a certain Nordic touch. I'm sure we'd have looked much more villainous in the dock than our recent clients. I can see Colonel Rostwood pointing at us and thundering denunciations until—'

'You ought to go and see him, sir,' Post repeated obstinately.

'Well, I won't, Mr P. So let us get down to some work and forget about it.'

But it was impossible to forget about it with Post's sullen, accusing face bowed over the typewriter all the long grey afternoon; with his monosyllabic answers and his refusal to be laughed and joked back into a good humour. At five o'clock Kaye had given up, risen to his feet and flung down his pencil. 'All right, then! All *right*! I'll see him. It doesn't matter to *you* that we're very busy and that it's late and cold. Nothing matters except that— Oh hell, go and get the car!'

They drove silently, each unhappily aware of the other's resentful irritation, and after calling at a PX for some otherwise unprocurable essentials—soap, razor blades and, in Post's case, gum—they arrived at the prison in the dank last dusk of twilight. High dripping stone walls, ponderous gates, rubber capes gleaming under the thin rain as their documents were scrutinized—it was not easy to gain admittance to condemned prisoners awaiting execution, even for J.A.G. personnel.

'I don't quite see—' said the assistant governor, a British major, politely—'why you need your corporal with you, Captain Kaye.' Though senior in rank to the American officer he was some years younger and had a proper awe of the Judge Advocate General's Office.

'Corporal Post is the instigator of this whole macabre expedition,' snapped Kaye. He was very put out and had every intention of showing it, for he had much of that particular characteristic of the inverted intellectual bachelor—a peculiarly tender sensibility which could make him, when aroused, excessively squeamish, and when ruffled extremely ill-natured.

The prison hospital was brightly lit, sterile and deeply depressing. It smelled of ether and disinfectant and was walled with that ornate ceramic tiling which Captain Kaye was wont to term 'Gothic lavatorial style.' Before being admitted to Kümmerol's room they were met by a young white-coated doctor who looked them up and down with suspicious dislike. 'I hope you aren't going to upset him still more. He is not in a state for visitors and I'm not at all sure—'

'He asked to see me—' said Kaye more loudly than was necessary— 'and I've come. I can assure you, Doctor, that it is very inconvenient for me indeed. But if you say we can't see him I'll very willingly accede to your veto—very willingly indeed.'

'Please lower your voice. There are sick men here trying to rest. You are not supposed to see him without the presence of a medical orderly. At the moment there is not one available, so I shall accompany you myself. Come this way, please.'

Another corridor; their footsteps echoed loudly on the tiles. A locked door and the young doctor's hand upon the key . . . Kaye felt the sweat damp in the palms of his hands as the door opened and he preceded Post into the white room.

Kümmerol sat facing them. He wore his uniform but without a tie and with the white collar of his shirt over the blue one of his jacket. His face was a colourless sallow grey, but his eyes burned out from dark pits with such terrified despair that it took all Kaye's willpower to move the four or five steps towards him. For a moment he stood foolishly in front of that small seated blue figure and felt the numbing horror of foretasted death reach out its icy tentacles to touch him. Then —'*Alors, me voici.*' For there could be no banal words of greeting; any words except those as terse and clear as the orders to a firing squad would be both horrible and meaningless here this evening.

Emil's eyes dropped to his hands, folded across the curved handle of his stick, as if he knew already the effect they had on others. When he spoke it was with what seemed a physical difficulty, as if his vocal cords were so stiff that he could only use them with a painful effort. 'I want to make one last appeal to—to common sense. You know that I am guiltless. You explained this very well to the Court. It was so clear that I cannot see—' he shook his head slowly, weakly—'how they can have condemned me. Somewhere there has been a terrible mistake —that is obvious. I—I am sure that there must be someone *somewhere* who can understand the simple facts.' He breathed in slowly in a long, sighing, shuddering gasp. Then—'It is not, monsieur, a question of asking for mercy. It is not even a question of asking for justice. It is merely to ask a reasonable man to look at the facts—nothing more. I can do nothing; I am locked in. I have no voice to use but yours. You must do this.'

Captain Kaye had managed to recover himself a little during this speech. He was too shocked and unnerved by Emil's appearance to feel pity—perhaps that would come later; but as a barrister he was capable of quick thought and an outward semblance of self-control. He wondered if the doctor, standing to one side and a little behind him, spoke French. 'To whom do you suggest that I make this appeal?'

The answer, when it came, left him momentarily speechless. 'To the King of England.'

'But—but—'

'You do not think he is reasonable? He is not intelligent; but that, of course, is not the same thing.'

Captain Kaye took a deep breath. 'Kümmerol,' he said carefully, 'I want to—I must—explain something to you. Dr Stusser should have done it, but as he has not . . . You were convicted according to the indictment. Do you remember the words of the indictment? That you were, in violation of the Laws and Usages of War, concerned with the killing of members of the crew of the steamship *Maréchal Oudinot*. That you *were* concerned with the killing of those men you admitted yourself. That this was a violation of the Laws and Usages of War was, unfortunately, held by the Court to be fully proven. Your conviction was thus legally justifiable.'

Wearily, as from a great distance, Emil said, 'Yes, yes. All that I understand. All that Dr Stusser explained—even though I understood it before. But you know why we had to do what we did and why I myself had to obey the orders I was given. You explained it to the Court. They did not believe you, but other people might. The English King might. After all, it is customary, is it not, for men sentenced to die by his Courts to appeal to him? Often, I have heard, they are successful.'

'Those are civilian criminal cases tried under British Statute Law. And that is something quite different. I doubt very much whether you have any right to appeal to King George under the new procedure.'

'I do not think anyone else can save me now.'

Someone was nudging his back urgently but the Captain took no heed. For something strange had happened to him in the last few seconds, something had snapped.

Captain Kaye was pre-eminently a civilized man, a cultured and erudite intellectual. His days, until the commencement of the war, had been carefully constructed to cater for and to augment his culture, erudition and interests. His life had consequently been pleasant and fulfilling and he had firmly suppressed certain instincts which might have endangered it. He had thus made his limited obeisance, sardonic and formal, to the society in which he moved and in return that society had made a place for him and had accepted him, if not exactly at his own valuation at least at a level which was by no means insulting. And it was this dignified society with its fastidious values and discreet wealth which the Third Reich had called decadent and set out avowedly to overturn and destroy by violence—uncontrolled, brutally destructive, vandalistic violence. The case of the *Maréchal Oudinot* had been a peculiarly flagrant example of this violence. That the defence brief had offered a magnificent opportunity to exercise forensic skill did not alter that fact at all. Captain Kaye had told Eugen Kielbasa that, whatever he might think to the contrary, his order had outraged the spirit of humanity. That was true; it was also true that it was an outrage against western civilization—that civilization of which Captain Kaye justly considered himself both an exponent and a beneficiary. He had found his clients interesting, and in some ways he had admired Kielbasa; but he had never liked either of them. And now, suddenly, he was filled with a peculiar mixture of anger and revulsion. Anger, because Kümmerol had succeeded all too well in projecting his own agony of trapped despair on to someone else—someone whom he believed most erroneously to be his friend. Revulsion at the way in which someone who must so recently have been a handsome and probably charming boy had been reduced to this sweating, abject cripple with the terrified eyes, struggling hopelessly to avoid a cruel judicial death. Kümmerol had negated the dignity of civilized mankind by his actions, and now it was negated in his own person.

Briefly, coldly (surely it was kindest to be honest), Captain Kaye said, 'No one can save you now. For your own sake you should try to understand that. It is stupid to talk of the King of England. You forget, too, that he is also a sailor and thus unlikely to feel much toleration for what you have done. No, I cannot help you. If there had been any possibility of doing so I should have been notified of it before the sentence was confirmed. As it is, I—'

But Emil had lifted his eyes and was staring at him in a way which made it impossible to continue. Captain Kaye broke off, and turning so quickly that he nearly knocked down Corporal Post, made for the door. He felt the sweat cold on his forehead and jerked his handkerchief from his pocket. As he did so something hit him violently in the small of the back. It was Kümmerol's stick. He swung around to see the small blue-clad figure trying to struggle erect, the livid face convulsed with rage. 'Go, then! Go! You know the truth, but you will not tell it! You betray me! You have only *pretended* to help! You—always you knew they would kill me. You—you . . . Go! Go!'

Then he was outside in the tiled passage with the door mercifully shut behind him and the doctor was saying with barely controlled anger, 'I must say you deserved that! Why the devil couldn't you have told him that you'd contact the King of England—or the Emperor of Peru, if necessary? Anything to keep him quiet and let him hope for a little longer. Have you no feelings at all? Can't you imagine what it is like to sit there waiting? No, of course you can't. Well, you'd better go. I must say, if ever *I* want a lawyer I shan't come to you in a hurry!'

Eight feet away, beyond the closed door, Emil, shivering and weeping, crawled over the floor to regain his stick. Before he reached it his palm pressed down painfully on something small and oblong on the floor near the door. It was a packet of PX razor blades which had fallen from Captain Kaye's pocket when he pulled out his handkerchief.

Twelve

In the cold darkness of approaching winter Europe slept as the turning globe swung the battered continent through slow night towards another dawn. Dying was easy for many already weakened by long hunger, imprisonment and unhealed wounds. Some, sick and sleepless in the darkness, longed for death, others regarded its approach indifferently. There did not seem to be much left to live for; tomorrow, now coming greyly out of the east, would only be darker, colder, shorter yet.

And then 'tomorrow' was 'today' and, though it could not break through the low sullen clouds blanketing Europe, the sun shone down on more favoured continents to the south, first in the bright radiance of morning and then in the long, drowsy calm of golden afternoon. . . .

Late afternoon sun over Masondi, hot and still and quiet. In the garden of the District Commissioner's house the Shellybeares wandered slowly under the double lines of Uganda flame-trees which led from a disused summer-house to a disused lily-pond. Unlike many of their kind they were not fond of gardening, though Mrs Shellybeare possessed a formidable pair of pruning shears with which, from time to time, she ruthlessly amputated the limbs of any plant which dared to encroach upon the gravel walks. The result was that the plants generally died and left legacies of large patches of dry, dusty earth. As her husband remarked—she made deserts where roses had blossomed.

This afternoon they were talking of Masondi's one wartime adventure, the German submarine. Since the trial of Kielbasa and Kümmerol it had been a source of constant conversation among everyone in the town. 'And to think—' Mrs Shellybeare was saying—'that you nearly helped the little beast to escape over the border!'

'I know, I know!'

'And we were actually going to have him to dinner. Thank heaven we never did! I don't know what we could have done now if we had —how we could ever have explained it away . . .'

'He took me in completely, I admit.'

'He didn't take in Tony.'

'No. Tony comes very well out of the whole thing. I always thought him intelligent and perspicacious. Well, I believe he'll get a district of his own next year. He deserves it. I've given him a splendid report.'

'Emerald comes out of it very badly. *Very badly indeed.*—Remind me to deal with this poinsettia tomorrow, it's quite out of hand.— Why, when she was doing so well with Tony, she had to fall for that wretched German creature . . . Tony won't have anything to do with her now. I don't blame him, I must say.'

'Poor Emerald! She is *persona* somewhat *ridicula* at present, isn't she? I'm rather sorry for her.'

'Well, I'm *not*! The whole thing was—was disgraceful, really. I told Patience Singlefield so yesterday. I said that I'd always thought Emerald an *odd* girl in many ways. We'd always tried to be nice to her, I said, but really—there comes a *time* . . . there is a *limit* . . . Patience said she wasn't at all surprised. She'd always known Emerald was capable of anything. She said—you know how everyone thought that Emerald wanted to study zoology and we thought it was only old Zared's meanness which prevented her? Well, Patience said that far from wanting to be a zoologist, Emerald wanted to be a prostitute.'

'No! How could Patience—'

'Emerald *told* her so.'

Thirteen

Late sunlight, warm and orange-golden, fingered its way through the fretted leaves of papaw and hibiscus, falling in chinks and fragments of brightness on to the dark, fig-perfumed earth below the dusky shade of giant banyans. A sunset breeze from the south-west, from Cape Delgado far away, swayed the long plumes of the high palms and rustled dryly over the dirty leaf-strewn floor of the abandoned bungalow. Emerald, still as the dusty mummy of the dead rat below the window, stood in the open doorway, legs apart, hands in pockets, staring across the room at the sagging bed. Nearly eight months ago—but it seemed only yesterday. Now—never again.

Everybody had followed the trial—which, owing to the nature of its local interest, had been fully reported in the Dar-es-Salaam press—with gasps of horror and indignation. Emerald, professing utter in-

difference, had followed it secretly and sullenly, abstracting the papers
from her father's desk long before his carnivorous curiosity was
satisfied and locking herself with them in the lavatory. So *that* was
Emil's real reason for trying so hard to escape. Well, she had always
known without resentment that it was not herself. She had asked a
good deal from Emil, but not that he should love her. She had been
content that he should obey her and let her love him. He had done
both; she had no reason to complain. She had been unbelievably,
dazzlingly happy for a short, a very short, while with her mutilated little
war criminal. As to what he had done—what did that matter to her?
It was not anything particularly dreadful, either, when compared with
the revelations, now filling the papers, of what had gone on in the
death camps. Anyway there was nothing she herself would enjoy more
than casting Tony adrift on a raft in mid-ocean, after firing a shotgun
into his belly—small birdshot, just enough to puncture and rupture
his intestines and ensure gangrene.

Dr Zared wanted Emerald to proclaim that her visit to the submarine had been on purpose to search for the hidden log, and to say
that she had always intended to take it to the authorities—was indeed
on her way to them with it when she had encountered Tony on the
dock. 'Why should he get all the benefit, eh? You could get in the
papers, Emerald—and your picture. "Doctor Zared's Daughter Helps
Bring War Criminals to Justice" . . . something like that. I could
probably get promotion, or at least a raise in salary . . . something,
anyway,' he had added a little forlornly.

'You can get stuffed!' Emerald had said. She had learned the
expression from Mr Spencer, who had picked it up in Dar-es-Salaam
on one of his visits.

She had no friends now, except Mr Spencer, who was often away,
and the orderlies, Latif and Rami, with whom she held long discussions about Emil and the trial. Neither of the Indians was very
shocked at the shooting-up of the *Maréchal Oudinot*'s survivors, though
they clicked their teeth and shook their heads and said 'That Emil!'

And now Emil was to die—and very soon. It had come as a jolt to
read that; sitting in the lavatory with the sunlight pouring through the
frosted glass window. There had been a sanctimonious section in the
leader column praising Tony, and British Justice, and someone called
the Judge Advocate, and a great many abstract values and ending up
with some poetry about 'hearts at peace, under an English heaven' . . .
'Very beautiful'—Dr Zared had said at lunch—'very true. That's real
good writing. What did you pay for this lettuce?'

But that night Emerald had dreamed of Emil. She often did—but this dream was different. For in it she *was* Emil. She was locked in a small bare room, and she was going to be killed very soon. It was silent, and she had been walking up and down on bare feet, padding unceasingly up and down, up and down, as Rose had padded up and down her cage—looking for a way out. And then—still far away, but approaching, she had heard other footsteps. And there was *no* way out, and they were coming for her—closer and closer, louder and louder, thunderous beyond the locked door. She had screamed out in white-hot terror and awakened dripping with sweat. Was it like that— Oh God, was it like that for Emil, far away under the unimaginable grev skies of unknown Europe? Was he locked in alone and frightened beyond all bearing? No, no. It could not be like that because dreams never were like reality. She had lain awake trembling all night, but by dawn she had convinced herself that whatever was being done to Emil could not be like her dream. Probably it was all very quick and painless and not . . . horrible, really. She had seen sick animals shot. They never knew what hit them. They felt nothing.

And now, very soon, it would be over. She did not know when for she refused to ask anyone about it. Yet she knew, somehow, that Emil's death must be very close. So she had come to visit this abandoned old house. It would be the last time. For once she knew—the papers would certainly report it—that Emil was dead she would leave Masondi. She could not stay any longer in this place where everyone except Mr Spencer and two Indian orderlies disliked her so much. How she would leave—where she would go—she did not know. There were cousins in India; her father seldom spoke of them but she knew they existed. She started suddenly at the sound of a car turning into the overgrown driveway. Who could be coming here? And what for? Emerald moved quickly to one of the broken windows and stared out through the warped louvres of the shutter. It was Mr Spencer, and she breathed a sigh of relief and went out to greet him.

They met at the top of the veranda steps in the orange glow of the falling sun. Mr Spencer looked neater and smarter than ever. A pistachio silk shirt, beige trousers white-suede-belted, and with white suede shoes. His wavy black hair glinted with brilliantine and his dark eyes sparkled. Except for his limp—his sciatica cure at Dar-es-Salaam had greatly increased the pain and frequency of his ailment—one would never have believed he was so old and of Eskimo, or possibly penguin, parentage. Yet soon he, too, would be gone—to a bigger agency in Dar-es-Salaam.

'Dear Emerald! How lovely you look!'

'How lovely *you* look, too. What are you doing here?'

'The Baumgartens are coming back. I had a letter yesterday. They asked me to have a dekko at the place and see what needed doing before they could move in. I've got to make an estimate.—What are *you* doing?'

'Me? I come here often. There's a dead rat I'm interested in. I estimate it.'

'I always said you had a zoological brain.'

'Anyway, now the Baumgartens are coming back I suppose they'll want to get rid of it. Why can't they go and get stuffed?'

'Ah, why indeed! Shall I tell them to leave your rat? "Emerald's rat," I shall say to Frau Baumgarten, "is sacred. Emerald is my dear and lovely friend and"— Oh, I nearly forgot.' Mr Spencer's brow clouded in quick doubt. Then he said, 'I don't know whether I shall upset you. Tomorrow is the day on which they are shooting poor Emil.'

But Emerald hardly heard him.—'*My dear and lovely friend,*' he had said. He could take her away. He was said to be rich. He had always been exceptionally kind to her. And he always did as she asked. He didn't *look* his age, after all.

'Tell me,' she took his hand and examined his gold bracelet. It had no name, initials, date. Mr Spencer remained inscrutable even in his most personal possessions. 'Would you like to marry me?'

'Immensely. Can you think otherwise?' But she could see he thought she was joking.

'No—I mean really. I don't see why not. I am your dear and lovely friend—you just said so.' Looking up from the bracelet she read dawning consternation in Mr Spencer's dark eyes. '*I'*d like to marry *you*—I think.'

Mr Spencer giggled. 'Well!' he said. 'Well! I've never been paid such a compliment! I don't know what to say!'

'Say "yes"—that's all. Go on.'

'Are you— No, surely you're not really serious, Emerald?'

'I am—truly. I am seriously proposing to you.'

'I—I—' Mr Spencer looked away and was silent a long moment. His swarthy skin was visibly paler. Then, quite roughly, he pulled his hand from Emerald's. 'You are being somewhat silly, I think. I am old enough to be your father. My—my words were not meant at all in the way you took them. I should not have uttered them, but they were diversion only. What you suggest is—is absurd.'

'Why?'

'Well, it is. Such a thing is ridiculous! It would be a—a most ineluctable espousal.' Mr Spencer quickly patted Emerald's shoulder but his eyes flickered away from her face. 'No, no, dear Emerald. Let us remain friends always, yes. But let us keep, equally, our sense of portention. Some things are fitting. Some—even among dear friends—are not. And now I find that, after all, I must go. I have quite forgotten that there is a most important telephone call coming through to me from Dar-es-Salaam.' He patted her shoulder once more, turned and ran lightly down the steps to his car. It was surprising how little his sciatica seemed to irk him.

Emerald walked slowly back into the dark, draughty coolness of the house. As the noise of Mr Spencer's motor faded down the road towards the town silence ebbed back again into the old rooms, so long abandoned, so soon to be inhabited once more. She looked back, as if over centuries, to the early spring, and to all the eighteen years beyond. Everything dwindled down to a tiny bright focus like the spot of light under the lens of her father's microscope. Tomorrow, far across the world, they were going to kill the only living being who had ever been more to her than a sounding-board for her own personality. Mr Spencer was right not to marry her; it would not have done at all. It would, she saw now, have been excessively ineluctable. But his refusal left her curiously empty and a little frightened. She longed, with an aching distress, for Emil's presence beside her here in the evening calm. Very slowly in the silence she said his name 'Emil'—standing alone in the house with only the sea breeze, the dry rustling leaves, and the dead rat.

Fourteen

Once more the short European day was fading from evening into premature darkness. For some minutes before it sank the sun had penetrated the heavy blanket of cloud and thrown its weak and watery winter light across the wounded city, across the distant suburbs and the looming bulk of the prison. In the streets some passers-by looked up at the rent clouds and thought that tomorrow, perhaps, would be a fine day; but few, burdened as they were with poverty and hunger and bereavement—or the worse uncertainty of sons and husbands still unaccounted for—cared about the weather.

Some four kilometres beyond the city limits a square-shouldered, heavily built man in his late thirties who wore the crowns of a British major on his khaki raincoat and the badge of the Royal Military Police in his hat, stared long at that yellow gap and hoped it indicated better weather on the morrow. He was standing on a barren stretch of heather-covered moorland directing a small squad of five men who were engaged in taking measurements with a surveyor's tape. The spring-roller was held by a red-capped corporal who stood between two newly planted posts set firmly ten feet from each other in well-tamped earth. Heavy, black and rough, the sets of regular rust-stained holes near their tops proclaimed them to be disused railway sleepers, and some fifteen yards behind them rose a tall artificial hill of gravelly shale.

When the tape had been unwound to a length of twenty-five yards Major Steward lifted a hand and the sergeant who had been walking backward with the tape's end halted. The Major strode up to him, turned and frowned consideringly back at the corporal who stood motionless between the grimy old posts. 'That'll do, Milne. Put in the pegs. Not so deep they can't be seen and so some fool falls over them.'

A sudden gust of cold wind with a spattering of raindrops blew from the east and the Major hunched his shoulders under his upturned collar and shivered. 'God, I hope we get better weather tomorrow!'

'So long as it's not foggy, sir,' said Sergeant Milne, pegging down the tape with the blade of his jack-knife and rising to his feet.

That was a new thought for Major Steward, who rasped a hand across the short bristle of moustache on his upper lip and swore softly but obscenely. 'All right. Put in provisional pegs at—at say, twelve yards.'

'Bit close, sir.'

'Better that than the other way about for all concerned—not least me. And I'm going to use targets. It's not usual, I know, but I want the bullets in the proper place this time—not all around their bloody balls. If I find a single bullet-hole below the navel I'll have the whole squad on extra range practice for a fortnight. I mean that, Milne—so tell them to watch it! Right. Now you and Corporal Maynard get those pegs in while I and the others measure up the sides for roping off. There'll be at least thirty people here, probably a lot more—and most will be civilian cameramen. They've got to be kept out of the bloody light. I'm going to station men down the inside of the ropes to see they *are* kept out of the bloody light, too. I'm not having any bloody *unofficial* corpses on my hands. But I bet they'll try. You ever seen any American cameramen in action, Milne?'

'No sir. Don't particularly want to, neither.'

'Well, want to or not, you will tomorrow. And you bloody well watch them like a cat watching mice. They'll do anything—anything at all—to get good pictures. If it was allowed they'd lie flat on their bloody bellies right under those posts taking close-ups. Then one gets killed and it turns out that he's a top performer from the New York *Screamer* or some bloody thing and on Christian-name terms with all their bloody generals—and we're dropped properly in the shit.'

'Can't have that, sir.'

Major Steward grunted morosely and started to walk towards the 15 cwt truck parked, ugly and mud-coloured, by a battered corrugated hut which had once held flags and markers. Then he turned back. ''Nother thing, Milne—'

'Sir?'

'These cameramen. They'll probably want to take close-ups afterwards. Well, afterwards in this case does *not* mean while everyone's ears are still ringing with the denonation. There's to be no scrambling under the ropes. First *I* go up—see? And unless it's obvious that I've got to go quick, I'm going to walk slow. 'Cos if I run it'll start a bloody rush sure as fate. Well, I have a look and then the M.O. does his check. And then, and *only* then, is anybody allowed on the—' the Major grinned briefly—'the course. As soon as the M.O.'s satisfied he'll tell me and I'll give the word to drop the ropes. You watch me—got it?

'Right. Then let's get cracking with these bloody pegs and posts and get back home.'

And in another fifteen minutes of measuring, hammering and desultory swearing the work was done. It was raining lightly and very cold out here on the bare moorland. The squad of military police piled thankfully into their truck and as soon as Major Steward, shaking the raindrops from his cap, had clambered into the narrow seat beside the driver the vehicle lurched off into the gathering dusk.

A bird called mournfully from a short line of stunted fir-trees to the left of the butts and a gust of thin, misty rain from the north-east whistled through them until they hissed and bowed like a rank of Japanese generals in surrender. Black and wet, the twin posts gloomed against the darkening sky.

Fifteen

They took Emil back to the cells after dinner. At seven o'clock he was still in the bare but not forbidding brightness of the hospital wing. At eight he was in a stone cell clamped by a heavy automatically locking door fitted with a glass spy-hole. Wooden plank bed, small hard pillow, two coarse sheets and one dark prison blanket—a lavatory pan in one corner, a small board table clamped to a wall, an iron stool. It was here, under the bright glare from an electric lamp deep set behind a grille in the ceiling, that he would spend the last night of his life.

He had hardly slept or eaten during the last forty-eight hours and now he was mentally and physically exhausted. This afternoon there had been a discreet visit from a priest. Emil, born and reared a Roman Catholic, was indifferent to whether or not he died one. Perhaps it was safer. He had listened vaguely to the priest, nodded, shrugged. Whatever state he was in, it was certainly not one of Grace as the priest wished. 'I would have you die serenely and at peace . . .' Emil had glanced at him with weary, bitter resentment. 'Perhaps some people die serenely and at peace in their beds. I don't know. I do know that I am not going to die that way, Or, at least—' Emil had cut himself short. 'Well—do you—do we . . . When—?'

'Tomorrow morning early.'

'It is better now.'

'But—' the priest had demurred gently—'you will eat again before the end. And—'

'No, I shall not. Tomorrow'—Emil had shuddered, licking his dry lips—'tomorrow I shall not be in a state to think of anything or to listen to anything. So—'

The priest, looking at him, had agreed. Someone in violent terror was in no fit state to accept the last rites of the Church. 'Very well, but I shall come again in the morning. Until then—all night—I shall pray for you. And now . . .'

So now in his cell Emil had his spiritual passport to the next world—on the highly dubious assumption that one existed. In any case he was about to leave the present one—and by his own hand. With his packet of dropped razor blades Captain Kaye had put the means of suicide within Emil's power and in doing so had temporarily calmed him. For though a forced death at twenty-one was an atrocious prospect, a private death in bed with life ebbing away from gashed wrists as the blood pumped out soaking mattress and bedclothes was less terrible than the gruesomely prearranged public spectacle which was being prepared for him beyond the prison walls.

For an hour Emil sat quietly on his narrow bed gazing unseeingly at the opposite wall and the guards, glancing in through the peephole, sighed with quick relief, for it had been indicated by the hospital staff that this one would probably give trouble.

But Emil was only waiting, lost in a tired reverie of his short life, for a reasonable time to pass before he could go to bed without causing undue suspicion from outside. His eyes half closed, he let his mind wander far from the eight-foot by twelve-foot cell to the wide sea-ways of the South Atlantic; to the night breeze, the star-covered sky and the phosphorescent wake at the U-boat's low stern. There would be sailors out there now; sailors no longer manning darkened ships or prowling, surfaced submarines, but lounging safe and unworried on the cargo hatches below their masthead lights, sure of their destination and secure in the knowledge that tomorrow would bring only the sun and the sparkling sea, the blue sky and the cries of the wheeling gulls. And somewhere far away to the south-east lay Madagascar and the loom of Cape Delgado. Somewhere in Mozambique Kalewski was free this night to wander the streets of Beira or Lourenço Marques . . . He would know all about the trial and the sentences . . . He would grin and shrug—and go on living. And beyond . . . Masondi . . . Emerald . . . Mr Spencer . . . Latif and Rami . . . All there, all alive and all to remain alive—to be allowed to go on living as if it were no special privilege but a right. Even the birds and animals released from Emerald's zoo—even the pangolin, horny and cold—would sleep tonight, tiny hearts beating under feathers, fur, scales, to awake to tomorrow's dawn. While he—while he . . . Emil could think of no one, not the least creature, without an anguished envy which took away his breath. He sat still, his trembling hands clasped between his knees, for what seemed an endless hour. Then slowly he rose. Very slowly, for the last time, he took off his uniform and shirt. He no longer had pyjamas, they were only supplied when in the hospital. For a moment he stood in his singlet and shorts looking down at his scarred misshapen leg. Then he clambered into the bed and felt quickly under the pillow for the razor blades.

There was no point in waiting any longer. He guessed that the initial cut would hurt badly, but one wrist, with the main veins open, would be enough. Once it was done he would have to lie still; he

would be dead, he thought, in fifteen or twenty minutes. Under cover
of the bedclothes he tore the paper envelope from one blade; then he
raised his knees so that the blanket formed a hump, a hollow space
over his stomach, and gripping his lower lip tightly between his teeth,
holding the blade between the thumb and forefinger of his right hand,
he brought it, sharp and deep, across the inside of his left wrist.

The pain stung like a hornet's jab and as the steel grated on bone
Emil's stomach turned and bile seared his throat, filling his mouth.
His face contorted and he jerked his head sideways to the wall. Then
it was over. His left arm burned with a fiery pain but even through the
shock he felt that pain lessening every instant. Hot wetness was soaking
through his thin underclothes in sticky warmth. He had done it.
Relief, and panic at approaching death, filled him equally. He panted,
moaning gently, eyes shut, sweat dripping down his face. Then the
door was thrown open. . . .

Outside in the stone-flagged passage Lance-Corporal Godkin had
glanced in through the spy-hole as Emil got into bed. Well—that was
something to be thankful for. Once the poor little bastard was asleep
it would be possible to nip down to the guards' restroom for a mug of
tea and a cigarette. Godkin made his measured way to the end of the
long passage, turned and came slowly back. He was glad that it was
not going to be his duty to take part in the actual execution tomorrow. Once he and Corporal Lake had got Kümmerol up, dressed
in the dung-coloured denim shirt and trousers which tomorrow would
replace his blue uniform, and taken him, handcuffed, to the courtyard
and the waiting van, their job would be over. For tonight it just
meant . . . He halted again at the cell door and peered through the
thick glass. In bed. Good. Not asleep yet, of course. Could one sleep
the night before? And he'd got his hands under the bedclothes. That
was forbidden. Prisoners, at least the condemned, were to sleep with
their hands above the covers—that was orders. And—God, what a
look on his face! Screwed up as if he'd got a bloody stomache-ache
second to none. And perhaps he had! Christ Jesus! had the bastard
taken something? Poison . . . Been in the hospital for days . . . an
open cupboard—someone's back turned . . . Christ! Godkin rammed
the heavy key in the great lock, turned it viciously and flung the door
open.

Kümmerol stared up, white-faced and sweating from the bed—
knees drawn up. He *had* taken something! With one step Godkin was
across the cell. One big hand gripped blanket and sheet. Kümmerol

was trying to hold on to them but his puny strength was hardly noticed by the burly guard. With one rip the bedclothes were down to his ankles and . . . *Oh, Jesus bloody Christ!* Godkin leapt to the door and yelled, 'Corporal! Corporal—quick!' He jerked the lanyarded whistle from his pocket and blasted out a high shrill call. Then he swung back to the bed. 'You would, would you, you little bugger! Oh no! Not here you don't! Stay still! Stay still or I'll knock you cold!' He grasped Emil's struggling crimson body, slimy and hot with fresh blood. His hands slipped and slithered but clamped on the left arm above the elbow. Vicelike his fingers gripped, pressing the brachial artery against the bone, cutting off quickly the red jet spouting from the slashed wrist.

Kümmerol was struggling weakly, weeping, trying to pull away. Godkin, never releasing the steely grip of his left hand, drew back his right fist and slammed a quick hard punch to the belly. Kümmerol doubled up with a choked grunt and spewed out the watery contents of his stomach over the stone floor, over Godkin's shiny boots, sabre-creased trousers. 'You filthy bastard!' Godkin hit him once more, this time in real anger, in the face and then the pounding boots of Corporal Lake and three other policemen thundered along the passage outside. 'What's up? What the fuckin' hell's going on here? Godkin—Christ, Godkin—you'll be arse over tip in the shit for this! Jesus, you will!'

'Bugger'd got a razor blade, Corporal. Not my fault. Lucky I got 'im in time . . .'

'Whose fuckin' fault don't matter! Quick, get a proper tourniquet on! Tauchner—get the doc. Double! You, Roberts—get his feet. Back on the bed—that's it! You hit him, Godkin? Good—best to lay him out. O.K., tighter! Pull it tighter! Christ, that's stopped it, anyway. Wow, what a fuckin' mess!'

'Think 'e'll live, Corp?'

'Bloody *got* to! Bastard! Drop us all in the shit, eh? Christ, I'll tell the doc he can fill him up with *my* fuckin' blood if that'll get him on the range tomorrow.'

'Not my fault, Corp. Like I says—'

'Doesn't *matter!* Doesn't fuckin' matter *whose* fault—see? So long as he lives. So long as he don't— Here comes the doc!'

Emil lived. Despite the gory state of the cell he had lost less blood than it had appeared at first sight. In the operating theatre they sutured the slashed veins, stitched the gaping wound and bound it tightly. Great lamps over a white table shone down on Emil's small, exhausted face; even anaesthetized it did not lose its look of horrified innocence.

The doctor, drawing strong sedative up into a glass syringe, paused, momentarily tempted. A little more, an extra two or three cubic centimetres and Kümmerol would never wake. But the doctor was a Catholic, too. Besides, it would be the military police who would be blamed. It would not be fair to them. No, no—out of the question. He pressed the plunger until the level of the drug was well within the safety margin.

And half an hour later Emil was back in a cell—a different, clean cell and lying on a clean bed. Both hands, one with a heavily bandaged wrist, lay outside the carefully turned-down sheet. On the plank table against the wall lay the folded canvas shirt and trousers, new and stiff, which tomorrow he would wear for the first and last time.

On the iron stool facing the bed sat Corporal Lake, big, immaculate, silent. He read slowly from a battered paperback novel with a garish cover, but he was on the alert none the less, and though the doctor had said that Kümmerol would not wake until morning the military policeman was taking no chances and his mind was not really on his book. From time to time he lowered it and stared from cold pale eyes at the pallid, tearstained, blood-smudged face turned unseeingly upward to the glare of the ceiling lamp. And, his own breathing momentarily suspended, he listened to the slow, deep breathing from the bed. Tomorrow—he thought—tomorrow you'll have to go through it all over again. And serve you fucking well right, you little murderer! Drop us all in the shit, would you? Fuck you—for a start!

Sixteen

In another cell, high up in the great irregular stone block of the prison, Eugen woke soon after dawn. He had not intended to sleep on this last night. He wanted to sit and think; to tie up in his mind all the loose threads of his thought, as he had dealt equally tidily and to the best of his ability with such material things as remained to him. But he was tireder than he had realized. He had spent the last day writing a voluminous letter to Viktoria in far-away Brazil; a painful business, but for that very reason one to which he felt it necessary to give his full concentration. Also he had a cold and no one would give him any clean handkerchiefs. He had to use the lavatory paper to blow his nose, which was now red and sore like his eyes. He had taken off his glasses, put them on the table and leaned back upon the hard bed. Very soon he had found it more comfortable to lie down and inevitably he had gone to sleep.

And now—he glanced at his watch—it was the day. The day itself. A shudder passed through him and he felt the sweat prickle out under his arms, over his chest. In a few hours' time there would be no more Eugen Kielbasa—only a bloody, bullet-broken body in a rough coffin ... He caught himself abruptly. That—thinking like that—was the one thing he must not do. No, no. Listen: Everybody has to die. Everybody waking today must die. Practically all the books you have read have been written by men who have died. Everything you have used in your life from a penknife to a periscope has been the invention of men long dead. They came—and went. It is just as natural and inescapable as being born. How you die does not matter any more than how you are born. When you die matters no more than when you were born. Both life and death may be entire illusions ... And there was Epicurus, too. Staring unseeingly up at the never-extinguished light, Eugen quoted mentally to himself—'He is foolish who says that death should be feared, not because it will be painful when it comes, but because it is painful to look forward to; for it is vain to be grieved in anticipation of that which distresses us not when it is present. Death, then, the most dread of all evils, is nothing to us, for while we are here death is not, and when death is here we are not.'

That was better. For he had always prided himself on being a rational man and therefore he must take a rational view of death and meet it in a rational manner—not with any stupid, willed courage or shaky dignity, but with the calm resignation of acceptance. 'Yes,' said a voice within him—a calm and logical voice—'but is that itself rational? If so, what becomes of the fundamental instinct of self-preservation— the natural, rational instinct which is the real reason that you are here now? Is an animal not being rational, in the way Nature intended, when it fights hopelessly and with abandoned fury for its own life? Would you yourself not be acting more naturally if you tried to strangle the next guard who enters the cell, or attempted to seize the rifle of one of the firing squad?' And—'No,' he answered himself, '—not necessarily, because ...'

It was speculations of this sort which were responsible for the calmness, the indifference, which impressed the prison guards and which, meeting in the passages, they compared favourably with Emil's behaviour. And yet ... 'There's something fuckin' cold-blooded about it, i'n't there? I mean to say it just don't seem to worry him. Don't *care*, like. 'Course it's easy to understand how he did what he did once you've seen him. I can just *see* him killing those poor fuckin' sailors! He'd do it just like killing ants. No malice, like—just thought it necessary. Worked it out that it'd be better—and then went and did it. Now the other, the little 'un. *He's* shit-scared, if you like!'

Yet deep within him Eugen was very frightened indeed. But he knew that for his own sake he must keep that fear suppressed; once let it seep up to conscious acceptance and he would suffer hideously, uncontrollably and unnecessarily—as he guessed unhappily that Emil was probably suffering. For Eugen, once sentence was passed upon him, had never had the slightest doubt that it would be executed. He knew exactly why this was so and understood its inevitability. He had written it clearly into his memorandum and his long letters to parents, sister, brother-in-law. But for Emil, on the other hand, he had confidently looked for commutation. The confirmation of Emil's sentence had come as a genuine shock. For, theoretically at any rate, he himself had had an option open to him when he gave that order on the submarine's bridge; whereas, again in theory, Emil had not. To kill Emil was *illogical*. When one took into account his age and his maimed leg it was also mercilessly savage, but it was the illogicality which characteristically upset Eugen. He had often asked about Emil, but the guards, who approved of him and who had no desire to alter his quiet behaviour, only said, 'Your mate? Not too bad. Been in hospital with a nasty cold, I believe. Looking after him well, they are, I understand.' Eugen had not entirely believed them but he could do nothing to ascertain the truth.

And now he slowly rose, ran the tap into the small steel basin and washed his face. His chin rasped under the rough towel but today he doubted if they would send the barber to shave him. Then the door opened and the guard called Roberts came in.

Eugen put on his glasses and said, 'Good morning.'

'Hallo.' Roberts, looking uncomfortable, dropped something on the bed. 'Look—you got to change into these here.'

'What?' Eugen blinked down at the brown canvas shirt and trousers. 'Why?'

'Orders. We got orders to have you and your mate in this rig first thing this morning.'

Eugen's pale face flushed slowly. So the British would not even allow them to die in their own uniforms, but in this dress of common felons. 'No. That is out of the question! These are—are criminal's uniform, is it not?'

Roberts shook his head patiently. 'No it ain't—honest! It's fatigue dress is all. What we wears—well, *I* don't because I'm a corporal, see, like all us Red-caps—but what ordinary squaddies wear when they got jobs to do—cleaning and such-like. They ain't criminal's uniforms —honest!'

'Well—I am not a soldier. I am a sailor. And more—I am an officer. I will die in my proper uniform!'

Roberts, six feet tall and two hundred pounds, folded his arms and shook his head gently. 'Can't be done, mate. Sorry. Orders is orders.'

'No. Send for an officer—someone of authority. Let me talk to—'

Roberts unfolded his arms and took a step towards Eugen. He put out one hand and undid the top button of the blue jacket. 'I'll send for someone all right if necessary,' he said softly. 'But not an officer, see? Just a couple more of us chaps to help me, see? 'Cos you got to get changed—an' there it is. Now—' his voice took on a wheedling, almost genial tone—'you always been a quiet, sensible sort of chap, you have. So don't let's have no trouble now, eh? 'Cos it won't do no slightest bit of good, I'm telling you. What's got to be has got to be —an' there it is.'

Eugen swallowed, backed away, and stood staring down at the mud-coloured shirt and trousers. Then he looked at Roberts. It was point-less—Roberts was twice his size—and he'd send for the others. . . .

Shakily he undid the other buttons of his coat and took it off. 'That's it,' said Roberts approvingly, 'that's the idea.' And staring up at him, pulling the white shirt from his trousers, Eugen said venom-ously, 'One day the Russians will do the same to you!'

Seventeen

At five minutes past noon Major Steward, driving the police 15 cwt himself—officers were not supposed to drive military vehicles, but this regulation did not, of course, apply to the Provost Corps— roared on to the firing range and braked viciously. He banged open the door and clambered out on to the damp heath. Everything had been ready for hours, and now . . . He cursed the Navies, both Royal and U.S., with that satisfying virulence which only a soldier can achieve, and stormed over to the corrugated iron shed where Sergeant Milne, Lance-Sergeant Spicer and Corporal Maynard were standing together with the drizzle gleaming on their rubber capes. There was someone with them, too, an American soldier; and since at his approach the four men slammed to attention and saluted rigidly, it must be a non-com. Major Steward's feelings for the Americans were particularly harsh at the moment but he was slightly mollified by that snapping salute. Yanks were, in his experience, sloppy and disrespectful to British officers. 'Postponed *another* two hours,' he growled at Milne. Then—'Who the hell's this?'

Once more the American, young, blond, in a smart gaberdine raincoat, saluted impeccably. 'Post. Corporal, J.A.G.'s staff, sir.'

'J.A.G.? What are you doing here?'

'Representing Defence Counsel, sir,' said Post smoothly.

Major Steward shrugged. 'Well, you're going to have a bloody long wait, Corporal. Nobody tell you about the postponement? No, of course not. Nobody told *me* until half an hour ago. Well, there it is, anyway.'

'Sir.' Woodenly in acceptance from Milne. Steward nodded glumly and the young American suddenly spoke again in a voice which seemed oddly strained. 'Major, sir. Does this—does this mean that it's been reconsidered?'

Steward stared at him. 'Don't get you.'

'I mean—maybe the sentences are being com—commuted?'

'Oh—oh, I see. No, no. It's just that two senior naval officers—one of them yours as it happens—can't get here until fourteen hundred. That's all. Don't ask me why, 'cos I can't tell you. Nobody's thought it worth telling *me*. I'm only the bloke in charge, after all! I suppose they want their lunch first.—Milne, I've brought up the food for you men in the back of the truck. You'd better unload it. There's enough for the Corporal too, if he'd like some.'

'Thank you very much, sir.'

Steward nodded, turning on his heel. 'Right. Well, I'll be getting back. See you later.'

'Sir.' The M.P.'s and the American clicked and saluted sharply, and then relaxed. Corporal Maynard followed the D.A.P.M. to collect the hot dinner from the back of the truck and Sergeant Milne turned to Post. 'Well, young feller. You'll have to manage with British grub today. Nothing like what you gets in the ordinary way, I 'spect.'

'Chow up,' said Lance-Sergeant Spicer trying unsuccessfully to adopt an American accent.

Post smiled. 'Maybe I won't worry. I don't feel hungry. It's good of your major, but—'

'Come on, boy; no need to be bashful. There's plenty of it—such as it is.'

'It's not that.' Post licked his lips. 'I—I just don't like this waiting.'

'Ah!' said Sergeant Milne wisely. 'I knows how it is. You never been to one of these things before, eh?'

'I guess not—no.'

'And don't fancy it, p'raps? Well, it's not pretty—that's true enough. But it's over pretty quick. Young Maynard—he's never seen one, neither. Don't feel so good himself, probably. So you got company.'

Together they entered the shed and sat down on a rough bench. Corporal Maynard came in carrying a metal container and a couple of web packs. 'Might've brought us something to fuckin' drink,' he said morosely.

'Plenty of water.'

'Don't mean water, Sarge.'

'Well, if you *must* know, he has.' Sergeant Milne pulled a small flask from one pocket of his battledress. 'Rum. If you knew more you wouldn't have asked. 'Cos we always get it for these do's. But you're not having none yet, see? Not with two bloody hours to go. This here—' he tapped the flask and thrust it back into his pocket— 'is to sustain morale of personnel—see? You'll get your tot when I see everyone coming. Not before. Now hand them plates round 'fore everything gets cold as a baboon's balls.'

Corporal Post accepted a plate of thick stew and ate without appetite but with an appearance of enjoyment. His manners had always been excellent. They were the origin, still more than his blond good looks, of his position as Captain Kaye's clerk. And now that position was terminated—or very nearly. It was a pity, but in the circumstances inevitable. As the British policemen ate in silence Post looked back over his association with Captain Kaye with a mixture of regret and yet relief. He had enjoyed himself working for the big, bearded lawyer and, far more important, he had learned a great deal. He had been taken for a little while into the engine-room of that society of which he had always considered himself a sworn enemy. A small compartment of that engine-room, perhaps—and under the guidance of a somewhat esoteric engineer—but a place of importance. He had watched the administration of law. The only real mistake he had made —the one which was responsible for the termination of his employment—was that he had supposed that he was watching the administration of justice. It was, he saw now, a stupid mistake and one for which he really had no excuse since Captain Kaye had often said that the two were not the same. It was useless to blame his employer for what had happened; he saw that now. He himself should never have pressed the Captain to go to the prison to see Kümmerol. For he was to blame for that dreadful interview, and Kaye had blamed him. Not openly and in anger, but in a cold silence, an obvious dislike for his company which had replaced all the genial kindness of the months before. Since that interview he had never been 'Mr P' again, but 'Post,' or still more forbiddingly 'Corporal.' Yesterday he had asked Kaye for a transfer and the Captain had at once agreed. 'Yes, of course, Post. I'll put it through at once.'

'I—I'll certainly stay until you've got someone else. I don't want—'

'That will be quite all right. I can manage easily enough.'

'I mean—this Reynolds case.'

'Don't let that worry you. I can get a typist from the H.Q. pool.'

So there it was. When this morning he had asked for the day off it had been granted with the same cool indifference. 'Certainly, certainly. I've no objection at all.'

And so he had come here; hitching a ride out of the city in an army truck and clambering up the narrow path through the damp heather. Why? He was still a little uncertain of his own motives though he knew that somewhere they existed and that they were powerful. One of them, he thought, was based on a remark an old and shabby school-teacher had once made to the class of small children in their first year, of whom he had been one of the worst disciplined. She was an eccentric old creature with a hair-do like an owl's nest and pince-nez which, unlike Captain Kaye's, made her look ridiculous rather than formidable. She was thought to be a witch and known to be a vegetarian. 'If you—'she had said one day in answer to a question on this latter point—'visited a slaughter-house you wouldn't eat meat, either. Everyone who eats meat ought to be made to visit a slaughter-house.' And perhaps, thought Post, everyone who is involved in a capital trial ought to be made to watch an execution. If Captain Kaye —let alone Colonel Rostwood, the President and the Court—were all brought here today, could they still maintain the mechanical dis-passion of the trial? There were to be plenty of witnesses up here on the range at two o'clock, but they had had nothing to do with the verdict or the sentence. It was the Court who should be here, to watch with their own eyes their orders being carried out.

Yet putting aside all such philosophical theories it did seem to Post that someone from the Defence should attend. The Defence had failed to save the two prisoners but it had tried its best. There had been conferences, consultations, conversations with the two accused. A relationship partly of trust, partly of hope and confidence, had been established, and despite Captain Kaye's views Post could not agree that the verdict and sentences had terminated it. He had no idea whether Kielbasa or Kümmerol would be in a state to notice any of the spectators this afternoon, but if they were he felt that they should see at least one known and friendly face among the curious and condemning ones of total strangers. It was not much, but it was the only remaining thing which might be done for them in their fear and misery.

But now that he was here; now that he had finished as much of the stew as he could manage and refused any of the peculiar doughy substance which his hosts called 'duff,' Post wondered whether he himself could sustain his self-imposed task. After all, unlike the policemen among whom he now sat, he *knew* Kielbasa and Kümmerol. He had listened to them and watched them for days. He had sat at tables in the lawyers' room at the prison with them, sharpened pencils for them, handed them papers and law books—he had even been sent out to buy them the new black ties they had worn in court. More—much more—than all these things, he had followed the whole case from its beginning and he believed that both men were being wrongly put to death—being judicially murdered for motives of vengeance for which a watertight legal technicality had been found. They were to be made a slightly oblique but none the less object lesson against the practice of unrestricted submarine warfare. That was why two senior naval officers and their staffs were attending.

'Smoke?' asked Sergeant Milne, belching slightly and pushing his plate away.

'Thanks.' Post took a cigarette and Corporal Maynard said, ''Nother hour to go. Still. I 'spose *they'll* be here before that, won't they?'

'Should be. Major'll get the squad up half-hour early in any case.'

'Looks like it's stopped raining outside.'

Post stretched his legs and rose. 'Guess I'll just walk around a bit, then. See you, fellers! Thanks for the lunch.' He smiled, nodded quickly and left the hut.

For a moment no one spoke and then Lance-Sergeant Spicer grinned. 'Think he's scarpered, Sarge?'

'Could be. Can't say I blames him if he has. Not his job—this sort of thing.'

'What is he?'—from Maynard.

'J.A.G.'s clerk—far as I can see.'

'Do we have 'em?'

'Course we has 'em! Ours don't get detailed for these do's, though. Leastways, I've never heard of it.'

'Started to rain again,' said Maynard.

Eighteen

Major Steward led the small convoy from the prison at 1.35 and it left the main road and ground up the hill to the range at 1.50. Behind the 15 cwt rumbled a big three-tonner which contained the squad and this was closely followed by a coffee-coloured closed van whose small, frosted glass windows were protected by heavy wire mesh. Two red-capped motor-cyclists brought up the rear.

Once the firing range came into view Major Steward began to curse again. For though there were a great many people to be seen it was obvious that the Navy had not arrived. Drab khaki alone moved and eddied over the drab heather of the range.

'Not come yet, sir.' Beside him his driver voiced his own thoughts.

'Damn them to hell!' grunted the Major briefly and swung open his door as the truck ground to a halt. Sergeant Milne ran up, slammed to attention, saluted. 'Sir!'

'All correct, Sergeant?'

'Yes, sir. Ropes all up and everyone behind them. The cameramen wanted to get closer. I told them it wasn't allowed. Said they'd like to speak to you, sir.'

'They won't like it if I have to speak to *them*,' said Steward grimly. 'They'll do as I say or get the hell out of it.'

'I wasn't certain what to say, sir. I'm not sure what equivalent rank we give them.'

'If in uniform they're camp followers—if not, they're just bloody civilians. As far as I'm concerned they rank the same as natives employed to clean troops' latrines abroad.'

'Yessir.'

'Ropes ready?'

'At the posts, sir.'

'Targets?'

'Here, sir.' Milne tapped his breast pocket.

'Good. Then I'll stay here. As soon as the Navy comes I'll bring the van up to the posts. You wait there with the others. When we bring

them out you and Spicer take the left post, I and Maynard will take
the right.'

'Very good, sir.'

'Well, then—' Major Steward relaxed slightly—'we'll just have to
wait still longer, I suppose. The Navy! Christ—the only sailors who
aren't late are our two poor buggers in the van!' He glanced moodily
at the low sky in which, to the west, one pale watery yellow streak
shone among the wide dull greyness. 'Filthy day. Has it rained up
here?'

'A bit sir—on and off. Sort of thin drizzle, like. Cold, though.'

'Umm.' The Major nodded morosely, watching the cameramen
who were plainly worried about the light. They examined small black
gauges, turned their lenses this way and that and shook their heads.
At a little distance six American army officers stood in a small tight
bunch and two dozen or more newspaper reporters prowled up and
down behind the roped-off area, stopping from time to time to make
notes. Steward saw the young American corporal whom he had met
on his last visit standing by himself behind the rest on a small hillock of
rubble composed of the spoil from a set of trenches near the butts. His
hands were in the pockets of his raincoat and his face looked pale and
pinched. An unhealthy sort of life—always in offices, thought Steward.
Still, someone had to do it. We all had our jobs. Even—his eyes
turned to the blank dun-coloured van whose paintwork gleamed in
the damp air—even those two in there had once had a job to do.
It was a job which had brought them here this afternoon.

Nineteen

The grey daylight penetrated with difficulty through the gridded
opaque windows of the closed van. Without movement forward the
small fan ventilator in the roof did not turn and the air was at once cold
and stuffy. Eugen's eyes moved involuntarily to the sack and the pile
of paper which had been taken in quickly, almost furtively, at the
prison before they had left. The sack contained sawdust and the paper
was of the thick coarse variety butchers used to wrap their meat.
When Eugen had realized that these were to prepare the floor of the
van for the return journey he had only just prevented himself from
vomiting; even now to look at them made the bile rise burningly in

his throat and black, smothering terror racked him, contracting his muscles, halting his breath.

He and Emil faced each other in the half-light. They sat on opposite benches, each between two big red-capped guards. Eugen was hand-cuffed, Emil attached by his unwounded wrist to the guard on his right. They had been in the van for over an hour.

Eugen guessed that they had arrived at the range and that death was imminent—a matter of minutes away. Under the hard canvas shirt his heart was beating fast and irregularly and his mouth was dry, his throat constricted. What frightened him most was the immense difficulty of concentrating his mind. His conscious thought plunged and veered, throwing up words, disconnected sentences, sudden flashes of memory—a rapid kaleidoscope of accelerating nonsense which he seemed unable to control. The calm inward voice which had guided him ever since adolescence, the voice which said, 'If such and such is so, therefore . . .' the voice of reason, appeared to have deserted him. He struggled in panic to hear its tones above the shrill gibber of nonsense which filled his head. For it was no longer of the slightest use to pretend that death was not dreadful. Epicurus had written his lines in the calm of his own benign thought—he was of no use now. Rather Dostoevski, reprieved at the last minute from before another firing squad, who had subsequently written that at the last, in the ultim-ate agony, a man would choose life under even the most terrible con-ditions—to stand for ever on bare rock in total darkness—rather than accept the black extinction of death.

And yet if there was anything worse than death it must be insanity —with the broken mind screaming and beating itself to pieces in a living human head. With an immense effort Eugen calmed himself by concentrating on the slumped figure of Emil opposite. For Emil, he saw now, had passed through this that he was now suffering a long time, days, perhaps, ago; and by pre-living this last agony had drained almost dry his capacity for any feeling at all. He already looked corpse-like, sitting there in the gloom, his eyes two black holes burned in dead-white paper. A curiously neat and clean corpse though, for he had been unable to dress himself and the guards had done it for him— and done it, automatically, with impeccable smartness. His canvas shirt and trousers were too big for him, but every crease had been aligned, the sleeves rolled to exactly the same level above the elbows, the belt lashed tight and firm with its hasp gleaming in the dead centre below his breastbone. They had even oiled and brushed his black hair and polished the single shoe and the thick-soled surgical boot. The effect was ghoulish in the extreme, and if the authorities had decreed this execution dress as a sort of degrading *samarra*, their minions, by smartening it up, had added a last touch of horror.

Eugen leaned forward in the chill dusk and took Emil's left hand gently between his own fettered ones—it was cold, damp and unresisting. The guards moved restlessly, one cleared his throat and then they turned their eyes away, embarrassed and unhappy. 'Emil—' Eugen's voice was low and harsh with the effort of forming words '—it won't be long now.'

'I know—not long.'

'It won't hurt. It will be nothing. The waiting has been the worst and that is over now. It is all nearly over—nearly finished. Only this last . . .' From somewhere outside, muffled by the metal walls of the van, came the noise of approaching cars. 'They've done all they can now. This last part is over so quickly . . . and then we are free of them for ever.' Eugen saw the bruised white face nod gently in the gloom.

Weakly, tonelessly, Emil said, 'I'm not frightened any longer. I don't care now. I don't care whether it hurts or not. I only want to get away. They are doing what I want now.' He paused. Outside the cars had stopped. Eugen heard the rattle and click of rifles brought to the salute. He guessed what rifles they were and he felt the short hairs on the nape of his neck rise prickling. He pressed Emil's hand, his own damp fingers rubbing Emil's cold lax ones.

Emil did not seem to hear anything outside the van. Quietly, slowly, almost in a whisper he went on speaking. 'For me there was nothing left anyway. Kaye said so; he told them. They are not taking much from me. Once—in hospital in Africa—I thought that perhaps I had found . . . but that was long ago. It means nothing now.'

With a muffled roar the van's engine started up and suddenly they were in motion, bumping and swaying over the uneven ground. Eugen tried to retain Emil's hand in his but it was impossible. The guards on each side steadied their manacled prisoners gently between them.

And now—the moment had come. The van was slowing . . . braking . . . had stopped. Hurriedly Eugen said, 'When—when it's going to happen, don't look at them. Don't look in front. Look at me.' And then the door swung open and the sudden daylight, grey as it was, seemed bright in their eyes; the air, cold and dank, felt fresh on their faces as they saw the British major and his men standing below. 'All right—bring them out!'

Two steps to the end of the van. Guards' hands under their shoulders, supporting and steadying them. 'That's it. Careful, now.' The damp springy heather . . . a low grey sky . . . cold. Eugen shivered, looking around. Yes, it was just as he had imagined it so often, except that there were so many people. People lined behind ropes and craning forward staring. A subdued buzz of noise, the clicking and whirring of many cameras and the sudden popping of flash bulbs making miniature, unreal lightning glares against the dull afternoon sky.

Emil's face was greenish-grey rather than white. They lifted him down carefully and handed his rubber-shod stick after him, though it was unnecessary since he would only have to walk half a dozen paces to the posts and he could be supported for these.

The Major's voice again, urgent and brusque. 'All right! Quick now! Driver—get the van out of the way!'

The big hands of the guards gripped Eugen's arms, but gently and only for support—just to help him take these last few steps out of life. 'Take his handcuffs off.' And a guard's voice, low and a little shaky— they knew he spoke some English—'Move back a bit. Lean back on the post. That's right, mate. Now—your hands behind.'

And immediately they had drawn his arms behind him, behind the thick post, and were tying his wrists. Eugen wanted to wipe his sore nose—and a drop of sweat from his forehead had fallen on to one eyelid and could not be rubbed away. For his hands were finished; he would never use them or see them again. He swallowed, shutting his eyes behind his glasses, shuddering in one fearful last spasm of unendurable fear. Ropes tightened around his ankles, his knees, his waist. 'Nearly done, mate. Nearly done.' How odd that guard's voice sounded. He longed for them to finish—to take their hands away. A rope was passed behind the post and through the crook of his elbows which were suddenly, savagely, wrenched back as it was pulled tight, snapping his shoulders back against the post and arching his back so that now he stood at a bound and rigid attention, as stiff and still as a soldier on ceremonial parade. He could move nothing but his head.

Now the Major was in front of him, smelling of stale tobacco, a square of thin greyish cardboard in his hands. For a second Eugen saw its face—the circles and disc of a practice rifle target. Then, with a swift jab, it was pinned to the front of his shirt.

He turned his head to the right and there stood Emil, small and rigid, his well-brushed black hair gleaming in the damp, his shoulders stretched back hard against the high wooden stake, bound and still. A guard was moving away carrying his heavy walking stick.

'Emil!' But even as Eugen spoke the Major lifted a hand and quickly, carefully, removed his glasses. At once Emil became a figure blurred slightly at the edges, indistinct of feature. 'Emil—look at me! Don't look at them!' And obediently the blurred head moved and the white face—surely it was smiling—turned towards him. If only he could see properly . . . Somewhere in front orders were being shouted and the rattle and click of arms answered them. 'That's right, Emil, that's right. They didn't hurt you—your wrist?'

'No. I'm all right. I—'

A high shout. An enormous, world-shattering concussion . . . unbelievable, blinding, searing agony—and no breath. No wish to breathe. A sick, vertiginous, vanishing fall . . . Emil. Odd jumbled images, meaningless and fading as the pain ended in dissolving darkness. . . .

Twenty

From his vantage point on his gravel mound Corporal Post had watched the Navy cars drive up and the gold-braided officers descend, returning salutes, nodding, staring briefly around them as the magnesium bulbs exploded like toy grenades. They were presumably here to represent—in some way difficult to comprehend completely—the sailors who had struggled in the South Atlantic under the U-boat's gunfire last January. Post doubted briefly if they were quite the sort of representatives the dead sailors would have chosen for themselves. Then he turned his eyes back to the van as it lurched the twenty-five yards to the two gaunt black posts, while the firing squad at the picket line brought their rifles smartly down from the 'present arms.' The rear door of the van opened and at once a cluster of red-capped khaki uniforms surrounded it. Then more khaki emerging . . . where was the blue of naval uniform—the gold stripes and stars of officers of the onetime Kriegsmarine? Surely— But yes, on the ground now, both of them, in those overalls. Post's stomach turned over. Was one, then, specially dressed for death? How diminished they seemed; so small, somehow, among those tall policemen. He wished that they would look up and see him since that was largely what he had come for. They knew him, and he them. Of all the men assembled on this forbidding piece of moor only he and they had this bond. He longed for them to see him, to feel at least the tiny touch of comfort which one known and friendly face might bring. He thought momentarily of climbing down the hillock of gravel in order to approach more closely, but if he

did so he would be blocked from view by all the others. No, he must
stay where he was.

He was sweating heavily and his stomach was a tight knot of panic,
but overriding even this was his passionate desire to make them *see*
him; to take, if possible, some of the fear from them, to lighten that
load of terror which must be pressing so unbearably upon their racing
hearts behind the black-circled cardboard targets. But, roped and fast
to their stakes now, they only looked at each other. White faces
turned sideways from each post, disregarding the squad twenty-five
yards away whose front rank knelt, whose rear rank stood, who now
levelled their arms. 'I'm here!' shouted Post wordlessly. 'I'm here
with you. You are not alone.' And then the volley crashed out and the
blast of it made Post rock and slip on the unstable gravel. For a long
moment his eyes were upon his scuffling, sliding feet as he strove to
regain his balance, and when he was once more back upon the crest
and looked again it was all over and he knew that they were dead.

They had not moved, for they were too rigidly tied to have even
jerked under the impact of the bullets. Only they no longer looked at
each other and both heads, the blond and the black, hung down upon
their chests. Stiff and still they stood, heads bowed too deeply for shame
or penitence but bent as if in profound contemplation of some mystery
unknown to all others here but they. Flash after flash of magnesium
light flared out at those two still bodies with the hanging heads. From
both sides the big black eyes of recording cameras whirred, halted,
and whirred again as photographers changed places, knelt, jostled
around the ropes.

And now Major Steward approached the posts at a quick walk,
holding a blue-black service revolver ready cocked in one hand. He
took a brief look at Kielbasa, then turned and strode to Kümmerol.
This time he seemed unsure. Post watched, breath held and sweat
popping out all over him, as the police officer put one hand under the
chin and lifted the fallen head. Mouth and chin were crimson and
dripping. The Major dropped his hand, the head sagged down again
and Post, reeling back over the other side of the gravel mound, sank
to his knees and started to vomit.

How long Post stayed there behind the gravel ridge, weakly retching, spewing up the pre-execution dinner which the police had given
him, he never knew. He went on coughing and jerking out half-
digested food until he sank on all fours and then, empty at last, rolled
over on to his back and lay panting and staring up at the low grey sky,
listening to the diminishing noise of auto engines descending to the

main road and feeling the thin drizzling rain cool and damp on his hot face. Breath after slow shuddering breath and the easing of his hammering heart. At last he sat up, loosened his collar and felt for a handkerchief. He wished he had a glass of water and wondered if he could get one from the police guards at the iron hut where he had eaten with them. Empty, drained of all feeling, aware only of weakness and thirst, he rose wearily to his feet and walked around the artificial hillock. Then he stopped and blinked. For the range was quite empty. No one . . . no vehicles . . . nothing. A battered cigarette packet, a carton which had once held film crushed in the heather, a scatter of burned-out bulbs—and the two posts, silent and gaunt, looming up out of a rapidly falling mist of low cloud blowing over the moor.

Slowly he walked towards them, approaching the one to which Kümmerol had been tied—ten minutes?—half an hour?—ago. There was a splintered gash on one side and a long smear already diluted under the thin rain. At the base the thin wiry heath was covered with a thick spattering of blood drops.

Before he reached the second stake Post's foot crunched on something brittle and looking down he saw Kielbasa's horn-rimmed spectacles. He took his foot away as quickly as if it had been resting on a snake. Then he stood where he was, half-way between the two black baulks, and turned to look up the range to where the squad had been. But the white pegs had been removed and the mist was thickening so fast that he could no longer be sure of the place.

Alone in the silence he stood under the increasing rain, and he felt many things that were too confused for immediate comprehension yet which he knew he would recall later and understand. But beyond them all, soberly and compassionately, he saw plainly the immense fallibility of mankind—something which he would never now forget; a legacy, perhaps, from the dead men. That he had been born into an age as stupid as it was wicked he had guessed darkly from his earliest years. In common with Kielbasa and Kümmerol he had lived his short life in a society largely dominated by the cruel and corrupt generation which had striven so ignobly in the mud of Flanders thirty years ago; a generation so maddened by the memories of what it had done that it had been forced to re-enact the bloody horror as a murderer is driven to return to the scene of his crime. He had feared and hated the men of that era who ruled, ordered and controlled the powerful institutions of Nation, State, and Army—great capital letters as heavy and black as the execution stakes between which he now stood. But from today the hatred would change to a sad contempt, the fear dwindle and disappear entirely—for he had seen a summary of all these things in action and he knew them, at last, for the stupid, childish mockery of what they were popularly supposed to be. Behind all the pomp and glory and rhetoric and high-minded speeches there was nothing but a narrow, dull and dirty room, in which an idiot child crawled over a cold floor crushing small spiders with its fingers.

He drew a deep breath and shivered, hunching his shoulders. Suddenly, to his own surprise and, it seemed, quite involuntarily, he said, 'I was here, but you didn't see me—either of you.' Then he turned quickly and walked away into the mist in the direction of the main road under the soft whispering of the rain.

Twenty-one

That rain swung in a great grey scythe moving across Europe from east to west. Over the long north coast of Belgium and the sodden fields of Flanders it blew coldly, and on into northern France.

Gaston, returning that evening from a walk along the deserted beach beyond Dieppe, felt its approaching coldness upon his face. The east was dark and only behind him in the west a few bars of clouded yellow light rifted down on to the grey seas of the Channel.

He had been home for nearly twenty-four hours, arriving yesterday an hour and a half before his old father died upstairs in the little room in the Rue Jehan Ango where he himself had been born twenty-one years ago. The telegram had reached him at the hotel in Germany where he had waited in expectation of what, he knew, had happened today without his presence.

There had been no choice except to leave at once, but it had been a bitter decision for all that. In taking it he had felt that he was somehow betraying the hope and trust of all those companions who had died ... Monsieur Lagny, with his melancholy face and collection of carved ivories. Captain Crawshaw, with his lost wood ... Brian Slater, Lin Hsiang under the red sail, Roldan—and poor, innocent, battered Rayner. Most of all, of course, Philippe, whom he had last seen clearly, a small, gaunt olive-brown figure as he stood on the prow of the raft, happy in the belief of imminent rescue.

For nearly a year he had borne on his own shoulders the piled debt of all their deaths, swearing that he would see it discharged upon their killers who should surely die. He had thought of almost nothing else for so long that in the end it had seemed as personal and heavy a weight as some ceremonial medieval vow taken before a great congregation in a hushed cathedral. It had to be fulfilled. Yet in the end, and after so long, he had been robbed of the final fulfilment.

But even so, the debt had been discharged in actual fact. With difficulty and at considerable cost he had made a long-distance telephone call earlier that afternoon and he knew now that the matter was concluded. Emil and his captain had died soon after two o'clock. He had wanted more details but the weak tinny voice so far away could supply none. Everything had gone as ordered except for a couple of hours' delay due to the luncheon engagement of two important witnesses. Death had been immediate in both cases; there had been no reason for the *coup de grâce*. The bodies had been brought back and were even now being burned in the prison crematorium . . . It was accomplished.

And for Gaston this meant more than the punishment for a brutal crime or vengeance exacted for atrocious suffering—it meant the end of the long war. Yet now, freed from the responsibility he had carried so long, he felt a strangely puzzled loss. He had suddenly realized that his father's death meant infinitely less to him—was entirely overshadowed by Emil's. He had been fond of his old father in an unthinking, casual way, and he had hated Emil with a terrible concentrated bitterness. So now, paradoxically, he missed Emil far more than his father. For if old Monsieur Guéroult left a small sad gap in his son's life, Emil's death took away its purpose. Without that purpose, Gaston thought as he trudged home below the towering flint-lined cliffs towards the darkening east, he would not have survived those weeks on the raft. If another—Slater, perhaps, or the Captain—had been called on board the U-boat instead of himself, the German crew would have been entirely anonymous, a faceless mass symbolized only by their submarine. And you could not feel about a U-boat as you could about a person. It was Emil—the first friendliness, the cognac, the French voice and manner, the offer to take Philippe on board, and then the horrifying, murderous betrayal—it was these things and the fiery emotions they had provoked in his own tempestuous spirit which had kept him alive as much as anything.

And now—now he must start again. Now he must reorientate himself to a new, and perhaps more difficult, world. He would have to put all that had happened behind him and turn firmly into the future if he were not to become like those most tragic of all ghosts—the unfallen dead of a world war.

It was growing dark now and the wind was rising; the choppy sea to his left glittered icily in the last metallic light. He must return to his weeping mother, to the sad house, the broken, battered town in which he now knew so strangely few people, for all the friends of his youth were gone—swallowed up in the war. But he did not need friends; he was sufficient to himself Or at least there was only one whom he would have wished . . . He shivered, hunching his shoulders beneath his upturned coat collar, and from the dark east the wind blew more strongly, bringing the rain . . . bringing the cold . . . bringing the winter.